Hidden Beauty

LUCINDA EDMONDS

POCKET BOOKS
New York London Toronto Sydney Tokyo Singapore

First published in Great Britain by
Simon & Schuster Ltd, 1993
First published in Great Britain by Pocket Books, 1994
An imprint of Simon & Schuster Ltd
A Paramount Communications Company

Simon & Schuster Ltd
West Garden Place
Kendal Street
London W2 2AQ

Simon & Schuster of Australia Pty Ltd
Sydney

A CIP catalogue record for this book is available from
the British Library

ISBN 0-671-85088-1

Typeset by Florencetype Ltd, Kewstoke, Avon
Printed in Great Britain by HarperCollins
Manufacturing, Glasgow

Acknowledgements

I would like to thank everyone at Simon & Schuster for their continued faith and support, especially my editor, Maureen Waller, who has been of such great help during the past year, and Lucy Ferguson.

Also my literary agent, Arthur Goodhart; Katie Pickering, Hugh Bache, Nigel Coleman, Jim Cunningham and Catherine Byron for their friendship, advice and hard work on my behalf.

Lastly, Janet and Don, my parents, and Georgia, my sister, who have all been there for me during the ups and downs of the past year. And my husband, Owen, whose unwavering belief in myself and the book has been an inspiration.

For my mother and father

Prologue

THE OLD WOMAN stared at Leah, then smiled and her face creased into a thousand wrinkles. Leah thought that she must be at least a hundred and fifty years old. All the children at her junior school said she was a witch and they howled like banshees as they passed her derelict cottage on their way home through the village after school. To the adults, she was old Megan, who took in injured birds and used herbal concoctions to mend their broken wings. Some said she was mad, others that she had the gift of healing and strange, psychic powers.

Leah's mother felt sorry for her.

'Poor old biddy,' she'd say, 'all alone in that damp, dirty cottage.' Then she'd tell Leah to collect a few eggs from the hen-shed and take them round to Megan.

Leah's heart always beat with fear when she knocked on the crumbling door. Usually, Megan would open it slowly, peer round and grab the eggs out of Leah's hand with a nod. The door would close and Leah would run as fast as she could back home.

But today, when she had knocked, the door had

opened much wider so that Leah could see behind Megan and into the dark recesses of the cottage.

Megan was still staring at her.

'I . . . I . . . Mum thought you might like some eggs.' Leah proffered the box and watched the long, bony fingers close around it.

'Thank you.'

Leah was surprised at the gentle tone. Megan certainly didn't sound like a witch.

'Why don't you come in?'

'Well, I . . .'

Already an arm had closed around Leah's shoulder and was propelling her inside.

'I can't stay long. Mum'll wonder where I've got to.'

'You can tell her you were having tea with Megan the witch,' she chuckled. 'Sit yourself down over there. I'm about to brew up.' Megan pointed to one of the battered armchairs placed on either side of a small, empty fireplace.

Leah sat nervously, her hands clasped under her legs. She looked around the small kitchen. On every wall, there were shelves filled with old coffee jars full of strange coloured concoctions. Megan pulled a jar down, opened it and put two teaspoons of the yellow powder into an ancient stainless-steel teapot. She added water from the kettle, placed it on a tray along with two cups and set the tray down on a table in front of Leah. Slowly, Megan lowered herself into the other armchair.

'Will you pour, dear?'

Leah nodded, leant forward and poured the steaming

4

liquid into the two chipped china cups. She sniffed. The liquid had a strange, acrid smell.

'It's all right, I'm not trying to poison you. Here, I'll sip mine first and you can see if I die. It's only dandelion tea, do you good.' She took the cup in both hands and drank. 'Try some.'

Leah tentatively put the cup to her lips, trying to breathe through her mouth, the pungent aroma too much for her. She sipped, and swallowed without tasting.

'There now, that wasn't too bad, was it?'

Leah shook her head and put the cup down on the table. She fidgeted in her chair as Megan drained her cup.

'Thank you for the tea. It was very nice. I really must be going. Mum'll start to . . .'

'I've watched you pass here every day. You're going to have extraordinary beauty when you're older. It's already starting to show itself.'

Leah blushed as Megan's piercing green eyes scanned her from top to toe.

'It may not be the blessing the world thinks it is. Take care.' Megan frowned, then reached across the table. Leah shuddered as the bony fingers locked in a claw-like grip around her hand. Panic rose inside her.

'Yes, I . . . I must go home.'

Megan's eyes were staring far beyond Leah, and her body was taut. 'There is evil, I can feel it. You must be on your guard.' Megan's voice was rising. Leah was paralysed with fear. The grip around her hand tightened.

'Unnatural things . . . evil things . . . never mess with nature, you upset the pattern. Poor soul . . . he is lost . . .

doomed . . . he will come back to find you on the moors . . . and you will return of your own free will. You can't alter destiny . . . you must beware him.'

Suddenly, the grip around Leah's hand slackened and Megan crumpled back into her chair, her eyes closed. Leah jumped to her feet and ran to the front door and out into the street. She did not stop running until she reached the hen-shed at the back of the small terraced house she shared with her parents. She opened the latch and slumped down onto the floor, causing the hens to scatter.

She leant her head back against the wooden wall and allowed her breathing to slow.

The villagers were right. Megan was mad. What had she said about Leah taking care? It was scary. She was eleven years old and she didn't understand. She wanted her mother, but she couldn't tell her what had happened. Mrs Thompson would think she had made it up and tell her that it wasn't nice to spread nasty rumours about a poor, helpless old lady.

Leah stood up and slowly made her way to the back door. The secure smell of home calmed her as she stepped into the warm kitchen.

'Hello, Leah, just in time for tea. Sit yourself down.' Doreen Thompson turned and smiled, then a frown of concern crossed her brow. 'Why, Leah, whatever is wrong? You're as white as a ghost.'

'Nothing, Mum. I'm fine. I've just got a tummy-ache, that's all.'

'Growing pains, most likely. Try and put some food inside you and I'm sure you'll feel better.'

Leah crossed to her mother and hugged her tight.

'Now, what's all this about?'

'I . . . I love you, Mum.' Leah nestled into the comforting arms and felt much better.

But the following week, when her mother asked her to take the eggs round as usual to Megan, she adamantly refused.

Megan died six months later and Leah was glad.

Part One

Yorkshire, June 1976

1

ROSE DELANCEY DROPPED her slim, sable brush into the jar of turpentine. She put down her pallet on the paint-spattered workbench and sank into the threadbare armchair, pushing her heavy, titian hair away from her face. She picked up the photograph from which she had been working, and compared it with the completed painting resting on the easel in front of her.

The likeness was excellent, although she found it difficult to distinguish between one sleek mare and the next. However, while she was trying to gather a collection of work to show at the London gallery, paintings like this paid the bills.

The work had been commissioned by a wealthy local farmer who owned three racehorses. 'Ondine', the chestnut mare staring soulfully at Rose from the painting, was number two. The farmer was paying her five hundred pounds for each painting. This would allow her to replace the roof of the rambling stone farmhouse where she and her children lived. It wouldn't stretch to solving the deteriorating damp problem, or make any headway into the dry-rot and woodworm, but it was a start.

Rose was banking on the exhibition. If she could sell just a few of her paintings, it would make all the difference to her mounting debts. The constant promises to the bank manager were wearing thin and Rose knew she was treading a very fine line.

But it was a long time since she had shown. Almost twenty years. People may have forgotten her since those heady days when she was adored by critics and public alike. Young, beautiful and immensely gifted . . . then it had all gone wrong and she had stopped painting and moved from London to live in seclusion here, in Sawood, on the rolling moors of Yorkshire.

Yes, the exhibition in April next year was certainly a gamble, but it had to pay off . . .

Rose stood up and manoeuvred her large frame expertly through the clutter of her small studio. She stared out of the picture window at the serenity beyond. The view never ceased to fill her with peace and was the main reason she had bought the farmhouse. It was perched on top of a hill, with an uninterrupted view of the valley below. The sliver of silver water known as Leeming Reservoir far beneath contrasted well with the thorough greenness of its surrounds. She'd hate to lose this view, but she knew that if the exhibition failed, the farmhouse would have to be sold.

'Damn! Damn! Damn!' Rose slammed her fist down on the solid grey stone of the window-sill.

Of course, there was another option. There always had been another option, but it was one she had resisted taking for nigh on twenty years.

Rose thought of her brother, David, with his penthouse in New York, country residence in Gloucestershire, a villa on an exclusive island in the Caribbean and the ocean-going yacht moored somewhere along the Côte d'Azur. Many were the nights when she had listened to the drip-dripping of water into the metal saucepan placed to the right of her bed, that she had thought of asking him for help. But she would far rather face eviction than ask him for money. Things had gone too far, too long ago . . .

She had not seen him for many years, only kept track of his meteoric rise in the corridors of power through newspaper articles. She had read with little sadness of the death of his wife eight months ago, which had left him widowed with a boy of sixteen.

And then, a week ago, she had received a telegram.

'Dear Rose stop I have severe business commitments for the next two months stop my son Brett is out of boarding school on the twentieth of June stop I don't want to leave him alone stop still mourning the death of his mother stop could he come to you stop country air do him good stop pick him up end August stop David.'

The arrival of the telegram had prevented Rose from entering her studio for five days. She had taken long walks over the moors, trying to reason why David was doing this.

Well, there was little to be done. David had presented her with a *fait accompli*. The boy was coming, probably a spoiled brat with airs and graces who would not take kindly to staying in a crumbling farmhouse with nothing to do save watch the grass grow.

She wondered how her own children would feel about

the arrival of a previously unknown cousin. Rose had to work out a way of explaining the sudden appearance of, not only Brett, but an uncle who was probably one of the richest men in the world.

Miles, her tall, handsome nineteen-year-old, would nod and accept it without question, whereas Miranda . . . Rose felt the usual tinge of guilt as she thought of her blonde, wilful, adopted daughter.

Rose worried that it was due to her that Miranda was such a handful. Miranda was spoilt, rude and deliberately fought against her will. Rose had always tried hard to show her as much love as Miles, but Miranda instinctively knew that she could never compete with the bond between mother and son, flesh and blood.

So instead of Miranda helping to bring security and a family atmosphere into the house, she only created tension. The mixture of guilt and continual exasperation at the lack of communication between them was not a recipe for a good relationship. The most that could be said was that they tolerated each other. Yet Rose had tried so hard to love Miranda, to do her best.

Rose knew how impressed Miranda would be by Brett's arrival and his father's amazing wealth. No doubt she would flirt. She was a very pretty girl with a long line of broken hearts already behind her. Rose wished that she wasn't so . . . obvious. At fifteen, her body was well developed and she made no attempt to conceal it. Rose had given up forbidding the bright red lipstick and the ridiculously short skirts, as Miranda would sulk for days and the atmosphere in the house lasted as long.

Rose checked her watch. Miranda would be arriving

14

home from school shortly and Miles was on his way from Leeds, where his term at university had just ended. It would be good to see him and she'd asked Mrs Thompson to lay on a special spread for tea.

Rose would join them and announce the impending arrival of her nephew as though it was the most natural thing in the world for her brother's child to stay with them during the holidays.

Rose steeled herself. She had a part to play. For he must never know . . .

2

'LEAH, HOW DO you fancy coming to help me up at the big house today? Mrs Delancey has a guest coming to stay tomorrow and I have to open one of those upstairs rooms and give it a good clean. Thank goodness it's summer. If we open some of the windows it should clear the room of that awful damp smell.' Mrs
Thompson wrinkled her nose.

'Of course I'll come,' said Leah, studying her mother. Doreen Thompson had thick brown hair worn in a sensible, short style. The recent demi-wave meant that the curls were far too tight on her forehead and at the nape of her neck. Years of hard work and worry had kept her statuesque figure slim, but had added too many lines to the thirty-seven-year-old face.

'Good. That's settled then. Go and put on your oldest jeans, Leah. It'll be filthy dirty in that room. And be quick about it. I want to leave as soon as I've prepared your dad's lunch.'

Leah needed no further bidding. She raced up the stairs, opened the door to her shoe-box of a room and scrabbled in the bottom of her small wardrobe for a pair

16

of tatty, ancient jeans. She found an old sweatshirt and pulled it on, then sat on the end of her bed so she could see in the mirror to plait her waist-length, mahogany-coloured hair. With the heavy braid hanging down her back, Leah looked younger than her fifteen years, but as she stood up, the mirror reflected the gently developing contours of a much maturer girl. She had always been tall for her age, taking after her mother, but in the past year she seemed to have shot up. Now she was a good head and shoulders above the other girls in her class. Her mother was always on about her growing out of her strength, which made Leah feel a bit like a sunflower, and urging her to eat more to fill out her skinny frame.

Leah found her trainers under the bed and quickly tied them up, anxious to be off to the big house. She loved it when her mother took her up there. The farmhouse had so much space, compared to the cramped two-up, two-down that she lived in. And Mrs Delancey fascinated her. She was so different to anyone else Leah knew, and she thought how lucky Miranda was to have her as a mother. Not that she didn't love her own mother, but what with her father in his wheelchair and her mother working all day, Mum would sometimes get bad-tempered and shout. Leah knew it was only because she got tired, and she tried to help her with the chores as much as she could.

Leah could only vaguely remember her father when he could walk. He'd been stricken with rheumatoid arthritis when she was four and had spent the past eleven years confined to a wheelchair. He had left his hard, manual job at the woollen mill and her mother had gone to

17

work as housekeeper to Mrs Delancey to bring in some pennies. In all that time, she had never heard her father complain, and knew that he felt only guilt for the way his wife had to look after him and earn them a living.

Leah loved her father dearly, and spent as much time as she could keeping him company.

Leah ran downstairs and knocked on the door of the front room. When her father had become sick, the sitting room had been turned into her parents' bedroom and a shower and toilet had been installed by the council in the walk-in pantry just off the kitchen.

'Come in.'

She opened the door. Mr Thompson was sitting in his usual spot, by the window. The brown eyes that Leah had inherited lit up as he saw his daughter.

'Hello, pet. Come and give your dad a kiss.'

Leah did so. 'I'm going to the big house with Mum to help her.'

'Right, lass. I'll see you later then. Enjoy yourself.'

'I will. Mum's bringing in your sandwiches.'

'Lovely. 'Bye, pet.'

Leah closed the door and went into the kitchen, where her mother was covering a plate of spam sandwiches with greaseproof paper.

'I'll pop these in to your dad and we'll be off, Leah,' she said.

It was a two-mile walk from Oxenhope up to the tiny hamlet of Sawood where Mrs Delancey's farmhouse sat on top of the hill. Mrs Thompson usually cycled, but today, as Leah was with her, they walked briskly away from the village and up the hill towards the moors.

The sky was a delicate egg-shell blue with wisps of white clouds flying across it. The sun was shining and the day was warm and balmy. Leah had slung her anorak over her shoulder, knowing that the temperature on the moors could drop suddenly and that she might need its warmth for the walk back later.

'I think we're in for a scorcher this year,' commented Mrs Thompson. Mrs Delancey told me it's her nephew that's coming to stay. I didn't know she had one.'

'How old is he?'

'In his teens. It'll mean Mrs Delancey has a house-full, what with Miles home from university and Miranda breaking up from school. And her in the middle of getting this exhibition organized.'

'Mum?'

'Yes?'

'Do you . . . do you like Miles?'

Mrs Thompson stopped and stared at Leah. 'Of course I do. I've helped bring him up, haven't I? Why do you ask such a silly question?'

'Oh, no reason,' said Leah, seeing the fiercely protective look on her mother's face.

'Now, if you were talking about that little madam of a sister, well, she needs a good spanking and no one will convince me otherwise.'

'Why doesn't Mrs Delancey spank her then?'

'I don't know, Leah. It's not my place to interfere. I'd like to know whose child she really was. Came from bad stock, if you ask me. Flaunting herself around the village in those get-ups. It's not decent for a girl her age.'

Leah rather admired the daring outfits Miranda wore

and she looked on with admiration as the boys at Greenhead Grammar School, where she was in the same year as Miranda, flocked round her. Leah sometimes saw Miranda heading for Cliffe Castle Park after school with a group of the boys from the year above her. She wondered how Miranda managed to look so pretty and grown up in the dull, regulation school-uniform, when Leah's own only served to accentuate her lankiness. Although only a month younger than Miranda, Leah felt like a kid beside her.

'I know you say that Mrs Delancey has no money, but Miranda always has new clothes. And they do live in that big house.'

Mrs Thompson nodded knowingly. 'It's levels, Leah. Now, take our family, for example. We don't have two ha'pennies to rub together, same as Mrs Delancey says she doesn't. But she used to be rich, really rich. So, compared to that, she thinks she's poor. Do you understand?'

'I think so.'

'Miranda complains if she can't buy a new outfit to go to a party. You complain if there's no food on the table for tea.'

'Why isn't she rich any more?'

Her mother shrugged. 'Well, I don't know what she did with all her money, but she only started painting again a couple of years ago, so she probably didn't sell anything for a long while. Now, enough of this chatter. Hurry your step, lass, or we'll be late.'

Mrs Thompson opened the back door of the farmhouse which led directly into the kitchen. The room was larger than the entire downstairs of Leah's house.

Miranda, attired in a bright pink satin dressing-gown and furry mules to match, was sitting eating breakfast at the long, scrubbed-pine table.

'Hello, Doreen, you've arrived just in time to make me more toast.'

'Well, you can sing for it today, young miss. I've got my work cut out preparing that room for your mother's guest.'

'Then I'm sure Leah wouldn't mind, would you, darling?' drawled Miranda.

Leah glanced at her mother, who was preparing to retort, and quickly said, 'Of course I don't mind. You go up, Mum, and I'll join you in a minute.'

Mrs Thompson frowned, then shrugged her shoulders and disappeared out of the kitchen. Leah popped a couple of slices of bread into the toaster.

'You grow every time I see you. Your tits have sprouted too.'

Leah blushed and her hands went instinctively to cover her newly formed chest.

Miranda appraised her slowly. 'Do you diet? You're very thin.'

'Oh no, Mum calls me the gannet. I'd lick the plate if she'd let me.'

'Lucky old you. I just have to look at cream and I put on pounds,' said Miranda mournfully.

'But you have a lovely figure. All the boys in our year say so.' Leah jumped as the toast popped up behind her.

'Use the low-fat spread, and only a thin layer of marmalade. What else do the boys say about me, then?' asked Miranda nonchalantly.

Leah blushed. 'Well, they say they think you're . . . very pretty.'

'Do you think I'm pretty, Leah?'

'Oh yes, very. I . . . I like your clothes.' Leah put the plate of toast in front of Miranda. 'Do you want another cup of tea?'

Miranda nodded. 'Well, you should tell dear Mama you like my clothes. She goes mad if my hemline's above my ankles! She's such a prude. Why don't you pour yourself some tea and keep me company while I eat this?'

'I'd better not. I've got to go upstairs and help Mum.'

'Suit yourself. If you have time later, come to my bedroom and I'll show you the new outfit I bought last Saturday. It's terriff.'

'I'd love to. See you later, Miranda.'

'Sure.'

Leah went up two flights of creaking stairs and found her mother vigorously shaking a threadbare rug in the wide corridor.

'I was just coming to find you. I need help turning the mattress. It's got mould on one of the corners. I've lit the fire in the grate to try and dry the room out a bit.'

Leah followed her into the large bedroom and took one end of the heavy double mattress.

'Right, lift it onto its side . . . that's right. I hope you won't make a habit of letting that madam downstairs treat you like a servant. Give an inch and she'll take a mile. Next time you say no, lass. It's not your job to fetch and carry for her.'

'I'm sorry, Mum. Miranda's so grown up, isn't she?'

Doreen Thompson caught the admiration in her daughter's eyes.

'Aye, that she is, and no role-model for you, miss. If you ever came home looking like a tart, Dad and I'd have your guts for garters. Now, that looks better. We won't put the sheets on it till the last moment. Give it time to dry out. The poor lad'll probably go down with pneumonia after sleeping on that. There's some window polish in that box. Give those filthy panes a good scrub will you, pet?'

Leah nodded, found the polish and a clean cloth and went to the leaded window. She ran a finger through the dust on the pane, dislodging a small spider from its web.

'I'm going downstairs to get the hoover.'

Mrs Thompson went out of the room and Leah set to work on the dirty panes, smearing the polish and scrubbing until the cloth was black. When she had cleaned four small, square panes, she peered out. The view over the moors was magnificent, reaching down into the valley, where she could see the chimney-tops of Oxenhope village on the other side of the reservoir. The sun was shining and the moors were bathed in light.

Then she noticed a figure perched on top of a hillock, perhaps a quarter of a mile away from the house. The figure was sitting with his arms around his knees, staring down into the valley below him. Leah recognized the thick, black hair. It was Miles.

Miles frightened her. He never smiled, never said hello; he just stared at her. When he was home, he seemed to spend hours alone on the moors and occasionally she would see him, a black silhouette against the sun, trotting across the top of the valley on one of Mr Morriss's horses.

Suddenly, Miles turned round. And, as if he had known that Leah was watching him, he fixed his black eyes directly upon her. Although he was some distance away, Leah felt as though he was penetrating her. She stood perfectly still, unable to move, then shuddered and moved quickly away from the window.

Mrs Thompson had arrived with the hoover. 'Come on, Leah, jump to it. You've not cleaned more than a quarter of those panes.'

Reluctantly, Leah moved back to the window.

The figure on the hillock had vanished.

'I wanted to ask you, Doreen, whether Leah would like to earn a bit of pocket-money?'

Leah was sitting in the kitchen with her mother, having a cup of tea before the walk back to the village.

Mrs Delancey was standing in the kitchen doorway in one of her smocks covered with a variety of bright, oily colours. She was smiling at Leah.

'Well now, I'm sure that sounds like a fine idea, doesn't it, Leah?' said Mrs Thompson.

'Yes, Mrs Delancey. What would you want me to do?'

'You know I have my nephew, Brett, coming to stay tomorrow. The problem is that I'm deep in the middle of painting for my exhibition. I'm going to have little enough time as it is without having to cook meals every day. So I was wondering if you would like to come and help your mother keep the house tidy and make some breakfast and an evening meal for myself and the children. My own are perfectly capable of fending for themselves, but my nephew . . . well, let's just say he's used to a far grander lifestyle. Obviously I'll pay you more for the extra hours, Doreen, and give Leah something too.'

Mrs Thompson looked at Leah. 'As long as one of us is around to cook supper for Dad, I'd say it was a fine idea, isn't it Leah?'

Leah knew her mother was thinking how the extra pennies would come in handy. She nodded. 'Yes, Mrs Delancey, I'd like it very much.'

'Good, that's settled then. I've got an old bicycle in the barn you can use to get up here. Brett arrives tomorrow afternoon and I'd like you to prepare something special for dinner. We'll eat in the dining room. Get the Wedgwood service out and make a list of the groceries you'll need for the week. I'll ring the farm shop and ask them to deliver. Now, I really must get back to my studio. I'll see you tomorrow.'

'Right, Mrs Delancey,' said Mrs Thompson.

Rose turned to walk out of the kitchen, then, in afterthought, turned back.

'If my nephew seems a little . . . different, take no notice. His mother died not long ago and, as I mentioned, he's been used to the best. Well, as I said, see you tomorrow.' Rose went out of the kitchen and shut the door.

'Poor mite, him so young and his mother dying.' Mrs Thompson rinsed the tea-cups in the sink.

The door opened and in flounced Miranda, dressed in a tight red mini-skirt and a low-cut cheesecloth top.

'I thought you were coming to see my new outfit, Leah,' she said petulantly.

25

'Well I . . .'

'Never mind. I've come to model it for you. What do you think? Isn't it great?' Miranda smiled and twirled.

'I think it's . . .'

'I think it's high time we were leaving to get your dad's tea,' cut in her mother.

Miranda ignored her. 'I got it from that new boutique in Keighley. I'm going to wear it to dinner tomorrow night for the arrival of my darling cousin. You know his father is one of the richest men in the world, don't you?'

'Now don't you go making up stories, young lady,' reproached Mrs Thompson.

'Oh, but it's true, honest injun.' Miranda sat down in a chair and swung her legs onto the table, revealing a large expanse of white thigh. 'Dear Mama kept that one quiet, didn't she? Her brother is David Cooper. I mean, *the* David Cooper.' She stared at them, waiting for their reaction, and pouted when there was none. 'Don't tell me you haven't heard of him? He's world-famous. He owns Cooper Industries, one of the largest companies in the world. God only knows why we have to live in this heap, when dear old Rosie has David Cooper for a brother.'

'Don't call your mum Rosie, madam.'

'Sorry, Mrs T,' Miranda replied. 'And here was me thinking that nothing exciting ever happened around this dump when, out of the blue, I discover I have an uncle who's loaded, and his son is arriving here tomorrow. And the best news of all; he's sixteen. I wonder if he's got a girlfriend?' she mused.

'Now, you treat him nice, Miranda. Poor thing, he lost his mother not long ago.'

Miranda grinned. 'Rest assured I will, Mrs T. I'll make sure he gets as much comfort as he needs. Oh well, I'm going to try out my new face-pack. See you.' Miranda stood up and skipped out of the kitchen.

Mrs Thompson shook her head. 'Come on, Leah, we'd best be going. It'll be a busy day tomorrow.' She wiped her hands on a tea-towel and inclined her head towards the door. 'And I smell trouble.'

3

THE LONG, BLACK limousine made its way smoothly through the small, Yorkshire villages. People stared at it curiously and tried to make out the shadowy figure behind the tinted glass.

Brett Cooper stared miserably back at them, making grotesque faces that he knew they couldn't see. The sky had just clouded over and it had begun to rain. The moorland around him looked as desolate as he felt.

Brett stretched forward and pulled a can of Coke out of the mini-bar. The interior of the car reminded him of a luxury tomb, with its plush leather wall-coverings and blinds to all sides so his father could shut out the world.

Brett pressed a button. 'How far now, Bill?'

'Only another half an hour, sir,' the metallic voice replied.

Brett released the button, stretched out his long, jean-clad legs and sipped his Coke.

His father had promised to collect him from school, and drive with Brett up to Yorkshire to introduce him personally to this aunt of his. But when he had eagerly climbed into the back of the car, he'd found it empty.

Bill, his father's chauffeur, had told him that Mr Cooper sent his apologies, but he'd had to fly off to America sooner than expected.

On the five-hour drive from Windsor up north, Brett had experienced anger towards his father for repeating, once more, the pattern of his childhood; fear at having to face this unknown aunt alone, and overwhelming sorrow that his mother was not here to stop him feeling as though his father didn't give a damn about him.

Tears filled Brett's eyes as he thought of this time last year. He had flown directly to Nice airport where his mother had met him at arrivals. They had driven to the villa she had rented in Cap Ferrat and spent a glorious summer together, just the two of them. His father had visited a couple of times, but had spent the days locked in his office or on the yacht entertaining important business associates who had flown over to see him.

And then, three months later, his mother was dead. He remembered being shown into his housemaster's study to be told the news.

Brett had gone to his empty room, sat on the edge of his bed and stared into space. All that money and luxury, and yet it had not stopped his mother dying. And she had died alone. He hated her for not telling him there was something wrong. Didn't she know how he would feel about not being there with her at the end?

And his father, he had known. So why the hell hadn't he been with his wife when she needed him?

Brett knew it was a ridiculous question to ask: business. The only thing in the world his father cared about. Brett wondered why his father had ever got married. He didn't need a wife, just a female secretary who could screw and type memos at the same time. That would suit David Cooper down to the ground. And yet, his mother had been so loyal. She never complained that she rarely saw him, that she and his son seemed to be at the bottom of his list of priorities. He had only heard them arguing once, when he was a child of four.

'For God's sake, Vivien, please think about it. New York is a marvellous place to live. When Brett goes to prep school, he can still fly over for the holidays. The apartment is wonderful. At least come and see it.'

His mother had replied in her quiet even tones, 'No, David, I'm sorry. I want to stay in England so that I'm here if Brett needs me.'

Brett had started to realize, as he had grown up, that his mother had made a choice that day. And that choice had been him. His father had come home less and less after that, basing himself in New York and never pressing his wife to join him there again.

When Brett had first started at Eton, boys had asked him what his famous father was like. Brett would answer 'great', or 'a really good sport', but the truth was, he really didn't know.

When he was thirteen, David had taken to pulling Brett aside and showing him plans for a new apartment block under construction. Brett would try to look interested in what his father had to say.

'As soon as you've left Cambridge, you'll be coming into the business to learn how it runs. One day, it'll be yours, Brett.'

Brett would nod and smile and inwardly grimace. He

didn't have the least interest in understanding his father's business. He had no head for figures and found statistics impossible. He had only scraped through the common entrance exam to Eton by gaining such high marks in his English paper.

In the past two years, Brett had started to wake up in cold sweats as the future that had been mapped out for him by his father began to dawn on him. Last year, in Cap Ferrat, he had opened his heart to his mother about how he felt. He had also shown her some of his paintings. She had stared at them in surprise.

'Goodness me, darling, I had no idea you could paint like this. They're exquisite. You have real talent. I must show them to your father.'

David had glanced cursorily at them and shrugged. 'Not bad. It's good for a businessman to have a hobby that relaxes him.'

Brett had put his watercolours and easel away. His mother had tried to comfort him and encouraged her son to continue capturing the splendid view from their villa.

'It's pointless, Mother. He'll never let me go to art college, never. He's got it all planned. He's so certain about me getting into Cambridge that he never thinks for a minute I might flunk my Oxbridge.'

Vivien had sighed. For they both knew that if the worst did happen, a place could easily be arranged by a generous donation to the right college.

'Look, Brett, I promise I'll talk to him for you. You are only fifteen. I'm sure that we can make him understand when the time comes. You must continue painting, darling. You show real promise.'

Brett had shaken his head. Then a month later he had gone back to school and painted his mother sitting on the swing in the garden of their Gloucestershire home. He had copied it from his favourite photograph of her, showing her delicate beauty at its best. He had planned to give it to her for Christmas. But by Christmas she was dead and the painting was still gift-wrapped under his bed at school. He had refused to step into the art room since.

After eight months, Brett still felt as though she had died yesterday. His mother had been the centre of his world, his rock and his security. He felt so vulnerable now that there was no mediator between him and his father.

He had presumed that he would go home to the house in Gloucestershire for these summer holidays, or maybe Antigua. So when he had received the letter, typed by Pat, his father's personal assistant, telling him that his father was packing him off to Yorkshire to stay with some aunt he'd never heard of, it had only added to his despair. He'd tried in vain to contact his father in New York and protest, but Pat had intercepted his calls.

'Your father is adamant you should go, Brett dear, as he has such a busy schedule for the next couple of months. I'm sure you'll be fine. I'm cabling five hundred pounds over to you as spending money. Let me know if you want more, won't you?'

Brett knew there was little point in arguing. What David Cooper wanted, he got.

The intercom buzzed. 'Another five minutes, sir, and we'll be there. You can see the house from here. If you look to your left, it's the one perched on top of the hill.'

Brett looked, and through the drizzle, he saw it. A large, greystone building, set alone in the surrounding moorland. It looked desolate and terribly unwelcoming, like something out of a Dickens novel.

'Bleak house,' he muttered to himself. His heart started beating faster as the limousine climbed the hill. For the thousandth time, he wished his mother was sitting next to him, telling him that everything was all right.

The car came to a smooth halt in front of the house. Brett took a deep breath. His mother wasn't here, and he must face this alone, like a man.

Rose heard the car draw up. She peered out of the corner of her studio window and saw the grand limousine. The chauffeur was getting out of the front seat and walking round to open the passenger door. The windows were tinted and she couldn't see inside. She sucked in her breath as a tall young man got out. She continued holding it as the chauffeur took forever to shut the door.

'Thank God,' Rose breathed out. Then, from her unseen vantage point, she studied her brother's son.

Rose recognized the titian hair as her own colour. The boy turned round and she saw David's deep, blue eyes and strong jawline. Brett was an extremely handsome young man. She watched him nervously fiddling with something in the pocket of his jacket as the chauffeur unloaded the suitcases from the boot and walked towards the front door. Something about the boy struck Rose as forlorn. Poor thing, he's probably far more nervous than I am, she thought. The bell rang, and Rose quickly checked her appearance in the mirror. She heard Mrs

33

Thompson open the front door, just as Rose had told her to. She had packed Miles and Miranda off horse-riding for the afternoon, wanting to have some time with Brett alone.

She heard a voice uncannily like David's talking quietly to Mrs Thompson as she led him through to the sitting room. Rose opened the door and walked down the hallway. The chauffeur was bringing in the last suitcase.

'Ms Cooper, I presume.'

'No, it's Delancey actually.'

'Sorry, Ms Delancey. Mr Cooper sends his thanks. He also asked me to give you this to cover Brett's keep.' The chauffeur handed Rose an envelope.

'Thank you. Would you like a cup of tea and something to eat? It's a long drive back.'

'No, Ms Delancey. Thanks for the offer, but I've got to push straight off. I'm picking some people up from Leeds Bradford airport at five.'

'Sounds as though David works you too hard.'

'He keeps me busy, but I enjoy it. I've been with him for nearly thirteen years and I've known Brett most of his life. He's a good kid and he won't cause you any trouble. If he seems a bit quiet, well, he's not had an easy time of it. He adored his mother. It was such a tragedy.'

'Don't you worry, I'll take care of him. I'm sure we'll get along fine. Drive carefully.'

'I will.' Bill tipped his hat. 'Goodbye, Ms Delancey.'

Rose closed the front door and heard the limousine drive off. She tore the envelope open and found a 'Cooper Industries' compliment slip and a thousand pounds in cash.

34

'My goodness,' she whispered, 'I'll have to feed him caviar and champagne every night to get through this much.' Rose tucked the envelope into a pocket of her voluminous skirt, wondering how soon she could get the builder in to quote for the roof, and opened the door to the sitting room.

Whatever Brett had expected his unknown aunt to look like, it was certainly not the woman who walked through the door.

His mother had always wondered from whom Brett had inherited his unusual red-gold hair colour, and now he knew.

His Aunt Rose was a large lady, dressed in a brightly coloured blouse and a peasant skirt. Brett could see that she had once been a very beautiful woman before she had gained weight. As he looked through his artist's eyes, he saw the fine bone structure, the prominent, high cheekbones, still refusing to be engulfed completely by fatty tissue. Her huge green eyes dominated her face and she shared her wide, sensuous lips with his father. She smiled at him, showing an even set of white teeth. Her face looked familiar, and Brett was sure he'd seen her somewhere before, but he couldn't place it.

'Hello, Brett, I'm Rose.' She spoke in a rich, deep voice that suited her bulk.

Brett stood up. 'I'm very pleased to meet you, Aunt Rose.' He held out his hand, but, instead of taking it, she clasped him in a tight embrace. He smelt strong perfume and something else . . . yes, he was sure that it was the distinctive smell of oil-paint. Rose let him go, sat down on the sofa and patted the seat next to her. He sat down and Rose took his hand in hers.

'It's lovely to have you with us, Brett. You must feel a little strange at the moment, having to come here and stay with relatives you've never met before. I'm sure you'll soon settle down. You must be hungry after that long drive. Would you like something to eat?'

'No, thank you. Bill filled a hamper for me to eat on the way up here.'

'Perhaps a cup of tea then?'

'Yes, that would be lovely.'

'I'll tell Doreen to bring some through.'

While Rose went to the kitchen, Brett looked around the room. It was untidily crammed with old furniture and bric-à-brac, but what caught his attention were the distinctive paintings on the wall . . .

'How long did the journey take?' Rose sat next to him once more.

'Oh, about five hours. The traffic was good.'

'You must be tired though.'

'I am, a bit.'

'I'll show you up to your room after we've had some tea. The house is very quiet as my children are out riding. Maybe you'd like to have a lie-down before dinner.'

'Maybe,' said Brett.

There was a pause as Rose tried to think of something to say.

'Ah, here's Doreen with tea. Do you take sugar?'

'No thank you, Aunt Rose.'

'Oh, for heaven's sake, drop the "aunt" part, will you?' Rose smiled. 'You're almost grown up now and it makes

me feel ancient. My children call me Rose too. I so hate
Mother or Mum.'

Rose bit her lip as she watched the anguish on Brett's
face. The confident, arrogant boy whose arrival she'd
expected could not be more in contrast to the shy, tense
young man who was so obviously still grieving for his
mother.

'You'll meet Miles and Miranda at dinner tonight. Let
me warn you about Miranda. She can be a bit of a madam
on occasions, but you mustn't take her too seriously.
She's fifteen, only a few months younger than you, so you
should be able to keep each other company.'

'How old is your son?'

'Miles is twenty and just home from his second year at
Leeds University. He doesn't say much, so don't worry if
it takes time to get to know him. I'm sure you'll get along
fine.' Rose could hardly believe she was having this conversation. 'Well, if you've finished your tea, I'll take you
upstairs to your room.'

Brett followed Rose up two flights of creaking stairs
and along a lino-clad passage-way.

'Here we are. I'm afraid it's basic, but the view from
this window is the best in the house. Well, I'll leave you to
unpack. If you need anything, Doreen is usually in the
kitchen. I'll see you at eight for dinner.' Rose smiled at
him and closed the door.

Brett looked at the room that would be his for the next
two months. There was a double bed, with an old patchwork quilt thrown over it. The linoleum covering the
floor-boards was worn and there were large cracks in the
plaster on the ceiling. Brett walked to the window and

looked out. The drizzle had turned to rain and grey clouds were covering the tops of the hills in the distance. He shivered. The room was cold and smelt of damp. He heard a faint dripping sound and noticed a small puddle of water near the door. The ceiling above the puddle was sagging heavily.

Brett felt a lump come to his throat. He felt deserted, utterly miserable and completely alone. How could his father have sent him here, to this terrible, desolate place? He threw himself face down on the bed and started to cry for the first time since his mother had died.

He cried for a long time, then, realizing that he was physically shivering, climbed under the quilt, fully clothed, and fell into an exhausted sleep.

That was how Rose found him, three hours later. After shaking him gently and getting no response, she tip-toed out of the room and closed the door.

4

BRETT WOKE TO a blinding light piercing through his closed eye-lids. He opened his eyes and blinked as the rays of golden sun streamed in through the window. For a moment, he couldn't remember where he was. As he came to, he sat up and looked out of the window at the beautiful greenery beyond. He could hardly believe that the sun could turn a desolate landscape into a scene of such tranquillity.

He turned over and stretched. Then he saw her.

She was standing by the door, holding a tray in both hands. She was tall, but almost waif-like in her thinness, and she had a head of the most glorious dark brown hair, reaching nearly to her waist. Her eyes were also deep brown, with long, black lashes framing them. Her face was heart-shaped, with lips of a natural red, and a small, retroussé nose.

With the sun shining directly onto her, sending dancing lights through her hair, she looked so perfect and pure that Brett wondered if he was seeing a vision of the Madonna. Then he realized that Madonnas didn't usually carry breakfast trays or wear sweatshirts and jeans, so she had to be real. She was the most beautiful girl he had ever seen.

'Hello,' she said shyly. 'Mum thought you might be hungry.'

The girl spoke in a soft, Yorkshire accent. So this was Miranda, thought Brett. Wow, two whole months with her for company. Maybe this holiday wasn't going to be quite as bad as he'd anticipated.

'That's very kind of her. Actually, I'm starving. I think I missed out on dinner last night.'

'You did.' She smiled, showing her flawless, pearl-white teeth. 'I'll put the tray on the end of the bed. There's bacon and eggs under the dish, and some toast and tea.'

Brett watched as she moved gracefully towards him and set the tray down.

'Thanks, Miranda. I'm Brett, by the way.'

Her lovely face creased as she frowned and shook her head. 'Oh no, I'm not . . .'

'Was somebody mentioning my name?' A girl with bright blonde hair, a pair of tight riding jodhpurs and a T-shirt that showed a large amount of rapidly developing cleavage burst through the door. The girl would have been very pretty if her face had not been plastered with unsubtle make-up. She bounced over to him and sat on the edge of the bed, sending the tray skidding onto the floor with a clatter of breaking china.

'Sod it! Who put that tray there? Clean it up will you, Leah?' She smiled at Brett as the other girl knelt on the floor. 'Miranda Delancey, your cousin, or should I say step-cousin, as dear old Rosie adopted me when I was little.'

Brett's heart sank. He watched the girl called Leah struggling to pick up the shards of china from the mess of bacon and eggs on the floor.

'Good to meet you,' he said to Miranda, then jumped out of bed. 'Let me help you with that.' He knelt beside Leah.

'Let her do it, it's what she's paid for,' said Miranda, swinging her legs onto the bed in a provocative pose.

Brett watched a glimmer of anger cross the brown eyes as he handed Leah the last shard of china from the floor.

'It's done now,' said Brett, standing upright.

'I'll go and get a broom and a cloth from downstairs to clean up the mess. Will you be wanting your breakfast up here still?'

Brett looked into Leah's clear eyes, thinking that breakfast was the last thing on his mind. 'No, I'll come down for it.'

Leah nodded, picked up the tray and left the room.

'Who is she?' Brett asked Miranda.

'Leah Thompson, the housekeeper's kid. She helps around the house during the holidays,' said Miranda dismissively. 'Now, onto more important things, like what you and I are going to do today. Rosie has put me in charge of the Brett Cooper entertainments committee, and I intend to see to it that you are not left alone for a minute.'

Brett was taken aback by the predatory look in her eyes and the obvious innuendo of the statement. He was unused to girls of his own age, being at an all-boys school and spending most of his holidays in the company of adults. Some of his class-mates at school boasted about

41

their blossoming sexual activities, but the stories were always about how the chap had sweated over how to get the girl alone and make her kiss him. Miranda, lying provocatively on his bed, looked as though she was ready and willing to be taken there and then. She was looking him up and down and Brett felt himself blushing.

'Well? What do you want to do today?'

'I . . . well . . . I –'

'Do you ride?'

'Yes.'

'That's settled then. When you're ready, we'll go over to old Morriss's place and take a couple of horses out on the moors for a nice long ride. Get to know each other better.' Miranda swept her hand through her hair and stared at him.

'Fine. Er, could you tell me where the bathroom is? I think I ought to wash and change out of these clothes.'

'Down the passage, second door on the left. What happened to you last night? I got all dressed up for dinner especially,' Miranda pouted.

'I . . . well I was tired from the journey I think.'

'I hope you don't usually make a habit of sleeping in your clothes.' Miranda winked at him and jumped off the bed. 'I'll wait for you downstairs. Don't be too long, will you now?' She disappeared from the room.

Brett padded along the corridor, found the bathroom and turned on the taps to run a bath. The water coughed and spluttered and when it finally made an appearance, it was a strange yellow colour.

Brett took off his crumpled clothes and climbed in, trying not to notice the brown, gritty sediment lying along

42

the bottom of the ancient iron tub. He closed his eyes and could only see a picture of Leah, standing in the doorway of his room. He felt overwhelming disappointment that she was not the girl he would be spending the holiday with.

Brett got out of the bath, dried himself and went back to his room to find his riding jodhpurs, still packed in one of his three cases. He emptied each one hurriedly and twenty minutes later was sitting in the comfortable kitchen eating a large plate of bacon and eggs. Miranda was chattering ten to the dozen about her plans for the next two months, and Leah was helping her mother with the drying up.

'Right, time to be off,' said Miranda. 'It's only a half-mile walk to the farm. We could cycle if you want.'

'No, a walk would do me good.'

Miranda led him out of the kitchen door and Brett stopped and turned round. ' 'Bye, Leah. See you later.'

''Bye, Brett.'

'Do you not think I should say good morning to Aun . . . I mean Rose before we go?' Brett asked Miranda, who was striding down the hill at a brisk pace.

'God no. She's locked away in her studio and it's on pain of death if you disturb her. She only comes out to eat.'

'What kind of studio?'

'Oh, didn't you know? Rosie used to be a famous painter back in the dark ages. She hasn't done anything for yonks, then a couple of years ago she cleared out one of the downstairs rooms and turned it into a studio. She's having an exhibition in London next year. Her big come-back or something. Personally, I think she's wasting her time. I mean, who's going to remember her from twenty years ago?' Miranda sniffed.

Things were falling rapidly into place as Brett walked down the hill. That smell of oil-paint when she had hugged him, the paintings on the wall in her sitting room, and Rose's face . . . of course!

'Is Rose's second name Delancey?'

Miranda nodded. 'Yes, why?'

'Miranda, I can tell you now that your mother was the toast of the art world twenty years ago. She was the most famous female artist in Europe, then she suddenly disappeared off the scene altogether.'

'Personally, I can't stand her paintings. They're so strange,' said Miranda. 'Anyway, you seem to know a lot about her. Interested in art, are you?'

'Well yes, I am actually.' Brett felt terribly excited, but puzzled. He wondered why on earth his father had never mentioned before that Rose Delancey was his sister. It was something to be tremendously proud of, surely?

'I'm sure Rosie will be able to spare a couple of seconds to discuss her favourite subject with you. Now, how good a horseman are you? The gelding's a brilliant ride, but unpredictable, and the mare . . . well, if you want an easy trot, I'd go for her.'

They had reached the stables and Miranda was leading him along the loose-boxes.

'I'll take the mare, thanks, Miranda.'

The horses were saddled up and the picnic that Mrs Thompson had made them stowed away in the gelding's saddle bag.

44

The two of them trotted at a relaxed pace in the direction of the moors.

'I just can't believe that this is the same place I arrived at last night. I don't think I've ever felt quite so depressed. It was all so black and gloomy.'

'It's like that up here. The weather can change in an instant. It's amazing how different the moors look when the sun's shining,' agreed Miranda.

'Who owns all this land?' enquired Brett.

'Farmers mostly. They graze their sheep on it.'

'It looks like it stretches for miles.' Brett gazed across the valley as they trotted onto the open grassland and began an ascent up-hill.

'It does. That's Blackmoor over the other side of the reservoir. It goes right to the edge of Haworth, three miles away. It gets pretty desolate in the winter up here, you know. We've been snowed in hundreds of times.'

Brett suddenly experienced a sense of well-being. He felt glad he had come. And he couldn't wait to get back and talk to his aunt.

'Phew,' said Miranda, wiping her forehead. 'It's a hot one today. When we get to the brow I think we should sit and have a drink.'

'Fine.'

Fifteen minutes later, the horses were tethered and Brett and Miranda were lying high up the hill in the rough grass, drinking Coke.

'Oh look,' Miranda shot up, 'there's Miles, down there, on the horse.'

Brett sat up and looked down the valley in the direction Miranda was pointing. He saw a small figure in the distance trotting across the moors on a big black horse.

'He spends most of his time riding on the moors when he comes back from university,' Miranda said softly, with a touch of wistfulness in her voice.

'What's he studying?'

'History. I miss him when he's not around.' Miranda tugged at a lump of grass. 'We used to spend a lot of time together when he was at home. Miles is different from other people . . . so quiet . . .' Her voice trailed off, then she turned to Brett and the seriousness left her face as she smiled. 'Me, I like lively people, lots of noise and action, you know. I'm moving to London as soon as I leave school. It's so dull here, nothing ever happens.'

'I think it's quite beautiful,' murmured Brett.

'Yes, but you don't have to live here, do you? I mean, I'm sure you go to fancy parties and famous restaurants all the time.'

Brett thought of the number of times he had done that, being paraded around at a function of his father's like a prize poodle, desperate to get home and out of the stiff, formal suit his father liked him to wear.

'Really, Miranda, those kind of things aren't all they're cracked up to be.'

'Well, I want to try them for myself. I want to be super-rich one day, then I can buy anything I want. I'd have a whole room full of designer clothes, and shoes to match. I'd have a huge house, and a Rolls-Royce, and . . .'

Brett lay back in the grass and wondered why the entire world thought that money bought happiness. He knew it didn't.

Later, they took the horses back across the moors to the stable and walked home.

Mrs Thompson was in the kitchen, preparing supper.

'Have a good ride, both of you?' she smiled.

'Great,' answered Brett.

'Mrs Delancey wants to have dinner in the dining room again tonight, as you missed out on it yesterday. It'll be ready for eight. Now, how about a nice cup of tea?'

At eight o'clock that evening, Brett wandered downstairs and into the dining room. It was deserted, so he went and sat down in an old leather chair, placed by the big, mullioned windows.

Leah came in, carrying a tray of soup bowls, which she proceeded to place on the scratched oak dining table.

'Here, let me help you, Leah.' Brett stood up.

'No, I can manage fine. Mrs Delancey'll be in in a minute.' Leah seemed nervous.

'Do you live here, Leah?'

'Oh no, I live in the village with my mum and dad.'

'I see. Miranda was saying today that Haworth is not far from here. I'd love to go and see the Parsonage where the Brontës lived.'

Leah's eyes lit up. 'Oh yes, you must visit it. I've been lots of times. I've read all their books, I think they're wonderful.'

'So do I. Which is your favourite novel?'

'*Wuthering Heights*,' said Leah without a pause. 'It's so romantic.'

Brett watched her blush prettily and move towards the door.

He put a hand on her arm to stop her. 'Well, as you seem to be the expert, maybe you could take me up there one day and show me round.'

She looked at him, paused, then smiled. 'Well, yes, if you'd like to, Brett.'

'I'd like to, very much.'

Rose appeared at the dining-room door and Leah scurried out of the room. She sat down at the top of the table.

'So, Brett, feeling better after your long sleep?' Her eyes twinkled.

'Much. I am truly sorry about last night. I don't know what hit me.'

'The Yorkshire air, probably. Miranda tells me you've been out riding today. It seems to have done you good. You looked so pale when you arrived. Are you settling in all right?'

'Yes, fine.'

'I must apologize for the leak in your room. The builder is coming to take a look at it tomorrow. I'm afraid the whole roof needs replacing.'

'No problem,' said Brett politely. 'Rose, Miranda was telling me today that you have started painting again. I know your work from the fifties and I was wondering if I could come and have a look at your new work sometime.'

Rose's face lit up. 'Of course. You're interested in art, then?'

'Extremely. I had no idea that you were Rose Delancey. I presumed your surname was Cooper, like Dad's.'

'I have been in retirement rather a long time. I'm flattered that you know my work. If you'd like to come to the studio after dinner, I'll show you what I've done so far for my exhibition.'

'Great, I'd love to. But I have to admit that I don't understand why Dad has never mentioned you before, especially with me being so interested in art.'

Rose opened her mouth to answer, but at that moment, Miranda bounced through the door. 'Hi, you two.' She was wearing the tight red mini-skirt and cheesecloth top. She sat down along one side of the table and patted the chair next to her. 'Come and sit next to me, Brett.'

Brett did so as Rose clucked. 'Really, Miranda, that skirt . . .'

'Sorry I'm late, everyone. I hope that the meal hasn't been held up on my behalf.'

Brett stared at the man in the doorway. He was immediately reminded of his conversation with Leah earlier. The man's tall stature and black hair and eyes reminded him instantly of his imaginary vision of Heathcliff. Brett watched him as he kissed his mother and sat down at the table next to her.

Brett recognized, as men could in another male, that Miles was devastatingly handsome. But there was something wild about him, in his eyes, as he focused them on Brett. Then his face broke into a wide, friendly smile and he extended his arm across the table.

'Miles Delancey, pleased to meet you, Brett.' For an instant, Brett felt the power of the well-muscled frame as Miles gripped his hand, then released it.

'And you.'

Leah entered the room with the soup tureen and began serving Rose. Brett watched her, and as he did so,

49

he noticed that someone else was watching her too. Miles was staring intently at Leah as she moved around the table. He didn't take his eyes off her once, and Brett saw the slight nervousness as Leah moved next to Miles to serve him. He continued staring at her, as she poured the soup into his bowl.

'How are you, Leah? You seem to have done some growing up since last time I saw you.' As Miles' eyes bored into Leah, Brett watched her give an almost unnoticeable shudder.

'I'm fine, Miles.' Leah quickly moved away towards the door with the empty soup tureen and Miles averted his eyes.

'Do begin, everyone,' said Rose, picking up her spoon.

'Now, I hope you all realize that a big event is going to take place on the twenty-third of July,' said Miranda. 'I'll be sixteen years of age, and we all know what an important birthday that is, don't we?' Brett felt a hand slide down his thigh. He turned and stared at Miranda, hard, and the hand was quickly removed. 'Rose, darling Rose, could I have the teeniest of parties to celebrate?'

Rose looked doubtful. 'Miranda, I have so much work on, the last thing I need is a house full of teenagers.'

'You asked Miles if he wanted a party when he was sixteen.' Miranda's eyes glistened with anger.

Rose knew she was cornered.

'All right, Miranda, you can have a few friends round on the Saturday night.'

'Thank you, thank you, Rose. You wouldn't fancy going out to the pictures or something for the evening, would you?'

50

The look in Rose's eyes made it clear that she would not, and Miranda knew not to push it any further.

'Mrs Thompson and Leah can make some food and serve it, can't they?'

'Don't you think that Leah should be a guest? After all, she is in your year at school,' Miles said quietly.

Miranda looked at Miles as he smiled at her. She nodded immediately. 'Of course. Now, I shall have to buy a new dress and I think I'll have my hair cut like Farrah Fawcett Major's . . .'

Miranda chatted happily away through the rest of the meal. Miles didn't say another word, and once dessert was finished, he stood up from the table.

'Do excuse me, everyone, but I have some work to do. Good-night.' And he left the room.

'Is Miles going to study?' Brett asked politely.

'No, Brett. His big passion is photography. He spends most of his time out on the moors taking photos, and he's turned one of the smaller rooms upstairs into a dark-room. I expect that's where he's gone now. Some of his photographs are quite beautiful.'

'I should like to see them.'

'Then you must ask Miles to show them to you, Brett. Now, how about you coming with me to my studio?'

'Yes please.'

'Oh Brett, I was going to take you upstairs and play you the new Abba album I bought on Saturday,' Miranda sulked.

'I'm sure Brett can listen to your album another time.' Rose stood up from the table and walked towards the door. Brett followed suit, but Miranda tugged at his sleeve.

'I'm sure I'll still be awake by the time you come up,' she whispered.

Brett gave a false smile and followed Rose out of the dining room and along the corridor to her studio. The room was in darkness, and Rose switched on the light.

Brett breathed in the familiar, comforting smell of paint and white spirit. The studio was not particularly large, and was cluttered with canvases stacked against the walls. There were the usual artist's brushes, pallets and tubes of paint strewn on a work bench along one wall.

Brett walked towards the large easel and studied the canvas resting upon it. There was only a basic outline, painted in thick, black strokes and Brett could not make out any particular shapes.

'Don't waste your time looking at that. I only started it this afternoon. Come and have a look at one of the finished products.' Rose was removing one of the canvasses from against the wall.

Brett knew that it would be recognizable anywhere as a Rose Delancey. The realist style was still the strong theme of the painting, but the colours were softer, more muted than the harsh, sometimes frightening, paintings that Rose had become famous for.

'What do you think?' Rose asked anxiously.

Brett thought how strange it was to have the great Rose Delancey asking him for an opinion on her work. Realism was not his own style; his own work reflected the English Impressionists, but he had always admired Rose's work for its strength and individuality, and he could see that her new painting had all that, and more.

'I think that it's wonderful, Rose, really. It is different

from your old work, but it has a subtlety to it that makes you want to look closer.'

Rose breathed a sigh of relief. 'Thank you, Brett dear. I've shown these to nobody else, you know. It may sound silly, but I was frightened that I may have lost my gift for painting.'

'No, certainly not. I can't say how valid my opinion is. I mean, I'm only a novice myself, but I think you should have every confidence about showing this to someone whose opinion does matter. Can I see the others?'

For the following hour, Rose and Brett pored over the eight other completed paintings. Rose explained each one in detail and the two of them discussed colour, shape and form. Rose explained how she felt she was moving out of the medium of realism for which she had become so famous.

'It's most odd,' Rose mused. 'When I was very young, I painted in a truly representational style. I was almost too romantic about my subject-matter. Then, as I matured to adulthood, I could only see the cold, hard seams and faults of everything I painted and I wanted to highlight this in my work. Critics used to comment that my work was almost masculine. I was also surrounded at the Royal College by the Kitchen Sinkers. And I was heavily influenced by Auerbach and Kossof, and Graham Sutherland's work. But since I've returned to painting, that feeling has left me. I want people to see beauty, too.'

Brett noticed Rose's eyes had become misty.

'They will, Rose. I promise.'

Rose turned to Brett and smiled. 'Your father loved . . .' she broke off mid-sentence and shook her head.

53

'I must be boring you. I'm sorry. Come on. Let's go and get some coffee from the kitchen, shall we?'

Brett helped Rose stack the finished paintings back against the wall.

'Why did you stop painting, Rose?' They were sitting at the kitchen table sipping their coffee.

Rose's face clouded over. 'It's a long story, Brett. Let's just say I was drained, that I felt as though I had nothing further to put on canvas. I had success so young. It's very unusual for a painter to do that, you know.' She sighed. 'I just woke up one morning and didn't want to paint any more.'

'And it took almost twenty years for the urge to come back?'

'Yes. But I can't tell you how much more pleasure I'm getting from painting now. In those days I felt like a machine, churning the work out, working to deadlines for galleries and collectors. Now, there are no expectations from others, only my own need to paint.'

'I bet you had no trouble securing an exhibition at a gallery,' smiled Brett.

'Actually, it was all rather a coincidence. I'd started painting again last year, and had just finished my first work, when I got a call from an old friend of mine who was at art school with me. He's opening a gallery in London in the New Year and asked me if I was painting again. I told him I was and he immediately suggested that I have an exhibition at his gallery. First of all I said no, then after I'd finished the second painting I thought, why not? It also comes down to lack of funds, Brett dear. This house need thousands spending on it and my coffers are empty. I need to earn some money, and painting is the only thing I can do well.'

'I'm sure the interest will be enormous.'

'Thank you for your confidence, Brett, but remember that the public has a short memory. Anyway, enough of me. Have you always been interested in art?'

'Oh yes. It's . . . it used to be my hobby.' Brett checked himself.

'Well, I really do think that you're too young to retire just yet,' Rose laughed.

Brett tried to think of a simple way to explain why he had tried to forget about his ambition, about the painting of his mother and how he couldn't face putting brush to canvas because it was all so hopeless.

'The thing is, Rose, my father isn't at all keen on the idea of me becoming an artist. He's got my future all planned. Cambridge, then going into his company to learn the business so I can take it over when he retires. My mother knew that I wanted to go to art college and she was going to talk to my father about it when the time came. But now . . .' Brett shrugged and looked so forlorn that Rose stretched her hand across the table and took his.

'Brett, whatever the problem, and believe me, no successful artist is without them at the beginning, you must keep painting. You might even find it gives you comfort. It certainly did me.'

'Yes, but there seems no point. My father, he . . .'

'He is a very complex man. I understand, more than anyone else, how he can be.' Rose paused and stared deep into her coffee-cup. 'However, hold onto your dream, Brett. Now, I think it's time we both went to bed. Tomorrow, come to my studio and I'll dig you out an easel, some paint and paper. Why don't you spend some time up on the moors? There are lots of splendid views to draw and I want to see if I'm to have competition in the future!' Rose stood up. 'Good-night, Brett dear. Sleep well.'

Brett sat for a long time alone in the kitchen, before he slowly made his way upstairs to bed.

There were so many things he had wanted to ask Rose. He wanted to know why his aunt had been kept a secret from him, but the look of sadness in Rose's eyes as she talked about her brother had prevented him from voicing those questions.

Brett switched out the bedside light.

Rose was right. He must continue painting. Although Rose had not actually told him that she too had faced problems when she was younger, he knew instinctively that she had. He suddenly wondered whether the fact that his father seemed so intent on ignoring his artistic leanings had something to do with Rose.

There was a mystery that he wanted to unravel, but in the meantime, he must paint.

And he knew exactly who he wanted to start with.

5

'YOU'LL HAVE TO amuse yourself today, Brett darling.
I'm off to Bradford to buy something incredible to wear
to my sixteenth birthday party and have my hair done.
Anyway, I'm fed up with sitting on a pile of sheep-doings
while you sketch some mouldy old view.'

Brett breathed a sigh of relief. Having Miranda with him
while he was trying to paint was proving to be an irritating distraction. But apart from that, during the past ten days he had
felt happier than he had since his mother died. He had completed four paintings. Doing what he loved most, combined
with the constant fresh air had provided a healing tonic.

Miranda got up from the table in the kitchen. 'I'll be
back for tea. See you later.'

When Miranda had gone, Brett surreptitiously turned
round and watched Leah who was quietly drying the
dishes with her mother.

What with Miranda, who was proving an able body-
guard, he had had little opportunity to speak to her. He
knew he must seize his chance.

'I was thinking I might go up to Haworth to see the
Parsonage today. Trouble is, I don't know how to get there.'

57

'Oh, it's easy. You just get on the Worth Valley railway from the station in the village. It's only ten minutes to Haworth and the ride is lovely. If you hurry, you might get the ten o'clock,' said Mrs Thompson.

'Great. I was wondering if I could borrow Leah to show me round? She seems to be the expert on the Brontës and I don't want to miss anything.'

Mrs Thompson frowned. 'Well, Mr Brett, I don't know about that. We've got all the upstairs sheets to change and . . .'

'Oh please, Mum. You know how I love Haworth.' Leah's eyes pleaded with her mother.

Mrs Thompson thought about how hard her daughter had worked for the past two weeks. She was a good girl and deserved a treat.

'All right, lass. As long as you're back by four to make your dad's tea. Have you got the train fare?'

'Don't worry about that, Mrs Thompson. I'll pay, as I've asked Leah to come with me.'

'I've got enough, Mum. Thank you.' Leah's eyes were sparkling.

'You'd better make it sharpish if you're to get the ten o'clock, mind.'

A few minutes later, they were hurrying down the hill towards the village. Now that Brett was actually alone with Leah, he felt completely tongue-tied.

They just had enough time to purchase their tickets from the quaint ticket office when the train pulled in. Brett opened the door to a carriage full of visiting German tourists and found two seats.

Brett could not help but stare at the beautiful girl sitting next to him. Leah was looking out of the window and he noticed that she had a faultless profile.

The rest of the journey was conducted in total silence and Brett realized that Leah was as shy as he was.

On arrival in Haworth, they followed the crowds of people off the train and walked along the road towards the centre of the village.

'This way,' said Leah, and Brett followed her as she moved gracefully up the steep, cobbled contours of the High Street. It was packed with people bustling in and out of the many gift and souvenir shops.

'We'll probably have to queue. They only allow so many people in at a time,' Leah remarked.

Brett nodded, realizing that he was making a complete ass of himself, unable to think of anything to say. Leah led him up some steps at the top of the High Street and along a narrow path, flanked by a graveyard on the left-hand side.

'There it is. Isn't it beautiful?'

The Parsonage stood tall and proud, washed by rich golden sunshine. Brett found it hard to believe that so much tragedy had taken place inside.

The queue was not as bad as Leah had anticipated, and within ten minutes they were in the sitting room staring at the chaise-longue where Emily Brontë had taken her last breath.

Leah immediately came to life, leading him from room to room and chattering incessantly. Brett relaxed too, asking Leah questions and receiving knowledgeable and interesting answers.

'I find it so difficult to believe that Charlotte Brontë

was so tiny. That dress looks as if it would only fit a doll. I feel like an elephant compared to her.'

The two of them were standing in front of a glass cabinet containing items reported to belong to the famous Charlotte.

'I can assure you that you don't look like an elephant, Leah.'

Brett smiled and Leah blushed heavily.

An hour later, they were in the gift shop, where Brett insisted he buy a stack of postcards to send to his chums from school.

'Now, I would like to treat my tour guide and fount of knowledge to lunch. Can you recommend anywhere?'

Leah was nonplussed. Whenever she came up here, she brought sandwiches and had never been out to eat in a restaurant in her life.

'Er, well, not really.'

'Not to worry. Let's walk down the High Street and see what we can find.'

What they found was the Stirrup Café, which provided lunches of traditional Yorkshire fare. They found a table at the back of the crowded room and placed their orders. Leah felt awfully grand.

'So, what does your father do?'

'Nothing. He has very bad arthritis and can't walk.'

'I'm sorry, Leah.'

'That's okay.'

Two Cokes arrived with the waitress and they both took a sip.

'Do you always spend your holidays working for Rose?'

'No. It's because of the exhibition and you being here.'

'I'm sorry I ruined your holidays, Leah,' Brett smiled.

'Oh no, I didn't mean it like that. I meant, we need the money and . . .' Leah stopped herself. She'd heard Miranda talk about how rich Brett's father was. He wouldn't understand. 'Are you enjoying staying up here? she asked.

'Very much. Especially today. Thank you for coming with me. I've been trying to get a chance to talk to you, but Miranda . . .' Brett's voice trailed off.

'She's very pretty, isn't she?'

Brett looked at the completely natural beauty sitting opposite him and smiled. 'Yes, if you like that sort of thing. I think you're much prettier.'

Leah looked down and blushed once more. The arrival of two shepherd's pies spared her from having to think of a reply.

'God, this is good.' Brett tucked in hungrily. 'They really know how to cook up here. I didn't want to come here for the summer when my father told me, but I'm so glad I did. It's a beautiful part of the world.'

'Yes.' Leah felt young and unworldly next to this boy who spoke so eloquently in his clipped English. It was hard to believe that he was only a few months older than she.

'When we've finished this, is there anywhere else we could go? I fancy a walk.'

'We could go up onto the moors at the back of the Parsonage. Or there's the ruins of Top Withens, which is the farmhouse they think Emily based Wuthering Heights on, but we won't get there. It's too far.'

'Well, we could just see how far we get,' shrugged

Brett, desperate for the day not to be over yet and for them to have further time alone together.

The two of them retraced their footsteps back to the Parsonage and set out across Haworth Moor, both of them lapsing into silence once more as they walked side by side.

After a while, Brett threw himself into the grass.

'I must be getting old,' he quipped. 'I'm exhausted.'

Leah sat down, a fair distance away from him. Brett shielded his eyes against the glaring sun and stared at the imposing house they had left behind in the distance.

'The Parsonage looks quite beautiful today, but I can imagine how bleak it must be up here in the winter. You can almost hear Heathcliff knocking on the window.'

Leah nodded. Brett looked at her, staring out across the moors, hands gracefully wrapped around her knees.

'You remind me of Cathy, sitting there. Apart from the T-shirt and jeans,' Brett laughed. She smiled at him and all he wanted to do was to pull her into his arms and kiss her. But he couldn't pluck up the courage.

Leah was thinking how romantic it would be if he were to take her hand. She'd never had the least interest in boys before, but Brett . . . no, she was just a poor Yorkshire girl from a small village. Surely, the sophisticated Miranda was much more his type?

They sat like that for a while, Brett willing himself at least to move closer to her. Eventually, he did so, and sat there, tearing at the grass with his hands.

'I . . . I've really enjoyed today, Leah. I hope that we'll be able to spend some more time together. Actually, I've got something to ask you.'

'What is it?'

'You can say no if you want, but I'd really like to sketch you.'

'Sketch me?' the astonishment in Leah's voice was plain.

'Yes. I think you're . . . very beautiful.'

No one had ever suggested to Leah before that this might be the case.

'Would you let me, please?'

'Well, if you really want to. I don't have much time, mind. Can't you paint Miranda instead?'

'No.' It was now or never. Brett reached towards her and put his hand on top of Leah's. 'It's you.'

Leah thought she might die of pleasure as she let Brett take her hand in his.

Spurred on by this, Brett moved closer and put his free arm around Leah's shoulder.

'I'd prefer it if Miranda didn't know, or she'll want to come too. I'd like it to be just you and I while I paint. Why don't we arrange a place on the moors near the house? We could meet there every day for an hour or so. When is best for you?'

'The afternoon. About three o'clock.' Leah hardly knew what she was saying as she felt the warmth of his body next to hers.

'That's settled then. We'll find a good place on the way back.'

Leah looked at her watch. It was gone half past two. Although she wanted to stay here for ever, she knew they must be getting home.

'We have to go.'

'Okay. But first . . .' he kissed her chastely on her closed lips, wanting to open them and kiss her more deeply, passionately. But he understood he must go slowly. So he drew his mouth away, put both arms around her and held her in a tight embrace.

Leah wondered if she was having a lovely dream as she sat with her head on his shoulder, eyes tightly closed. Her first kiss, in a place she loved with a boy so different to any of the brash, uncouth lads in her class. It felt so wonderful she wanted to cry.

Eventually, Brett released her and they walked hand in hand down the hill. Silence, so uncomfortable at the beginning of the day, now completely natural for the two of them experiencing their first taste of love.

6

'OH, MUM, I haven't got anything to wear to Miranda's party next week,' wailed Leah.

'You've got the dress you wore to Jackie's party last year. That'll do fine.'

'But Mum, I've grown since then and that dress is so babyish.'

'Listen, madam, you're only fifteen and . . .'

'Sixteen on the eighth of August,' put in Leah.

'You're only fifteen and that dress will be fine if I let it down,' said her mother firmly.

'Can I just go into Bradford and have a look? I've got some money saved from working up at the house. Please, Mum.'

'You've never been interested in clothes before, my girl.'

'I know, but I'm growing up now, and all Miranda's friends will have beautiful clothes.'

'They've got the money. We haven't.' Mrs Thompson looked at her daughter's crest-fallen face and her heart softened. 'Tell you what, we'll go into Keighley tomorrow and see if we can find some material that I can turn into something quickly. Will that do?'

'Oh, Mum, thanks.' Leah gave her a hug.

'Right. I'm off to the big house. You get your dad's tea sorted and I'll see you later.'

Mrs Thompson went out of the kitchen door and Leah got on with peeling the potatoes for tea. Once she had put them on to boil, she sat down at the table. A smile lit her face as she dreamily remembered the afternoon she had just spent with Brett.

Every day, at half past two, Leah would leave the big house as if she was going straight home, then scamper across the heather as fast as she could. They had found a lovely, concealed spot on the moors and Brett would be waiting for her, sketch-pad and charcoal in hand. Leah would sit very still for half an hour as Brett sketched her. After that, Brett would put his arms around her and they would lie back in the rough grass and talk. Leah would still pinch herself to believe that this was really happening. She could no longer think of him as Mrs Delancey's nephew, or the son of a very wealthy man. He was just Brett, who talked to her about how much he wanted to be an artist, how heart-broken he was about his mother dying, and how he was dreading returning to Eton, leaving her and Yorkshire behind.

Leah sighed and got up from the table to turn the potatoes down. She wondered what Miranda would say if she knew what was going on. It was obvious that Miranda liked Brett a lot, and Leah still couldn't believe that Brett preferred her to Miranda.

Leah took the toad-in-the-hole out of the oven, mashed the potatoes, adding lots of creamy butter, doled them out onto two plates and called her dad to say that tea was up.

Harry Thompson wheeled himself skilfully along the narrow corridor and tucked himself into the kitchen table.

'Mmn, this smells good, lass. You're getting to be as good a cook as your mum.'

'Thanks, Dad.' Leah sat down opposite him. 'Tuck in before it gets cold.'

'Aye, lass. So. How's it going up at the big house?'

'Fine. It's nice to have the extra pennies.'

'And what's this rich young nephew of Mrs Delancey's like then?'

'Oh, he's very . . . nice.'

Harry did not miss the look in his daughter's eye. He'd had his suspicions over the past three weeks, seeing the spring in her step, the flush in her cheeks and the dreamy expression on her face when she thought no one was looking.

'I see. Anything you want to tell me?' He smiled at Leah.

Leah blushed a deep red. She'd never been able to keep anything from her father.

'Oh Dad, promise you won't tell Mum. She mightn't let me work up there if she knew and . . .'

The whole story came tumbling out. It was such a relief to tell someone.

'I don't know how I'm going to live when Brett goes away,' Leah finished, tears coming to her eyes.

'You've got me, pet. You can cry on my shoulder,' Mr Thompson replied. 'Look, Leah, I know even Mum says what a little gentleman he is, but he's from a different world. Don't let yourself get hurt by him, will you, pet?'

'Brett would never hurt me,' Leah said defensively.

'I'm sure he wouldn't, lass. You enjoy yourself. Being in love for the first time is magic. If you ever want to talk, I'll always be there to listen.'

Leah nodded, stood up and moved round the table to give her father a hug.

'Thanks, Dad. I love you very much, you know. Now, you go and watch *Coronation Street*, I'll do the washing up and bring us in a cup of tea.'

Harry nodded and pushed himself out of the kitchen, troubled by the obvious strength of feeling his innocent daughter had for a boy that would walk out of her life in less than six weeks' time.

'Wow, this summer's turning out to be one of the hottest ever,' said Brett, staring up at the perfect duck-egg blue sky.

Leah nodded, shifting her position in Brett's arms to become more comfortable.

'You swear you're going to write to me at least every day when I go back to Eton?'

'Only if you do the same,' answered Leah.

'And I was thinking, I could come and spend the half-term up here, and maybe Christmas.'

'Yes.' Leah just couldn't bear to think about Brett leaving. She changed the subject. 'When are you going to let me see the sketch?'

'When I've finished it. You are impatient, aren't you, madam?' Brett leant above her and began tickling her unmercifully.

68

'Stop it! Stop it!' laughed Leah, loving every moment of it. She wriggled away from him across the grass and looked at her watch with a sigh. 'I ought to get going. Dad'll be wanting his tea.'

'Okay, but first . . .' Brett grabbed her and pulled her into his arms. He kissed her, feeling the soft outline of her breasts beneath the flimsy cotton blouse she was wearing. His hand caressed her neck, then travelled down to the soft swelling. He closed his hand over it, sighing with relief that Leah did not stop him. Tentatively, he undid the top button of her blouse, and his hand moved slowly underneath.

'No!' Leah pulled away from him angrily.

'I'm sorry, Leah. I thought you trusted me.' Brett groaned in frustration.

'I do. But I've told you, I don't want to go any further.'

'Don't you like me enough? Is that what it is?'

'Of course I like you. But Mum's warned me what trouble a girl can get into.'

'Leah, honestly. Do you think what we're doing can get you into trouble? I mean, Miranda must have been up here on the moors with half the boys in Oxenhope from the way she carries on and . . .'

'Then why don't you go and find her?' Leah's eyes filled with tears. She stood up, and began to run down the hill.

'Leah, I . . .' Brett sighed and sank down onto his haunches as he watched Leah running gracefully over the moors away from him. He felt rotten. The last thing he had meant to do was to upset her, but she was driving him crazy. He was glad of the stone-cold bath water in the morning, for his dreams were filled with erotic fantasies

69

of Leah naked, and him making passionate love to her in bed, on the moors, in the bath, anywhere . . .

'Damn!'

Of course he understood. She was so innocent, so naïve and seemed so much younger than he. But the contours of the body that he felt beneath her clothes portrayed a different story altogether. It was a woman's body, in the first bloom of maturity, and he could not help but respond physically.

She was in his thoughts night and day. He wanted to take her, ardently, but also protect her. She knew so little about the world, which made him feel manly and strong.

He was in love with her. And he would tell her at Miranda's party next week.

Leah kept running until she was far enough away from Brett, then she threw herself down on the moors to have a good cry. It was so unfair. Brett knew she didn't like him to touch her there, and yet she ended up feeling so guilty when she stopped him.

'And what's wrong with you?'

A shadow came across the bright sunlight and Leah looked up. Miles was on a big, black horse staring down at her. The same involuntary shiver ran up her spine as he dismounted. She wiped away the tears from her face and stood up, desperate to get away.

'Nothing. I'm fine. I've got to go home now.'

'Had a row with your new boyfriend, then?'

'I . . . what do you mean?' Leah stood stock-still, his hand burning into her shoulder. She did not want to turn round and look into those jet-black eyes.

'I've seen the two of you on the moors together in the afternoon. You have grown up, haven't you?'

She was rooted to the spot, paralysed with fear. He let go of her shoulder and walked round to face her.

'Don't worry, I won't tell anybody. It can remain our little secret, can't it?' He smiled at her. 'Go on, run off to Mummy.'

Miles reached out his hand and ran his fingers down her neck to her waist, lightly touching the contours of her left breast. This movement galvanized her into action and she ran, as fast as her legs would carry her, across the moors and down towards the familiarity and safety of home.

That night, Leah had a terrible nightmare. A man was chasing her over the moors. She knew what he would do if he caught her, and he was gaining on her. Her legs were getting slower and slower and there was Megan's voice saying, over and over, '. . . evil things . . . doomed . . . you can't alter destiny . . . you must beware him . . .'

7

'WELL NOW, DAD, doesn't our Leah look a picture?'
Mum was smiling with pride.

'She does indeed. That dress is quite beautiful. It looks
like it's out of one of those fashion magazines. You're
right talented with a needle, aren't you, love?' Mr
Thompson gazed fondly at his wife.

Leah stood in her mother and father's bedroom, staring at the mirror in disbelief. The dress was very simple,
made of cheap, white cotton, but her mother had managed to fit it so perfectly to Leah's tall, graceful body that
it did indeed look like a designer dress. It was sleeveless,
with a boat-neck, a nipped-in waist with a pleated skirt.
The dress would have looked like a child's party frock on
anyone else, but Leah's height and slimness added just
the necessary degree of sophistication and in turn made
her look years older.

'Now, young lady. You just make sure you behave yourself. I'll be serving the food and drinks so I won't have time
to watch you. Mrs Delancey's invited half of South
Yorkshire, and her complaining she has no money all the
time,' Mrs Thompson clucked. 'Anyway, no slinking into

the toilet to put some of that war-paint on your face, young miss. That pale lipstick is enough for a girl of your age.'

'Yes, Mum,' Leah said obediently. 'We'd better go.'

'Go and get your coat, Leah. It'll be cold on that walk back.'

Leah retrieved her coat from the hall and went back into the bedroom to kiss her father good-night. It broke her heart sometimes to leave him alone.

''Night, Dad,' she kissed him.

''Night, love. You look quite the little grown-up miss in that. Have a good time and behave yourself.' He smiled and winked at her.

'I will.'

The two of them left the house and started the walk up the hill in the sultry July air.

Miranda finished outlining her lips with 'strawberry red', put a tissue between them and pressed hard. She looked at the outline on the tissue and wondered for the thousandth time why Brett was not bursting with desire to kiss them.

She had tried everything from outrageous flirtation to demure stand-offishness, but nothing seemed to work.

Miranda stood up and surveyed herself in the mirror. Perfect. The tight black dress showed off her voluptuous body, and surely tonight even Brett would not be able to resist her.

What Miranda wanted, more than anything else in the world, was wealth. She wanted out of this dump of a house, out of the small, repressive village full of nobodies leading boring, little lives.

She already knew how to use her face and curvaceous body to make the boys at school prepared to do anything, just for one touch of her breasts or a look at the suspenders she wore under the innocence of her school uniform. Miranda was not top of her class academically, but she knew how the world worked.

Money equalled power and control, and there was only one way women could get it.

Love, well, she didn't believe in that. Love was for the foolish. It made you powerless, and stopped you from getting what you wanted. Miranda didn't ever intend to fall into that trap.

But Brett's reaction had disconcerted Miranda. He wasn't behaving in the way she thought they all behaved, wasn't falling under her spell the way all the boys had so far. She had to have him. He was her passport out of here. However, she hadn't played her trump card yet. No, that was being saved for tonight.

Miranda smiled at her reflection as she stood up. Brett didn't stand a chance.

'Thank you, Rose, it looks quite lovely.' Miranda surveyed the barn that had been cleared by men from the village and festooned with streamers. The mobile disco was being set up at the front and Mrs Thompson was busy in the kitchen preparing the food.

Rose looked at her daughter, wishing she had the courage to tell her that the skin-tight, short black dress, overdone make-up and the high stilettos, made her look like a little tramp. However, Rose had put a lot of effort into this party, hoping that it might make Miranda easier

74

to deal with, and the last thing she wanted was to argue with her.

'That's all right. Now listen, Miranda, a few ground-rules for you and your friends. They're allowed into the house to go to the bathroom, but the rest of it is off-limits and I don't want anyone sneaking off into the other barns. And apart from the fruit punch, which does have a little wine in, I don't want anyone drinking alcohol. I'll be in the sitting room with the adults and as long as there isn't any trouble, I'll stay there. But . . .'

'It's okay, I understand,' Miranda interrupted impatiently. 'You just enjoy your party and I'll enjoy mine. Do you like my outfit, by the way?'

Rose gritted her teeth. 'Yes, it's . . . very . . . stunning.'

'I thought so too. I'll see you later. I just want to go and check my make-up before everyone starts arriving.'

Miranda made her way upstairs as best she could in the tight dress and stilettos. She walked along the corridor to the bathroom, passing Brett's bedroom. The door was slightly ajar and she could hear him whistling. She crept to the door and peeped through the crack. Brett was sitting on his bed, with his back towards the door, wrapping a flat, rectangular object in an old blanket. She knocked and walked into the room.

Brett was obviously startled, for he jumped, quickly slid the object under the bed and turned round.

'Jesus, Miranda, you shouldn't creep up on people like that.'

'Sorry, darling.' She sat on the bed and crossed her legs, revealing the top of one of her black stockings. 'Was that my birthday present?'

'Er, no. But this is.' Brett passed a neatly wrapped package to her, hoping that it would defer Miranda's interest in what was under the bed.

'Can I open it now?'

'If you'd like. Happy Birthday.'

Miranda tore at the wrapping paper, finding a blue velvet box inside. She opened it and looked at the dainty gold locket. Not her scene at all, but obviously worth a packet. She took it out of the box and laid it across her fingers.

'Thank you, Brett. It's lovely.' Miranda fiddled with the clasp of the locket and managed to open it. 'See, I can put a picture of someone in here and wear it next to my heart. Do you have a picture of yourself I could put in?'

'No, not one small enough anyway. I'm glad you like it, Miranda. I didn't know what to get you, so I asked Mrs Thompson to help me.' Leah had chosen it, actually, but Brett didn't think Miranda would be too pleased about that.

'Could you put it round my neck and I'll wear it tonight.'

'Of course.' Brett knelt on the bed behind Miranda and fastened the clasp. Before he could move, she swung round and put her arms around him. Her face was inches away from his, and he could smell the heavy scent she was wearing.

'I think I should give you a kiss for that, don't you?' Miranda locked her lips against his, her tongue trying to probe into his mouth.

'No, Miranda, I . . .'

Before he could move, her other hand swiftly took his up towards her breast and placed it on her fullness.

The feeling of her breast under his hand made Brett's body react immediately. He couldn't help himself after all those fruitless afternoons on the moors and erotic dreams night after night. He relaxed his lips and let Miranda's tongue into his mouth. His hand roamed over first one breast, then the other. Miranda did not stop him when he slipped his hand inside her dress and felt the heavy nakedness against his palm. He groaned, knowing that this was wrong, dangerous, but his body, not his mind, was in control. He slipped Miranda's straps off her shoulders and bent his head to kiss the large, pinkish nipples. He pushed her back on the bed, his hand travelling to her covered thigh, his mouth on hers. The pleasure he was feeling was intense as Miranda's hand encased his own and led it up her thigh. He felt the clasp of her suspenders before she took his hand again and placed it on the line of her underwear. He encased her mound and felt the heat coming from inside. His fingers slipped under the silken material and he felt her wetness. He explored her, pushing his fingers up inside her, this further adding to his own physical pleasure.

Brett was rigid, bursting. He felt a hand rubbing against his crotch, then slowly undoing the zip of his trousers.

'Oh God,' he moaned as the hand slipped inside and began massaging him through his underpants. Feeling a women's touch for the first time was unparalleled and carried an already intensely aroused Brett beyond the point of no return.

Pent-up passion spent, Brett was aghast. He could only think of getting away from Miranda as quickly as possible.

He wrenched his mouth away from her vice-like kiss and moved off the bed towards the door.

'Miranda, . . . I . . .'

There was the light of victory shining in her eyes.

'I'm sorry.' It was all he could think of to say as he bolted for the bathroom and locked himself in.

He sat on the edge of the bath with his head in his hands. How could he have done that, after all he'd said to Leah? It was as if, in those few minutes, he'd been possessed, not himself, unable to think about anything else except his own physical gratification. The wet stickiness, slowly drying against his skin, was proof of his weakness. Were all men like this? Did they all become powerless when faced with their own need for sexual relief? Was this why he was constantly reading of ruined careers after involvement with unsavoury women?

He couldn't tell Leah. She would never, ever forgive him and he wouldn't blame her.

He had been so excited about tonight, for he was going to tell her that he loved her and give her the finished charcoal sketch. He had found a hidden spot in one of the barns, and when Miranda had burst in on him he was wrapping the sketch in a blanket, ready to sneak it downstairs into the barn to show Leah later.

Brett stood up, undressed and washed his body, face and hands, as if to cleanse himself of Miranda's touch. He took a deep breath and decided that he couldn't lose Leah, that he would just have to live with his secret and make it up to her in other ways.

She immediately became a shining icon in his eyes;

pure, untouched, innocent, so unlike Miranda who had tempted him and succeeded.

'Shit! The sketch!'

Brett unlocked the door and ran back down the corridor to his bedroom, which was empty. He checked under the bed and to his relief, the sketch was still there. He hoped that Miranda had forgotten about it, for he was aware that while she could not harm him, she could harm Leah.

It was the first thing Miranda had done when Brett had left the room. Happy in her triumph, in the knowledge that however much money, wealth or power men had, they were all the same underneath, she reached under the bed and drew the object out.

The shock was terrible. Miranda turned ashen and anger burned inside her. Leah's beauty and innocence, captured so perfectly by Brett, shone out from the sketch.

But Miranda couldn't see it. All she could see was the mousey kid who washed Rose's dishes to earn some pin money.

'Bitch!' she said under her breath. That was probably why Brett had been so stand-offish with her, 'cos he was getting it from that common little brat.

Miranda's first instinct was to smash the frame and tear the sketch to shreds. No, Brett would know it was her. There had to be a better way for her to get revenge.

'I'll fix you,' she said to the sketch as she wrapped it and replaced it under the bed. Then she stood up, tidied her hair in the mirror and went downstairs to greet her guests.

*

'Dancing Queen' burst through the speakers in the barn as the disc jockey welcomed everyone to the party. A few people edged onto the make-shift dance floor and started to move to the beat.

Miranda was surrounded by friends handing her presents when Brett entered, fresh from secreting Leah' sketch in the spot he had found in the end barn right on the edge of the moors.

He searched for Leah, unaware that his activities previously had been watched from start to finish.

'There you are. My, don't you look beautiful.' Brett kissed Leah and wrapped an arm round her shoulder.

'Brett, don't, Miranda's just over there and she might see.'

'I don't care any more. She can't stop us.'

'No, but . . .'

'Sshh. Come on. Let's go and dance.'

The barn was filling up. Some boys from the village had brought cider and beer and Miranda was drinking from their proffered bottles. She looked round, the sight of Leah and Brett on the dance floor heightening her anger.

'Come and dance with me.' Miranda grabbed the nearest male, pulled him onto the dance floor and jived seductively to the music, swigging the bottle of cider with one hand.

Brett had his arms round Leah and they were swaying slowly to the music.

'Are you happy, Leah?'

She looked up at him. 'Yes.'

'Good. I've got something for you. It's in the last barn

on the edge of the moors. We'll have to go there separately so no one sees us, but will you come? I promise to behave myself,' he pleaded.

'All right.' Leah smiled.

Mrs Thompson was bringing in the food from the kitchen and putting it on the trestle table at the back of the barn. She immediately espied Leah dancing with Brett.

'That'll lead to trouble,' she muttered under her breath. Once the song had finished, she clapped her hands together and shouted, 'Food up!'

People drifted over to the laden table, and Mrs Thompson was kept busy serving the sausages, baked potatoes and salad.

'I'm keeping my eye on you,' Mrs Thompson whispered to Leah, as she filled her plate.

Leah looked at the floor in embarrassment. 'Honest, Mum, we were only having a dance, that's all.'

'See that it stays that way. No disappearing.' Mrs Thompson passed onto the next hungry customer.

Miles watched Leah and Brett from his vantage-point in the corner of the barn. She was turning into such a beautiful girl, just as he had known she would. But that boy she was with . . . he wasn't good enough to lick her boots, even if his father did own half the world.

Miles had photographs of her, taken secretly from the time when she was a tiny, delicate five-year-old, pottering around the farmhouse behind her mother. The camera loved her, her ethereal beauty enhanced by the sharpness of the lens.

And now there was a pretender to his throne. He was looking forward to seeing that portrait, to tearing it to shreds like the heap of shit it was.

Brett had to understand. She was pure and perfect. And she was not ready yet. He had known this when he had touched her the other day. He'd had to mark her for his own.

Miles sauntered out of the barn, heading towards the edge of the moors; a dark, solitary figure in the moon-light.

Leah entered the end barn, having slipped out the minute her mum had taken a pile of dirty dishes back to the house. There was only the ghostly moon-light to see by and she hoped that Brett had got there first. She felt relief as she heard a noise from the far end. Then the sound of something smashing.

'Brett, Brett, are you all right?' She stumbled in the direction of the noise and saw a circle of light shining on the floor. It was immediately switched off and everything was silent.

'Brett, where are you?' She had reached the spot where the circle of light had been and she could hear someone breathing. She reached out and put a hand on something warm.

'Thank goodness, Brett, what was that noise?'

The arms reached out for her and she snuggled into them. But something didn't feel quite right. She looked up, her eyes now adjusted to the dim light, and screamed.

A hand covered her mouth, and she struggled, but he held her tight.

'I'm not going to hurt you, Leah. Stop struggling, for goodness' sake.'

Feelings of revulsion and fear rose in Leah.

'No!' She wrenched herself away with all her might. The motion toppled her backwards against the wall. She heard the tear of material as her dress caught on something and she slid down to the ground.

'Leah, Leah, are you okay? Damn, I can't see a thing!'

Leah picked herself up and ran towards the shadowy figure of Brett standing near the entrance to the barn. She threw herself into his arms, sobbing loudly.

'What on earth's the matter?'

'Over there . . . he was in here and I thought he was you and . . . he wasn't.'

'Okay, okay, calm down. I'm here now,' soothed Brett. He looked towards the back of the barn and could see nothing.

'You stay here, and I'll have a look.'

'No! Let's just go.'

'But there's something I wanted to show you.'

'I want to go back to the house. Now. My dress is all torn and . . .'

'Okay, I can show you another time.'

Brett turned her round to walk out of the barn and saw Miranda standing there, arms folded.

'Well, well, well. We've had a busy night, haven't we, Brett?' She looked at the tear in the dress across Leah's shoulder.

'Hello, Miranda. I wanted to tell you about . . .'

'About the fact that you've been screwing her as well as me?' Miranda's words were slurred.

'Shut up, Miranda.'

'Oh no, I think little Leah has a right to know where lover-boy was earlier this evening, don't you?' She laughed viciously.

Leah was standing there silently, staring straight ahead, not wanting to hear.

'Go on then, Leah, ask him. See if he denies it,' she taunted.

Leah looked up at Brett, her eyes begging him to do just that. But she didn't have to ask. The guilt was written right across his face.

She gave one huge sob and ran out of the barn, straight into the arms of her mother.

'COME ON NOW, Leah, tell Mum what happened.' Mrs Thompson wrapped a cardigan round her daughter's shoulders. The girl was shivering violently and she couldn't get a word out of her. Mrs Thompson had sent Brett back to the disco. She'd had a quick word with Miranda, who had obviously been drinking. Miranda had said she'd heard screaming and found Brett and Leah in the barn alone together.

Mrs Thompson looked at her daughter's torn dress and feared the worst.

'Did he, did Mr Brett . . .' Mrs Thompson could not speak the words. Thank goodness she'd gone looking for Leah once she'd noticed that she and Brett were missing.

Leah did not reply. If that boy had touched her daughter, well . . . there'd be hell to pay, however rich his father was.

'Leah, did Mr Brett . . .?'

'No, Mum.'

'Then what happened? How did your dress get torn?'

Leah sat, tight-lipped and pale as a ghost. Mrs

Thompson realized that she would get no more out of her tonight.

'All right, love. We'll talk about it tomorrow. I think we need to get you home and tucked up in bed.'

Mrs Thompson didn't want Dad knowing about any of this, not with his health the way it was. She went into the sitting room where Rose was entertaining her guests and asked Mr Broughton, a local farmer, whether he'd mind giving Leah a lift down the hill as she wasn't feeling too well. He agreed, and Mrs Thompson bundled Leah into the back of the car, and told her to go straight upstairs to bed when she got home.

She went back to the kitchen and started making headway into the large pile of dishes in the sink. The kitchen door opened and Brett came in, looking shame-faced and ashen.

'Is she all right, Mrs Thompson?' he asked quietly.

'She is. I've sent her home to bed.'

'I didn't touch her, you know, really. I wouldn't. I like her too much to do anything to upset her.'

'That's not what Miranda said when I asked her. She said she heard screaming and went to the barn to find you and Leah alone together.'

Brett ran a hand through his hair. 'Oh God, did she?'

'Yes, she did. Any road, I'll be speaking to Leah tomorrow and she'll not be back working up at the house for the rest of the summer. I think you've caused enough trouble for one night, young man. I'd take yourself off to bed if I were you.'

'Yes, you're right. Please, Mrs Thompson, send Leah my love and my apologies.'

Mrs Thompson said nothing, just continued with the dishes.

Brett slunk miserably up the stairs. Everything was ruined. And he was to blame. If only he'd been stronger, if he'd resisted Miranda, then none of this would have happened. As for what went on in the barn, it was his word against Miranda's. She was paying him back for deceiving her, and he knew Leah would never want to see him again.

Brett undressed and lay miserably under the covers. He closed his eyes and dreamt of his lost love.

Miranda lay in bed in an alcohol-induced sleep. Someone was entering her room and climbing into bed next to her. He was touching her in intimate places and telling her that he loved her. She felt his hardness sliding up and down inside her. When he had finished, he kissed her and left the room.

Miranda turned over.

She'd had that dream many times before.

9

DAVID COOPER SWIVELLED his chair away from his desk to gaze out of the full-length glass window overlooking Central Park. The trees were like tiny, green dots far below and the cars looked like dinky toys.

He thought how his physically elevated position reflected his standing in life. He rarely came into contact with any of those normal, everyday people far below him, rushing about their business along Fifth Avenue. Everyone he met these days was very rich, very powerful; a mirror-image of himself.

He wondered why the pleasure of making money had stopped for him on the day his wife died. He'd loved her, in a way, but never to the extent of the feeling of loss he was now suffering. And he'd had countless affairs while he was married. Disposable sex. You used them one night and threw them away the next morning. But he hadn't touched another woman for the past nine months.

Vivien's death had devastated him. Totally. It had brought back the realization of his own mortality.

David knew his son didn't think he gave a damn about his mother dying. He'd only seen Brett twice since she'd died, once at the funeral, and at Christmas. But they'd not grieved together.

He wondered how Brett was getting on in Yorkshire with Rose. Rose . . . having not seen her for over twenty years he still maintained the image of the exquisitely beautiful girl she had been in her twenties.

David was thinking of the past a lot these days. Having survived only by blocking it out, he had spent his life planning the future. But now he was starting to look backwards, to let old memories resurface.

Some of them were painful, too painful to be unlocked, but others, well, the retrospectiveness so far as his business was concerned had made him realize just how far he had come in the last twenty-eight years.

David sat there, in his forty-foot office, remembering the time when he had run his business from the sitting room of his tiny flat in Bayswater.

He had started with a run-down tenement building in Islington at the beginning of the fifties, buying the land it stood on for a song and refurbishing the building into four, smart studio flats. Young people didn't buy property in those days, so he had rented them out and used the money he received to buy another, similar building. By the mid-fifties, he had twenty such buildings, providing him with enough steady monthly income to ask the bank for a larger loan really to get to work.

There were still sites in the centre of London untouched since the war on which he built office blocks and sold them for a fortune to the growing number of companies opening at the time.

By the mid-sixties, he had the largest construction company in Britain. He began to look abroad, at the newly growing holiday market, and bought sites along the beaches in Spain, the Balearics and Italy. He built hotels on the land, holding on to portions to sell back to the governments five years later for triple the price.

Now, ten years on, he owned land in almost all the major developed countries and was starting to look to the Third World for business opportunities.

He had been named as one of the top ten richest men in Britain and in the top fifty in America.

One hell of an achievement.

The thrill of a successful business deal had made up for the part of him that couldn't function. He knew his colleagues and his wife and son saw him as a cold man; emotionless.

Now that she was dead, David wished that he'd had the courage to confide in Vivien, to tell her why he'd been incapable of affection . . . but it was too late.

He knew that this sudden memory surge was the reason he'd decided Brett should go to Yorkshire.

David was not going to pick up his son from Yorkshire. He had given himself the pleasure of knowing it was an option, but seeing her again after all this time . . . he wasn't up to it at the moment. He might pop into that little gallery he'd just bought in London when she held her exhibition there, just to see.

David turned and studied the painting on the wall behind his desk. He sighed. He sometimes felt sad at the easy way that everything could be bought and sold, especially people. David stood up and picked up his slim,

Cartier briefcase. He had to be at Sardi's in thirty minutes for lunch with a newly elected senator.

As he left his office and waited for the elevator, he wondered briefly what this man's price was.

10

'WELL, BRETT, IT's been lovely to have you with us. I do hope you'll come back and visit soon.' Rose kissed him. 'And keep up the painting. The ones I've seen show great potential.'

'Thanks, Rose. I've enjoyed being here. I'll try and get to your exhibition.'

Bill and the limousine were waiting outside for him.

''Bye, Brett, it's been nice knowing you.' Miranda came running down the stairs and gave him a peck on the cheek, but Brett couldn't bring himself to do the same, so he smiled and waved and got into the back of the big car.

'Have a nice holiday, sir?' Bill asked on the intercom. 'You look well on it, I must say.'

Brett thought about the past two months. The first five weeks had been wonderful, with his re-discovered painting and Leah. But the past month had been dreadful, with him unable to get her out of his mind.

As promised by Mrs Thompson, Leah had not been up to the house again and he had not seen her since the night of the party. He had spent most of his time on the moors at the spot where Leah and he had met every day, hoping and praying she would come. He had asked Mrs Thompson time and again how she was, but she would just purse her lips and say, 'Fine', and that would be the end of the conversation.

He'd been so desperate in the last week that he had gone down to the village just to see if he could catch sight of her, but he didn't.

'Yes, Bill, it was . . . different.'

'Good, sir. Your father sends his regards. He'll be down to visit you at half-term. He's in South America for the next six weeks.'

Brett felt lower than he had when he'd arrived in Yorkshire. As the miles increased between him and the girl he loved, he thought his heart might break.

''Bye, Leah, I'll never forget you,' he whispered as they crossed the Yorkshire border into Derbyshire and sped down the motorway towards Windsor.

11

ROSE SHIVERED VIOLENTLY, despite the three sweaters and scarf that she was wearing. She blew on her hands, which were numb from the cold and becoming too inflexible to paint.

The snow was piled in great drifts outside her studio window. The thaw had begun yesterday, but it always took longer before the snow on high ground began to melt.

Rose stoked the small, ineffectual fire and warmed her hands. The freezing January weather made her feel miserable and depressed.

She turned to look at the painting on the easel. Self-doubt hit her once more.

'Oh,' she groaned. 'Is it worth it? Can I still do it? Am I going to be torn to shreds by the critics?'

Come on, said a voice inside her, as she plugged the old kettle in. Just think of the central heating you could install if the exhibition is a success.

Rose sat in front of the fire, warming her hands on the coffee cup and drinking from it slowly. She sighed, picked up her brush and pallet and walked back to the easel.

'Think positive, Rosie, old girl. Two more to go and you're there. And this painting must be worth at least four and a half radiators.' She smiled and began to paint.

An hour or so later, there was a knock on her studio door.

'Come in.'

'Rose, can I see you for a moment, please?' Miranda was standing at the door, looking unusually pale.

Rose had noticed how quiet she'd been for the past few months. It had, in fact, been a blessed relief. In the four and a half months since Brett had gone home and Miles had gone back to university, Rose had virtually managed to complete her work for the exhibition.

Now she wondered whether she had missed something. Miranda looked quite dreadful. She put down her brush.

'Of course, darling. Come and sit down. What is it?'

Miranda promptly burst into tears. Rose could never recall seeing Miranda sob in front of her before. She knelt next to her and put a comforting arm round her shoulder.

'Whatever it is, I'm sure it can't be as bad as all that.'

'It is, it is,' Miranda sobbed.

'Come on then, tell Rose what the problem is.'

'I think I'm pregnant.' The words burst out in a rush.

Oh my God, thought Rose. I should have seen this coming. One of the village boys, perhaps, when I was locked away in my studio.

'Have you missed your last period, darling?'

Miranda nodded. 'And the one before that, and the

one before and . . . I don't know how many.' She looked up and Rose could feel nothing but sympathy. After all, she herself had been through this.

'Try to think clearly, darling. There's probably still plenty of time to . . .'

'About five, or maybe six . . . I don't know.'

'Well, what I'm going to do now is telephone a very good clinic I know in Leeds. I'll make an appointment for tomorrow and if the snow will let us, we'll go and see them. You may not be pregnant at all. It could be some kind of woman's problem and . . .'

'Feel this,' Miranda's hand took Rose's and led it under the layers of sweaters to her stomach. Rose felt the definite bulge.

'Why didn't you come to me before, Miranda? Surely you must have realized a long time ago?'

This induced a fresh stream of tears. 'I know, but I kept hoping that I was wrong and thinking that next month it might be all right.'

'Okay, okay,' soothed Rose, remembering so vividly the self-same nightmare. 'Don't worry, we'll sort it out. Now, how about a nice cup of tea?'

She led Miranda into the kitchen and boiled the kettle. Miranda's usual high-handed attitude had disappeared completely. There was a frightened little girl sitting at the kitchen table.

Miranda sipped the tea while Rose made an appointment at the clinic for the following day.

'Right, all fixed up. We're going to see a lovely woman doctor called Kate.'

'Thank you, Rose,' Miranda said quietly.

'What for?'

'For being so nice. I know I'm a pain sometimes and I'm sorry.'

'That's okay.' Rose was desperate to ask who the father was while Miranda was being so pliable, but she thought it better to wait until they had seen the doctor tomorrow.

'I'm scared.'

Devoid of the usual make-up, Miranda's eyes looked very big and blue and young. Rose went to her and gave her a hug.

'Don't worry, darling, we'll sort it out.' Rose spoke with as much confidence as she could muster.

'I'm afraid you're over six and a half months pregnant, Miss Delancey. Only two weeks below the allowed limit for termination by the National Health Service and, in my opinion, too near to risk it. The baby is due on the twentieth of April.'

Rose sighed deeply. It was no less than she had expected.

Miranda sat stock-still, staring at the doctor.

'So you're saying I can't get rid of it?' Her face was deathly pale.

'I'm saying that in my opinion it would be a risk to your health that I wouldn't like to take.'

'Absolutely,' said Rose. 'I'm not putting you in jeopardy. I'm afraid you're going to have the baby, Miranda, dear.'

'Does the father know about this?' asked Kate softly.

Miranda stared at her hands and shook her head.

'Do you know who the father is, darling?'

Miranda looked at her mother and for an instant Rose saw the flicker of fear run through her daughter's eyes. It vanished in an instant and Miranda stared silently ahead.

'No.'

'But darling, I think that . . .'

'No! It's nothing to do with him.'

Rose saw Kate send a warning glance in her direction.

'All right, Miranda. If you don't feel like talking about it at the moment, that's fine. Now, so far as the procedure for ante-natal care is concerned, I want you to come back tomorrow and I'm going to give you a full check-up. You have only three months until the birth of the baby and we need to look after you both. Do you smoke, Miss Delancey?'

Rose drove her ancient Land Rover back to Oxenhope with a silent Miranda next to her. During the drive, she racked her brains to try to think of one particular boy that Miranda had mentioned during the past few months. If she was over six months pregnant now, that would mean that conception had been in the middle of July . . . of course, Miranda's birthday party. Rose knew that Miranda had been much the worse for wear by the end of the evening . . . it might have been any one of the twenty or so young boys that had turned up. Perhaps Miranda couldn't even remember and that was why she was being so cagey.

'You're going to have to leave school, darling, at least for the time being. I shall postpone my exhibition until the baby's born and you're settled.' Rose was desperate to tell her how stupid she'd been not to confide in her

98

before so they could have done something, but her guilt over her self-centredness of the past few months prevented her from doing so. Rose felt it was her fault and, therefore, her responsibility.

Miranda only nodded and continued to stare out of the window.

When they arrived back at the farmhouse, Miranda went straight up to her room, threw herself on the bed and lay staring up at the ceiling. She needed so desperately to confide in someone, to tell them the awful truth. But she knew she could not. No one would ever understand, least of all Rose.

The father? Should she tell him? Surely he'd understand, help her?

Miranda sat up, jumped off the bed and searched for a notepad in her chest of drawers. Armed with a biro and paper, she lay back on the bed again, propping herself up with pillows.

'Dear . . .'

Miranda threw the notepad onto the floor with a cry as tears streamed down her face.

She couldn't tell him. She couldn't tell anyone.

And she could not admit the truth to herself.

12

LEAH SAT IN her tiny bedroom staring into space. The news had been all round the school today. Miranda Delancey was pregnant and was leaving until after the birth of her baby. There were all sorts of ideas on who the father was; Miranda was never short of admirers, but no one was absolutely positive.

Leah knew for definite.

The tightness in her chest increased and the lump in her throat produced one small tear that sailed slowly down her cheek.

'Nothing more than I expected,' clucked Mrs Thompson when she'd returned home from the farmhouse with the news. 'That one's always been trouble. A right little madam. That poor wee mite inside her, not knowing who its dad is. Mrs Delancey told me Miranda is refusing to say.'

Leah understood why Miranda wouldn't say anything to Mrs Delancey.

Brett. The father of Miranda's baby. The boy Leah thought had loved *her*.

Leah had spent the past six and a half months believing that she was the unhappiest girl alive. Her young heart had been so consummately, completely given to Brett, that she doubted whether she would recover.

Knowing that Brett was still living not a mile away had been the hardest part. Imagining Miranda in his arms had been terrible too. At least when her mother had said that Brett had left to go back to school, the distance had eased the pain slightly.

Leah had swung from the terrible anger of being deceived to the devastation of knowing she would never see Brett again.

There had been times when she had imagined that Miranda had been lying, just to get her own back, but now Leah knew that Miranda had been telling the truth.

Leah wished that she could hate Brett. Really, truly hate him so that the longing in her heart would go away. But, even now, she could not.

She still loved him.

Leah, always quiet before, had retreated further into her own world. She was studying for O levels, and had found these a means of taking her mind off her broken heart. Her mother had assumed that her long silences at supper were to do with 'growing pains', as she put it, but her father knew. He would wink at her and tell her funny stories to try to make her smile. Leah felt awful that she couldn't talk to him about what she was going through, but no one could understand. Dad would tell her to forget him, and that was something she couldn't do.

Ever.

13

'KEEP PUSHING, THAT'S a good girl, nearly there now. Come on, just one more push and . . .'

Miranda, red-faced, exhausted and with not an ounce of energy left, gave one final push. As she screamed, her cry mingled with that of the first sounds of her newly born child. She saw the strange blueish thing being held by the midwife and sank back, uninterested in anything else except closing her eyes.

'Come on now, dear, hold baby.' The midwife pushed the bawling infant into her arms. 'It's a beautiful little girl.' The midwife smiled as Miranda looked down at the tiny creature with the ugly, screwed-up red face.

She'd wondered how she'd feel when she held it in her arms for the first time. Fear, maybe? Or love. Miranda felt neither. She felt nothing at all.

She handed the screaming bundle back to the midwife. 'Too tired now,' she said, and closed her eyes once more.

The midwife clucked in disapproval, but carried the baby off to the nursery.

Rose came rushing through the door five minutes

later. She stroked her daughter's sweat-matted blonde hair away from her face.

'Well done, darling. I've just seen her and she's absolutely beautiful. I'm so proud of you,' she smiled.

Miranda nodded, keeping her eyes firmly closed and wondering why people kept saying that the baby was beautiful. She didn't think it was.

'Anyway, I'm going to let you get some sleep now, darling. I'll be back to see you later.' Rose kissed her daughter gently on the cheek and crept out of the room. After checking with the doctor that mother and baby were going to be fine for the next couple of hours, Rose left the hospital, retrieved her car from the car park and set off towards Oxenhope. She hadn't been home for twenty-four hours, since she had found Miranda standing in a pool of water in the kitchen and in a terrible state of panic. Rose had managed to keep her calm on the journey to the hospital, inwardly feeling as frightened as Miranda, remembering the pain of childbirth and wishing she could endure it for her.

Thankfully, however, although long, the birth had been straightforward and Rose found tears filling her eyes as she neared Oxenhope. It was a glorious April day and the fresh smell of spring hung on the air.

'New life, rebirth,' Rose whispered emotionally. She thought of Miranda's real mother and wished that she could see her beautiful granddaughter.

'I'll do the best I can, I swear,' murmured Rose, knowing the problems were only beginning.

Mrs Thompson had offered to take over the day-to-day care of the baby when and if Miranda returned to school.

Rose somehow doubted that Miranda would do so, never having been academically inclined. And the attitude from the other students in her year, especially the boys, was enough to deter the most confident girl.

But there was no doubt that Doreen Thompson would prove useful. She had been very good with Miles when he was small.

Rose had managed to delay the exhibition only until the beginning of August, and Mrs Thompson's help was going to be invaluable while she was in London.

She drove up the hill and parked the car in front of the farmhouse. The builders were still at work on the roof of the house, and the barns adjacent. Rose had hired them out to a local farmer for a little extra monthly income, so they were being cleaned out and swept ready for the herd of cows to take up residence.

'Mrs Delancey, how did it go?' one of the builders shouted from the roof as she stepped out of the car.

'Just fine. It's a little girl and both mother and baby are doing well.'

'That's cracking news,' he smiled. 'I've left something on the kitchen table for you. One of the lads found it while he was clearing out the barns. He thinks it might be one of your paintings.'

Rose frowned and nodded. 'Thanks, Tim.' She opened the door to the kitchen, thinking the painting may have been junk stored there by the previous owner.

It was lying on the table, frame smashed, but sketch untouched. Rose gasped. It was the most exquisite charcoal drawing of Leah. She picked it up, carried it into her studio and placed it on an easel. Then she sat down and studied the signature in the right-hand corner. 'B.C.' Of course, it was Brett's work.

Rose was completely dazzled by the sketch. Brett had shown her his landscape work and she had been impressed by his obvious talent, but this . . . it had a maturity and depth to it that belied the artist's age and experience. The face staring out at her was one of great beauty. The eyes, my, they were hypnotic. You could hardly drag yourself away. In them, Brett had caught Leah's innocence and maturing sexuality perfectly.

And she knew that it had been painted through the eyes of love.

Rose sighed and wondered why Brett had never shown this to her. Why, if she had seen this, recognized the talent that he had inherited from his aunt, she thought proudly, then she would have given him more encouragement.

Rose's eyes filled with tears as she stared at the sketch. It reminded her so much of a drawing she had done when she was younger, when she too had been in love.

David must not be allowed to discourage his son. She went to a drawer, pulled out a pad of writing paper, found a paint-splattered biro and sat down in her chair.

After staring at a blank page and chewing the end of her pen for five minutes, she put the pad down.

No, she had a much better idea of how to help Brett.

14

'ROSE, DARLING, HOW absolutely marvellous to see you again, after all these years.' Roddy clasped her in a tight bear-hug, then pulled back and looked her over from top to toe. 'Mmn, still the same beautiful Rosie.'

'It's very kind of you to say so, but I think I've put on as many pounds since you saw me over twenty years ago,' she smiled wryly.

'Darling, it suits you. You always were far too skinny. Oh!' Roddy clapped his hands together, 'I can hardly believe you're here.' He put his arm through Rose's. 'Follow me. I've a bottle of your favourite Veuve Clicquot chilling in my office. We'll take a look round the gallery later. Your paintings arrived safely yesterday, by the way, and I have to admit I was tempted to look at them immediately.'

Rose walked through the spacious, newly fitted gallery with Roddy, its plain white, deserted walls a reminder of why she was here. Butterflies jumped in her stomach.

'To you, my darling. I just know that the exhibition will be a huge success,' said Roddy, handing her a champagne flute.

Rose lifted her glass and drank, vaguely wondering how Miranda and little Chloe were doing. She'd felt so guilty leaving them, but with Mrs Thompson clucking round them like a mother hen, Rose knew that they'd be fine. She only hoped Mrs Thompson didn't do all the work, as Miranda used her as an excuse to have as little to do with the child as possible.

'Of course, you're going to come and stay with me in Chelsea for the next week.'

'Well, actually, Roddy, I've booked myself into a hotel and . . .'

'Bugger the hotel, I insist you stay with me. I have a super flat that I bought a year ago. It's divine and I'm looking forward to cosy nights in front of my roaring fire while you tell me everything that's happened over the past twenty years.'

Rose had to smile at her friend. He was completely unchanged by the years except for the fact that he was sporting a toupee. His wiry frame was, as always, dressed immaculately in a designer suit. She wondered which rich lover had bought the flat for him as a token of thanks for Roddy's constant ministrations to his every sexual whim.

She had met Roddy in 1948. He had been in her year at the Royal College of Art. Then, it was as if he had sensed the secrets in her past, and never once had pried into those things that were too painful for her to remember.

In return, she had moved into his comfortable flat in Earls Court when she'd finished college, and provided a listening ear to the complications of Roddy's sex life. He was outrageously camp and proud of it. He came from

107

dubious nobility in Devon and had been a well-known figure at the Colony Room and French's where up-and-coming artists gathered in the fifties.

Having discovered he had little talent for painting himself, but loving the atmosphere and the people, he had concentrated on putting his more libidinous talents to good use. It used to be a joke in their tightly knit crowd that the only well-known young artist in London Roddy had not seduced was Rose herself. When Rose had left for Yorkshire, he was off in the South of France living with a very wealthy art dealer.

'Who owns this gallery, Roddy?' she asked. 'It's in a prime location.'

Roddy filled her glass to the brim once more. 'Well,' he said, 'I got a call from a company in New York offering me a job as manager at this plush new gallery in Cork Street. I was at a bit of a loose end, so I came to see the place. I mean, back then, ooh my dear, you should have seen it. A shell, that's what it was. Anyway, I called them in New York and told them to contact me when they'd refurbished it. I said that I couldn't say yes or no until I'd seen the finished product. Then they told me I could have *carte blanche* to design it myself, money no object. Of course I couldn't resist. A very nice gent from New York flew over to take a look at the finished product. He loved it, I'm glad to say. In fact, it was his idea that I should have an exhibition of fifties artists. It's all above board and everything. We pay our VAT and tax on time, so you're all right, dearie. It's not being funded by Mafia money or anything. To be honest, it's a perfectly wonderful arrangement. They just let me get on with it.'

'Are you doing well?'

'We've only been open since the New Year, and you're our sixth showing. But with my connections? Of course we are going to. I intend to bring the fun back into the art world. It's become so staid and snobby since our merry little band grew up and went their separate ways. I've invited everyone to the private viewing. Sontag, Lucie-Smith, and I think a few others might just pop along to say hello to their old stable mate. People are going to pour in, just to see if you really are still alive.'

'Oh dear, Roddy, you make me feel like an ancient monument. I'm only forty-six, you know,' Rose sighed.

'Sorry, sweetie, but people do love a mystery. No one knows why you ran off into the deep blue yonder at the peak of your career.'

And God help me, I hope they never know, thought Rose.

'I've arranged lots of interviews for you. There's the *Guardian* tomorrow, the *Telegraph*, and John Russell on Thursday. The . . .'

Rose listened as he reeled off a lengthy list of newspapers and wondered what had possessed her to do this. Could she handle it? Could she keep her cool and lie smoothly to journalists trained in the art of interrogation?

She had to. Twenty years of self-denial was too long a punishment for her crime. She owed it to herself to grasp at this chance. So she nodded and smiled and went with Roddy to see her paintings.

Roddy spent a long time studying the paintings, as Rose sat nervously sipping champagne. Finally, he turned to her, his beady eyes surveying her face. 'I think I detect a touch of romanticism in this one. Have you fallen in love, darling?'

Rose laughed and shook her head. 'No, Roddy. I know my new work is softer, the colours less stringent and the lines muted. Oh dear, you do like them, don't you? Or have I lost my touch?' Rose bit her lip, hating the old feelings of insecurity as someone surveyed her innermost thoughts on canvas.

'Well, they are different from your previous work, but still with the same great Rose Delancey touch. You've matured. Maybe the break you've taken was the right thing to do, because these . . .' Roddy swept his hand along the length of the paintings '. . . are wonderful.' His eyes greedily devoured the twenty paintings. Rose could almost hear the cash register ringing inside his head.

'Now, I'm going to take you out to lunch at San Lorenzo, then we'll come back here and set to work on placing the pictures round the gallery. How does that sound?'

'Just fine, Roddy, just fine.' Rose's relief was evident as she smiled at him.

They took a cab to Beauchamp Place, and Lucio, the maitre d', settled them at a discreet table under the large sycamore tree that grew inside the restaurant. Over a sumptuous lunch of grilled red mullet with fennel seeds, and veal San Lorenzo, accompanied by a bottle of Frascati Fontana Candida, Roddy went through the list of paintings, and they discussed a rough price guide.

'Do you not think we're being a little over-ambitious, Roddy? After all, I have been off the scene for twenty

110

years and my style must be dated compared with what the youngsters are doing these days.'

'Absolutely not, darling. For starters, the more figurative work you're doing is immensely popular at present, and look at Lucien's work! He sells for a fortune. We have to make you exclusive, to make the dealers and collectors feel as though they will be buying a piece of British art history. People want to pay for the pleasure of owning something rare, they don't want to feel as though they got something in the bargain basement, lovie.'

'I suppose not,' sighed Rose, realizing that she was out of touch with the market place. The figures Roddy was quoting her seemed absurdly high and would replenish her bank account to an extremely comfortable level.

'I still think it's a gamble to put myself in the price bracket of some of the top artists around today.'

'Trust me, Rose. You're my number one project and my establishing the gallery depends on your success. By the time I'm finished with you, every art collector from here to the Poles will know you're back in business. I intend to make you bigger than you were in the fifties.'

'Well, let's just see how the exhibition goes, shall we?' Rose was determined not to get carried away.

'Okay, darling, I understand your apprehension. Now, I'll order coffee and then you can tell me about the land of mists and damp and sogginess.'

'Oh, well, I have a farmhouse there, and two children, and I've just become a grandmother.'

'Rose!' Roddy almost choked on the dregs of his glass of Frascati. 'I didn't know you were married.'

'I'm not. Oneof my children, Miranda, is adopted.'

'I see. And the father of the other one?'

'Someone, just someone.'

'The lady of mystery once more,' Roddy smiled. 'Ah well, I shan't interrogate you. But surely, Rose, you could tell me why you disappeared the way you did? I promise not to say a word to anyone. I've been theorizing along with the rest of the art world for the past twenty years. Rumour had it that you'd run off to some harem in the Sahara with that sheik who kept buying your paintings. Someone else suggested you'd been kidnapped by the German count, and there was an idea that . . .'

Rose chuckled and shook her head. 'Nothing so exciting, Roddy. I went to Yorkshire, that's all.'

'I have to tell you that when I arrived back from France and found your note saying you were running out on me and the flat without so much as a good-bye or a forwarding address, I could have happily killed you. And, of course, you left me to deal with the trail of broken hearts you left behind. It was over a year before you wrote to me from Yorkshire, and that was only so I could send your post on. But no matter, I forgive you, I suppose.' Roddy sniffed.

'I am sorry, Roddy. I felt terrible about it but it was what I had to do, I'm afraid.'

'But why, Rose? Everything was going so wonderfully. Your career, all those simply gorgeous, wealthy men desperate to marry you. Especially that young French aristocrat that kept carting you off to his little shack in the Loire. Now, what was his name . . .?'

'Jean, Jean de Plessey,' murmured Rose. Oh yes, she remembered him. How could she forget?

'That was the one. We all thought you were about to get hitched.'

Rose took a sip of her coffee. 'Enough of the past. All I can tell you is that I'd run out of steam. I needed time to sort myself out and I didn't want to paint any more, okay, Roddy?'

Roddy looked at the frown across Rose's brow and knew that he'd dug deep enough. 'Of course. Let's finish our coffee, then go back to the gallery and set to work.'

Rose found the rest of the afternoon exhilarating as she and Roddy spent hours hanging paintings in one order, then deciding they looked wrong and taking them down and starting all over again.

'God, I'm exhausted. Time for a break.' Roddy went off towards the small kitchenette at the back, and re-appeared two minutes later holding a small frame.

'I think we've missed one out. I found it in the store-room where the others were. Let's have a look at it.' Roddy removed the sheet and placed the sketch against a wall.

'Surely this can't be yours, Rose darling?'

'Er, no. But what do you think of it?'

Roddy studied it thoughtfully. 'I think it's quite lovely. And the girl is stunning. Who's it by?'

'A friend of mine. He doesn't know I've brought it here, but I thought the same as you and wanted a second opinion. The artist is still very young.'

'Do I smell a protégé here?' smiled Roddy.

'Not exactly, no. He's my nephew actually.'

'Ahah! David's son, is it?' Roddy stared at her for a reaction, but got none. 'Looking at it again, I have to say

113

that there is a similarity between you, not in your style of course, but in its mesmeric quality. I'll hang it if you like, round the corner. It can start my small section of new artists.'

'Oh well, all right then. But it's not mine to sell.'

'Of course not. We'll hang it and see if there's any interest in it.'

'Fine. Now, how about that cup of tea?'

A week later, Rose stood in front of the wall-to-wall mirror in Roddy's guest suite, and studied her reflection. For the first time in twenty years, she rued the fact that she'd let her lithe figure slip away. In Yorkshire, there had seemed little point in caring what she looked like. No one had been around to notice. But tonight the vultures would be out in force, and it wouldn't just be her work that was on show.

She straightened the belt of the loose-fitting black gown and decided that she looked like a madam in a bordello. The Dior dress, dreadfully expensive, was covered with tiny, sparkling sequins. When she had tried it on in the salon, she had thought that it made her look sophisticated and perhaps slimmer, but as she looked at it now, she knew it had been a mistake.

'Shit!' Rose tore the dress off, left it in a heap on the marble floor of Roddy's bathroom, and hunted through the wardrobe for one of her favourite caftans. It was years old, picked up at an ethnic shop in Leeds for thirty pounds, but she felt comfortable in it. She stood once again in front of the mirror and felt immediately better. The dark green of the caftan set off her emerald eyes and

114

titian hair. She added some heavy gold chains and a couple of thick, gold bangles.

Rose took deep breaths to try to calm herself. She was as nervous as a kitten.

'Come on, girl, you've been through much worse. This is your night tonight. Think of the money and try to enjoy it.'

Rose walked down the corridor to find Roddy, decked out in a dinner jacket, waiting for her in the sitting room.

'Do I look okay, Roddy? Tell me honestly.'

Roddy held out his hands to her. 'Stunning, absolutely stunning. That caftan is wonderful. Balmain, or Galanos, perhaps?'

Rose smiled and took Roddy's hands. 'Neither, I'm afraid. These days, Marks and Sparks are above my price range.'

'Ahh, you just wait until after tonight, as the art world greets the return of their very own prodigal daughter. You'll be able to buy the entire range of any major fashion house you choose. Right, the taxi's outside. I suggest we go. And don't worry, my darling. You'll be coming back to this flat a queen.' Roddy touched Rose's cheek gently and proffered his arm. She smiled and slipped her arm through his.

By nine o'clock, the gallery was jam-packed. Champagne was flowing freely and Rose was surrounded by faces she hadn't seen in twenty years. With one eye cocked on the art critics, slowly perusing each of her paintings, she chatted away calmly to the many people who had come to support her. It was like being in a time-warp; the same faces around her, in the same atmosphere, and yet, so much had changed. The silver hairs and lines creeping onto the faces of the people with whom she'd partied until dawn years ago were testament to that. It was strange to see many of the young, devil-may-care artists she had known transformed into sober-suited males with responsible jobs and wives to match.

Everyone asked her the same questions, time and again. After a week of practice with the media, she was adept at answering, the rehearsed words falling smoothly and naturally off her tongue.

She glanced around and saw Roddy talking earnestly to an art collector whom she knew from the fifties. He had been wealthy then, and had bought three of her paintings. She only needed someone as influential as he to take the plunge and the rest would follow suit.

She checked her watch slyly, wondering where on earth Miles had got to. He had promised to be here by eight thirty and there was no sign of him.

'Rose, darling,' Roddy interrupted her thoughts. 'Didn't I tell you? I just knew that you would be a great success. Now, I want you to come and say hello to Peter. You must remember him. He bought three of your paintings years ago and is oh so interested in buying two of this collection. So be nice to him and . . .'

Peter Vincent was the collector Rose had seen Roddy with before. She put on her most charming smile and went to shake his hand.

Miles entered the gallery. The waitress offered him a glass of champagne, but he refused and took orange juice instead. He glanced around the packed room and spotted his mother deep in conversation.

He hated crowds like this. It made him feel claustrophobic and unimportant. Just another sliver of humanity carved off the main joint. But his mother had begged him to come and he could hardly refuse. Also, he had been in London for the past two days hawking his portfolio of photographs around magazines and newspapers.

And this afternoon, he had found himself a job. Only a temporary contract, but it was with an important fashion magazine and he was flying off to Milan next week to cover the haute couture fashion shows for next year's spring and summer range. Not exactly taking the pictures, but as an assistant to one of their hottest photographers, Steve Levine. In between changing rolls of film and carrying equipment around for Steve, he just might get a chance to do some of his own stuff.

Miles wandered around, looking at the paintings hanging on the wall. He found his mother's work strange, and could not associate it with Rose. He could see her talent, but he preferred the uncomplicated reproduction of reality that his photographs showed.

He turned a corner, glad that this part of the gallery seemed to be less crowded than the rest, and found himself looking at the sketch of Leah. Her beautiful face shone out at him, but he knew that this was nowhere near as good a representation as the many photographs he had taken of her over the years.

'Bastard,' he muttered under his breath.

'Pardon?' A fair-haired man was standing behind him studying the painting.

'Sorry, I didn't say anything,' said Miles.

117

'Oh, I thought you did. You don't by any chance happen to know who this girl is, do you?'

'I think you'd better ask the gallery owner. Sorry I can't help you further.' Miles moved away.

Steve Levine shrugged and stared at the sketch again. The girl was radiant. Youth, innocence and beauty, just what Madelaine looked for on every street corner every day of her life. And the kind of face that Steve dreamed of photographing. He pushed his way through the crowd and found Roddy standing with Rose Delancey.

'Steve, lovie.' Roddy kissed him on both cheeks. 'Have you met Rose Delancey?'

'Yes,' smiled Steve. 'Years ago, but I'm sure she won't remember me. I was nothing but a starving photographer desperate to make a crust in those days.'

'Oh, but I do remember you. You took a photograph of me walking in Regent's Park with a man I was trying to keep under wraps and sold it to half of Fleet Street,' chuckled Rose.

'Oh God, you do remember me!' Steve put his hands up in mock horror. 'Guilty as charged, I'm afraid.'

'I'm sure Rose will forgive you. You know Steve is now *the*, I mean *the* top photographer in London. Even the society hags are turning to him instead of Bailey,' pronounced Roddy.

'Mmn, I manage,' he smiled. 'Actually, I was wondering if you could help me, Roddy. There's a charcoal sketch round the corner of the most stunning girl. Do you know who she is, because I'm sure Madelaine would love to get her hands on her.'

Roddy shrugged. 'I'm afraid I don't. How about you, Rose?'

'As a matter of fact I do. But who's Madelaine?' she asked suspiciously.

'The *châtelaine suprême* of the biggest model agency in London,' said Roddy.

'Oh. Well, the girl in the sketch will only turn seventeen next week and . . .'

'Perfect. We like 'em young these days.'

'Her name's Leah and as a matter of fact she's my housekeeper's daughter.'

'Real Cinderella time,' smirked Roddy.

'If you wouldn't mind, Roddy, I'd like to bring Madelaine in to show her the sketch tomorrow. See what she thinks. Then we could get the girl to come to the office and . . .'

'Just hold on one moment,' interrupted Rose. 'The girl, Leah, lives in Yorkshire and is just about to start her A levels. I hardly think her parents would like her to go skipping off down to London.'

'In that case, Madelaine'll have to come to Yorkshire. She's got dealing with difficult parents down to a fine art, I can assure you.'

'Let's just slow down here. You know nothing about the girl, you've never seen her in the flesh and . . .'

Steve interrupted her. 'If she's half as lovely as she looks in that sketch, she'll be as big as Jerry and Marie in a couple of years. You've seen her, Rose. How tall is she?'

Rose sighed, knowing that the fact that Leah must be over five foot nine would make Steve's eyes light up further. She imparted the news reluctantly.

'This girl gets better and better,' Steve smiled. 'Well, good to see you after all these years. I hope you've forgiven me for the shot in Regent's Park. That photo was actually what gave me my big break. I'll bring Madelaine along tomorrow to see the sketch, if that's okay with you, Roddy.'

'Perfectly. Then I can announce that not only did I rediscover one of the greatest living artists, but I helped launch a young model on her way to a glittering career.'

Steve waved as he left the gallery. Roddy hugged Rose tight. He was tingling with excitement. 'Well, there's an almost definite sale from Peter on two, I've got an American who's coming back tomorrow to study "Light of my Life", and a collector from Paris who is a dead cert for "Tempest". You may have made a fortune tonight, darling. Let's mingle and see if we can spot any more would-be purchasers. The night is still young, Rose.'

As Roddy led her across the still-crowded gallery, Rose allowed herself a small smile. It was good to be back.

15

'WHAT CAN I say, my dear? I think a triumph would sum it up. You're back, Rose.'

She could see Roddy grinning from ear to ear as she listened to his voice on the telephone.

The day after the opening of the exhibition, Rose had insisted on getting a morning train home to Leeds, concerned about Miranda and the baby. Roddy had protested heavily, saying that there were still buyers he wanted her to meet, but Rose would not be swayed.

She was sitting in her studio, surrounded by the Sunday papers, most including good to glowing reviews of her exhibition.

'Thank you, Roddy, for all your help.'

'Don't thank me, darling. You're the artist. I think you could probably afford to go out and buy yourself some new canvas and brushes. We've sold six of your paintings, for a grand total of fifteen thousand pounds.'

'My God, that's incredible!' said Rose.

'Nothing to what you're going to earn in the future. but it's a start. Now, the other thing is that Steve brought Madelaine in to the gallery yesterday to see the sketch of

Leah. My dear, Madelaine nearly orgasmed on the spot when she saw it.'

'Please, Roddy!'

'Sorry. Anyway, Steve's off to Paris on a shoot next week, but he wants to bring Madelaine up to meet this little girlie of yours in the flesh when he gets back at the beginning of September. I thought I might tag along to see where my number one artist lives and works. We'll drive up in the Jag and be there for lunch. How does that sound?'

'Fine, Roddy, but I'm really not sure what Leah's parents' reaction will be to all this.'

'I suggest that you ask Leah and her mother to come round after lunch. Then Madelaine can set to work.'

'I don't know whether I want to be a part of all this. Leah is due to start the new term at school soon and . . .'

'Look, give the girl a chance to make up her own mind. She can always say no to Madelaine if she wants.'

Rose sighed. 'All right, Roddy.'

'That's my girl. Tell Leah it's a huge honour that Steve Levine is prepared to drive up to the wilds of Yorkshire *avec* Madelaine Winter in tow.'

'I'll see Leah's mother tomorrow and ask her.'

'Great. And I may have some more good news for you about your paintings. I've someone coming to the gallery tomorrow who's interested in three of them. I'll be in touch. *Ciao*, my darling.'

The telephone clicked off. Rose wandered into the kitchen where Miranda was sterilizing bottles for the baby. Little Chloe was gurgling happily in her carry-cot on the kitchen table.

'Hello, darling,' Rose cooed at the baby, who grasped

122

her finger in one of her tiny hands. 'She's a strong little mite. That grip is incredible. I'm sure she's grown since I've been away, haven't you, beautiful?' Rose picked Chloe up and hugged her.

'If you say so,' said Miranda morosely.

Rose looked at her daughter and sighed. Since the birth of Chloe, Miranda had become a different girl. All her spark seemed to have left her and from being almost obsessive about her appearance, Miranda never bothered to put make-up on. Her lovely blonde hair was scragged back in a tight ponytail. She'd been wearing the same pair of jeans for weeks.

'That was Roddy on the telephone. I've had a piece of good news. He's sold six of my paintings for a large sum of money. I think that calls for a celebration. Tomorrow, I'm taking you into Bradford on a spending spree.'

'And what about the baby?' Miranda picked Chloe roughly out of Rose's arms and sat down at the table. The baby spluttered as Miranda rammed the bottle into her mouth.

'I'm sure Mrs Thompson won't mind baby-sitting. You know she adores Chloe. Anyway, I've got to speak to her about Leah.'

Miranda looked up. 'What about Leah?'

Rose knew she had to play this very carefully. Her daughter was demoralized as it was. 'It seems a photographer might be interested in taking her picture. It's a friend of Roddy's and he's coming up here in September for lunch.'

'How come this man knows what she looks like?' Miranda's eyes were hard, questioning.

'There was a sketch of her at the exhibition,' said Rose

123

quickly. Embarrassed, she stood up. 'I'll see you later, darling.'

Miranda closed her eyes as Rose left the kitchen. She listened to her daughter suck contentedly on her bottle.

She hated the permanent smell of dirty nappies, talcum powder and the milky sick that pervaded all her clothes. She hated getting up at all times of the night to feed the bawling Chloe and having her life ruined by someone that depended on her for her every need.

Sometimes, Miranda even hated Chloe herself. She was only seventeen and she felt her life was over before it had begun.

The whole episode had taught her a lesson. She hated men. Hated them with a vengeance. Why wasn't the father's life being ruined like hers was? A year ago, she'd had her future mapped out. She was going to control them, use them to get what she wanted. Now, she was the victim.

She took the empty bottle away from Chloe's mouth and heaved the baby onto her shoulder to wind her.

Chloe's arrival had started her thinking about her own mother. For the first time in her life, she was wondering who she was, why she'd abandoned Miranda when she was so small. Sometimes, Miranda wished she could do the same with Chloe.

But she understood now. Everyone was selfish, out for what they could get. There was nobody who really gave a damn about her.

All her dreams of a better life had been ruined by Chloe's arrival.

Tears of self-pity plopped slowly down her cheeks.

16

ROSE SAW THE green Jaguar pull up at the front of the
farmhouse. She eyed the woman who was emerging from
the front passenger seat.

Madelaine Winter, ex-model and owner of the most
successful modelling agency in Europe, was still a very
beautiful woman. Rose knew that Madelaine was older
than she was but had to admit she looked younger. Her
thick, black hair, worn in a tight chignon, betrayed not a
hint of grey, and the figure that had graced all the major
catwalks into the early sixties was still perfect. The red
suit she was wearing was Chanel and her make-up was
impeccable. Rose felt, once again, frumpy and old, and
determined to go on an immediate diet.

'Darling! We made it! Grief, it's like the end of the
world up here! However do you stand it!'

Rose smiled at Roddy, kissed him, then shook hands
with Steve and Madelaine and led them into the sitting
room.

'What a fabulous view,' said Madelaine, looking out of
the window.

'It is, indeed.' Steve joined her.

'I must say, I hope this girl is worth it. We got held up in a jam on the motorway and it'll take hours to get back,' Roddy moaned.

Rose thought how strange it was to have these three smartly dressed Londoners standing in her sitting room. They looked totally incongruous with their surroundings. Leah was going to be overwhelmed and Rose wondered whether she should have encouraged Mrs Thompson to let her daughter meet them.

'I've prepared a light lunch, but I suggest we have a drink in here first.'

'Sounds perfect. I brought a tiny bottle of champagne with me to celebrate the fact that I sold your tenth painting yesterday.' Roddy produced a magnum from the plastic bag he was carrying.

'Congratulations, Rose. London is still talking about your exhibition.' Madelaine smiled, showing a perfect set of neat, white teeth.

Rose found some glasses and Roddy proposed a toast to her.

'And to Leah,' interrupted Steve.

'Now, talking of Leah, her mother is in the kitchen preparing our lunch. Leah's joining us later. Doreen's not too happy about all this so I'd tread very carefully if I were you. She's a straight up and down Yorkshire woman and a damn good housekeeper. I wouldn't like either Doreen or Leah to be coerced by you.'

'Don't worry, Rose. I'll tread carefully, I promise,' Madelaine smiled.

'Well, I think it's about time we went into lunch and you can meet Doreen,' said Rose.

At that moment, the door opened and Miranda entered the room. Rose drew in her breath. Her daughter was wearing one of her tight, short mini-skirts and a low top. Her face was once more plastered with make-up. She looked very pretty in a cheap, plastic sort of way, but Rose couldn't help but feel embarrassed.

'Miranda. This is Madelaine Winter, Steve Levine and Roddy Dawes. Everyone, this is my daughter, Miranda.'

Miranda smiled and posed in the doorway for a second, before coming into the room. 'I thought I might join you for lunch, if that's okay by you, Rose.' Miranda had lowered her voice and was speaking in a slow, husky drawl.

'Of course, darling. Miranda has just presented me with a beautiful granddaughter.'

Miranda shot Rose a look of venom across the room.

'Let's go and have something to eat, shall we?' said Rose quickly.

They settled themselves down in the dining room, Miranda pointedly waiting until Steve had taken his seat before placing herself next to him.

'Ahh, here's Doreen with the soup. Doreen, I'd like you to meet Steve Levine. He's the gentleman I was telling you about.'

'Good to meet you, Mrs Thompson. I'm looking forward to meeting Leah immensely.'

Mrs Thompson nodded.

'And me. My name's Madelaine Winter. I run Femmes, a modelling agency.'

'Nice to meet you, Mrs Winter,' Doreen croaked, overwhelmed.

Rose felt immense sympathy for the woman. She knew that if Madelaine wanted Leah, there wasn't a damn thing Mrs Thompson could do to stop her. She would be out-manoeuvred and brushed aside as a small irritation.

Mrs Thompson finished serving the soup and left the room.

'I have a surprise for you, Steve,' said Rose.

'And what might that be?'

'I hear *Vogue* has hired an assistant to help you in Milan.'

'That's right. Jimmy, my loyal and faithful servant for two years, has left me in the lurch to start up on his own. Diane at the magazine said she'd find me someone at short notice. I just haven't the time to start conducting interviews. It's only for a week. If he's awful, I can always find someone else when I get back.'

'I hope you don't think he's awful, because he happens to be my son, Miles,' smiled Rose.

'Your son?' Steve was amazed.

'I know. It's a total coincidence. I didn't realize until Sunday night when he told me on the telephone he was working for you in Milan.'

'Is he here?'

'No. He's in London. I'm sure you won't be disappointed with him. He's a very talented photographer and he's been told to be on his best behaviour.'

'Small world,' mused Steve.

Rose watched Miranda all through lunch. She was appalled at her behaviour. She was flirting outrageously with Steve, tossing her hair and leaning forward so that the entire table received an excellent view of her cleavage.

128

'Does your daughter know she's on a loser?' whispered Roddy. 'Of course, he has been known to dabble with women, but take it from me, he's as gay as I am.'

Rose nodded as they went through to the sitting room to have coffee. She squirmed as Miranda sat impossibly close to Steve on the sofa.

Mrs Thompson followed them in five minutes later with a tray of coffee and a terrified Leah trailing behind her.

Miranda looked at Leah. She couldn't understand why Steve was interested in her. Leah was just a thin, lanky kid with no tits or sex appeal, not a patch on her.

'I think it's time you fed Chloe, darling,' said Rose.

Miranda scowled. 'She'll be fine. She's fast asleep upstairs.'

'Well, go and check her, will you?'

Miranda stood up reluctantly.

'I'll see you later, Steve.' She shot him a winning smile and left the room.

Steve was staring at the girl in the doorway. She had on a pair of old jeans and a T-shirt which she wore with effortless grace. Her hair was wonderful. Long, lush and a natural burnished mahogany. Her face was perfect for the camera, with its high cheekbones and big brown eyes. And to top it all, the girl was at least five foot nine and wafer thin. He watched Madelaine staring at the girl, and when she shot him an almost imperceptible nod, he knew that he'd found something special.

'Leah, let me introduce you to Steve Levine and Madelaine Winter.' Rose stood up and steered Leah over to first Steve, then Madelaine. Leah shook their hands shyly. 'Now, come and sit down by me, and you too, Doreen. Madelaine would like to talk to you both.'

Madelaine smiled at Leah kindly. 'Leah, do you know anything about the world of modelling?'

Leah shook her head. 'Not really, no.'

'Well, you must have seen all the models on the covers of glossy magazines?'

'Yes.'

'Well, Steve here, who takes those pictures, and I, think that you could be on the covers of magazines too.'

'Me?' Leah said, astonished.

Steve nodded. 'Yes, you, Leah. That's why I brought Madelaine up to see you for herself. She runs one of the biggest agencies in London.'

'What's an agency?' enquired Leah.

'Well, I have a number of girls that I look after. I find them modelling work, I agree the money they will be paid and make sure that they get it,' said Madelaine. 'And I would very much like to look after your career, Leah.'

Mrs Thompson was sitting silently next to her daughter. Leah looked at her for help, but there was none forthcoming. Mrs Thompson was as overwhelmed as she was.

'But I'm just about to start my A levels,' Leah managed, and her mum nodded in agreement.

'Well, there's no reason why you couldn't continue your course in London. You'll have plenty of time to study when you're travelling,' reassured Madelaine.

Fear filled Leah's eyes. 'I'd have to leave here and move down to London then?'

Madelaine nodded. 'Yes, but you'd be able to visit your

parents as often as you wanted, and I'm sure you'd have a lot of fun with the other girls,' she soothed.

'But, I . . .' Leah searched desperately for another excuse. 'I only turned seventeen three weeks ago.'

'The perfect age, my dear. I much prefer to take girls from scratch and build them. That means they don't have any bad habits from other agencies.

'Oh,' said Leah. 'I . . . what do you think, Mum?'

Mrs Thompson sighed. 'I'm not sure, Leah. I don't know anything about this modelling business. And I'm not keen on our Leah going down to London and living by herself.'

'You could go with her to start off with, Doreen,' said Madelaine.

'No I couldn't. My husband, Harry, is in a wheelchair. He has arthritis and needs constant care.'

'Oh, I'm sorry.'

Rose noticed the flicker of interest that passed across Madelaine's elegant brow.

'Well, I can certainly sort out somewhere for Leah to live, probably in a flat with another of my models. Of course, another point that must be taken into consideration is the fact that Leah would be earning quite a lot of money if she does well. I bet you'd like to be able to help your mother with your father's care, wouldn't you, Leah?'

Madelaine smiled sincerely at Leah. Rose was aghast at the merciless emotional blackmail that Madelaine was employing. She watched as Leah wavered.

'Of course, but . . .'

'I think the best thing to do would be to have Leah and

Doreen come down to London for a couple of days, and see how Leah likes it,' cut in Rose firmly.

'Good idea,' said Steve. 'I can take some shots of Leah to see how they turn out. Then Doreen and Leah could visit your offices, Madelaine, and have a chat.'

'That sounds fine. Then I can go into more detail with you both about the way the industry works.' Madelaine was beaming. She knew that once she got them to London, she was well on her way to securing a contract with Leah.

'Great. Now, I really think we should be thinking of getting back to London. We're going to hit the rush hour head on and I have a dinner engagement at eight.' Roddy stood up and Steve and Madelaine followed suit.

'I'm off to Milan for the fashion shows next week, but Madelaine will call you and we'll arrange a date for the week after. Good-bye, Leah. I look forward to seeing you again very soon.' Steve shook Leah's hand.

'Good-bye, my dear. We'll be seeing you shortly.' Madelaine smiled at Leah, then followed Rose, Roddy and Steve out of the door. Leah and Mrs Thompson were left alone in the sitting room .

'What do you think, Mum?' Leah's eyes were wide.

'I think we could both do with a nice cup of tea. Come on, love.' Mrs Thompson put an arm round her daughter's shoulder and they went into the kitchen.

'Rose, promise me you'll work on that mother in the next week. Leah is sensational. I must have her,' pleaded Madelaine.

'I'll do what I can, but I rather think it's Leah you'll

have to work on. She didn't seem too keen on the idea of leaving home.'

'Honestly, all the girls who are desperate to become stars and we have to pick the only girl who doesn't have a clue what she has to offer,' said Steve.

'Ah, but that's part of her beauty. We don't want to lose that. Anyway, thanks for lunch, Rose. *Au revoir.*' Madelaine got into the car and Roddy kissed Rose good-bye.

'I'll be in touch soon if there's any further develop-ments on the sales of your paintings. Now you get back into that studio of yours and start work. I'll be needing plenty more Rose Delanceys to sell in the next year,' smiled Roddy.

Rose waved at the car as it disappeared down the hill, then went back into the house. Leah and Mrs Thompson were sitting in the kitchen drinking tea.

'I don't know, Mrs Delancey. What do you think about this modelling carry-on?'

Rose shrugged. 'Well, Doreen, Leah ought to feel very honoured that the best photographer and agent in the business came all the way up here especially to see her.'

Leah blushed. 'I can't believe they think I'm pretty enough to be a model, Mrs Delancey.'

'Let them worry about that. These people are profes-sionals. They wouldn't waste their time if they didn't think you'd be successful.'

'I don't know,' Mrs Thompson was shaking her head doubtfully.

'Look Doreen, I think you should go down to London with Leah and then decide. What I will say is that

Madelaine is the best in the business and she really looks after her girls. And if Leah does make it as a successful model, she could earn a lot of money.'

'I wouldn't like to be in London by myself, but on the other hand, if I made some money, then Dad and you . . .' Leah's voice trailed off.

'Now don't you go making your decision on the money. Apart from the fact that it would be yours anyway, me and Dad've managed just fine up until now, and I daresay we'll continue to do so,' said Mrs Thompson firmly.

Miranda entered the kitchen with Chloe on one shoulder.

'Hello, my pet,' cooed Mrs Thompson, taking the baby from Miranda.

'How's the new Twiggy?' drawled Miranda.

'She's hungry, same as your baby,' said Mrs Thompson sharply. 'Why don't you nip off home, love?' she said to Leah. 'You could tell your dad all about Mrs Winter and get started with the tea. I've got to clear up here.'

'All right, Mum. 'Bye, Mrs Delancey, 'bye Miranda.' Leah opened the kitchen door and set off on the walk home.

Outside, she breathed in the fresh autumn air. She loved the beginning of September, when the moors were beginning to turn a soft gold and she awoke in the morning to see the mist hanging gently over the hills.

How could she leave all this? And what about her mother and father? They would be left all alone if she went off to London. On the other hand, if what Mrs Winter said was true and she could earn a lot of money, it

134

would be so nice to help them. They'd struggled for such a long time.

But the sudden realization that she might lose every bit of what she had taken for granted for the past seventeen years made her suddenly intensely grateful for the life she led at present.

Leah passed the spot where Brett and she had spent such wonderful times together. She stopped and sat down. Twelve months and still no respite from waking every morning fresh from vivid dreams of him. She felt haunted by a boy she truly wanted to hate, but could only love. Maybe going away would help her forget.

When Leah arrived home, she went straight to her father's room. He had fallen asleep while reading a book and his glasses were perched right on the tip of his nose. Leah felt a surge of love as she studied him.

Mr Thompson stirred and opened his eyes. He smiled when he saw his daughter standing in the doorway.

'Hello, love. How did it go up at the big house with those folks from London?'

Leah went and sat on the pouffe by his side. 'They want me to go to London and be a model.'

'Do they now? And what do you think about that, then?'

Leah shrugged. 'I don't know, Dad. Mrs Delancey says it's a big opportunity, but I'd have to go and live in London. I'd miss you and Mum and Yorkshire something rotten.'

Mr Thompson looked at his beautiful daughter and smiled at her concerned face. He'd been so worried about her for the past year. The lass had taken her first affair of the heart very hard. But he knew she'd get over it in time and this modelling business seemed like just what was needed to bring back her confidence. It would break his heart to see her leave, but he knew that Leah had something special and had to go out into the world and find her future.

'Well now. I know you'll miss Mum and me, pet, but employment's bad up here and someone's offering you a job. And a glamorous one at that.'

'I'd have to leave school, and I worked so hard to get good results in my O levels. I want to take my As and think about university if my results are good enough.'

'Well, it's a decision only you can make, Leah. But don't look a gift horse in the mouth, will you? Opportunities like this don't come along very often. I'll support you whatever you want to do. You're a good girl and although I don't want you to go, I think you're worth more than ending up in an office as a secretary with a brood of kids. And you're a lovely looking lass, Leah. Take after your dad, of course.' Mr Thompson smiled. 'Come and give me a hug.'

Leah put her arms around his neck and thought how wonderful it would be to be able to shower him with presents in return for the kindness he had shown her. She held him tight. 'I love you, Dad.'

Mr Thompson felt a lump in his throat. 'Go on now, go and put the tea on. Your dad's hungry and you're not a superstar yet, you know.'

He watched Leah leave the room and reached in his cardigan pocket for a tissue to wipe his eyes. Leah was what he lived for. And he knew he was going to lose her.

17

'THEY'RE ABSOLUTELY FABULOUS,' Madelaine said excitedly, as she spread the photos across her desk for Leah to see.

'Are they really me, Mrs Winter?' Leah said in amazement as she looked at the beautiful girl in the pictures.

'Please, call me Madelaine, and yes, they are you, Leah. It's amazing what a good make-up artist and photographer can do, isn't it?'

'I look so much older.'

'Well, I would say you look more sophisticated, yes. And the clothes you're wearing help too.'

Mrs Thompson was touching the photos reverently. 'I must admit that Mr Levine's done a good job. I can hardly believe this is our Leah.' She smiled proudly.

Madelaine breathed a sigh of relief. Having spent a large amount of money putting Mrs Thompson and Leah up at the Inn on the Park for the past three nights, hours reassuring Mrs Thompson that she'd personally take care of her daughter when she was in London alone, and even paying for a nurse to stay with the crippled husband, she was delighted to see that familiar look of motherly pride. Now it was only Leah she had to convince.

'Did you enjoy the photo session, Leah? Steve said you both had a good time.'

'Yes, I did, Mrs, er Madelaine. Steve's a very nice man.'

'So, do you think you're prepared to do this kind of thing full time?'

Leah looked at Madelaine. Guilt for all the money she had spent putting her and Mum up in that plush hotel, and the thought of how she could help her mother and father with what Madelaine had said she could earn made it difficult for Leah to say no.

This was exactly what Madelaine had intended.

'What about my A levels?' She looked at her mother.

'Well, as Mrs Winter has said, you could try modelling for a year, and if you really didn't like it, you could always do the exams next year. It's a wonderful chance, Leah,' Mrs Thompson encouraged.

'Well, I suppose I could try it for a while to see how I got on,' she said slowly.

'That's fine, Leah, although I'll have to sign you up to the agency for a year. Standard procedure, I'm afraid.' Madelaine picked up the contract and handed it to her. 'Now, why don't you sign that and then we'll all go out to lunch and celebrate.'

Leah looked at the five pages of small type in front of her.

'Go on, dear, I'm sure Mrs Winter would understand if you really didn't like it and wanted to come home.'

'Absolutely, Doreen,' nodded Madelaine.

Leah took the heavy gold pen that Madelaine handed her uncertainly.

'Do I need to read it through first?' she asked.

'No, it's all legal gobbledegook, but it basically says that Femmes will be your sole representatives and will take a percentage each time we get you a job.'

Leah took a deep breath and scribbled her signature in the appropriate place.

'Wonderful!' said Madelaine. 'Now, before we get down to the hard work, let's go and enjoy ourselves.'

Madelaine took them to a plush restaurant just around the corner from her office in Berkeley Square. She ordered champagne, and over some very strange food – which Madelaine told Leah were something called 'hescargo' and looked like snails – she talked to Leah about the future.

'This afternoon, I'm going to take both of you round to meet Jenny at her flat. She's one of my up-and-coming young models and has a spare room. She's a couple of years older than you and a nice, sensible girl. She can look after you and show you round London. I'm sure you'll both like her,' beamed Madelaine. 'Tomorrow, I want you to come into the office at nine o'clock. I'll book a hair appointment with Vidal and send you off to Barbara in the afternoon. She'll teach you how to do your make-up. And I might send you to Janet, a friend of mine who teaches elocution, just to get rid of that Yorkshire accent.'

Leah listened as Madelaine planned her life, and watched her mother agreeing with everything she said.

'Doesn't it all sound exciting, Leah? Say thank you to Madelaine for all she's done for you.'

'Thank you, Madelaine,' Leah repeated.

'I'm going to try and book you for the ready-to-wear collection in Milan next month. It's where most of the girls start. The fashion editor of *Vogue* won't even look at you until you've made it in Europe.'

Madelaine continued to chat away in the taxi on the way to visit Leah's new home. It was in a place called Chelsea and the taxi stopped outside a grand white house.

'It's a very safe area, Doreen, so there'll be no worries on that score.' Madelaine pressed a bell and a girl in an old tracksuit answered the door.

'Madelaine, darling.' The girl kissed her on both cheeks. 'Come in. And this must be Leah. Hi, I'm Jenny. Come up.'

As the three of them followed Jenny up the two flights of steep stairs, Leah thought that Jenny was the prettiest girl she had ever seen. She was about the same height as Leah, with long blonde hair and a pair of huge blue eyes. Much prettier than she was, Leah thought.

Jenny showed them round the flat, which was small but elegantly furnished. Leah's bedroom was no bigger than a broom-cupboard, but it was prettily decorated with candy-stripe wallpaper and matching curtains.

Mrs Thompson's 'oohs' and 'ahhs' as she looked round the tiny kitchen, furnished with every appliance on the market, made Leah long for the basic but cosy kitchen at home.

Jenny suggested coffee as Madelaine and Doreen went into the sitting room and sat down.

'Stay and help me make it, Leah. You look scared stiff,' Jenny smiled.

140

'I am, a bit.'

'Don't worry. I was just the same when Madelaine found me walking along a street in Bristol. I'd never even been to London before.'

'Nor have I,' said Leah.

'Madelaine'll look after you, and I'll be here to show you the ropes. Just keep your head down and do what Her Majesty asks you to.'

'Her Majesty?'

'Yes, all the girls on her books call Madelaine the Queen behind her back,' said Jenny conspiratorially.

Leah giggled and carried the tray of coffee into the sitting room feeling a little better.

However, she did not feel that way as she stood on the platform of King's Cross station that evening, sobbing her heart out.

'Come on now, Leah. Anybody would think you weren't ever going to see me or your dad again. Madelaine says you can come up next weekend if you want to visit us.'

'Oh, Mum,' Leah wailed, hanging on to Mrs Thompson's coat.

'Honestly, you're acting like a ten-year-old. Pull yourself together and think how many other girls would give their eye-teeth for the chance you're getting,' Mrs Thompson chastised.

Leah blew her nose hard and walked down the platform to see her mother onto the train.

'Don't bother waiting for the train to go out. You go and get in that taxi. It must be costing Madelaine a fortune.' Mrs Thompson kissed her daughter and opened the door to a carriage.

''Bye love. Be a good girl and do everything Madelaine tells you to. I'll write as soon as I can.'

'Send my love to Dad, won't you?'

''Course I will. Make us both proud of you, pet.'

The tears were coming into Mrs Thompson's eyes. She waved hastily and disappeared inside the carriage to find a seat.

Leah walked miserably back up the platform towards the waiting taxi, tears blurring her eyes. She opened the door of the big black car and jumped in.

'Where to, miss?'

She read out Jenny's address and the taxi set off, taking Leah to begin her new life.

18

'IT'S GOOD OF you to see me at such short notice, but I wanted to catch you while you were in Washington, Mr Cooper.'

David studied the heavy-set man with the distinct accent. 'What exactly is it that you want to discuss?' David felt slightly irritated. He'd an important business meeting and he was not interested in some Third World charity organization, probably here to beg for money. Pat usually dealt with this kind of thing and he wondered how this one had slipped through the net.

'First, Mr Cooper, I have to apologize. I am here under false pretences. I do not work for the organization you think I do.'

Jesus, this was all he needed. David sighed. 'Okay, so who do you work for?'

'Would you sit down, Mr Cooper, and I shall explain.'

As the man began to talk to him softly, all David's irritation vanished. The colour drained from his face.

When the man had finished, David sat in silence, staring into space.

Eventually, he said, 'How did you find me?'

'One of our organization recognized your face from a news cutting. He knew you many years ago.'

'What do you want?'

'We know that you are about to start doing business with this man.' He passed David a file with the name of the man on the cover.

'It is the man you are dealing with, is it not?'

David nodded slowly. 'Yes. What is the problem?'

'Have you met this man yet?'

'No. I've corresponded with him quite heavily and spoken to him briefly on the telephone. We're due to meet for lunch in a couple of weeks' time.'

'Then I'd like you to read that file. It is, of course, highly confidential and should any word of this leak out, thirty years of intelligence work will be for nothing. I will leave it with you. I want you to read it from cover to cover and I think you might find what it contains a little disturbing. When you have finished, I would like you to ring me on this number. There is a man who would be pleased to meet you, if you are agreeable.' The man stood up and held out his hand. David shook it.

'Good-bye, Mr Cooper.'

The man left the room and David went across to the drinks cabinet. He poured himself a large Scotch with ice and settled down in the comfortable hotel chair to read the file.

An hour later, tears were pouring down his cheeks and he was on his fifth Scotch.

'Jesus,' he moaned. He went into the bathroom and splashed his face with cold water.

So many years ago, so much pain. All these years of
blocking out the past and now . . .

He wandered back into the sitting room of the hotel
suite and poured himself another Scotch.

David knew he had to make the biggest decision of his
life.

Then he remembered the vow he had made when he
been so much younger.

His hands were still shaking from shock. His mind
forced him back into the past, opening doors into the
dark recesses of his memory that he had not entered in
all that time . . .

19

WARSAW, 1938

'MAMA, MAY I go and see Joshua? He has a new trainset and has asked me to help him play with it.'

Adele smiled fondly at the boy in front of her. No one could resist him, herself included. He was so clever and had the kind of cherubic, innocent face that made it impossible for a bad or evil thought to pass behind.

'Of course you may, as long as you have finished the reading that Professor Rosenberg set you.'

'Oh yes, Mama, I finished it hours ago. English is such a strange language. It has words which mean more than one thing. It confuses me sometimes.'

He spoke so seriously, so fluently for a boy of ten. His teachers were predicting a great future for him.

'All right then. You may ask Samuel to take you round in the car. I will want to hear you play your violin when you return.

'Of course, Mama.'

'Give your mother a kiss, David,' she beckoned.

He came forward and planted a kiss on her forehead.

'Good-bye, Mama,' he smiled, and walked out of the drawing room.

Adele sighed contentedly and thought once more how lucky she was. And how glad that she had taken such a dreadful risk over ten years ago and eloped from Paris with the young Polish artist with whom she had fallen so deeply in love.

In the summer of 1927, Adele had been on a tour of Europe with her maiden aunt, Beatrice, before returning home to England to be married to a man deemed suitable by her father and packed off to India as his wife. While visiting Paris, Beatrice had gone down with a bad attack of food poisoning, leaving Adele free to explore Paris by herself. She had chanced upon Montmartre, sat down to cool herself with a *citron pressé*, and listened to the noisy chatter of a group of artists sitting at the neighbouring table. One of them had asked her to help settle an argument they were having over whether Picasso or Cézanne was the greatest artist of their time. Adele had done so, joined the table, and there she had been introduced to Jacob Delanski. Adele had been spellbound by the tall young Pole, with his blond hair, penetrating blue eyes and infectious laugh. Jacob had asked if he could paint Adele, and for the following week, she had left the comfort of her suite at the Ritz Hotel to go to Jacob's cramped attic on the rue de Seine.

Jacob, with his charismatic personality and sheer exuberance at being young, talented and in the most exciting city in the world, had overwhelmed Adele. She'd been used to her regimented, Victorian-style upbringing, and the formal, stiff young army officers in England thought suitable by her father to escort her to balls.

Now here she was in a Montmartre studio, drinking wine at three o'clock in the afternoon, listening to Jacob telling her he loved her, that he wanted to marry her.

Adele had protested that it was impossible, but Jacob had silenced her, telling her that she was wrong, that destiny had taken a hand. He'd made love to her then, and she'd known Jacob was right, that they must never be separated again. Adele knew that her father would come searching for her in Paris, so the two of them had decided to travel to Jacob's native Warsaw. Adele had left the Ritz in the early hours with one small valise, the overwhelming passion she felt for her beautiful, talented lover blinding her to the momentous decision she was taking.

When Jacob and Adele had arrived in Warsaw, they had taken shelter with one of Jacob's oldest friends in Wola, an artisan district of Warsaw.

Their first priority was to get married, but this was a problem. Jacob was Jewish and Adele was a British Christian. There was not a rabbi nor a priest in the city that would marry them. One of them had to change religion and Adele agreed that it should be her.

She went to preparation classes as Jacob struggled to find work so that they could eat. He also went to see his father, who would have none of him unless he denounced his ambition to paint and assumed his rightful position at the family bank. Jacob refused and found himself a job at a library, which gave the two of them enough money to find a room of their own and throw a small celebration after their wedding, which his parents did not attend.

148

Things had been dreadfully hard at first, but they'd survived on love, with Jacob never failing to bring a smile to her face when she felt low. His lust for life was infectious, and Adele learnt that there wasn't a problem that couldn't be solved. A year after their marriage, Adele gave birth to a baby boy, whom they named David. Their one room was filled with soaking nappies and the smell of paint, as Jacob determined to make a success and show his parents he didn't need their help.

Jacob had then been asked to paint a portrait of one of his friends' wealthy relatives and they'd had enough money to move to a two-roomed apartment. Three months later, Jacob was asked to paint another member of the same family and word soon started to spread. Jacob was able to give up his job at the library and work full time on his paintings.

By the time Adele gave birth to Rosa in 1931, they had moved from the overcrowded city to Saska Kepa, a housing district joined to the centre of Warsaw by the new Poniatowski Bridge. Jacob was establishing an excellent reputation as a portrait painter, his good looks and charm earning him commissions from middle-aged matrons anxious to be flattered both on and off canvas.

As Jacob's fame and prosperity grew, his parents, although uncomfortable about his choice of career and gentile wife, softened in their feelings towards their son. They too moved away from the city and joined Jacob and Adele in Saska Kepa and communication was re-established. As they saw the care Adele took to bring up her children in the Jewish tradition, and hearing that she had been of noble birth in England, they accepted her and doted on their grandchildren.

Adele had been quite prepared to understand why Jacob could not give up his religion for her; it would have been like asking him to change his nationality, but she was determined that her children would grow up knowing something of her own heritage. So, since they'd been babies she had spoken English to them, and French had been the common language between Jacob and herself as she struggled to get to grips with the Polish language. And now, at ten and seven respectively, David and Rosa could converse with ease in three languages.

When they lay tucked up in their small beds at night, Adele would sit and tell them stories of her life in London; of the big house overlooking Hyde Park that she had lived in as a child. She told them of Big Ben, the Houses of Parliament and Old Father Thames running through the capital of the world. She promised, as their eyes hung heavy with sleep, that one day she would take them there.

Often, Adele would think about her mother and father and what had happened when they learnt of her disappearance. She had felt dreadful leaving poor Aunt Beatrice to break the news, but she had had no choice. By now, they probably thought she was dead.

Adele was brought out of her reverie by a knock on the drawing-room door.

'Enter.'

Christabel, the round-faced nanny, led Rosa towards her by the hand.

'Hello, darling.'

The little girl, a minute replica of her mother with her thick, titian hair, held her small arms up. Adele lifted her and hugged her tight.

'Tell Mama what you have to show her,' said Christabel fondly.

Rosa's large emerald eyes grew wide and she reached a hand out towards Christabel, who handed her a piece of paper.

'Here.' She presented the piece of paper to her mother, who put Rosa down and studied it.

On the piece of paper was a painting of a bowl of flowers. Adele drew in her breath as she realized that this was her seven-year-old daughter's work. She could hardly believe it. The use of colour, shape and intricate detail showed the hand of a far more mature artist. Adele questioned whether she was looking through an unbiased eye, looked again and knew she was.

Rosa was standing patiently in front of her, arms folded neatly over her spotless white pinafore.

'Why, darling, this is wonderful! Are you sure you are telling me the truth? Did you really paint it yourself?'

Rosa nodded. 'Oh yes, Mama, I really did.'

'I can vouch for that, ma'am. I watched her with my own eyes. And she has a drawing book full of them upstairs.'

Rosa watched as Nanny and Mama exchanged knowing glances, the ones grown-ups often used in front of her and David.

'Well, Rosa, I think we should take this to show Papa, don't you?'

'Yes. And can I show David?' Rosa's eyes lit up.

'Of course you may.' Adele was always touched by the closeness of her two children, she herself having been an only child.

When Jacob saw his daughter's painting, he felt awed. He knew that within his daughter lay talent that paled his own into insignificance. He set about harnessing it immediately. Rosa was sent to his purpose-built studio at the back of the house for two hours every morning. He taught her everything he knew and watched with pride and amazement as her talent and effortless grasp of what he imported far outstripped her tender years. Although unspoken to Rosa, whose sheer delight in her ability to bring things to life on a sheet of paper was part of her gift, Jacob and Adele acknowledged that she did indeed have a prodigious talent.

And David was showing a flair for the violin. On his tenth birthday in 1938, Jacob and Adele had bought him the Ludwig, a rare and valuable Stradivarius. The four of them sat, night after night, listening to their son drawing melodious sounds out of the rare instrument.

'I told you, didn't I, that our best chance of happiness was in being together?' Jacob would whisper when they climbed into bed.

'Yes, my love. Life is perfect.'

They would fall asleep, in each other's arms, innocently, unaware of the horrors to come.

On 1 September 1939, Germany invaded Poland. Over a million men, fully equipped with superior air power, easily overcame Poland's inadequate army. Two weeks later, Russia sent her troops into Eastern Poland. Polish forces crumbled completely and Poland was divided between Russia and Germany.

The battle for Warsaw raged on. Jacob, Adele, David and Rosa sat huddled in their cellar. Jacob was filled with horror and growing fear. He'd heard of the atrocities committed against the Jews in Berlin and had watched as anti-Semitism took on renewed fury in Poland. A policy of 'evacuating' the Jews from many of the small Polish towns and villages had sent them flooding into Warsaw to escape brutal pogroms. Thousands of Jews had died already, yet as Jacob listened to the explosions that rocked Warsaw day after day, he knew that this was only the beginning.

On 27 September, Warsaw surrendered. For the first time in a week, Jacob ventured outside, horrified by the devastation wreaked on the once-magnificent city. The Royal Castle had been burnt to the ground and the newly refurbished Central Railway Station had been badly damaged.

The streets were deserted as he hurried to his parents' house. His heart lurched as he saw the next-door building still smouldering, its innards hanging out.

'Dear God, Jacob. What is to become of us now the Nazis are here? You should have got Adele and the children out while you had the chance.'

Jacob sighed, as he gazed at his mother's white face. 'I know, Mama, but Adele refused.'

'Well, she's missed her opportunity. Now she'll have to stay here and die with the rest of us.'

'Mama, do not talk like that! There are three million

153

Jews in Poland. Even the Nazis cannot kill all of us. We shall stand up and fight back.'

Surcie Delanski considered her son's defiant face, his youth and strength. But she knew, deep in her heart, that the battle was already lost.

After Warsaw surrendered, the Polish government went into exile in Paris. The Generalgouvernement of Poland was formed and Hans Frank, the governor general, issued orders for the Jewish community in Warsaw to set up their own council, under German instruction.

Jacob's father was a member of the Kehillot council. Jacob listened as his father related the latest set of German instructions to be implemented amongst the Jews.

'As from tomorrow, all Jews will have to wear identifying armbands. Parts of the city will be closed to us.'

'Papa, I can hardly believe this! Is the council not fighting back?'

'How can we, when the Nazis are already subjecting our people to a reign of terror? Random shootings, Jews being bundled into lorries and taken to labour camps? Thousands have died already and there will be worse to come.'

'You say we are not allowed access to certain parts of the city? It is almost ghettoization.'

Samuel Delanski nodded sadly. 'Yes. And we believe that is exactly what they want. My son, I implore you to sell what you have now. Raise as much money as possible before it is too late. Thank God I had the sense to withdraw the funds from my account at the bank. I knew the

Nazis would close it. Some of my friends have lost everything. The net is closing in. I advise you to insist that Adele leaves the city with the children. She still has her British passport, does she not?'

'Yes, Papa.'

'And neither David nor Rosa looks Jewish. You must get them out, David. You know they will stand a much better chance of survival without you.'

'Adele will not go without me, but I shall try to persuade her one last time.'

'Good. I have a friend who is helping people to make their way to Gdynia. There are a few boats still sailing to Denmark. When they reach there, they can go into hiding until a boat sails for England.'

That night, Jacob related to Adele what Samuel had told him. As he knew she would, Adele adamantly refused to leave without Jacob.

'But do you not see, Adele, that without me, you have every chance of reaching safety? With your passport, you and the children are English and no one need ever know that you converted when you married me.'

Adele's eyes were full of tears. She shook her head. 'I will not leave if you do not come with me. I cannot abandon you here to face possible death.'

Jacob looked at his wife. The love he felt for her burned stronger than ever. She had the chance to escape this madness – after all, it was not her war – and yet she was prepared to stay and suffer with him.

He had one last try. 'Adele, *kochana*, you understand that I cannot possibly come with you. If we were caught we would face immediate death and that is too much of a chance to take. But think of the children. Think of how they will suffer if they stay. *Please*, Adele, I beg you.'

She sighed, stared upwards, then stood up slowly and knelt at his feet. She took his hands in hers.

'Jacob, that day when we ran from Paris to be together, you begged me to follow my heart. I did so, and at that moment, I knew that I had sealed my fate. There is no going back. I took my decision to be your wife and convert to your faith and it would be as if I was denying you and our love if I pretended otherwise. So please, my darling, accept that we must be together, as a family, until the day we die.'

She put her arms around him and he grasped her tightly to him.

He nodded slowly. 'Until the day we die.'

As Samuel Delanski had predicted, orders were given by Hans Frank that all Jews in Warsaw were to be sealed inside an area in the northern part of mid-town Warsaw by the end of November 1940. Having prior warning of this, Samuel had managed to organize a small apartment inside the ghetto area in the brushmaker's district on Lezno Street. It had only three rooms; one for Jacob and Adele, another for Samuel and Surcie, and the sitting room provided enough space for two mattresses for David and Rosa. Compared to the conditions others were living in, the apartment was a palace.

Jacob had sold everything he owned to raise cash. Pooled with Samuel's money, they reckoned they had enough to keep them in food for two years or more.

Four hundred thousand Jews were sealed in the area,

three quarters of a mile square, and stretching only twelve blocks from Jerozolimska Street to the cemetery.

The overcrowding in the ghetto was unimaginable, the sanitation appalling, and already there were food shortages. Adele spent most of her mornings queueing outside one of the few licensed ghetto bakeries to bring home bread.

Jacob and the Kehillot Council tried hard to bring some kind of normality to the ghetto citizens. Schools were set up and ran without fail every day; debates were organized, theatre groups formed and a fine symphony orchestra gave weekly concerts.

But by the end of 1940, the number of Jews forced out of the villages from the provinces had swelled the population to over half a million. Rations to the ghetto had been decreased and were barely enough to feed half the population; many were dying of starvation and disease and the black market was rife. Those who made the dangerous run out of the ghetto to bring back supplies were charging outrageous prices. The Delanskis had no choice but to pay or starve.

It was a strange life, fraught with terror as friends disappeared and the streets rang with the sound of Nazi bullets, but Adele and Jacob desperately tried to keep some kind of routine for the children's sake.

David and Rosa attended school in the morning, then Jacob sat with Rosa in the afternoon and painted, using the backs of old paintings to extend the life of their small supply of fresh paper. It wiled away the hours as Adele tried to cook a palatable dinner out of her supplies of potatoes and a few old vegetables. Nine-year-old Rosa seemed blissfully unaware of her surroundings, although she sometimes crept into David's bed when the sound of gunfire frightened her. Her sweet nature endeared her to the neighbours who would find her a spare apple if she sketched them.

At night, the family would huddle together around the small fire. David would play his precious Stradivarius, which Jacob had not been able to bring himself to sell.

The following April, Surcie Delanski went down with an attack of typhoid that was sweeping the ghetto. She died a week later. Samuel Delanski followed her in July.

Unable to speak from grief, Jacob hauled his father's body onto one of the carts provided for the purpose. It was already overflowing.

After the death of his parents, Jacob became quiet, withdrawn. He stopped painting and would sit for hours, staring out of the window on the dreadful poverty and suffering in the street below their apartment.

Adele despaired as she watched her beloved, exuberant husband retreat further into himself as each day passed. He would stare at her when she tried to talk to him, comfort him, as if he did not know her. All he could say was, 'Sorry, I'm so sorry', as tears came once more to his eyes.

Adele was left to care for the children, to try to organize a supply of food. Try as she might, she could not shake her husband out of his increasing misery.

Already weak from lack of food and caring for two fatally ill people, she passed out in a dead faint on the floor of the tiny kitchen.

Horrified, David had picked her up. She was light as a

feather and he could feel the bones beneath her worn dress. He spoon-fed her a little broth that was simmering on the stove. Davidsuddenly realized that his mama had been neglecting her own rations to feed her family.

Tears came into Adele's eyes as she watched her son.

'Eat this. All of it,' he demanded.

'No, David.' She pushed the bowl away.

'Mama, it is all right. From now on, I'm taking charge. By tonight, I promise there will be fresh food on the table.'

David left the apartment half an hour later. At six he returned with a sack of fresh food.

From thenceforth David would go out once a week and not return until the dusk was falling, with a sackful of supplies. He always smelt fetid and Adele guessed that he was making the journey through the sewers to reach the outside of the ghetto.

Rosa never questioned how he got the food. She knew David was subjecting himself to terrible danger and she couldn't bear to think about that.

The winter of 1942 wiped out thousands more in the ghetto. Coal was virtually impossible to get hold of and even David, with his now excellent knowledge of the black market, was struggling. The money was starting to run short and he reckoned he only had enough to feed the family for another few months. He was unable to talk to anyone in his family about this, or about the risk he ran once a week. If he was caught on the outside, he would be shot. He was only thankful that spring was on its way.

David's black market connections and trips to the other side also provided him with a useful amount of intelligence. He heard from one of his sources that the ghetto of Wartheland had been emptied, with Jews deported to Chelmo, and that the same was happening in Lublin. There were dreadful rumours that Chelmo was a death camp, where the Nazis were annihilating Jews by the thousand.

David longed to confide this news to his father, to hear him say that David's information *must* be wrong, but Jacob was confined to his own world. These days he rarely got out of bed. So David shouldered his terrible fear alone.

In July 1942, on the day of Tish B'ab, a Jewish holiday to commemorate the destruction of the Temple in Jerusalem, David was making his way back to the apartment with a precious haul of five potatoes.

A German patrol, an everyday sight on the streets of the ghetto, whisked past him, and stopped in front of the building housing the Jewish council. David did not think much of it, guessing that the Germans were continuing their round-up of Jews for their forced labour battalions.

So he did not pause to listen to what the Commandant had to say. The golden rule was to keep as far away from Germans as possible.

Later, as the four Delanskis were sitting eating their paltry meal, there was a knock on their door.

David went to open it and found a pale-faced friend of his who lived with his family in the apartment below theirs.

'Come in, Johann. What is wrong?'

'My father sent me to warn you. Today he saw the Germans rounding up old people and tearing children out of their mothers' arms. Those they rounded up in the Umschlagplatz were marched to Stawki Street near the railway sidings where there was a line of freight cars. The old and young were bundled into the cars and the train left. Nobody knows for sure where it was heading. There is panic on the streets. People have heard rumours of death camps. David, keep Rosa inside. She should not attend school. I must go. There are others who need to be warned.'

'Thank you, Johann. I will indeed keep Rosa home.'

David shut the door, his heart thumping. The liquidation of the ghetto, as at Wartheland and Lublin, had begun here.

Adele knew the minute she saw her son's face that something was wrong. Later, when Rosa was sleeping, and Jacob was in his bedroom, Adele beckoned David into the kitchen.

'What is it, David? What did Johann want?'

David explained what Johann's father had seen. Adele's green eyes darkened with fear.

'David, I have seen in your face that you know more about what is to become of us than you say. But you must tell me now all you know. We shall share it between us. Rosa is too young to understand and Jacob . . . well, it is better if he does not know. So, David, is this rumour about the death camps true?'

David looked at his mama and nodded slowly. 'Yes. People believe so.'

Then he sat on the floor with his arms around Adele

and told her everything he had heard. He wept at the relief of confiding his terrible knowledge.

Adele sat silently, listening to him.

Then she said, 'I admire your strength and your courage, for shouldering this alone. I want you to know that it was my decision to stay in Poland with your papa. He blames himself for what has happened to his family, but my love for your father . . . well, maybe one day you will understand why I could never leave him. He has only ever seen the beauty and joy of this world, always blocking out the bad things. But now there is no joy for him to see and the shock of this terrible reality has meant he has had to withdraw into himself to survive. He lives in the past, to stop the guilt. Do you understand?'

Suddenly, for the first time, David did.

'Now, I want to give you something, just in case we become separated. Here.' Adele took the gold locket from around her neck and handed it to her son. 'Open it.'

David did so. Inside was a photograph of Adele, taken when she was much younger.

'Take the picture out and turn it over.'

David saw the tiny writing. 'What is this?'

'It is the address of your grandparents in London. If by any chance we are . . . separated, you must try and get to them. God willing, they are still alive. Explain who you are. The locket will prove it. Memorize the address now and put it round your neck. And swear to me you will never take it off again.'

David put the locket round his neck and tucked it under his shirt.

'I swear. Mama.'

Adele stood up and fumbled in the back of one of the kitchen cupboards. She withdrew a slim, blue book. 'Here. I want you to keep this as well. It's my British passport. You can use it as proof of who you are, just in case.' Adele held out her arms. 'Come and hold me. If anything happens to me or your father, look after Rosa for us. She has a great gift and it will be up to you to help her develop it.'

Adele held her son for a long time and David knew then that the two of them shared an unspoken knowledge of the future.

Throughout the summer, the German patrols combed the streets of the ghetto, rounding up victims. The Delanski family stayed in their apartment twenty-four hours a day, with only David venturing out to find food supplies. The tension and misery in the ghetto was unbearable as the Germans took people at random and sent them off in their death trains.

Adele begged David not to leave the apartment, arguing that it was better for them to go hungry than for David to be caught and sent away, but they both knew the family had to eat.

After one fruitless expedition that had only yielded half a loaf of mouldy bread and two old carrots, David turned into Lezno Street in time to see four German patrols marching a group of people off down the road. Once they were out of sight, David flew along the street to the apartment.

Sobs consumed him as he entered the devastated, empty apartment. He sank to the floor, grinding his knuckles into his eyes.

'Mama, Papa, Rosa. Noooh!'

Eventually, he picked himself up and went into his parents' bedroom. Drawers had been opened, the contents flung all over the floor. His mama's jewellery box lay empty on the bed.

He felt inside his shirt for the locket, its presence comforting him slightly. Then, with a racing heart, he dived under the bed, hoping and praying they had not found it . . . no, the Stradivarius, with the passport hidden in the lining of the case, was untouched.

He brought the violin out and put it under his chin, still weeping. He lifted the bow, but as the first sweet sound filled the room, the familiar melody that brought back such powerful memories of his beloved family were too much for him to bear.

Then he heard the slight noise. So faint that he thought he had imagined it. He listened again. Yes, yes, it was someone crying, piteously.

It was Rosa.

'Rosa, Rosa, *kochana*, where are you?'

He stumbled round the room, following the noise to the heavy mahogany wardrobe. He opened it, but found it empty. Then he realized that the sound was coming from behind the wardrobe. With every muscle in his body straining, he managed to heave the wardrobe along the wall. Behind it, there was a small door, only two feet high.

He opened it and Rosa, shaking with fear and half hysterical, fell into his arms.

'David, David! Mama hid me in here before the soldiers came and took Mama and Papa away. I was so

frightened. It was so dark in there and I couldn't breathe
and . . .'

'Hush! David's here now. Hush.' He stroked her hair
gently, remembering the promise he had made to his
mama.

He vowed then that he would protect Rosa until the
day he died.

After two weeks of living in the sheer terror of being discovered, and surviving on the scraps of food that David
had found in the other empty apartments in the block,
David knew that he would have to venture out or Rosa
and he would face starvation.

Rosa refused to be left alone and would start screaming
the minute he left her by herself. Only when she at last
fell asleep, the mattresses pulled by David next to the tiny
cupboard just in case, could he leave her alone and ferret
for food.

'Sweetheart, why don't you draw me a picture? I have
to go out and find something to eat. I won't be long,
I –'

'*No!*' Rosa clung to him. 'Don't leave me alone, David,
please!'

It was no good. He would have to take her with him,
otherwise her hysterical screams would draw unwanted
attention.

'All right, you can come with me. As long as you
promise to do everything I say.'

He went to the floorboards, under which there was the
box where the money was kept. David groaned as he saw
how little there was left.

Then he had an idea. It was only a chance, but someone might be interested in it.

David picked up the violin case which contained his precious Stradivarius.

'I'm taking my paper and pencil in my bag, in case I see anything to draw on the way,' Rosa said pedantically.

David didn't argue. 'Right. Come on then. And remember, you must do exactly as I say.'

Rosa followed David into the deserted streets. It was a hot sunny day, which made the stench of the rotting bodies strewn everywhere almost unbearable. David darted across roads, pulling Rosa into the shelter of doorways if they heard footsteps. He only prayed that one of his contacts in the black market had escaped as he had. He felt all eyes were on him as he pulled a tired and sulking Rosa behind him.

When he arrived at the apartment of one of his suppliers, he found it deserted. The cupboards were bare and Rosa was complaining of thirst.

David sighed. It was impossible. Rosa slowed him down and made them so obvious. He would have to leave her.

He noticed a big teddy bear sitting on a chair in the bedroom. Rosa's eyes lit up as he gave it to her.

'This bear is called David too. He's going to stay here and look after you while I find us some supper. Now, no complaints. I'll be back before you know it, otherwise there's no water and nothing to eat for David Bear. You must not move from here and David Bear has promised to tell me if you so much as squeak.'

To his relief, Rosa nodded, completely entranced with her new toy. 'All right. I'll be good. I think I shall draw

David Bear as a present for you,' she announced.

David slipped out of the apartment and ran swiftly down the road.

He was back an hour later, still clutching the violin. It was hopeless. Everyone else was starving too and no one was interested in a musical instrument, no matter how precious it might be.

He opened the door to the sitting room and his heart stopped. Rosa was sitting, hungrily eating an apple, while a German officer studied a piece of paper. She looked up and smiled.

'Hello, David. This man gave me an apple. He liked my picture of David Bear and asked me to draw one of him while we waited for you to come back.'

The officer stood up, the squeak of his boots sending shivers up David's spine. He smiled, almost pleasantly.

'You are David Delanski, and this is your sister, Rosa.'

David nodded. He couldn't speak.

'Good. Your sister is a talented young lady. Her sketch of me is most accurate. I have heard of your father. He was talented too. Come, it is time for us to leave.'

The soldier clicked his heels and pulled Rosa to her feet.

'Can I take David Bear with me, sir?'

For a moment, David saw a fleeting glimpse of sympathy cross the Nazi's face as he stared down at Rosa's innocent face.

'Why not?' he shrugged. A few more hours of pleasure seemed little to ask.

They were bundled into the back of the Nazi's car and

driven to Stawki Street where the sight of the freight trucks sent shivers of terror through David.

The platform was crammed with frightened faces and the trucks were being filled to bursting point with humanity.

David got out of the car, and Rosa followed. She reached up to the German and planted a kiss on his cheek.

'Thank you for the apple,' she said.

The German watched as David and Rosa were bundled into an already packed truck.

He saw the little girl's face register fear as the sliding door of the truck closed.

He wandered back to his car, then stopped and said something to one of the guards, pointing to the truck housing David and his sister.

It was Rosa's kiss that saved her life.

David stared unseeingly out of his hotel window. He arose from his chair, his face betraying the dreadful suffering he had just relived, and poured himself a large brandy. He swallowed it in one.

As he picked up the receiver and dialled, he knew his life could never be the same again.

'For you, Rosa,' he muttered, as his call was answered.

20

'LAST CALL FOR Alitalia flight AZ459 to Milan. Please board at gate 17.' The robotic voice repeated the message as Leah and Jenny dashed through passport control, through the departure lounge and ran towards the gate.

'Shit! I knew we should have left more time. I just can't believe the traffic was so dreadful,' gasped a red-faced Jenny.

'Oh, Madelaine will never speak to us again if we miss this flight,' cried Leah.

'It's okay, we're nearly there, we'll make it,' said a relieved Jenny as they handed their boarding passes to the gate attendant.

Ten minutes later, the plane was taxiing down the runway and Leah's beautifully polished nails were dug into the sides of her seat.

'Here we go,' said Jenny gaily. 'I love this feeling, don't you?'

Leah closed her eyes as the engines roared and the plane soared into the sky.

'There, we're up. You can open your eyes now,'

laughed Jenny. 'Gosh, am I glad to be sitting down after all that running.'

'Would either of you like a drink, ladies?' asked the air hostess.

'Yes, I'll have a vodka and Coke. What do you want, Leah?'

'Just a Coke, please.' Leah was still trying to recover her stomach.

'Honestly, Leah, you'll have to be more adventurous than that when we hit Milan. Absolutely everyone drinks and they'll think you're an awful square if you don't.'

'I don't like the taste, Jenny.'

'Nor did I at first, but you get used to it after a while.'

'Anyway,' shrugged Leah, 'I'm under age.'

'So are most of the girls when they start, but that doesn't stop them. Cheers. Here's to your first assignment.' Jenny took a healthy slug. She turned round and surveyed the cabin. 'Oh look, there's Juanita. She's on Madelaine's books too. And Joe, he works for *Harper's*. The same crowd always end up on the same plane. You'll get to know everyone soon enough. I must just go and have a word with Juanita. Won't be a minute.'

Jenny slipped out of her seat and Leah closed her eyes, trying to will this terrifying new flying experience to be over as quickly as possible.

She found it difficult to believe that she'd been in London for over a month. The time had flown by, every day filled with photo sessions to begin her portfolio, make-up lessons, elocution and deportment. Leah hadn't had time to know whether she loved it or hated it and Madelaine had waited until now to send her on her first assignment. There was a whole new language she had learnt.

'It's not worth sending you on go-sees here until you've got some work in Europe behind you and some tears in your portfolio,' Madelaine had said. Jenny had translated 'go-sees' as showing your portfolio round photographers and fashion magazines, and 'tears' as pages from magazines in which you'd appeared that went in your portfolio.

Jenny had been marvellous, taking a sisterly interest in her and teaching her all sorts of things that she didn't know.

'What on earth are you doing, Leah?' Jenny had stood there one night horror-struck by the sight of Leah tucking into fish and chips. 'Give me those.' Jenny had grabbed the remainder of the chips and chucked them in the bin.

'What's wrong, Jenny? I'm starving.'

'Never, never, never eat chips.' Jenny waggled her finger at Leah. 'They make you fat, spotty and your skin becomes oily. Here, have an apple instead.'

Leah found it impossible to adjust to the different kind of diet. She'd often nip to the chip shop round the corner to eat a crafty bag when Jenny had gone out for the evening. She didn't know how Jenny survived. She seemed to live on fruit and muesli. When Leah tried it, she just became ravenously hungry.

'I give up,' said Jenny, when she came home one day to find Leah tucking into a huge chocolate eclair. 'What I hate about you more than anything else is that you can eat as much of whatever sort of food and never get spots or put on weight.' And she had stomped off to have a bath

171

and given up chastising Leah about her diet.

Jenny had tried to persuade Leah to go out with her in the evenings, but Leah was too tired and too shy to enjoy the round of parties and nightclubs that the other models went to. She usually sat at home and watched television, then spoke to her mum on the telephone.

She missed her parents something rotten and felt terribly homesick on occasions. Madelaine had vetoed the idea of Leah going back home just yet, worrying that it might unsettle her.

'The girls and I reckon you're the Queen's new protégée. I was thrown on a plane to Paris the day after she signed me. She's taking a lot more care of you,' Jenny had commented without a hint of jealousy.

Jenny did not need to be jealous. Her career had really started to take off over the past six months and when she returned to London from Milan, she was doing a six-page spread for British *Vogue*.

'Hi there. Can I come and keep you company for a while? You look a little lonesome.'

'Sure,' said Leah. Steve Levine sat down next to her. Leah liked Steve best of all the new people she had met. She had enjoyed his photo sessions immensely.

'Is it always like this?' Leah indicated the group that had gathered behind them, perched on the end of seats and arm-rests, smoking cigarettes and drinking.

'I'm afraid so. The fashion world is a very small place. Everybody knows everybody else. You'll get to know them soon enough. They're a nice bunch, but don't confide a secret to anyone. It'll be all over town the next day.'

'I'll remember that, Steve.'

'Good. Would you like a drink?' Steve was holding a bottle of wine and pouring himself another glass.

Leah sighed. 'All right then.'

'It's not in your contract, Leah. Don't have one if you don't want one.'

'I know. But I don't like drink, I don't smoke. Jenny says they'll all think I'm square.'

'Don't you listen to Jenny. You just carry on in your own way, Leah, and let them all accept you for what you are.'

'That's easy to say, but I want them all to like me.'

'Of course you do. It's terrible being the new girl, but they all have to go through it. They're bound to be a little wary of you at first. The word's out that Madelaine thinks you're destined for big things,' Steve whispered.

'I just hope I don't trip up on the catwalk and can remember everything Madelaine's told me.'

'You're a natural, sweetheart, you'll be fine. Just a couple of words of warning though. This crowd are mostly okay, but some of the girls are bitches. They'll stop at nothing to make you look bad. Also, be on your guard against anything you get offered at parties. And I mean *anything*. Milan is notorious for its eventful social life after the shows, but there's a side to it that isn't so pleasant. Stick with Jenny. She's fairly straight.' Steve smiled at the worry lines creasing Leah's beautiful face. 'I'd better go back.'

'Is Miles with you?' Leah knew that Miles had assisted Steve, although she'd never come across him at a shoot.

Steve frowned. 'No. That relationship didn't really work out. I've got a new assistant called Tony whom you'll love. See you later, cherub.' Steve chucked Leah's cheek and walked back to his seat.

'Poor little girl, she doesn't know what she's in for. It's like locking the Virgin Mary in a bedroom with Casanova for a week,' he muttered and took another slug of wine.

The taxi drove Leah and Jenny the six miles from Linate airport into Milan, the richest city in Italy.

Leah, having never been out of England, stared with excitement as the taxi negotiated the maze of narrow streets and squares; cars bumper to bumper, drivers tooting their horns and shouting out of windows. The atmosphere of the city was cosmopolitan and electric, with the mixture of skyscrapers, and the gothic pinnacles of the Duomo, dominating the skyline.

'Rush hour in Milan! This is all you'll see of the city, so enjoy it while you can!' laughed Jenny.

The taxi dropped Jenny and Leah off outside a large, white building in the Piazza della Repubblica.

'This is it, sweetheart. The Principe Di Savoia, the best hotel in Milan.'

They checked in and were shown to their rooms, planning to meet in the bar at half past seven.

Leah was overwhelmed by the luxury of her room and took ten minutes to explore, pressing every single knob, and jumping out of her skin when the television or radio came blaring out unexpectedly.

She lovingly hung up the clothes that she had brought with her. Madelaine had taken her out shopping when she first arrived in London and spent hundreds of pounds on a new wardrobe for her. She had suits by Bill

Gibb, cocktail dresses by Zandra Rhodes and a shimmering evening dress by Jean Muir.

'It's important to have a British model wearing British designers wherever possible. If Jean saw you in that dress, she'd have you on the catwalk tomorrow,' Madelaine had smiled.

Leah showered, put on the soft terry-towelling robe provided by the hotel, then sat down to do a light make-up the way Barbara Daley had taught her.

'When you're out in public, whether in a professional capacity or a social one, you must always look your best. The myth of a model is ruined instantly if the public see her looking like a hag in the supermarket on Monday morning. Wear what you want at home, but outside your front door, you're a professional model.'

Leah had nodded at Madelaine and said she understood completely. She brushed her long hair vigorously, turned her head upside down as Vidal had shown her, then threw it back. The light perm Vidal had put into her hair had given it more body, and three inches had been cut off so that it hung in a thick, glowing sheen round her shoulders.

Jenny had said that tonight was casual, just an informal drink in the hotel bar to which some of the designers turned up. She looked in her wardrobe and took out a black crêpe jumpsuit, chosen by Madelaine from Biba. She matched it with a thick, black belt and a pair of high-heeled pumps.

She studied her image in the mirror and felt reasonably confident about her appearance. However, being naturally shy and reserved, she was sure that she could never master the art of casual small-talk.

175

But she didn't want to let Madelaine down. So she took a deep breath and prepared to do her best.

Carlo Porselli watched the girl emerge from the lift. He'd always shrugged his shoulders when other designers had claimed that they had found their 'muse', believing that clothes should be made to make any woman feel good in them. But as the vision approached him, he swiftly changed his mind.

'Who is that? *Molto, molto bellissima.*'

'Madelaine's new model.' Jenny was sitting next to him in the bar, draining her fifth vodka and Coke. 'She lives with me. Her name's Leah. She's in your set, along with me, Juanita and Jerry. Hey, Leah, come and sit by me and meet Carlo Porselli. We're modelling his ready-to-wear on Friday. He's the hottest young designer in town.' Jenny pulled up a chair between herself and Carlo. The bar was crowded with models, photographers and fashion editors, chatting away loudly.

Carlo stood up, took Leah's hand and kissed it.

'*Buona sera, signorina.* It is a pleasure to meet you.'

'And a pleasure to meet you,' said Leah in a stilted voice. They sat down. Carlo clicked his fingers and a waiter came running. 'We shall all have champagne to celebrate Leah's first fashion show.'

'I'd prefer a Coke, if that's all right with you,' said Leah quietly.

'Ahh, the young girl, she looks after her so beautiful figure and face. *Per favore*, a Coke and a bottle of Berlucchi.' The waiter scurried away and Carlo turned his attention to Leah. 'So, it is your first time in Milan, *si*?'

'Yes.'

'It is the most beautiful city in the world, especially in late autumn, when the noisy tourists have gone home and the leaves are falling from the trees. You must allow me to show it to you.'

'I don't think Leah's going to have any time for sight-seeing, Carlo. As from tomorrow, we work night and day.'

'Time can be made,' said Carlo dismissively.

The drinks arrived and the waiter poured the champagne into three glasses. Leah picked up her Coke and sipped it.

'Here. You will insult my patriotism if you will not take one tiny sip of our best champagne.' Carlo held out a glass to Leah and she took it reluctantly.

'Okay. Just one sip.' She put it to her lips and took a sip. The bubbles raced down her throat and she spluttered helplessly.

Carlo threw back his head and laughed. 'Ah, well, it is not the reaction I had hoped for, but I can see we have to protect your innocence against the predators who would take advantage.' He looked at Jenny, who nodded knowingly.

'Carlo's talking about the playboys. They have a field day during this week. There is a line of Ferraris parked outside the hotel. You see those men talking to Juanita? And the three with the models at the bar?'

Leah nodded.

'Well, they are very rich international playboys. They'll take their pick tonight and then plague you with flowers and trinkets until you give in and go out to dinner with them. After that, they'll try anything to . . . well, you know.'

177

'Yes,' said Leah, blushing.

Carlo sighed. 'I'm afraid it is so. I apologize for the bad behaviour of my countrymen. But it is the Italian blood. We cannot resist a beautiful woman.' He stared hard at Leah once more. 'So, are you looking forward to this week?'

'I'm a little nervous.'

'But of course. That is only natural. I am sure that you will shine like a bright star in the sky. And now, I must take my leave and go back to work. There is much to be done before Friday. *Buona notte*, Jenny. You make sure that this little one is taken under your arm.' He kissed her on each cheek.

'Wing, Carlo, not arm,' giggled Jenny.

'Good-night to you, *piccolina*. I see you on Wednesday.' Carlo kissed Leah's hand and walked out of the bar towards the hotel entrance.

'Are you sure you don't want any champagne?' Jenny took the half-full bottle and refilled her glass.

Leah shook her head and watched Juanita being escorted from the bar by one of the young playboys.

'Tart,' muttered Jenny, noticing too. 'She's unbelievable, that one. She's meant to be engaged to that pop star and yet she goes for anything in tight pants with an overflowing wallet.'

'Carlo seemed nice,' Leah prompted.

'Oh, he is these days. But apparently he used to be just as bad as the rest of the young men in this town. Then he got into design four years ago and seems to have reformed. His father's stinking rich. Someone was telling me last year that he's in with the big "M".' Jenny leaned in close.

'Big "M"?' Leah whispered back.

'The Mafia,' Jenny hissed. 'Mind you, most of them here are. A lot of the modelling agencies are run by them. Last year, one agency which wouldn't go for a take-over deal was bombed!'

Leah's eyes were opening wider and wider. What she was learning today were things that Madelaine hadn't told her about.

'*Scusi, signore.* Can we buy you both a drink?'

Two good-looking Italians were standing behind them.

'No thanks, we're fine,' said Jenny firmly.

'Then could we at least sit down and have the pleasure of your company?'

'Actually,' said Jenny, 'we were just leaving, weren't we, Leah?' Jenny stood up and Leah followed suit. '*Ciao*, gentlemen.' Jenny smiled politely and set off towards the lifts with Leah in tow.

'I think an early night is in order for both of us. Call room service if you're hungry,' said Jenny as the lift opened onto their floor. ''Night, Leah. You've just completed lesson one and passed with flying colours. You're going to be fine.' Jenny kissed her and disappeared into her room.

21

'GOOD LUCK, DARLING, you'll do just great.' Jenny squeezed Leah's hand as the pulsing beat of their entrance music started. Leah was glad that the designer had placed her at the back, and she was modelling only two cocktail dresses.

'Go!' said the choreographer and Leah walked out into the blaze of lights behind the other girls. A round of cheers and applause came up from the audience. She followed the weaving pattern that the choreographer had taught her and managed to smile as it was her turn to walk to the front onto the circular platform to show the dress she was wearing. Flash-bulbs popped in her face as she turned and walked back up the catwalk and off the stage towards her designated dresser and hair stylist.

There was no rush for her, but she watched with interest as some of the older, more experienced models swore blatantly as they deftly changed into their next outfit, then rushed up the stairs to walk serenely down the catwalk.

The whole show was over in less than forty minutes and there was a lot of kissing and congratulations back-stage with the designer. There were drinks in the salon afterwards. The models had been asked to stay in their dresses. Leah was wearing a red satin halter top, and a heavy black satin harem skirt.

'Congratulations. I told you it was a cinch, didn't I?' Jenny said. She had been one of the two main models tonight and Leah thought she looked stunning in the pinstripe velvet dinner suit, with a silk, wing collar blouse and satin bow tie at her neck. 'Stay as close as you can. This is when things start to go wild.'

Leah nodded and followed Jenny into the salon. Jenny was immediately surrounded by a posse of photographers. She saw the fashion editor of *Vogue*, kissing and congratulating Jenny.

Leah took a glass of orange juice from a passing waitress and sipped it slowly, feeling uncomfortable. Everyone seemed to know each other and she knew no one.

'*Cara*, you were perfect!' Carlo swung her round and kissed her on each cheek. 'Of course, tonight's designer makes clothes that do not flatter a woman as I do, but still, I had eyes only for you.'

'Thank you.'

'I will be using you to show off your true potential on Friday. I hope you are not modelling too many dresses tomorrow night at *his* show?' Carlo indicated the world-famous designer standing behind him.

'I'm not sure yet.'

Carlo took her hands. 'I want you for me. All for me. You are the woman to take my designs into immortality.' He was staring at her again with those powerful brown eyes, and Leah was at a loss for words.

'Carlo *caro*!' A stunning woman with jet-black hair and flashing green eyes kissed Carlo directly on the lips. A conversation in fast Italian followed, Carlo pointing in Leah's direction a couple of times.

'Excuse me for being so rude, but I have not seen Maria for many months. She has been away in America earning lots ofdollars for a cosmetic company.'

'I pleezed to meet you, darleeng.' The look on the woman's face betrayed her words.

'Maria has flown over especially to do my collection. You will be working together on Friday.'

'I see you then, no?' Maria turned and kissed Carlo once more. As she walked away, she turned and looked at Leah, muttered something in Italian and disappeared into the crowd.

'Sorry about that. I got caught up by the photographers.' Jenny joined them. 'Was that Maria I saw walking away from you?'

Carlo nodded. '*Si*, Jenny.'

Jenny raised her eyebrows. 'Umm, now, we're off to the Astoria Club. Gianni's hired it for the night. Sally and I are going with him in his car.'

'Ahh, then I will drive Leah there. Do not worry, Jenny, I have her under my arm.'

'Wing, Carlo,' Jenny drawled. 'Okay, I'll see you there. Behave yourself, Leah,' she winked.

'Right. We go.'

'I must change first,' said Leah.

'Okay. I wait here.'

Leah went into the dressing rooms, took off the dress and slipped into her Jean Muir evening gown.

'Ahh, that is much more you. I like Muir's line. It is similar to mine,' Carlo commented as if the great British designer had copied *him*. He grabbed Leah's hand and pulled her through the crowd of people and out into the cool air of the via della Spiga.

'First, I want to take you somewhere. It is not far. We can walk.' Carlo set off down the street, his hand firmly holding Leah's. He saw Leah's worried look and smiled.

'It is okay, *cara*. Jenny trusts me, no? See, we are in the Quadlitalero. In these few streets is every great Italian designer.' Carlo turned right and they walked down a quieter street. Instead of the grand neo-classical, white *palazzi* and big luxury shops of the via della Spiga, the via Sant' Andrea was a tranquil, eighteenth-century world. Leah stopped to peer in the windows of an antique shop.

'Come, come. We have little time.'

'Sorry.'

'See, that is Giorgio's salon. You are there on Thursday, are you not?'

Leah nodded.

'We are here.' Carlo stopped two hundred yards further along the road. He pulled Leah up the steps. On the gold plate by the bell, it said 'Carlo'.

Carlo was unlocking the door. 'My assistant, Julio, will still be here and I want him to meet you. Wait here.'

Carlo indicated an ornate chair and took the grand steps in the centre of the salon two at a time. Leah looked round the room. It was incredibly plush, with huge chandeliers suspended from the hand-painted ceiling, and long, moiré silk curtains hanging from the tall windows.

Carlo reappeared on the steps with a short middle-aged man behind him.

'Leah, please, stand.' She did so. Carlo paused on the bottom step and looked up at the older man.

'Am I not right?' he said.

'*Si*, you are quite right.' The other man nodded slowly.

Carlo walked towards Leah. 'Leah, this is Julio Ponti. He has worked for many of the major houses in Milan, and I kidnapped him to come and work for me, just as I have kidnapped you tonight.' He paused, then turned to Julio. 'I want her to wear the wedding dress on Friday.'

Julio stared at Carlo as if he was mad. 'But we have fitted it exactly to Maria.'

'That is why I have brought Leah here tonight. I want her to put on the dress and you must re-fit it to her. I am sure there will not be that much difference.'

'Well,' Julio came down the steps reluctantly and surveyed Leah. 'Same height and hips, I think, but Maria . . .' Julio gestured with his hands, 'she has more here.' He indicated Leah's chest.

'Attch, that can be fixed in a *momento*. Leah, will you go into the dressing room on the right upstairs, where you will find the wedding dress. Please put it on. We will come up shortly.'

Leah nodded and started to walk up the stairs. Julio was talking in fast Italian, and Leah could make out only the name 'Maria'. She found the room, and opened the door.

The shimmering white dress was hanging in a corner, and Leah removed her own dress and slipped the gown over her head. Julio had been right. It fitted perfectly everywhere but on the bust, where it was only slightly too big. There was a knock on the door.

'I'm ready,' she called out.

Carlo and Julio entered and stood staring at her. Carlo nodded. 'I was correct. Leah must wear this dress on Friday. She brings to it the natural innocence and joy of a bride on her wedding day. Please proceed with the fitting.'

It took Julio only ten minutes to make the slight alterations. When he had finished, they left Leah alone to change, and she joined them in the salon.

'Now we go the nightclub.' He smiled at Leah, and she thought he looked like a little boy who had just succeeded in getting his own way.

'You will explain to . . .'

Carlo waved a dismissing arm in the direction of Julio as he took Leah's arm and led her towards the front door.

'I will handle it. There is no problem. *Arrivederci*, Julio.'

When Carlo and Leah arrived at the Astoria nightclub in his red Lamborghini, the paparazzi gathered round them. Carlo smiled, put an arm round Leah's shoulder and flash-bulbs went off again. He answered their questions in Italian, waved and ushered Leah inside. He pushed Leah into a seat.

'Wait there. I go for some champagne and, er, Coke.' He grinned and set off towards the crowded bar.

Leah, still dazed and feeling exhausted from the night's events, saw Jenny walking towards her, glass in hand.

'Wherever have you been? I let you out of my sight for a

moment and you disappear. I was worried sick,' said Jenny crossly.

'She has been with me, Jenny. And she is perfectly safe, is she not?' Carlo reappeared behind Jenny and shot her a winning smile.

'I suppose so, but next time let me know where you're going. I promised Madelaine I'd look after you. I want to go back to the hotel in a minute. And Leah looks exhausted.'

'Come, sit down for *un momento*, and let me show you what I have for you,' said Carlo. 'I know you like it and it is the best in Milan.' He produced a small phial from his top pocket and handed it to Jenny.

'I shouldn't. I've had enough already.'

'Then you keep it as a present, *cara*.'

'Thanks, Carlo.' Jenny slipped the phial into her evening bag, watching Leah's inquisitive eyes on her. 'I'll come back in half an hour,' she said, and left the table.

'Dance?' Carlo stood up and offered his hands.

'Okay.' Leah was wishing that she was tucked up in her comfortable bed back at the hotel. Her feet were killing her, but she knew that this was the kind of thing she had to do with grace, if she was to be successful.

As they stepped onto the dance floor, the music changed to a slower beat and Carlo pulled her into his arms. Leah smelt the strong aroma of his aftershave, then sniffed at the fug hanging in the air. It was a strange smell, something she didn't know.

'Oh *cara, mia cara*,' Carlo was murmuring. He tipped her face up to his and studied it. 'I will make you so famous. Our names will be joined for ever together. You

186

are my muse. Say you'll stay with me tonight.' He leaned
forward and kissed her on the lips, his tongue trying to
force her to open her mouth.

'No, Carlo, stop it!' She wrenched herself out of his
arms and ran towards the exit. She jumped into a waiting
taxi and gave the driver the name of her hotel. When she
was safely in the confines of her hotel room, she flung
herself on the bed and burst into tears.

It was all too much. A little more than a month ago
she'd been living with her parents in a small northern
town. She was seventeen years old and knew nothing
about the world. Now here she was, suddenly launched
into a glittering arena of unknown territory, trying to
ward off strange men who treated her like an adult when
she was only a child.

She felt completely out of her depth. She wanted to go
home to the safe world she knew.

There was a knock on her door and Leah held her
breath. The knock came again.

'Leah, it's only Jenny. Let me in.'

Leah stood up and unlocked the door. Jenny's eyes
were full of sympathy when she saw Leah's blotched face.

'Sweetheart, I'm so sorry. It was my fault. I shouldn't
have left you with him. Come on, you go to the bathroom
and wash your face, while I make you a cup of tea.'

Leah nodded silently. After she had washed her face
she felt a bit better. She opened the bathroom door and
Jenny handed her the steaming tea.

'What did he do to you?'

'He tried to kiss me,' Leah said quietly.

Jenny gave a sigh of relief. 'Thank God that was all. I've

known them try much more at a nightclub before. I'll murder him tomorrow. He promised me he wouldn't touch you.'

'It's not your fault, Jenny. I just don't think I'm cut out for this kind of thing, that's all.' Leah could feel a lump rising in her throat again.

'Don't you think we all feel that way when we start? Trust me, Leah, I was greener than you are when I first began and I really learnt the hard way.' Jenny's blue eyes saddened as she remembered.

'What happened to you?'

Jenny sighed. 'Well, remember I told you that Madelaine sent me off to Paris the day after she signed me?'

'Yes.'

'Well, I had no one to look after me or tell me that the model groupies will do or say anything to get you into the sack. So when this dishy French bloke started wining and dining me and sending flowers to my room, I believed everything he said. I mean, like you, before then a night out at the pictures with a spotty youth was my idea of romance. I was overwhelmed by the attention and the presents he showered on me. One night he fed me coke in a cigarette, took me back to his house and raped me. Three months later I was back in England and I discovered I was pregnant. I had an abortion, which Madelaine kindly paid for. It seems it's almost routine for her. By the way, coke is a drug, not something brown and fizzy that you drink,' added Jenny.

'Was that coke in the tube Carlo gave you?'

Jenny's mouth tightened. 'Yes. But don't you dare tell

Madelaine, Leah Thompson. If she found out I'd be off her books in a flash. I don't use it very often, but everyone does it in the fashion world. You can't avoid it.'

'But Jenny, if you say that man raped you after giving you that stuff, why . . .?'

'You get a taste for it, that's all. Anyway, I want you to tell me where on earth you and Carlo disappeared to earlier.'

'To his salon to try on a wedding dress. He wants me to wear it on Friday.'

'Jesus!' Jenny looked horrified.

'What's the matter?'

'Maria always wears the wedding dress for Carlo. She's been his number one model since he opened. And they had an affair for three years until she went off to America six months ago. Does she know about this?'

Leah shrugged. 'Carlo mentioned that he was going to tell her.'

'Oh dear, Leah. He's really dumped you in it. Carlo's a sweetie but he's so spoilt. He just brushes things aside to get what he wants and leaves other people to pick up the pieces. Seriously, you're going to have to be on your guard against Maria. She's a bitch at the best of times and this . . .' Jenny could not finish the sentence.

'Jenny, I just want to go home,' Leah said in a small voice.

Jenny came and sat beside her and put an arm round her shoulder. 'I'm sorry, darling. I didn't mean to frighten you. Of course you don't want to go home. To be chosen from nowhere by the great Carlo to model his wedding dress is the biggest honour you could have and means that you're going to be incredibly successful. It's a huge coup and all you must remember is that this game is a rat-race. You have to grow up very fast. If I can do it you can, darling,' Jenny squeezed her.

'But what if Carlo tries to touch me again?'

'Do you not like him? He's obviously fallen for you in a big way.'

Leah shrugged.

'Oh, Leah, just take a look at yourself in the mirror.' Jenny steered her towards it. 'Now, what do you see?'

'Myself,' shrugged Leah.

'Got it in one. And "yourself" may only be seventeen, but that reflection shows a sophisticated, beautiful woman who could pass for twenty-five, without the red eyes, that is,' Jenny joked. 'So remember that men see you that way and their bodies react accordingly, just as Carlo's did. Mind you, if you tell him you're only seventeen it'll make him even more rampant! Anyway, I must go to bed and so must you. You just stick to your principles as you're doing now and you'll be fine.' Jenny walked to the door, then stopped and turned.

'Madelaine's right. You are something special. Sleep tight.'

22

LEAH AWOKE TO her alarm call at ten to seven on Friday morning. She pulled her exhausted body out of bed and went to take a shower. As she came out, she heard a knock on the door.

'Who is it?'

'Reception with a delivery, Mees Leah.'

Leah opened the door, to find the bell boy struggling with a huge bouquet of white roses.

'*Grazie.*' Leah tipped the young boy and he handed her the bouquet. She shut the door and carried the bouquet to the bed. She opened the card and read it.

'Tonight will be a night you will never forget, my bride. Carlo.'

Leah had not seen Carlo since Monday evening. He hadn't turned up at any of the other designers' shows and Leah had been glad. She had spent the week on a steep learning curve and was starting to realize that modelling may be glamorous, but it was also a lot of hard work. Every day this week, she had been up at seven and in a designer's salon in the Quadlitalero by nine. The models had then been put through their paces for the

191

evening's show. They had rehearsals with the choreographer, trial runs with the hair and make-up stylist, and then a full dress rehearsal. They would usually have no more than half an hour's break to grab something to eat before getting ready for the evening's show.

Then there had been the socializing afterwards. Most of the models stayed out until the early hours, going to parties and nightclubs. Leah didn't know how they managed to look so fresh the following morning. There would be lot of groans and aspirin passed around first thing, but the previous night's hectic activities seemed to be something the girls took in their stride.

For Leah's part, she had got into the habit of having one drink at the party in the designer's salon afterwards, then quietly slipping back to the hotel, content to have a long bath and enjoy the splendour of her hotel room. She didn't feel part of the crowd, and although some of the girls called her a 'party pooper', mostly they left her alone.

Jenny would usually regale her with the latest gossip over coffee in her room the following morning. Leah had asked her why she thought that the playboys seemed to be leaving her alone and Jenny had smiled wisely.

'Carlo's put the word out that you're off limits. None of them would dare touch you. They're too scared of him. I told you that he and his father hold a lot of sway in this town.'

Leah had been grateful to Carlo for that. Wild parties and drink and drugs just didn't appeal to her, and she knew her mother would kill her if she got involved with anything like that.

Of course tonight would be different.

She had spent the week in the background watching the attention that the star models received and she thought she was ready to cope with it. She wondered what the other girls would think when Carlo announced that she would be wearing the wedding dress. The back-biting she had witnessed in the dressing room when a model got the best clothes had prepared her well.

'Keep your head, Leah, and be sensible,' she muttered as she went down the corridor and knocked on Jenny's door.

Jenny opened the door, looking ravaged and still dressed in her nightie.

'Come in. I'm running late. God, do I have a hangover! Put on the kettle for some coffee and I'll jump in the shower.'

Leah did so, then picked up Jenny's beautiful Chanel evening gown lying in a heap on the floor and hung it up.

'Mmn, that's better,' said Jenny as she sat naked on her bed and sipped her coffee. 'I met someone last night.' She eyed Leah over the rim of her coffee cup.

'But, Jenny, I thought you said that you wouldn't touch any of those playboys with a barge-pole.'

'He's not a playboy. He's a prince.'

'Oh.'

'Oh? Oh? Your best friend meets one of the world's most eligible men and spends the evening with him, and all you can say is "oh"?'

'I'm sorry, Jenny. Tell me about him.'

'His name's Ranu, and he's Crown Prince of somewhere in the Middle East. His father is reputedly the richest man in the world. The gossip columns are always full of Ranu holding huge parties on his yacht or private island in the Caribbean. You must have heard of him, Leah. They're always trying to marry him off to one beautiful woman or another.'

Leah shook her head. 'No, I haven't heard of him, Jenny. But what was he like?'

Jenny's face became dreamy. 'Oh, Leah, it was the most romantic night of my life. When Giorgio, the designer, said that Ranu was desperate to be introduced to me, I wasn't particularly thrilled. I mean, the man hasn't exactly got the best reputation. But then Ranu came over and . . . he's so sweet, Leah. Such a gentleman. We went to this party at a grand *palazzo* on the shores of Lake Como and he stayed by my side all evening. Then he brought me home and he didn't even try to kiss me. Can you believe it! Before I got out of the car he turned to me, and said in that terribly sexy voice of his, 'I want to see you again, Jennee'. Oh, I love the way he pronounces my name, with the accent on the "y".'

Leah thought she might be sick. She had believed that sweet, sensible Jenny was above being fooled by the things these men said.

'I know what you're thinking, but I just can't explain . . .' Jenny was pulling her faithful rehearsal tracksuit on. 'He's different, I know he is. He's coming to the party tonight and I want you to meet him and tell me what you think. Now, enough of me. Are you ready for your big day?'

Leah nodded. 'I think so.'

'Remember, ignore anything that the girls say. They'll

only be jealous because you've got a big break and you're new on the circuit. But just watch out for Maria. I'll be interested to see how Carlo handles her. Come on, we're going to be late.'

When Leah and Jenny arrived at Carlo's salon, most of the other girls were already there, drinking coffee and smoking.

'Okay, ladies, gather round. I want to go through the schedule, and Carlo wants a word with you all.' Julio was looking tired and red-eyed. Leah and Jenny took two seats at the back and Carlo climbed up onto the front of the catwalk that had been erected for the show.

'*Buon giorno*, ladies. I hope that none of you were later to your beds than midnight . . .'

A titter came up from the seats. Carlo raised his eyebrows and continued. 'Because we have a very busy day today. Julio, my assistant, will run through the schedule. This year the format will be slightly different, with one notable change. The beautiful Maria, who has so kindly joined us from America, has been asked by her company there to keep a low profile so as not to interfere with the marketing and promotion in the States. She will, of course, still be in the show, but under the circumstances we have decided that someone else must wear the wedding dress.'

'Good try, Carlo,' muttered Jenny, knowing that not a person in the room believed him.

'Having looked at all your measurements, the girl who has the closest to Maria is Leah. Therefore, she will wear the wedding dress tonight.'

An audible gasp went round the room. People began

195

nudging each other and turned round to stare at Leah, who blushed and studied her hands. Then they turned to gauge Maria's reaction. She was in the front row, shrugging her elegant shoulders and smiling graciously.

'*Va bene*, I leave you in the capable hands of Julio who will go through the running order, and Luigi, who is staging the show. *Grazie*, ladies.'

As Carlo left the stage, the girls began whispering. A few of the older models gathered round Maria, and others turned to Leah and whispered insincere congratulations. Maria stood up and walked over to Leah. Every single head in the room turned to watch.

Maria smiled and kissed Leah on both cheeks. 'Thank you, darleeng, for 'elping me out. These Americans are oh so possessive wiz me. Good luck. Eef you need any 'elp, you ask, okay?'

Leah breathed a sigh of relief as Maria went back to her seat and Julio climbed up on the catwalk to start going through the running order.

For the rest of the morning, Leah concentrated on learning her moves. She was partnered mostly by Maria, and the older woman could not do enough to help her. Maria fussed over her like a mother hen, brought her coffee when she was too busy to get it herself and generally treated her like a long-lost daughter.

At lunchtime, Leah and Jenny nipped out for a breath of fresh air.

'I can't get over the way Maria's looking after you. All the other girls have commented on it. I don't know whether she's being a little too sweet, though, so don't be totally taken in, will you?'

Leah shook her head, but had to admit that Maria's concern seemed genuine enough.

The thing that was frightening Leah most about the evening was the quick changes. She had watched the other girls go through them night after night, and marvelled at how they managed it. She was wearing ten outfits tonight, and she and the other girls knew that they were the plum dresses.

The dress rehearsal was a disaster. Leah missed two of her cues and Julio shouted at her.

An hour before the show, Leah was sitting having her hair styled, in a state of frenzy. Maria came up behind her.

'Ah, leetle one, you are nervous, no?'

Leah nodded as she stood up from the chair and the next girl sat down.

''Ere, I give you these to calm you down.' Maria handed her three small white pills.

Leah shook her head. 'No, thank you, Maria.'

'They are only aspirin. See, I take them too.' Maria popped another two white tablets into her mouth and reached for a glass of water to swallow them.

'Well, I . . .' Leah relented. She had a stinking headache from the bright lights and having her hair pulled this way and that. And Maria had taken them too, so they couldn't do any harm.

'Thank you, Maria,' she said as she took the glass of water and swallowed the pills.

Half an hour later, Leah was in her first outfit, a scoop-necked ribbed sweater and skirt, in the soft wool that had been so popular with all the designers that week. She was trying to keep calm. Ten minutes before the show began, Carlo appeared in the dressing room, resplendent in a white dinner suit.

'Good luck, girls. I am sure you will do me proud.' He made his way over to Leah and took her hands. 'You look incredible, *cara*.' Carlo kissed her on each cheek. 'In an hour's time, you will be the new star of the fashion world, trust me.'

'Okay girls, everyone in order, please.'

Leah took her place and as she did so, her stomach gave a giant somersault and her palms became clammy.

'It's nerves, Leah, really.' Jenny looked at Leah's pale face and the tiny line of sweat on her forehead. She touched her hand reassuringly. 'You'll be fine once you get out there, I promise.'

Leah nodded. Jenny was probably right, but her stomach really did feel very strange.

She moved to the entrance to the catwalk and listened to the hum of the audience. Tonight, she was the model leading the rest of the girls down for the first number. There was a hush as the compere spoke, then the familiar beat of the music. The pain in her stomach was getting worse.

'Okay, go!'

Leah walked out into the lights and received a round of applause. When the first number was over, she ran off towards her dresser, feeling a little calmer, but decidedly ill.

The next twenty minutes were a nightmare. She did six changes, feeling sure she was going to pass out at any moment. She desperately needed to go to the ladies, but she knew there wasn't a minute to spare. Somehow, she gritted her teeth and managed to smile as she went through her paces on the catwalk.

'It's nearly over, you're nearly there, just the wedding dress now,' she told herself as she rushed off the catwalk towards her dresser. She was halfway through taking off the evening dress, when she knew that she could hold on no longer.

'I'm sorry, I have to go to the ladies.'

Her dresser stood there holding the wedding dress in astonishment as Leah fled in the direction of the toilets.

'*Mamma mia*! What to do! What to do!'

Julio came rushing down the stairs from the side of the catwalk.

'Quick! There is no time to lose! Maria, come here and put the dress on.'

Maria gave a triumphant smile and sauntered over.

'But my compannee will not like it,' she drawled as the dress was put over her head. 'Attchh, it is tight around the top.'

'Take off your bra, quickly!' screamed Julio.

'But you can see my nipples . . .'

'No matter, just do it!'

A minute later, Maria walked onto the stage and an audible gasp went up from the audience, followed by thunderous clapping. The rest of the girls joined her, and a bemused Carlo jumped up onto the catwalk to receive an ovation.

Jenny found the pathetic figure in the ladies, crumpled in a heap in one of the cubicles.

199

'Oh darling, whatever is it? We must get you to a hospital immediately.'

Leah shook her head. 'I don't need the hospital.'

'You look ghastly, Leah. Where's the pain? In your stomach?'

Leah nodded. 'I just can't stop going. Excuse me.' Leah pushed Jenny out of the cubicle. She emerged five minutes later, doubled over, and sank to the floor again.

'It looks like you've got food poisoning. But you hardly ate anything today. I watched you. Can you think what it might be?'

'Did Maria wear the wedding dress?' asked Leah.

Jenny nodded. 'Yes. She caused a sensation. She couldn't wear a bra under the dress, so you could see her nipples peeping through the chiffon. I don't think it was quite what Carlo had intended, but it'll certainly make all the papers tomorrow morning.'

'She gave me some tablets. She said they were aspirin and took two herself. The pain started about an hour after I'd taken them,' Leah said quietly.

Jenny was dumbstruck. 'Oh my God, she's given you laxatives. I've heard about models doing that before, but I can't believe Maria would stoop so low. On the other hand, she did look pretty pleased with herself and I thought she was being too nice to you today. Do you really think it was the tablets?'

'Yes. I've eaten nothing today, and I haven't been sick or anything. I just keep wanting to go.'

'That bitch!' cried Jenny as Leah once again had to close the door and avail herself. 'Right. I'm getting your jeans and you can change while I call a taxi to take you back to the hotel. Then I'm going to see Carlo. Maria's not going to get away with this.'

'Leave it, Jenny. There's no proof,' said Leah from inside the cubicle, but Jenny had gone.

Leah lay in bed in her hotel room, feeling exhausted, ill and very sorry for herself. She'd only just made it back to the hotel in time to rush to the ladies, and had spent the past hour in her bathroom. She could hardly believe that anyone could do such a wicked, dreadful thing.

But tonight had confirmed her theory. She just wasn't cut out for this. Anyway, she'd been made a laughing stock in front of the entire fashion world and no one would ever want to employ her again. She decided that tomorrow she would buy a ticket home with her wages and go straight back to Yorkshire where she belonged.

A solitary tear rolled down her face, but she stopped herself crying by thinking that this time tomorrow she'd be tucked up tight in her own little bed, with her mother looking after her.

She drifted off to sleep, grateful that the worst seemed to be over.

A persistent knocking woke Leah from her dreams.

'Who is it?' she called weakly.

'It is I, Carlo. Please, let me in.'

'I'm not well. Go away.'

'*Cara*, I implore you. Open the door. I will not leave until you do.'

Reluctantly, Leah staggered to her feet, unlocked the

door, and only just made it back to the bed before her legs gave way beneath her.

Carlo came and sat on the end of the bed, his eyes full of anxiety. He took her hand. 'How are you feeling?'

'I'm okay. I think I feel a bit better than I did. I'm so sorry, Carlo.'

'Don't you dare apologize. Jenny told me what Maria did and a word in the right ear confirmed that it was indeed true. And it is all my fault. I was so stupid to think she would accept it with good grace. I am so, so sorry, *piccolina*.'

'It was a terrible thing to do, Carlo, but it made me realize that the modelling world isn't for me. I'm going home tomorrow,' Leah said sadly.

Carlo's brown eyes flashed. 'You will do no such thing! Here, take a look. He put a copy of a newspaper called *Il Giorno* into her hands. There, on the front page, was a big picture of Leah in her penultimate evening dress, with big words in block capitals running along the top of the photo.

'What does it say, Carlo?' She handed back the paper and he translated.

'It says, *Who Is She?* Would you like me to read the rest?'

'Okay,' Leah shrugged.

Carlo cleared his throat. 'This is the face of the mystery model who caused a sensation at Carlo's ready-to-wear collection last night. She did not appear at the party afterwards and no one has seen her out on the town on any night this week, apart from on the arm of Carlo himself at a nightclub on Monday evening. Even then, she stayed only five minutes before leaving alone. There is talk that she may be Russian aristocracy, descended from the Tsar himself . . .'

Leah could not resist a giggle at this point.

'No one in the fashion world can understand why the flamboyant Carlo allowed Maria Malgasa, his ex-love, to wear the wedding dress. Some suspect it was a peace offering to pacify the fiery Maria, as there is certainly no doubt of his new star. The mystery model's natural beauty and radiance on the catwalk only served to make the rather vulgar display of Maria's flesh – one could see parts of this lady that usually appear only in *Penthouse* – seem more contrived.'

Carlo grinned at Leah over the top of the paper. 'Do you wish me to continue?'

'No.'

'So, do you not see that Maria's plan has backfired on her? The fact that you did not wear the wedding dress and were absent from the party has only made the media's interest in you greater. It is good that you do not like the social life, as the others do. It has made you a mystery, and there is nothing the press likes more.'

'I'm still going home, Carlo.' Leah turned her head away as Carlo sighed.

'It is your decision. I understand that you are upset by the thing this woman has done. But do you not see the best way to pay her back? Become the star she is so scared of you being. Outshine her and the other girls. They do not like you because they know you are different. If you creep home, they will clap their hands thinking they have won. Do you understand?'

Leah nodded slowly, saying nothing.

'May I ask how old you are, Leah?'

'Seventeen. Just.'

'Ahh, my *piccolina*, now I understand. You are too young to have to deal with all this. But you will learn. You are a clever girl, I think, and sensible. And from now on, you will have Carlo by your side, protecting you, like the child that you are.' He brushed her hair away from her face. 'I am sorry for trying to kiss you. I thought that you were more than twenty, you look so *bellissima* and sophisticated. If you will stay, I promise I will never touch you again. You have my word on that.'

Leah turned round and looked at him.

'You must stay, Leah. It is your destiny.'

'Yes,' she said.

The next morning, Leah emerged from the lift to find a posse of photographers waiting for her.

Her new life had begun.

Part Two

London, August 1981

1

'THIS IS IT, chaps. Raise your glasses to our last week as carefree young men. Soon we'll all be getting up at dawn, instead of skulking out of bed at eleven just in time for the first lecture. We'll be working through until seven or eight at night, rather than sleeping off last night's hangover in the afternoon, and becoming pillars of this green and pleasant land, instead of drunken, irresponsible undergraduates!'

Each one of the five young men sitting round the table in the Savoy Grill groaned and raised his glass.

'And to think I complained about the amount of work my sadistic tutor piled on me,' moaned Rory.

'At least you get long lunches in the city, which is more than you can say for us poor old medical students,' grinned Toby.

'I think Brett's got the best deal of the lot of us. Working for Daddy on a starting salary that most of us will end our careers being pleased to earn. You've got a cushy number if ever I heard of one,' teased Sebastian, without a hint of malice.

Brett shrugged. 'I know, guys, it's tough at the top,' he

joked, wishing he could swap places with any one of them. His four good friends at Cambridge had all chosen their future careers, and gladly he'd have given up his fat salary to do the same.

Brett had enjoyed his three years at Cambridge and was enormously sorry to see the back of them. He had not worked particularly hard, finding the Law course unfulfilling and too pedantic for his artistic nature. But he had found his niche in the more bohemian quarters of the university, from which he had drawn the friends with him tonight.

He had become involved with the Footlights dramatic club, painting scenery and even performing in a couple of the reviews. And to his surprise, he had still managed to come out of Cambridge with a decent second.

He looked round the table sadly. First at Toby, who had made such a wonderful Dame in the Footlights' Christmas pantomime. At Rory, who had spent most of his three years getting paralytic in the student union bar and sleeping his way round Girton. At Sebastian, who had a superb singing voice and had sung with the choir at King's. And at Mark, his closest friend, who had written a wonderful play and had it performed by the Footlights' company.

And yet, not one of them had decided to take their particular talents any further. They had made their career choices and it was as if they accepted that the fun they'd had for the past few years came to an end the minute they received their degrees. Being an undergraduate at Cambridge and behaving in an outrageous manner was what was expected of them, before they settled down to leading nice, civilized lives in respectable professions.

Brett seemed to be the only one who could not accept this. Next week, he would begin working for his father. And he was dreading it. In the cloistered world of Cambridge, Brett had been just another undergraduate set on having a good time, but even now, two months after leaving, he could feel the difference between himself and his friends.

'I'll get this, chaps.' Brett opened his wallet, removed a gold American Express card and placed it inside the leather-bound folder. The men round the table were hardly paupers, coming from some of the most aristocratic backgrounds in Britain, but they knew and he knew that his father's wealth was on an entirely different level.

'Cheers, Brett,' Sebastian said casually. 'Now, I don't know how the rest of you feel, but I'm not ready to go home yet. And it just so happens that I have some invitations to the hottest party in town tonight. Bella, my sister, got them for me. The party's at Tramp, for the birthday of some model or other. Sounds like there'll be some hot crumpet on offer.' He raised his eyebrows.

Brett's heart skipped a beat.

No, she probably wouldn't be there, although he knew that she was hugely successful and reputedly one of the highest earning models in the world.

He had done his best to forget her, but with her face suddenly staring at him from the cover of every magazine during the past few years, it had made this somewhat difficult.

He had tried relationships with a number of nubile undergraduates, each one considered a catch for any young man at Cambridge, but that feeling he still harboured for his first love was never replaced, not even by the most sexually athletic activities. No matter whose soft, feminine flesh was beneath him, no matter how skilfully they touched him, he still closed his eyes and imagined Leah.

Rationally, Brett wondered if the experience of his first emotional involvement with a girl had been blown out of all proportion, but his heart still stopped every time he saw Leah's face and he found himself fantasizing about meeting her again one day.

'Come on, let's get a taxi. We don't want all the best girls being snapped up before we arrive.' Sebastian stood up from the table as the waiter discreetly returned Brett's gold card.

The doorman hailed them a black cab and they set off in the direction of Tramp.

'*Cara*, tonight you look more radiant than I have ever seen you.' Carlo stood on the doorstep of Leah's mews house in Holland Park and kissed her on both cheeks.

'Thank you, Carlo,' Leah smiled. 'Now come in and meet my mother.'

She ushered him into the hallway, the white dress he had designed especially for her tonight rustling slightly as she moved. Carlo followed her into the big, comfortable living room, where a woman in her forties was sitting, looking uncomfortable in a formal Yves Saint Laurent black dress.

'Mum, this is Carlo.'

'It's a pleasure to meet you, Mr Porselli. Our Leah's told me so much about you.'

'Don't you think Mum looks lovely? We went shopping yesterday and chose her dress specially for tonight.' Leah glanced at her mother proudly.

'Mrs Thompson, you look *bellissima*. I can see where Leah gets her beauty from.'

'Mrs Thompson fidgeted embarrassedly. 'Well, it's very nice of you to say so, Mr Porselli, but I'm much happier in a skirt and a pinny.'

'Pinny?'

'Mum means apron,' translated Leah. 'Well, I think that you look a picture. Here, champagne for both of you.' She handed them each a glass.

'Ah, *si*. It is a night of celebration, but also of sadness. For I am losing my muse to the Americans next week.'

'Honestly, Carlo. Don't be so dramatic! I'm moving to New York because of the cosmetics contract, but also because I seem to spend most of my time over there anyway. You know that's where the action is at the moment.'

Carlo nodded. '*Si*, Leah. But New York is far away from Milan and that is why I am sad.'

'I'll be over for your show in just over six weeks' time. Now, before we go, I've got something for you, Mum. I know it's my birthday, and you're meant to buy me presents, but before I give it to you, I want you to promise me you'll accept it.' Leah's face was serious as she went to the antique mahogany writing desk and took out an envelope. 'Here.' Leah handed the envelope to her mother.

'Go on, open it.'

Mrs Thompson fingered the vellum envelope and looked at her daughter's excited face. She opened it slowly and drew out a sheaf of papers. She stared at the incomprehensible legal language, and saw her own and her husband's names printed three or four times on the first page.

'What is it, Leah? It looks like a will,' frowned Mrs Thompson.

Carlo and Leah both laughed. 'It's not a will, Mum. It's the deeds to a new bungalow in Oxenhope. I've bought it for you and Dad.'

Mrs Thompson sat there silently, fingering the sheaf of papers. Leah walked over to her and knelt in front of her. Mrs Thompson looked up and saw the tears shining in her daughter's eyes.

'Leah, love, I can't accept this.' Tears were coming to her eyes too. 'You've given me and your dad so much already.'

'You must accept it, Mum. It's one of the reasons I model, to be able to give you and Dad presents. This bungalow has been specially adapted for Dad's wheelchair. It's brand new, with a nice sitting room, a big bedroom for you both and a spare room for when I visit.'

'Oh Leah.' Mrs Thompson promptly burst into tears and the two of them hugged each other tight.

'Thank you. I just hope you haven't used up all your money. You must keep it for yourself. You've earned it, after all.'

'Don't worry. I've got enough to keep me going for years and Carlo's shown me how to invest it,' Leah smiled. 'I'm going to come to Yorkshire this weekend and show you and Dad round,' she said proudly.

Carlo stood watching the tender scene in front of him, then coughed. 'Come, ladies, it is time to go.'

He had waited a long time for this night and he couldn't wait for it to begin.

Miranda followed the rest of the guests inside the famous nightclub. There was a crowd of photographers waiting outside. Miranda felt like a star and she loved it. Inside, the place was jam-packed and Miranda glanced at the banner hanging from the ceiling.

'Happy twenty-first, Leah, from all your friends,' it read.

Jealousy surged once more inside her. Miranda could hardly believe what had happened to Leah while she had been stuck at home with dirty nappies and boredom.

She had to admit that it had been nice of Leah to send 'Rose and family' an invite.

Chloe, Rose and herself had travelled down from Yorkshire yesterday. Rose had business to attend to with Roddy and had said that she would babysit Chloe at Roddy's flat so that Miranda could go to the party.

Well, tonight was her chance. And she meant to take it.

As Leah's limousine pulled up in front of the club, the paparazzi gathered round. The proprietor of Tramp greeted her on the steps. Carlo brought up the rear with Mrs Thompson, who was a bright shade of red.

'Carlo, give Leah a birthday kiss, will you?' one of the photographers shouted.

Carlo nodded, swept a surprised Leah off her feet into his arms and kissed her hard on the lips.

'Wonderful!' The paparazzis' flash-bulbs popped, just as the taxi bringing Brett and his friends pulled up behind the limousine.

Brett stood transfixed on the pavement as he watched the tall Italian place Leah's feet on the ground once more, put an arm round her exquisite, bare shoulders and disappear inside.

Brett felt sick. He had a sudden urge to run away from the club as fast as he could.

'Listen, chaps, I think I've changed my mind. I'm going to head off home. You four go, and I'll . . .'

A barrage of 'shut up, Brett' followed, and he was propelled up towards the doorway by his friends.

By the time they entered the club, Leah was surrounded by admirers. Brett slunk into a corner where he could remain unnoticed, and prepared to sulk the evening away.

Carlo watched Leah from a distance, wanting her to have this special evening all to herself. There would be time later to claim her for his.

He felt a surge of pride as he remembered the pathetic figure lying in the big bed in the hotel in Milan, determined to give up her career and return to Yorkshire and anonymity. The poised, elegant female, now at the peak of her career, with the crowd of admirers hanging on her every word, had been his creation.

Like a piece of raw silk, he had fashioned and shaped her into something extraordinary that betrayed its menial origins. He had done it with time, skill and patience, taking care to pay attention to detail, as all great designers should. For four years he had watched those long, sensuous limbs covered in his own garments, and he had never once touched her. But he knew that the time he had taken to perfect Leah to the peak she had now reached would be worth it later tonight.

She was twenty-one years old today and Carlo had waited long enough.

'Hello, beautiful. Want to dance?' A tall, older man was bearing down on Miranda. He had a strange, foreign accent.

'Why not?' she said. He guided her onto the floor and began moving to the beat in the strange way that older gentlemen, who have adapted their skills learnt as a teenager in the ballroom to the aggressive music of the disco, had of moving.

Miranda surveyed him. He was a big man, probably in his mid-sixties. He didn't have much hair, and his face was covered in small blue veins.

Well, he certainly wasn't love's young dream, but she noted the gold Rolex peeping from his sleeve and the well-cut, expensive suit. Miranda went into action, using all the tricks that she'd stored up for four long years. She moved sensuously, like an animal, brushing against him just close enough for him to glimpse her firm, round breasts, only partially concealed behind the tight gold lamé dress.

The music stopped and the man steered her over to the bar.

'Champagne?' he asked.

Miranda nodded

'So, what's a nice girl like you doing in a place like this?' he quipped as Miranda smiled seductively at him.

'I'm an old friend of the birthday girl.'

'Ahh, Leah. She is very beautiful, as you are too.' The man's finger traced the contours of her chest. 'Let's go and find a quiet corner and you can tell me all about yourself.' The man picked up the champagne and walked away from the bar, Miranda following him a step behind.

Leah came face to face with Brett, who had decided to take his leave minutes before, as she emerged from the powder room.

Her heart started to bang mercilessly against her chest as she willed herself to remember how Brett had betrayed her, but all she could see was the boy that had for so long been part of her dreams.

Brett had grown taller. His youthful features had defined themselves and he resembled Rose more than ever.

As they stood there, memories of those perfect days on the moors came flooding back, negating the terrible way they had parted.

'Hello,' they said together, and then laughed.

'Happy Birthday, Leah.' The sound of his voice saying her name after all this time sent a tingle up Brett's spine.

'Thank you.'

Brett racked his brains for something to say to keep her here.

'You're looking quite beautiful, Leah.' It was corny, but he meant every word of it.

Hearing those words from the lips of Brett meant more

216

to her than any of the hundreds of others who had told her the self-same thing.

'And you look well. Are you leaving?'

Shit. Extricate yourself from this one, old chap. Maybe she wanted him to leave.

'Er, well . . .'

'There's just about to be a toast for my birthday. At least stay and have some champagne,' Leah said too quickly.

Brett breathed a sigh of relief. 'Thank you, I'd be delighted.'

He followed her back inside, just as the music stopped and the club owner moved to the centre of the dance floor and clapped his hands.

'Ladies and gentlemen, if there are any present,' he laughed. 'I . . .'

'Leah, where have you been? Come with me.' Carlo was frowning as he led Leah off towards the club owner, leaving Brett alone.

Leah turned back and mouthed 'see you later' as Carlo pulled her onto the dance floor.

'I now hand you over to Mr Carlo Porselli,' a cheer went up from the crowd, 'who as I'm sure you all know gave our Birthday Girl her first big break and who is also our host for the evening.' Another resounding cheer went up as the assembled company took a sip of their champagne, courtesy of Carlo.

Brett could see the possessive way Carlo looked at her. He talked of Leah almost as if she was something he owned. Leah stood next to him, head down in embarrassment as Carlo extolled her virtues.

'*Prego*, will you raise your glasses in a toast. To Leah!'

'To Leah,' chorused the assembled company.

'To Leah,' whispered Brett, almost to himself.

'And now, I would like the pleasure of being the first man to dance with you since you have come of age.' Carlo held out his hand to Leah and led her to the centre of the floor. The crowd cleared around them as the slow, rhythmic beat of 'Woman', Lennon's huge number one hit, echoed out of the powerful speakers.

Brett cringed as Carlo put his arms round Leah and held her close. From the way they were dancing, it was obvious that the two of them were involved romantically. He couldn't bear to watch and turned away.

'Oh Leah, how long I have waited for this night,' Carlo murmured into her hair.

Something about the tone of Carlo's voice was different from the way he usually spoke to her. Like that first night he had tried to kiss her in Milan. She immediately felt uncomfortable.

The eyes of the circle of people around her were fixed on the two of them with interest. Leah could almost feel the sense of anticipation.

'Kiss me, Leah,' Carlo whispered, as he tipped her face up to his.

'Carlo, I . . .'

But his lips were upon hers before she could protest. She pulled away and buried her head in his shoulder as the crowd burst into a spontaneous round of applause.

'Please, Carlo, I'm embarrassed.'

'Still so shy, little one. No matter. There will be plenty of time to be alone later. I want you to come back to my hotel. I have your birthday present in my room.'

The song finished and the disc jockey began playing a Shakin' Stevens record. The floor became crowded with dancers.

'Excuse me, Carlo, but there is someone I have to see.' Leah extricated herself from his arms and looked around for Brett. She espied him heading for the exit. She moved quickly across to him.

'Trying to sneak out again?'

'Well yes, actually.'

For all her sophistication, Leah had no knowledge of how one casually gave the impression that she didn't want a man to leave.

'What about one quick dance before I go?' Brett said bravely.

'Aye aye. Don't tell me you've managed to scoop the belle of the ball tonight,' Brett's friend Toby joined them, with a dishevelled debutante leaning on one of his shoulders.

'Leah and I are . . . old friends. Come on, Leah.' Toby's appearance gave Brett the excuse he needed to take the delicate white hand and lead Leah onto the dance floor.

Brett wished with all his heart that fate had conspired with the disc jockey to put a slow song on his turntable so that he could hold her in his arms. Instead, the up-tempo disco beat throbbed unmercifully, with Brett unable to make Leah hear anything he wanted to say. She was smiling shyly at him, as she danced gracefully opposite him.

The song came to an end, and the haunting voice of Diana Ross, singing a duet with Lionel Richie, spilled out across the dance floor. Brett plucked up his courage and pulled Leah into his arms.

'It really is great to see you again after all this time,' Brett ventured.

'It's good to see you too,' came the reply.

Feeling the perfect body touching parts of his own was sending an electric thrill up and down him. He pulled her closer.

'I'd love to see you again, Leah. I'd like a chance to explain, about, well, what happened. The problem is, I'm flying to New York on Sunday. My father has his main office over there and I start work for him on Monday. Perhaps I could write to you?'

Leah giggled. 'Don't bother buying any air-mail envelopes, Brett. I'm off to New York, too. I fly out on Tuesday to start a campaign for Chaval Cosmetics.'

'Wow! What a coincidence! Where are you staying?'

'For the first couple of weeks I'll be at the Plaza Hotel, then I'm going to find an apartment with Jenny, my best friend. She's over there at the moment working for another cosmetics company.'

'Are you going alone or is Carlo coming with you?' Brett asked cautiously.

'Alone. Carlo has the shows for his collections coming up. He has to fly back to Milan tomorrow.'

'Could I call you at your hotel?'

'Yes.'

'Leah.' A hand roughly swung her round. 'I think it is time we went.' Carlo was swaying slightly and Leah could see he was drunk.

'Carlo, I'm afraid I'll have to go straight home. My

mother is staying with me, remember? You can give me the present another time.'

Carlo looked as though he was due to explode. '*Permesso*,' he said to Brett, and dragged Leah off towards the front door.

'Stop it, Carlo! You're hurting me!' Leah tried to free her wrist from his grasp.

'I am sorry, but you must come with me. I have it all arranged.' He was pulling her down the steps and Leah was only glad that the paparazzi had gone home.

'Carlo! I said stop it!' She tried to wrench her arm free. This was not the Carlo she knew and she felt a tingle of fear.

At the bottom of the steps, Carlo hailed a cab and Leah struggled helplessly to remove her arm from his vice-like grip.

'I'm not coming with you, Carlo. You're drunk.' He was trying to pull her inside the cab, and she was doing her best to resist.

'Leah! Will you get into the cab!'

'No!' she shouted in desperation.

Two strong arms clasped her shoulders from behind her and pulled her backwards and out of Carlo's grasp.

'I don't think the lady wants to come with you, Mr Porselli.'

Leah recognized the familiar voice and turned round to see Miles, three cameras slung around his neck, standing behind her. He pushed Carlo roughly inside the back of the cab and shut the door.

'Take this man to his hotel.'

The driver saluted Miles and the taxi moved off along the road.

'Thanks, Miles,' Leah said gratefully. 'I don't know what's come over him tonight. I've never seen him like that before.'

Miles said nothing. He just stared at her in that strange way of his.

'Leah. Are you okay?' Brett was running towards her, concern written over his face.

'Yes, I'm fine, thanks to Miles.'

'Hello, Miles. What are you doing here?' asked Brett curiously.

'Plying my trade,' said Miles coldly.

'Miles is a freelance photographer. His work is always appearing in the national newspapers.' Leah did not say that Miles spent his time hanging round the entrances of nightclubs and restaurants to catch the rich and famous committing *faux pas* on celluloid and selling them to the gutter press in Fleet Street.

'I'll find you a taxi,' said Miles.

'I have to go and fetch my mum. She's still inside.'

'I'll go and find her. You get in the car.' Miles flagged down a passing cab, opened the door for her, then disappeared inside the club.

'Good-bye Leah. I'll see you in New York,' Brett smiled.

'Yes, see you there.'

There was a pause as they stood alone on the pavement. Brett was just about to pull her into his arms and kiss her, when Miles emerged with Mrs Thompson.

Damn! Brett kissed her chastely on the cheek, waved good-bye to Mrs Thompson and Miles, and set off down the street.

The taxi containing Leah and her mother passed him

a hundred yards up the road. Leah looked at him, and gave a tiny smile and a wave.

Brett walked home to his father's small Knightsbridge flat, needing the cool night air to clear his thoughts.

Both of them in New York. It had to be fate. Carlo? Maybe he was too late already, but he had to try. He'd been offered a second chance. This time, he'd get it right.

Miles also walked home to his tiny rented flat in Chelsea, thinking of Leah. He found a half-full bottle of Scotch and poured himself a large glass to calm him.

He'd had to use the utmost restraint not to wring that bastard Carlo's neck. Did he not realize that Leah was special? A woman to be fêted and adored, not treated as if she were some cheap whore. Miles found the key to his special room, unlocked the door and went in. The photographs on the wall calmed him, as they always did. He knew with absolute certainty that, one day, she would be his. He fingered the bulge in his trousers, which was synonymous with being in this room.

Tonight, though, his own hand would not do.

He closed the door behind him and went across the sitting room towards the telephone. He dialled the number and a female voice answered. After a minute's conversation he replaced the receiver, glad that she lived only a few streets away.

He opened his cameras and stored the films in the fridge he kept for that purpose.

The doorbell rang and Miles went to let the girl in. Without any preamble he took her into the bedroom and removed his clothes as she removed hers. He switched off the main lights, only leaving the dim glow of the night-light next to his bed.

She was ready for him, her long limbs stretched in anticipation across the bed. This one had lasted longer than most of the whores he bedded. She enjoyed his rough games, was amenable to his unusual demands and had the added advantage of long, mahogany hair. In the half-light, with her hair partly covering her face, he could almost believe that it was Leah.

He massaged his hard penis as he knelt astride her, dominating, ruling the woman beneath him. She fingered her breasts as she knew he liked her to do. He never kissed her or any of the whores. This wasn't love. This was pure, hard sexual need.

'Say the words,' he ordered the girl.

'Fuck me,' she said, her hand moving to her own mound, her eyes closed in pleasure as she touched herself.

'Louder, bitch!' Miles' hand continued to work up and down his own shaft while his other hand roughly squeezed her breasts.

'Fuck me!'

He slapped her hard across her face and she screamed. 'Louder!'

Before she had time to answer, he had plunged into her, his own attention to his penis leaving him on the point of shooting. He almost tore her in two, enjoying her screams of pain as she writhed beneath him. He pulled out just before he was about to release himself into her.

'Turn over,' he ordered.

The girl looked frightened. She usually enjoyed their games, but tonight there was something evil, almost manic in his eyes.

'Miles, I . . .' She started to crawl across the bed, but he dragged her back and slapped her hard back and forth across her face until her lip began to bleed.

'Turn over, whore!'

Too frightened to do otherwise, the girl turned and watched the blood from her lip drop onto the pillow beneath her. Pain ripped through her as the huge shaft entered her from behind. His nails clawed at her breasts, breaking the delicate skin.

'Stop it, Miles! Please, stop it!'

Miles couldn't hear her. With a roar, he shot into her. As she lay whimpering, her face buried in the pillow, Miles stood up, went to the bathroom and shut the door behind him. When he came out, the girl was fully dressed and standing by the door, her face swollen, her eyes full of tears.

'You bastard! Men like you should be locked up. Don't ever call me again. If you do, I'll report you. You're going to kill someone one day.' She closed the door behind her and Miles heard her hurried footsteps walking down the two flights of stairs. He smiled, then shrugged.

He'd have to find a new one tomorrow. Well, that was no problem. Sex was easy to find. But it was always the same. None of them lasted for more than a few sessions, and he'd had high hopes for this girl.

Miles climbed into his crumpled sheets and distastefully pulled off the blood-stained pillowcase. He felt good now, and calm, and closed his eyes.

2

MIRANDA OPENED HER eyes and felt the thunderous banging of her head. Feeling disoriented, she sat up and looked around. The room did not look familiar and she struggled to remember where she was. She felt her body under the covers and discovered that she was naked. Her dress was thrown over a chair across the room, along with her underwear and shoes. On the bedside table was a note and a pile of money. She read it.

'Dear Miranda,
Thank you for last night. It was most enjoyable. I am entertaining this weekend on my boat in Greece and would very much like you to come along. Please be back here at six tonight so that we can go together to the airport. My assistant will call you. He is sorting out your passport. The boutique down-stairs will send up a selection of clothes for you to chose from. Buy yourself a present this afternoon.'

The note was signed with an illegible squiggle. Miranda racked her brains to try to remember the man's name and the events of last night. She recalled drinking a lot of champagne and the man leading her unsteadily out of the nightclub. After that, it was all a blur.

'Shit!'

Rose would be in a frenzy. She lifted the telephone by the bed, struggling to remember Roddy's number.

'Reception,' a crisp voice answered. Miranda realized that she was in a hotel.

'Er, yes. I wonder if you would call directory enquiries and get me a number.' Miranda gave the woman Roddy's surname and address.

'Certainly, madam. And can I order breakfast for you?'

The thought of breakfast made Miranda's stomach churn.

'No thanks. But some coffee would be nice.'

'Right away, madam. I'll call you back as soon as I have that number for you. And can I tell the boutique to send up the clothes you ordered?'

'Yes, thank you.'

While Miranda waited for the telephone to ring, she thought about what she was going to say to Rose. A girl couldn't turn down an opportunity of flying off to Greece to spend a weekend on a boat with an obviously very rich man. This was what she'd dreamt of all her life. She was joining the jet-set.

'Sucks to you, Leah!' she giggled as reception rang to give her Roddy's number.

Miranda thought for a while, then dialled the number. Roddy answered.

'Hi, Roddy, it's Miranda.'

'Jesus, Miranda! Thank God! Where are you? Your

mother's been half out of her mind with worry. She was just about to call the police.'

'I'm fine. Tell Rose I am twenty-one and I'm not a child any more.'

'You might have told us where you were going, sweetie. Rose has phoned everyone this morning and no one knew where you'd got to. What time are you coming here? Your mother wants to get back to Yorkshire with Chloe.'

'Actually, I'm not coming back with her. A friend of Leah's has invited me to a party for the weekend. Tell Rose I'm fine, that I'll see her on Monday, and ask her to kiss Chloe for me. 'Bye Roddy.' Miranda put down the telephone before he could say anything. A tinge of guilt about her daughter pricked at Miranda. But, she comforted herself, she had given all her attention to Chloe for the past four years, and didn't she deserve some fun too?

The telephone rang again. Reception announced the caller and Miranda had no idea who he was.

'Yes?'

'Hello, Miranda. My name's Ian Devonshire and I work for Mr Santos. He's asked me to sort you out a passport *toute de suite*. Do you have a passport at present?'

'No.'

'Good. That makes things simpler. I need to take your second name and a few details so that I can get hold of a copy of your birth certificate from Somerset House.'

'My surname is Delancey. My date of birth is 23/7/60.'

'Okay. I'll come by the hotel at midday with the forms. You can sign them and I'll take them to the passport office. I've a friend there who'll process your application this afternoon. Can you get two photographs of yourself done by lunchtime? There's a booth at Charing Cross station, just down the road from the Savoy.'

The Savoy. Was that where she was? A *frisson* of excitement ran through Miranda as she confirmed that she'd get the photos done and meet him in the bar downstairs at midday.

As she put down the phone, there was a knock on the door. She jumped out of bed too fast and felt dizzy and nauseous as she stood up.

'Just coming,' she called as she looked around the room in desperation for something to cover her nakedness. She ended up pulling the sheet from the bed and draping it round her, toga style.

The young man wheeled in a trolley containing the coffee, a red rose and a bottle of champagne on ice.

'I didn't order the champagne,' she said hurriedly.

'Compliments of Mr Santos,' the boy said.

There was another knock on the door.

'May I open it for you, madam?'

Miranda nodded.

Another porter in the same smart uniform wheeled in a large pile of boxes and bags.

'A selection of garments from the boutique. Mr Santos has asked you to choose what you want. If there is nothing here that you like, please come down to the boutique where I'm sure the manager can find something to suit you.'

Both men stood there staring at her expectantly and it suddenly dawned on Miranda that they were expecting to be tipped. She remembered the pile of notes by the bed, went over to them and picked them up. She gasped as she realized that the pile of twenty-odd notes were all fifties. She had no choice, so she handed the boys one note.

'Share it between you,' she said grandly, vaguely noting the look of disappointment on their faces. As they left the room, she supposed Mr Santos would have given them one each. Clutching the notes in her hand, she walked over to the heavy mahogany door on the opposite side of the large bedroom. She opened it, expecting to find a bathroom, but instead found herself in a sumptuous sitting room, with large picture windows flanked by gold damask curtains. She wandered over to them, threading her way through the heavy, expensive furniture.

Miranda drew in her breath as she looked out over the Embankment and the silver water of the Thames running far below her. This must be what they called a penthouse suite. She went back into the bedroom and grabbed as many of the boxes as she could. Having transferred all of them to the sitting room, she wheeled in the other trolley and poured herself a coffee.

She knelt on the floor, surrounded by the boxes, picked the largest and took the lid off. On the top, resting on the tissue paper was a small gold-edged card reading: 'The Savoy Hotel, with compliments'.

Miranda stood up and did a little jig around the room. She could hardly believe this was happening. Then she settled down again on the floor and pulled back the layers of soft tissue paper. Inside was the most exquisite evening dress she had ever seen. It was fashioned out of

230

black silk, and carried the name of a world famous designer on the label.

Hurriedly, Miranda divested herself of her sheet, put the dress on and went back into the bedroom to look at herself in the full-length mirror. The dress fitted her perfectly, and she twirled, with one hand holding her hair up in a knot on her head.

'Watch out, Leah, I'm coming to get you,' she giggled as she ran back to the sitting room to open the other boxes.

An hour later, the room was covered with open boxes, tissue paper and thousands of pounds worth of expensive clothes draped over the furniture. Miranda was sitting in black silk undies with a Hermès scarf tied round her neck, admiring the soft leather shoes on her feet.

Almost disappointedly, she noticed that there was only one small box left to open. She grabbed it and took the lid off. Inside were two leather-bound boxes, one smaller than the other. She opened that first, and found a pair of twinkling diamond earrings shaped like teardrops. In the other box was a fabulous necklace to match.

'Wow,' breathed Miranda.

Having recovered well and truly from her hangover, she went over to the trolley and poured herself a glass of champagne.

'Here's to you,' Miranda toasted herself. She took a sip and made room amongst the clothes to sit on the sofa. All this for a quick screw that she couldn't even remember. I must have been good, she giggled as she took another sip.

Miranda showered and chose a pink silk blouse

matched with a beautifully cut Chanel suit. She left the room, made her way downstairs and asked the concierge directions to the tube station.

A brisk walk down the road found her at Charing Cross station and she changed one of the fifty-pound notes at the ticket office.

Miranda checked her watch as she waited for the photos to drop out of the slot. Ten to twelve. Just enough time to get back to the hotel and meet Ian Devonshire in the bar.

Not really considering the possibility that there was anything strange about the morning's happenings – for Miranda had been quite sure for her entire life that some day this would happen to her – she walked back into the Savoy, went into the bar and sat down.

'Miranda?'

'Yes.'

A plain young man wearing a thick pair of glasses and dressed in a smart suit sat down opposite her.

'Ian Devonshire. Good to meet you. Drinks?'

'White wine for me.'

He ordered, then pulled a sheaf of papers out of his briefcase.

'I presume you know that you're adopted?'

'Yes. Have you got my original birth certificate there?'

'Yes. Here, take a look.'

Miranda gazed with interest at the piece of paper. 'So my real name was Rosstoff.' She glanced up at Ian, an idea running through her mind. 'I prefer my original name. Can I have "Rosstoff" on my passport?' Miranda was thinking that Rose would find it difficult to trace her if she decided to stay away for a little longer.

'I don't see why not. I'll ask my friend.'

'Good.'

'Now, I just want you to sign here.' Ian indicated the spot on the passport form. 'And check that the details I've filled in are correct.'

Miranda did so.

'Super. I'll get this off to the passport office straight away and have the documents back to you by four this afternoon.'

'Mr Santos must be a powerful man to be able to arrange all this for me,' Miranda fished.

Ian nodded his head. 'Absolutely. He's a very wealthy man. He doesn't visit London very often. He lives in South America.'

'Do you do this kind of thing for him often? I mean, arrange passports?'

'As I said, he's not here too often. Anyway, I'm afraid I must leave you and get on with the job in hand. It's nice to meet you, Miss Delancey. Have a good trip to Greece. Good-bye.'

Ian left the bar and Miranda sat sipping her drink thoughtfully.

Who was this Mr Santos? She racked her brains to try to remember if she'd ever heard his name mentioned on television or in the papers.

No. For a second, a flicker of doubt passed through her mind. Should she be going off with some strange man all alone? He could be part of the white slave trade, or the Mafia for all she knew.

On the other hand, here she was at the Savoy, dressed in hundreds of pounds of designer clothes. All the hotel staff seemed to know him and Ian had seemed very straight down the line.

Suddenly exhausted, Miranda stood up and walked towards the lift, too engrossed in her own thoughts to notice a man who had been sitting quietly in a corner of the bar stand up too. She called the lift and went up to her suite. The chambermaid had obviously been in, for all the clothes had been replaced in their boxes, and the bed made.

Miranda sank down onto the comfortable bed gratefully. She decided she would take a nap and then spend the rest of the afternoon preparing herself for Santos' return. She closed her eyes, her mind whirling from the events of the past few hours. Feeling more contented than she had ever felt in her life, Miranda drifted off to sleep.

3

'HELLO, DAVID.' The tall, bearded man shook David's hand warmly. 'How are you?'

'Well, thanks. I was beginning to think I wouldn't be hearing from you again. It's been over eight months since I last had contact.'

'There are reasons for that, I assure you.'

David sat down behind his desk and invited the man to take a seat, too.

'Did you proceed with the security checks we suggested?' asked the man.

'Yes. They've been over this office with a fine tooth-comb. I can assure you that it is perfectly safe to talk.'

'That is something that is never perfectly safe. However, I wished to see you at your office as it is always more sensible not to arouse suspicion. Underground car parks at midnight and arranged meetings on deserted beaches at dawn are for the movies. This is reality. I have come to see you today because things are beginning to progress, both on our side, and from your point of view. Am I right?'

David nodded slowly. 'Yes. I have done as you asked.

You can understand how difficult it has been for me. But the project began six months ago and I believe I am winning his trust.'

'I understand how hard it must have been. And I warn you; he is a clever man, David. But we hope that we are cleverer still.'

'You have been watching him for all these years?'

'Yes.'

'Then why has a move not been made before?'

The man shrugged. 'In dealing with cases like this, and I can assure you that there are many others, water-tight evidence must be gathered. Also, as time passes, they grow more confident, less careful and eventually they slip up. If it takes a lifetime, that is of little importance.'

David stared silently at the man. Then he said, 'Why me?'

'David, in a way you are similar to this man. You also have a past that you have chosen, understandably, to forget. You are powerful, well known and beyond reproach in your business dealings. Like with like produces a good bait. You also have a strong personal motivation to help us.'

'Yes, but I . . . I find it so hard to . . .'

'Hush! You have said enough. We ask you to continue your joint business venture and take time to get to know the man. Become his friend, as you are doing at present. To trap him, there are certain circumstances he must be under. You will be informed of these nearer the time.'

David tapped his index finger slowly on his marble-topped desk. 'I have to tell you that . . . on many occasions I've considered telling you no.'

'Mr Cooper, that would not only be foolhardy where your bank balance is concerned, as I'm aware that the project will be extremely lucrative, but it would also arouse unnecessary suspicion and complicate our plans. I do not wish to remind you of who you are, but . . .' the man shrugged his shoulders, and reached out his hand across the desk. 'Good-bye, David.'

He walked across the spacious office, opened the door and closed it behind him.

David sighed and rubbed his forehead. He felt drained and exhausted. He hadn't slept last night, his mind full of the meeting today.

Four years since the past had crept back into his life and he still awoke from the nightmares.

The memories were undimmed by the passage of time.

David ran a hand through his hair. They were expecting too much, surely? He was not only putting himself, but his entire business at risk.

But then, as always, David remembered the promise he'd made when he was fourteen years old . . .

4

POLAND 1942

DAVID FELT THAT even death could be no worse, as he sat, holding a weeping Rosa to him in a tiny corner of the truck, listening to the hum of the train as it rattled across Poland. Others in the truck had come prepared, with food supplies and drink, but all they had was the violin, some paper and pencils and Rosa's precious teddy bear. Only when Rosa screamed in her desperation for a drink and something to eat, did an older woman take pity on her and hand her a small phial of water and a cold sausage.

The heat in the closed truck was unbearable and the stink of excrement mixed with disinfectant and old straw would live on in his memory for ever. He talked little to the others, listening to their conversation as they pondered what faced them at the end of their journey. He already knew. He hoped it would be fast, however they did it, for Rosa's sake, if not his own.

The women were pulling their jewellery from their necks, arms and fingers and hiding it in their underwear.

David followed suit, secreting the precious locket with the passport in the lining of his violin case.

As the journey progressed, a man next to him keeled over from a heart attack and died in David's lap. A blessed escape, he thought quietly, as the man's wife cried piteously for the rest of the night, holding her dead husband to her bosom, the man's legs still straddled across David.

The train screeched to a halt. David peered through the tiny barbed-wire grille and saw a sign on the platform: 'Treblinka'. There were several railway workers outside and David could see some SS officers. The train started to move again, stopped, then lurched backwards, throwing the occupants of the carriage violently against each other.

David could see that their wagon and a few others were being pushed into a siding. The light faded as dense forest surrounded them, then some huts came into view, and behind them, a huge pile of shoes. The train entered a clearing and David saw barbed wire enclosing a camp. A strip of land broadened into a makeshift platform. There were SS men everywhere, carrying whips. Sentries stood in black uniforms by the fence, holding rifles.

As the train halted, the other occupants of the carriage piled behind David, desperately trying to see out of the grille.

Immediately, the doors to their wagon were opened, and the sentries clambered into the truck and started hurling them out.

'David! David!' Rosa's screams filled his head as she was dragged off the truck by a guard and disappeared into the mass of crying, screaming people on the platform.

Still clutching his precious violin, David moved along the platform as they were herded towards an open gate in the middle of the fence. He called Rosa's name over and over, but it was impossible to make himself heard above the dreadful noise of desperation.

'Oh, Mama, oh Mama,' he repeated as he was pushed towards a yard, the cries of 'Schnell! Raus!' resounding from the sentries.

As they entered a yard, women were being ordered to one side, and men to the other. The fence was covered with dry branches. David searched desperately for sight of Rosa amongst the women, but it was impossible. Unaware of the tears that were streaming down his face, he sat down with the other men and started to take off his shoes, as directed by a group of Jews wearing armbands. They were handing out bits of thread to enable the men to tie their shoelaces together.

As one of the men approached him, he looked down at the violin sitting next to David.

'Is that yours?' he asked in Polish.

David nodded.

'Do you play?'

'Of course.'

'I'll tell the guard.' The man continued handing out the bits of thread, then disappeared.

David could see that the women were being herded into a hut on the other side of the yard. It was not large enough to accommodate them and women were standing outside, removing their clothes.

A sentry ordered the men to do the same. As he was about to remove his trousers, he was hauled to his feet.

'Play!'

David turned round and saw an SS officer behind him, pointing to his violin.

Disoriented, David stood silently. A whip cracked across his bare chest.

'Play!'

David opened his case with trembling hands. He put the violin under his chin and picked up his bow. Try as he might, no tune would come into his brain.

The rest of the men stared up at him silently. They were all naked.

'Liar!'

As David watched the whip come towards him for a second time, a tune came into his head. He lifted his bow and began to play, the soft, soulful melody of Brahms' Violin Concerto filling the yard. The pitiful naked men around him wept openly.

'Enough! Wait over there!'

David was dragged by the arm and pushed into a hut. He peered through a hole and watched the yard empty as the naked men were pushed through an opening in the fence. The women had gone too.

Packages and clothes were strewn across the yard.

David sank to his knees, head in hands. For how long he didn't know. Weak from fear, lack of food and sleep, his mind wandered back to the times the family had gathered together in the drawing room and he had played the violin which had just saved his life. Then he noticed the terrible stench filling the air. Even in the ghetto,

David had never smelt the like.

His imagination could not begin to conjure up what was happening to his little sister, his precious Rosa. His only hope was that it was all over for her now and she was at peace.

He heard a noise in the yard. Then fifteen or so Jews appeared. Under the supervision and constant beating of the sentries, he saw the Jews start to clear the bundles of clothing.

David looked around the hut. There were piles of rags strewn over the floor; cups and plates and pyjama tops. He was obviously in some kind of dormitory. Shivering, he realized that he was still naked from the waist up, grabbed a shirt lying on the floor next to him and donned it. He noticed the material was good; the shirt almost brand-new.

The door to the hut opened and a stream of bleeding Jews entered, followed by a sentry.

'Follow me!' the Ukrainian sentry barked at David.

David crossed the yard. The Ukrainian led him towards another hut. Inside were groups of men dressed in all manner of strange attire. They were sitting at long wooden benches, eating hungrily from their bowls. The Ukrainian pointed to an older, familiar face sitting at one of the tables. 'Get your soup, then see Albert Goldstein. He is your conductor.'

Recognition crossed his face as David took a bowl of the delicious smelling soup from a woman standing behind a trestle table, then crossed to sit next to the great conductor.

'Mr Goldstein, I cannot tell you how honoured I am to meet . . .'

Albert Goldstein waved him quiet. 'Eat, then we'll talk.'

David did so, amazed at how palatable the soup was, better than anything he'd eaten during his time in the ghetto. The food nourished him and his dizziness abated.

'So, what do you play, boy?'

'The violin, sir.'

Albert wiped his mouth with his hand. 'I might have guessed. Our last violinist met with . . . an accident. Are you good?'

'For my age, I was considered so in Warsaw, sir. Sir, could you tell me, please, where we are and what will have happened to my sister?'

The older man stared at him, sorrow in his eyes.

'How old are you, boy?'

'Fourteen, sir.'

'Your sister?'

'Eleven, sir.'

'Come, we will go to our quarters.'

David followed Albert back across the yard and into another hut. This one was cleaner than the last. It also had thin mattresses on the floor.

'There. That was Josef's and now it will be yours.' The maestro pointed to an empty mattress.

'Josef?'

'Yes. The last violinist.'

'Please, sir, can you explain this place to me? Where did the other people from my train go?' David knew in his heart, but he had to have it confirmed.

Albert sighed deeply. 'To their death. You are in Treblinka. It is not a labour camp. It is a place where the

Germans exterminate Jews in their thousands. Your neck was saved by that.' He pointed to David's violin.

'My sister?'

Albert shook his head sadly. 'Women are of little use, especially children. Do not hope. It is best to understand now the mentality of our captors.'

A small cry escaped David's lips.

'Every single person still alive in this hell-hole has lost their families. We live with the guilt daily; that we are alive and they are not. But as you will see, your little sister may have had a blessed escape. What you will witness every day . . . it will turn your heart to stone.'

'What do you mean?'

'The orchestra of which you are now a member has to play as the Germans send our families to their deaths along 'The Road to Heaven'. We call it Death Avenue. It helps drown out the screams of those dying inside the gas chamber and keep those who are waiting their turn calm. You will see people in their thousands walking to their deaths, believing they are going to the shower.

'We also have to entertain the prisoners at roll-call in the evenings, and the German guards and their Ukrainian whores after dinner. Maybe now you see that you were not the lucky one?'

He watched quietly as David's face turned ashen.

'I am sorry, my boy, but you must know what this place is. The stench in the air is that of burning corpses. The Germans continue their massacre night and day.'

'My parents, they too were taken from Warsaw.'

'What is your name?'

'David Delanski, sir.'

244

Hope jumped into Albert's eyes. 'Your father is Jacob Delanski?'

'Yes, sir.'

'Ahh, then I have good news for you. Your father is alive. He is the camp painter. He lives in this dormitory and produces portraits for the Nazi pigs.'

David's eyes shone. 'Sir! I can hardly believe it!'

'Well, it is your talent that has saved your skin. Be grateful that God blessed you with it. However, I must warn you now that every second you live, your life is in peril. The Germans take pleasure in shooting for the sake of it. There is always another truckload of Jews to replace you with. And please, be careful of the deputy commandant . . .' Albert shuddered, 'Kurt Frankl. Never, never do anything to attract attention to yourself. He is the most evil, sadistic man I have ever had the horror to witness. Anyway, you will meet him shortly, but be warned. Now, let me explain the rules of the camp.'

David listened as Albert explained that his father, Jacob, was part of a small group of '*Hofjuden*', the privileged Jews, who performed services for the Germans. Among them were carpenters, mechanics, shoemakers and jewellers. There was no shortage of food, clothes or money, due to the large amount of supplies coming in daily to the camp with those who had no further use for such things.

'Physically, we are comfortable, more comfortable than perhaps you were in the ghetto, if you can avoid the beatings. They do not expect the workers to last very long in here, so they do not even bother to shave our heads. Stay out of trouble and try to hang on to your sanity. Now, let me hear you play. We will be called out soon for roll-call and we must play perfectly to avoid flying bullets.'

For the next two hours, the other member of the trio joined them and they practised well-known pre-war tunes that brought tears to David's eyes as memories flooded back.

Roll-call arrived and David followed Albert onto a small wooden platform, positioned in the middle of the assembly yard surrounded by huts. It was hardly big enough to hold the three of them. David looked down at the sea of faces lined up in front of them. Three names were called out by a German officer. The men stepped out of line, faces creased in fear. They were positioned in a line in front of the wooden platform and, one by one, thrown across a small stool and whipped.

David wobbled as faintness hit him. He thought he would fall off, but a vice-like grip on his arm stopped him.

'I said, do not draw attention to yourself,' muttered Albert harshly under his breath.

The SS guard turned towards the ragged figures on the wooden stand and nodded.

They began to play.

Twenty minutes later, they queued up in the mess hall for their food. David searched the room for sight of his father. He spotted him, sitting at the other side of the room.

'Papa!' David's joyous greeting seemed to have no meaning to the gaunt man sitting in front of him. Jacob took no notice of David and continued eating.

'Papa, it is I, David. Your son. *Jak się masz?* How are you?'

Jacob stopped eating and sat stock still. The man sitting next to him moved out of his chair to allow David to sit down.

'He doesn't hear us, but try again,' the man said softly.

David sat and put his hand on the thin wrist of his father.

'Papa, please. It's David.'

The hollow face turned towards his and David stared as the empty eyes filled with recognition and emotion.

'Is it really you, David? Am I dead and in Heaven?'

'No, Papa. You are alive. They let me live because I play the violin. Is Mama . . .?' David's voice trailed off.

Jacob looked past his son. 'She was taken.' He stared silently into the distance. Then his eyes landed back on David's face, as if remembering.

'Rosa?'

David shook his head.

'So young, so much talent. Why do we live?' Jacob searched his son's face for the answer, but found none. He stood up.

'Good-bye, David.' Jacob left the table. David was about to stand, but a hand pulled him down.

'Listen. You must understand that your father has lost the will to live,' the man whispered. 'He has stopped painting for the past two days. He just sits and stares at his easel. The Germans are growing angry. He has little time left.'

'Then I must help him.'

'There is nothing you can do. Rumour is that a new artist was brought in on the last train.'

'I am his son! I will go to him!' David pushed the man

roughly away and walked towards the door of the mess hall. Back in the dormitory, Albert and Johan, the other violinist, were getting ready for their evening session.

'Have you seen my father?' David asked Albert.

'Yes. He was wanted in the room where he paints. It's next door to the furrier's shop, just to the left at the end of this row of huts. You'll see an easel by the window.'

'Thanks.'

'Don't be late. We start in ten minutes!' shouted Albert.

David went outside and noticed that the fast darkening sky was lit by a terrific red glow. A dark, murky smoke was billowing out and the air was thick with the dreadful stench of death. He ran along the hut, saw the easel and entered the small room behind it.

Jacob was sitting on a chair, motionless in the dim room.

'Father!' David ran and knelt in front of him. As he did this, the door opened and an SS officer entered, carrying the easel and a painting behind him.

'Father, please,' he whispered.

'*Schnell!* Attention!!' shouted the officer. He put the painting on an easel and moved it next to another painting, which David recognized as his father's work, then left the room as another figure entered. This officer had an oil lamp swinging from one hand. There was another, smaller figure holding his other hand, hidden behind him.

He turned back to Jacob. 'Father, please, I . . .'

'And what have we here? Father, did you say? Rise, both of you!'

David stood up and found he was looking into a pair of such malevolently evil eyes that his body shuddered involuntarily.

'What did you say?' The SS officer's eyes were not inches away from his own.

'I said Father, sir.'

The officer's eyes darted in the direction of Jacob, who was standing, still staring straight ahead.

When he turned back to David he was smiling. He put the oil lamp on a table and its glow lit the room.

'Well, how touching. A Delanski family gathering.' The man's harsh German accent blunted the mellow language of David's homeland. He pushed the small figure behind him into the middle of the room.

'Say hello to your brother and your father, Rosa.'

David gasped as Rosa's terrified expression gave way to joy. She ran to him. He closed his arms protectively around her, hardly daring to believe that it was she. Then Rosa saw Jacob. His eyes were still fixed on a point above them.

'Papa!' she squealed. She threw her arms around his neck and covered him with kisses.

The officer seemed to be watching this scene with a degree of pleasure.

'Well, it seems as though you have solved my problem. I was going to call one of the *Hoffuden* to help me, but I believe that your opinion will be far more discerning. See here.' The officer pointed his stick at the two paintings on the easels, standing side by side. 'One is painted by your father, the other by your sister. One of the guards told me that your sister could paint, so I had her draw this for me this afternoon. It is a sketch of my dog, Wolf.'

The officer turned to face David. 'Of course, it is bad economy to have two artists in the camp. So, I would ask you to choose which painting you think best.'

It took David a few moments to comprehend what he was being asked to do. The horror of it struck him as he turned to see his sister, now clasped in the tight embrace of her father. Jacob was looking down at his daughter, caressing her hair disbelievingly.

'Well, Herr Delanski? Which is it to be? Rosa's, or your father's?'

David looked desperately round for help, heavenly guidance. There was none. Surely this wasn't happening. How could anyone make a decision that would send one of the two people he loved most in the world to their death?

'I want an answer, boy!' The officer was drawing out his pistol. Immediately David knew what he must do. He got down on his hands and knees in front of the officer.

'Take me, sir. Please, I beg of you. Then there will be one less mouth to feed, as you requested.'

The officer shook his head very slowly, a look of mock concern on his face. 'But we can't do that, boy. You are needed for our little orchestra. *Choose!*'

David was dragged to his feet by his collar and stood in front of the paintings.

'Help me, Mama!' It was an inner scream as he stared desperately, unseeingly at the two paintings.

'Well, boy. If you find it impossible to choose, I will understand that you think neither of the artists worthy and will have to look around for another from the next intake.'

250

'*No!*' David turned, his entire body shaking involuntarily, tears streaming down his cheeks. Rosa and Jacob were staring at him.

His father gave an imperceptible nod and, with a slight movement of his head, indicated Rosa.

David heard the pistol being drawn behind him.

His breathing was coming so fast he could hardly speak.

God, Mama, Papa, forgive me.

'Rosa.' It was no more than a whisper.

'I am sorry, boy. Did you speak?'

'Rosa.'

'Louder!'

'Rosa!' David screamed and turned towards the door. The SS officer who had brought in the paintings was blocking the exit. He pushed him roughly back into the room.

'Good. I agree with you. My dog's portrait is indeed excellent. Rosa! Come and stand by your brother. He has chosen you to continue your father's work.'

Jacob kissed the top of his daughter's head as she clung to him. Then he gently pushed her away from him. David held out his arms and she ran to them.

The officer pointed his pistol at Jacob. He fired three times.

The air was filled with Rosa's hysterical screams. The officer took hold of her arm and pulled her away from David.

'Please, sir, can she not at least stay with me for a short time?' David begged, as Rosa screamed his name over and over again.

'I will take care of our little protégée.' He pushed Rosa roughly out of the door and into the arms of the other SS officer. He turned back into the room.

'My name is Frankl. I will be meeting with you again soon, I am sure.' He smiled once more, then left David alone with the bullet-ridden body of his father.

David had little idea of the amount of time that passed. One day of terror, humiliation and pain melted into another. He knew it must be approaching winter when they awoke to frosts. The snow started to fall and David watched the naked men and women turn blue as they waited in line to go to their deaths.

Now he understood why his father had disappeared inside himself. The horror of what he witnessed daily was a surreal nightmare from which he never awoke. Every day he lived, he prayed to die. The number of men that hanged themselves with their own belts bore testament to the hell on earth in which they lived. Sanity was a precious commodity in Treblinka.

David would lie awake at night and ask God why innocent people were being punished in this way. There was never an answer and David had stopped praying. His faith disappeared along with reality.

His only consolation was that Rosa was alive and well. She was living in the Ukrainian women's quarters. Frankl, from whom he had witnessed unspeakable atrocities, seemed to have taken a shine to her. He had instructed his whore, a Ukrainian girl who worked in the kitchens, to take Rosa under her wing.

The girl, Anya, almost a child herself, was a very pretty,

sweet-natured thing who doted on Rosa. David believed that she was more frightened of Frankl than Rosa was.

David sighed and turned over, knowing he must sleep. But he was obsessed with plans for escape. He had managed to hide a pile of paper money, gold coins and jewellery under the floorboards in his dormitory. He knew all the other prisoners did the same. These things were found secreted in the possessions of those who had already died and Ukrainian guards were prepared to swap fresh fruit and meat for large amounts of money when rations to the camp were diminished. David thought of it as his passport once he got Rosa and himself away from the camp.

Tears stung David's eyes as he realized how useless it was. The dense forest and the treachery of the Ukrainians who lived outside the camp in the surrounding villages made escape almost impossible. Since he had been in the camp, every prisoner who had tried to escape had been captured, brought back and shot by Frankl in front of the rest of the camp. Frankl had then taken every tenth man from roll-call and murdered them too.

There had to be a way. If they stayed much longer, they would die anyway. David closed his eyes and tried once more to sleep.

'So Rosa, *Liebchen*. Let me see the picture you have painted today.'

Rosa stood nervously in front of Officer Frankl's desk and passed her canvas across the table. He took it and smiled.

'How pretty. I think you are getting better, yes? Come and kiss Uncle Kurt, Rosa.' He held out his arms.

Rosa walked round the table. She hated this bit. He liked her to sit on his knee and play with his thing until it squirted funny white stuff all over her hand.

Rose sat on his knee, legs akimbo across Kurt's body. As he fiddled with his fly and the pink thing popped out, he kissed her on the lips. One hand shook as he rubbed himself and it grew bigger. The other went up and under her skirt and found its way inside her knickers. He fiddled around, then roughly stuck his fingers up inside her. It hurt, but last time she had cried he had hit her very hard.

A hand grabbed hers and placed it round his thing. She rubbed it like he had taught her. He was moaning and saying something in German that she didn't understand. Her hand became numb as she rubbed faster, hoping it would be over quickly. The hot gush covered her fingers and Rosa breathed a sigh of relief.

Frankl smiled at Rosa. 'Good, good. You are getting better. Tomorrow I teach you another game you will enjoy.'

'Yes, Herr Frankl.' Rosa climbed off Frankl's knee and headed towards the door. Once it was closed behind her, she ran as fast as her legs could carry her to her dormitory, where Anya was lying on her mattress, her eyes closed.

'Are you feeling all right, Anya? You look unhappy.'

Anya opened her eyes and looked at Rosa. 'Yes, of course. I am fine. It is time you slept. I must get ready for this evening.'

While Rosa undressed and donned an oversized nightie, Anya put on a dress that she had found amongst

254

the piles of clothing brought in yesterday to the sorting hut. It said it was made by Chanel. She hoped Frankl would like it and it would hide the growing bulge in her stomach. If he saw that . . . she knew her life was over. She'd heard dreadful stories from others who had witnessed whores being shot by the SS officers when they grew tired of them.

She put on some lipstick and piled her soft golden hair on top of her head.

At fifteen years of age, Anya was already a grown woman. She had come into the camp a year ago, when her parents, half starved and desperate for money, had heard of a vacancy in the kitchen of the camp through a neighbour in their village. Her father had encouraged her, but her mother had begged him not to make Anya work for the Nazis.

'Hush! Do you not understand that the Nazis are doing us a favour by purging the world of the stinking Jews?'

Her mother, who had only sympathy for the poor souls who perished daily, had not replied. So Anya had begun to work at Treblinka.

A week after she arrived, Frankl had invited her to his quarters. He had offered wine and food of which she had never seen the like before. Then he had raped her and ordered her to live at the camp.

For the past year, Anya had been subjected to such acts of humiliation and indecency that she felt no more human than the Jews living in the camp. Sometimes, if she refused, Frankl would produce his pistol and make her do it to him with it pointed at her head. He had made her watch as he took Jewish prisoners of both genders, violated and then disposed of them with his pistol. Sometimes he'd even 'lend' her to other SS officers.

He showered Anya with presents, and in public treated her as though she was a goddess. The prisoners spat at her when they passed, but she knew that if she didn't give him what he wanted, then others would be chosen instead.

The only person that she had ever seen him show kindness towards was Rosa. Frankl had taken a shine to the girl from the moment she had arrived at the camp. She believed his affection was genuine and thanked God for Rosa's sake.

Anya had thought countless times of escape. Each night, as she lay on her mattress, mortified and ashamed of what Frankl had made her do, she vowed that it would be the last time. And now there was no choice. She was pregnant. She reckoned over five months gone and she could not hide it from him much longer. He liked her because of her slim, pubescent body, which was fast disappearing. He would never allow a Ukrainian whore to give birth to a child of the master race. Although it was likely Frankl was the father of her baby, it could be any one of the four other SS officers she'd been used by.

She had also heard him talking with the Commandant of the camp. They were discussing the fact that soon Treblinka would be only a peaceful farmyard with no trace of what had gone on before.

Anya saw the fear in her eyes as she applied lipstick in her precious, broken piece of mirror. If she went home, her father would send her back and she would be shot.

Sometimes she wondered if she would not be better off dead.

'Nooh! Please! Stop it! You're hurting me!'

Cold steel was placed at Rosa's neck.

'Shut up! Do not speak another word.'

Rosa closed her eyes and sank her teeth into her knuckles as Frankl moved violently behind her. In and out, in and out. It would be over soon and so would the pain. She had to keep quiet, otherwise she would die. Frankl screamed in ecstasy. Tears spurted out of Rosa's closed eyes as she endured the agony in silence.

Frankl removed himself and the gun from her body, pulled down her skirt and kissed the top of her head.

'Good, good for a first time, *Liebchen*. Here.' He handed Rosa an apple.

Anya knew something was wrong the minute Rosa walked into the dormitory. Her face was deathly white and her small hands were shaking.

'What is it, Rosa? Tell Anya.'

Rosa shook her head, not trusting herself to speak.

Then Anya saw the blood dripping onto the floor. At first she thought that it was . . . no, this was an eleven-year-old child.

Instantly she knew what had happened.

'Frankl. Did he . . .?'

Rosa did not have to answer. Anya swept Rosa into her arms and the little girl began shaking violently.

'Oh, my poor darling, my darling.' Anya stroked Rosa's hair.

Enough. Neither of them could take any more.

David took his usual place in the tailor's shop after dinner. The few prisoners in positions of authority were gathering in the shop, which was the largest and most pleasant hall in the camp.

Albert nodded in his direction and the three of them began to play. David thanked God for this time, for it was the one moment in the day when life came somewhere towards normality. People would smile and dance, and David could lose himself in the music and forget about his aching bones and how hungry he was. The trains had stopped coming and therefore so had the supply of food. Everyone in the camp was starving and the Ukrainians charged phenomenal amounts for smuggled supplies.

A few Germans started to drift in and began dancing too. Frankl entered the hall with Anya and joined the dancers.

Ten minutes later Anya walked over to David. 'Play *Blue Danube*, can you?' she asked, then leaned closer. 'I must talk to you. The furrier's hut tonight. I'll wait for you there. Thank you,' she said as she walked back across the floor to join Frankl.

The furrier's hut was in complete darkness.

'Anya,' he whispered hoarsely.

'Over here.'

He moved towards the sound of her voice and at last saw her, sitting against one of the mountains of fur coats.

'Why did you wish to see me, Anya?'

'Because Rosa and I must escape and we need your help.'

'What has happened, Anya? Is Rosa all right?'

'No, David. Frankl's interest in your sister is not innocent. He has been making her do indecent things and today he . . . well he violated her.'

A deep moan came from inside David. He doubled over as he retched.

'Oh, my God . . . that bastard! I'll go now and kill him with my own bare han –'

'Hush, David! I have a plan for escape. I too am at risk. When he discovers I am carrying a child, he will shoot me. Now, listen carefully, while I explain . . .'

Roll-call finished the following morning and the prisoners went off about their gruesome business. David's heart ticked steadily against his chest as he went back to his dormitory.

Everything was in place. He just had to time it right and in two hours, he should be leaving this hell. He knew other prisoners would suffer if he went; but he had to get out, if only to tell the world the madness that had existed here and have a chance to get Frankl.

He'd found the gasoline in the tool hut, only a small canister, but enough he believed to send up in flames the fence camouflaged in dry twigs that hid the gas chambers from view. In the confusion he planned to make his way to the truck on the train. He had to pass right below the watchtower, but he was hoping that all the attention would be on the fire, on the other side of the sorting area.

259

It was time to go. He walked nonchalantly across the path to the gas chambers and into the assembly yard, his violin in his hand. He dived into the hut that served as an undressing area for the women on their way to the gas chambers, and rooted under the wooden bench for the gasoline and the three matches. He knew that this was the most dangerous part of his plan. He had to get to the other side of the yard which provided no cover from the watchtower.

He peered out of the hut. Seeing that the yard was empty, he bolted across and sheltered underneath the five-metre high fence. He poured the gasoline on the dry branches and twigs nearest to him. He struck the match along the hard gravel floor. It lit, then went out. The same with the next one. He had one match left. He struck it, sheltering the flame with his hands, and put it to a twig. It caught with such fierceness that he jumped backwards in fright.

He heard a shout, turned and saw the men from the watchtower turn towards him. Bullets rattled around his head. The fire had taken a firm grip of the fence. The guards stopped shooting and began to scurry down the tower. David seized the moment and raced back into the women's changing room. He scampered down to the other end of the hut and peered through a hole. The train was in front of him. He watched as the surprised Ukrainians who were loading the piles of clothes dropped what they were doing and heeded the calls of the Germans to help them with the fire.

When the platform had emptied, David opened the door. Ten yards between him and the truck. He saw Anya already clambering inside.

'David! Come on! Quick! Cover yourself! Rosa is already buried.' David leaped across the platform, threw his violin case into the truck and jumped up inside. He plunged into the massive pile of clothes, trying to ease his breathing. A small hand was touching his shoulder. He wriggled round, grasped it with his own and squeezed it.

David listened as heavy boots landed inside the truck. He heard the door close and everything went silent.

After what David would always remember as eternity, the train began to move. Tears of relief came to his eyes. He held Rosa's hand tightly. She moved through the clothes and snuggled up to him.

'I love you, David.'

'I love you, too, Rosa. And one day I'll make that bastard pay for what he did to Papa, and to you, Rosa. I swear.'

She fell asleep as the train gently rocked her. David looked down at her sweet, innocent face and knew that he meant it with all his heart.

The intercom buzzed, bringing David sharply out of his reverie and back to his smart New York office. He wiped his sweating brow and dried his eyes.

'Yes?'

'Mr Brett Cooper is in reception for you, sir.'

'Thank you, Pat. Give him a coffee and tell him I'll be with him in five minutes.'

'Right you are, sir.'

'Damn!' For the first time, David wondered whether he'd taken the right decision to keep his past from his son. He'd done it out of the best intentions, wanting to protect him, but now, as it crept into his own future, changing him irrevocably, he wasn't so sure.

Of one thing there was no doubt. He was being given an opportunity to take revenge for his mother, father and his sister, as he had sworn to do. Whatever it cost him, David was prepared to pay the price.

He collected himself as best he could and pressed the intercom.

'Okay, Pat. Tell Brett to come in.'

Maybe one day he'd tell Brett, when it was all over. But this was his war, not his son's.

The door opened and his red-eyed, exhausted son walked across to his desk.

'Hello, Dad. Good to see you.' Brett stood with his hands in his pockets and admired the room. 'Wow, this is amazing. It's much better than the office in London.'

'Yes. You'll get used to everything being ten times larger than it is in England. How was the flight?'

'Okay. I was too excited to sleep. I got a taxi here straight from the airport. I feel a bit rough, though.'

David smiled. 'Well, I'm not going to suggest that you do a day's serious work here, but what I do suggest is that we spend an hour going through the plan I've drawn up for you, which will take us to midday. Then I'll take you to lunch at the 21 Club, after which I'm packing you off to my apartment to get some sleep. How does that sound?'

'Marvellous. I'm glad to be here, Dad.'

'And I'm pleased to have you, Brett.' David was relieved that Brett finally seemed to have accepted the idea of working for Cooper Industries, and had forgotten all those silly ideas about being an artist. At present, that was something that he couldn't deal with.

Brett's happiness was almost totally due to the fact that Leah would be arriving in New York in less than three days' time.

Father and son spent an agreeable hour going through Brett's work plan. David wanted Brett to spend four months in the New York office, learning how the hub of the business was run. Then he would be sent off for a year or so around the world to visit Cooper Industries sites in their various stages of development.

'I don't hold with any of this "starting in the post room" sort of business. Everyone in the company knows that one day you'll take over. However, you will not be officially given a position or title for the next eighteen months, during which I expect you to turn your hand to anything. The most important thing is to earn the respect of the people you will one day control. Humility and a willingness to learn are what I want to see. Don't put people's backs up. You are not here to comment or criticize. You're here to learn from every single person on the payroll. Now, speech over. Let's go to lunch.'

After a pleasant meal David and Brett hailed a cab and went back to David's brand-new, duplex apartment, situated on Fifth Avenue, six blocks from the offices of Cooper Industries.

'Now, I thought this could be your suite. It's got a nice view of the park.'

Brett looked around the grand sitting room, then wandered into the spacious bedroom, with marble bathroom en suite.

'It'll do fine. Thanks, Dad.'

'I thought of getting you a separate apartment, but I'm hardly here and you'll be off too in four months' time. There's also Georgia, the resident cook, who's always on hand to knock you something up.'

'It's great, Dad, really.'

'Right. I'll leave you to get some sleep. I'm out tonight at a business dinner, but I'll be around tomorrow morning. If you need anything, press the housekeeper's bell by your bed.'

'No problems.'

David turned to walk out of the room. He stopped and looked back at his son.

'I'm glad you're here, Brett,' he said simply, and left.

Brett sank onto the bed and closed his eyes. But although his body was begging for rest, his mind was too alert to allow sleep to come. Twenty minutes later, he gave up and decided to explore his new home.

The duplex was on a grand scale, with the formal sitting room and dining room on the top floor, opening onto a terrace overlooking Central Park far below. David's suite of rooms led directly off his comfortable office. The lower floor, where Brett's suite was, also housed the huge kitchen, three further suites and the servants' quarters. Brett was used to luxury on a grand scale, but even he had to admit that this was something else.

He wondered what Leah would think of it, then stopped himself. He was automatically assuming that she would want to see him again.

Brett wandered back into his suite, and once more lay down on his bed. Three days until she was here.

He finally fell asleep with his mind full of pictures of her.

5

'LEAH, DARLING! I can't believe you're here.' Jenny hugged her friend tight. 'I've missed you. Sit down and I'll order some champagne.'

'Mineral water for me, Jenny.'

'Oh, you bore! You simply can't sit in the Oak Room on your first night in New York and toast it with mineral water!' laughed Jenny.

'Okay. I'll have one glass.'

Jenny ordered a bottle from a passing waiter. 'Seriously, it is good to see you haven't changed, I just wish I had your discipline.' She smiled ruefully. 'Let me look at you.' Jenny surveyed her. 'Still as beautiful as ever. Not an inch of fat, or a touch of a crow's foot under your eyes. Lucky old you,' she sighed. 'I'm starting to really show my age.'

Leah studied her friend. Jenny looked tired and haggard. Her eyes were red and there was a noticeable roundness about the delicate contours of her face.

'You look absolutely fine. Just the same as ever,' Leah lied smoothly.

Jenny shook her head. 'I look like shit, Leah. Don't

266

worry, I can take it. I had a call from Madelaine this morning to say that if I don't lose half a stone and clean up my act, my cosmetics company aren't going to renew my contract next month. She wants me to go off to this health spa in Palm Springs for a week. Trouble is, you can't drink, or smoke, and you live on rabbit food most of the time.'

'Sounds like a great idea to me.'

'Anyway, tonight is special, and, as Snoopy says on my apron, my diet starts tomorrow.' Jenny lifted the glass of champagne that the waiter had just poured. 'Cheers, Leah. Here's to success in the Big Apple.'

The two girls clinked glasses and drank a toast to the future.

'I hope I've made the right decision, moving to New York. I mean, I've only a month's work to do for Chaval, then I'm back on assignments again.'

'Come on, Leah. Not only is the reported half a million you got for the year's contract pretty good for twenty-odd days' work, but your face is going to be all over America. You're already huge in Europe. Magazines and photographers will be screaming for you here. They did for me when I first arrived,' Jenny said sadly. 'Now, I want to hear all about your birthday party. I'm so sorry I couldn't make it. The stinky old company wouldn't rearrange a shoot,' she moaned, pouring herself another glass of champagne.

'Well, it was eventful,' said Leah, thoughtfully.

'Oh yes? And what do you mean by that?'

'I met Brett, a boy I hadn't seen for years, Carlo disgraced himself and had to be packed off in a drunken stupor to his hotel.'

Jenny giggled. 'Sounds like a good night.'

Leah sighed. 'Carlo was really weird, Jenny. You know how good he's been over the past few years. Never touching me, just being a great friend and supporter. But it was like he was a changed man that night. He tried to kiss me, then became abusive because I wouldn't go back to his hotel room. I don't know what's got into him.'

Jenny nodded her head slowly. 'I've always told you to watch him, Leah. The guy's madly in love with you, but not only that, he honestly believes that he made you, that it's all down to him that you've become so successful.'

'Well, he did give me my big chance.'

'Oh come on, Leah. It's your face and body that's put you at the top of your profession. From what you've said about the night of your party, I reckon Carlo is calling in his chips.'

'What do you mean?'

'You know what Italian men are like. Carlo wouldn't touch you until you're over twenty-one and have officially, in his eyes, become a woman. Come on, Leah, don't act dumb. He's behaved as if he owns you for the past four years and he's moving in to take what he believes is his due. The entire modelling world, plus the press, have assumed that you two have been at it for years anyway.'

'Jenny! Please! I'm grateful for what Carlo's done and I regard him as a very good friend, but I don't and never have felt . . . that way about him. I'm sure Carlo knows that.'

Jenny sighed. 'Oh dear, Leah. You may have grown up in some ways, but in others, you're terribly naïve. Anyway, let's drop the subject. The best thing that could have happened is you moving to New York, out of Carlo's clutches for a while. But believe me, Leah, everything in life has a price. Just as I know this glass of champagne will show on my hips and in my eyes, Carlo feels that you owe him something for how he's helped you.'

'That's a very cynical view, Jenny.'

'It is, isn't it? But it's a cynical world and I'm not usually wrong, especially where men are concerned. Anyway, tell me about this boy you met at the party. I noticed your eyes light up. Old flame, is he?'

Leah shrugged. 'Sort of. I met him when I was fifteen. He did the dirty on me, actually.'

'Well, I hope you didn't give him the time of day.'

'I'm afraid I did. We danced together and I said he could contact me here in New York. By coincidence, he flew out to work here a couple of days ago.'

'Don't tell me that the only virgin over twenty-one left in the Western world has had a stirring in her loins?'

'Honestly, Jenny. You make me sound like a relic. I haven't had time over the past few years and . . .'

'And you haven't been out of Carlo's sight for long enough to even think about other men, let alone do anything about it,' finished Jenny. 'You like this boy, don't you?'

Leah paused, then looked at her friend. 'I shouldn't, he did something absolutely rotten to me years ago, but yes, I do. Very much.'

Jenny took a healthy slug of champagne. 'Good. It's about time you joined the human race. It is perfectly natural to fancy a guy, you know.'

'Talking of men, how's your prince?'

Jenny poured herself another glass of champagne. 'Oh, okay, I think. He's not rung me for a couple of weeks. He's been with his father on some urgent family business. I'm sure he'll call when he hits New York.'

Leah was glad that Jenny had not seen copies of any recent British papers. Prince Ranu had been in most of the gossip columns, photographed entwined with the daughter of a wealthy European aristocrat. One columnist had even mentioned that there was talk of a possible engagement.

'You don't love him, though, do you Jenny?'

Jenny was silent as she traced the line of her glass. She sighed. 'As a matter of fact, I do. I adore him. Four years on and I still feel the same as the first night we met. If he asked me, I'd marry him tomorrow and get out of this stinking rat-race.' Jenny glanced at Leah ruefully. 'I know. You don't have to tell me. He's having an affair with that Princess De-La-Unpronounceable-Surname. It's not the first time, I can assure you. But he always comes running back to me in the end, begging for forgiveness.'

'Why on earth do you forgive him, Jenny?'

'Why are you prepared to forgive this boy you re-met at your birthday party?'

Leah blushed. '*Touché.*'

'I'm sorry. That was below the belt, but it illustrates the point. I love him. And he's rich. Very, very rich. He can have any girl he wants, when he wants. He doesn't need to be faithful, because there'll always be another younger, prettier girl in the queue behind me. So I figure that the only chance I have of eventually getting him is to hold on fast to my place in the queue.'

'Oh dear.' Leah did not know what else to say.

'Don't worry. You see this boy again, then you'll understand.'

'But I won't fall in love, Jenny.'

'Oh no?' Jenny's eyes twinkled. 'Famous last words, Leah Thompson,' and she ordered another bottle of champagne.

6

'LEAH, IT'S BRETT.'

'Hello, Brett.'

'You sound sleepy. Did I wake you?'

'Er, no. Sorry.' Leah sat upright on the big kingsize bed, her head still woolly, her heart pounding at the sound of his voice.

She had returned to the Plaza an hour ago after a heavy lunch with the PR people from the cosmetics company and an afternoon of press interviews. Jet-lagged and exhausted after a sleepless night, she had fallen onto the bed and closed her eyes.

'I was wondering if you fancied meeting for a drink tonight.'

Leah could see her pale face and dishevelled appearance in the mirror on the wall opposite. Getting ready and going out was the last thing she had on the agenda tonight. On the other hand . . . she hated herself for wanting to see him so badly . . .

'Okay.'

'Great. I'll meet you in the hotel lobby in forty minutes.'

272

'Fine.'

Leah sighed and lay back on the bed. She shouldn't even give Brett the time of day. He didn't deserve another chance, but maybe if she talked to him, spent some time with him, it would exorcise the ghost.

Forty minutes to transform herself. She'd better get moving.

After showering and drying her hair, Leah tried on her entire wardrobe of clothes, discarding one expensive outfit after another.

'Shit, shit, shit!' she screamed aloud in frustration. She spent her life being a professional clothes horse and tonight she was acting as though she was a teenager on a first date.

She finally decided on a favourite dress designed especially for her by Carlo. She then sat in front of the mirror pulling her hair into a myriad of different styles, all of which she was convinced looked dreadful. Realizing that she was already ten minutes late, she pulled her hair out of the top-knot and let it hang loose around her shoulders.

'You'll just have to do,' she muttered, grabbed her handbag and keys and headed for the lift.

Brett was standing nervously in the lobby, checking his watch as the lift opened and Leah emerged. As she came out, he noticed every male head turn and watch her. Brett felt a surge of pride as one of the most beautiful women in the world spotted him and walked towards him.

Brett thought she looked even lovelier tonight than on her birthday. She had a radiance about her, and with her long hair flowing naturally around her shoulders, Brett was reminded of the very first moment he had seen her, silhouetted by the early morning sun in his bedroom in Yorkshire. Of course, her beauty had matured: in her designer clothes, and with the polish of gracing catwalks for the past few years, Brett felt like a schoolboy as she casually kissed him on both cheeks.

'Hello.'

'Hello.' Brett could almost feel himself blushing. 'Shall we go to the bar here?'

'Yes.'

As they walked into the Oak Room, both of them tried to think of something to say, and ended up saying nothing. They sat down in silence.

'What would you like to drink?'

'Mineral water, please.'

'You don't drink?'

'Rarely.'

Brett ordered water and a beer, thinking how composed and cool she was. But it was understandable after what he had done to her all those years ago. He was going to have to work extremely hard to show her how he had changed.

'How was your flight?' they both said together and laughed, the ice broken a little.

'Fine,' said Leah.

'And mine. I'm still feeling slightly jet-lagged, though.'

'Me, too,' said Leah. 'I was awake all last night. I spent most of it staring out of my hotel window. This city just never sleeps.'

'Tell me about it. It has this permanent sense of

urgency, as though there are not enough hours in the day to do what has to be done. I keep feeling as though I want to take a shower. The grime and dust seem much worse here than in London. Anyway, cheers. It's wonderful to see you again.' Brett toasted.

'Thank you.'

'Amazing coincidence that we're both in New York at the same time.'

'Yes. Tell me what you've been doing in the past few years.'

Brett sketched an outline for her. He spoke of Cambridge and his friends with an obvious fondness. Clearly he'd not spent his time there pining for her, Leah thought irrationally.

'So I'm here in New York to start learning how my father runs his company,' Brett finished. 'Now, what about you? I mean, my life is dull in comparison. I could hardly believe it when I saw your face staring at me from the cover of *Vogue*. Tell me all about it, Leah.' He meant, tell me about Carlo, and the other men who have been part of your life. Her career rise had been better documented by the press than the Prime Minister's.

'Actually, there is one thing you don't know, that nobody knows, Brett. And that is that you are responsible for my being spotted.'

Brett looked amazed. 'How on earth do you mean?'

'Rose took the sketch you did of me on the moors and hung it in the gallery at her first exhibition. Steve Levine, the photographer, saw it, and here I am,' she smiled.

'Good grief! Where did Rose find it? Has she still got it?'

Leah shook her head. 'No. That's the mystery. It disappeared a few days after the exhibition. It's never been seen since. Everyone who saw it still raves about it, though. Do you still paint, Brett?'

'No, is the simple answer. I've grown up a little, realized that the world is not about silly childhood dreams and . . .'

'Your dreams were hardly silly. You had real talent, Brett. I think you should use it, if only as a hobby. You've obviously inherited Rose's gift.'

'Maybe, except our styles couldn't be more different. Hasn't she done well over the past few years? I wrote to congratulate her on the latest exhibition. I thought it was magnificent.'

'You should see the farmhouse these days. You'd hardly recognize it. All mod cons and Laura Ashley furnishings.' Leah took a deep breath. She had to know. 'And Chloe has shot up since I last saw her.'

'Chloe?'

'Miranda's daughter.'

'Good God. Is she married already?'

'No. And she won't say who the father is. Chloe's four now. Miranda told Rose she was pregnant just after you left Yorkshire.' Leah took a sip of her drink to give her something to concentrate on.

A cold chill ran through Brett's bones.

'Look, Leah, about Miranda. Will you let me explain?'

'If you want to. But it's pretty obvious. Chloe is your daughter, isn't she?'

Leah watched as Brett turned white.

'Don't worry, I'm the only one who knows.'

276

'No! No, absolutely impossible. No way, no how.'

'But Miranda told me that night that you two . . . oh Brett, please don't lie to me. Guilt was written all over your face.'

'Leah, I swear to you that Chloe couldn't possibly be my child. Miranda and I . . . oh dear . . . well, we kissed and cuddled and stuff, but not . . . you know.'

'Then why did Miranda tell me you did? And why won't she say who the father is?'

'The answer to the first question is simple. Miranda wanted revenge. The second, I honestly don't know.'

'Well,' sighed Leah. 'I'm afraid it confirmed your guilt when Miranda was so secretive about Chloe's father. I thought that it was because it was you and she was too scared to tell Rose.'

'Look, Leah. I can't prove it, but I swear to you, I am not guilty of that crime. I was stupid and selfish yes, but I paid for that when I lost you. Look, I understand how you must feel at the moment, but please will you give me a chance to prove that I really am a decent sort of a guy these days?' Brett pleaded.

Leah suddenly felt extraordinarily tired.

'I'm sorry, Brett, but I'm exhausted. I've got a very heavy day tomorrow and I really must get some sleep.'

'Of course.' Brett sighed. She hadn't forgiven him. 'But would it be okay if I called you again?'

'Yes. But I'm going to be pretty busy for the next week, and Jenny and I are going out apartment hunting at the weekend. The one she has at the moment isn't big enough to swing a cat in.'

'Will you let me know your new address and telephone

number?' Brett pulled a card out of his wallet and handed it to her. 'Leave a message with Pat, my father's PA, if I'm unavailable.'

'Will do.' Leah stood up. 'Thanks for the drink.'

He walked with her to the lift. 'You won't forget to call with your number, will you?'

'No.' The lift opened. 'Good-night, Brett.' She kissed him on both cheeks and stepped inside.

'Good-night.' The door closed and she was gone.

Brett sauntered outside and hailed a passing yellow cab. He checked his watch. Half past nine. Early. So much for his dreams of whisking her up to her hotel room and making passionate love until the dawn broke. Brett sighed. He had no one to blame but himself. Leah held all the cards and he would just have to wait in an agony of anticipation to see if she called.

7

MIRANDA STRETCHED LUXURIOUSLY, opened her eyes
and stared at the mirrored ceiling above her. She liked
what she saw. Her naked body was partly hidden beneath
the white satin sheets, and her blonde hair was splayed
across the pillow.

She sat up and looked round the comfortable bedroom. Her new home. All this luxury, a bank account
with as much as she could ever wish to spend, and a
wardrobe full of beautiful designer clothes. Miranda
smiled and hugged her knees. Everything she had ever
wanted had become hers in a matter of days. And it had
all been so easy.

Three short, painless fucks were the price for all this.

Santos had been so sweet to her while they were on his
boat, introducing her to his many associates, mainly
people who worked for him, who had flown in to Athens
and joined them at the port of Piraeus on Saturday morning to begin the weekend cruise round the Aegean.

Miranda had never seen such luxury before in her life.
She had imagined the boat to be a small vessel with a
couple of cramped cabins below deck, but this boat . . .

why, it was like being on the QE2. Three floors of sumptuous suites for the fifteen guests, a magnificent glass-enclosed sitting room and formal dining room, and five enormous sun-terraces.

For the two days she had been on board, Santos had showered her with gifts and affection, making it plain to the male guests that she was his. They had treated her with respect and deference, as if she was the hostess of the entire 'chabang'.

She had done her best to try to extract information on Santos from his friends, but had only come up with the fact that he lived in South America, was over sixty and incredibly wealthy, which she had gathered anyway.

When he had visited her in her cabin late at night, and climbed into bed next to her, he did not talk, only grunted as she teased his flaccid cock to life. Once she had steered him inside her, and he was happily bouncing up and down on top of her, Miranda shut her eyes and pictured her diamond necklace, her beautiful clothes and the luxurious private jet, occasionally emitting what she hoped were realistic groans of feminine pleasure. It had been over quickly on all three occasions. Santos would kiss her, put on his silk robe and depart for his own cabin.

On Sunday evening the boat had pulled gently back into Piraeus and the guests began disembarking and climbing into their waiting limousines. Miranda watched them wistfully from one of the upper sun-decks, thinking that it was back to Yorkshire and normality tomorrow. Santos came up behind her and handed her a key.

'Your limousine is waiting to take you to the airport, Miranda.'

'Are you not coming with me?'

'I cannot. I must go home. That key will open the door to an apartment in London. The driver who collects you from Heathrow will take you there. I will call you later.' He kissed her. 'Good-bye, Miranda.'

When Miranda had arrived at Heathrow, she was whisked through customs and out to a waiting Rolls-Royce. The car drove her through the darkening streets of London and stopped in front of a palatial white stucco building, which overlooked a park.

'If you'd like to follow me, madam,' the chauffeur said formally, and led her into a large lobby, up to the third floor in the small lift and opened the door on a tastefully furnished one bedroom apartment.

The chauffeur had taken her suitcases through to the bedroom, then tipped his hat.

'The number to call if you need me is on the list by the telephone. Good-night, madam.'

Miranda had got the feeling that the chauffeur had been through all this before and spent the following hour combing the apartment for any clues as to previous occupants, or to Santos himself. She had found nothing in any of the scented drawers nor down the back of the plush washed silk sofa. But she did find an envelope by the telephone addressed to her. She had opened it and inside found two thousand pounds cash plus notification that she would be receiving two credit cards in her name, charged to the account of Mr F. Santos, and a bank account opened for her, containing the sum of ten thousand pounds, an amount topped up on the last day of every month by another five thousand.

Miranda had sat in shock. This was better than she had even dreamt about. She was rich.

At nine o'clock that evening, the ornamental telephone had jangled loudly in the silent apartment. She'd picked it up.

'Hello.'

'Hello, Miranda. Have you found everything to your liking?'

'Yes. Everything's wonderful.'

'Good, good.' There was a pause as the bad line betrayed the distance between them.

'I hope that you understand that all these things come with certain conditions. I do not wish you to go out of the apartment at any time without calling for Roger, the chauffeur, to escort you in the Rolls-Royce. And no guests. Men are forbidden in your apartment, apart from Ian, whom you met at the Savoy. He will visit you from time to time and if you have any problems you must contact him. I will ring you at half past nine every evening to make sure you are well and happy. Maria, the housekeeper, lives in the apartment below you. She will cook all your meals and take care of household duties.

'One last thing. Always have a suitcase packed, for I may ring you at any time and ask you to join me abroad. Under no circumstances will you ever attempt to contact me. Well, I hope that those few little rules will not stop you enjoying your new home. There is champagne in the fridge. Drink a toast to us both. Good-bye, Miranda.'

The telephone had clicked and Miranda replaced the receiver. She had sunk down onto the sofa and tried to take in what Santos had said.

All this luxury came with a much higher price than she had at first thought. The cold truth dawned on Miranda. Santos had just bought and paid for her. She was his possession and, therefore, he had the right to dictate how she lived her life.

She was a mistress.

'Mistress.' Miranda uttered the word to see how it sounded on her tongue as she stared up at the mirrors on the ceiling.

After four days of being alone, Miranda was finding the silence in the apartment deafening. She was used to the morning sounds of Mrs Thompson bustling in the kitchen, Rose's loud singing as she painted, and the sweet, high-pitched voice of her daughter, Chloe.

She suddenly felt dreadfully homesick. She reached for the telephone by her bed and dialled.

The telephone rang and Rose hurried to pick it up.

'Hello,' her voice was hoarse from lack of sleep and too many cigarettes.

'Rose, it's me.'

Rose choked back a sob.

'Thank God. Are you okay?'

'Never been better,' the voice sang down the receiver.

Rose wanted to strangle Miranda. She had just spent the past four days going crazy.

'Where are you, Miranda? I've been worried sick. You might have called. We were expecting you home days ago and . . .'

'For God's sake, Rose, I'm twenty-one and I can take

283

care of myself. I'm in London and I'm absolutely fine.'

'You may be twenty-one, young lady, but you are still my daughter and . . .'

'Okay, okay. I apologize, Rose.'

'All right. Now what train are you catching? I'll pick you up from Leeds.'

'Actually, I'm not coming back to Yorkshire just yet.'

'Why ever not, Miranda?'

'Because I've met some people down here and I want to stay a bit longer. Will you take care of Chloe for a while?'

Rose bit her lip. 'Of course, Miranda. But . . . where are you staying? Can I have your number? Have you got enough money . . .?' Rose's attention was caught by a small plump hand pushing open the sitting-room door.

'Mummee? Where's Mummee?' The angelic face, a replica of Miranda's at the same age, creased into a frown.

'Come to Granny, darling.' Rose held out her arms and Chloe walked over to her. 'There's someone who wants to speak to you, Miranda. Chloe, say hello to Mummy.'

'Hello, Mummee. Come home.'

'Hello, Chloe darling. Don't worry, Mummy will be home soon.'

Rose settled Chloe on her knee. 'She misses you badly, Miranda. She asks every day where you are.'

'Yes, well. I have to go now. I'll ring again soon. Give Chloe a kiss for me. And don't worry, Rose. I'll be fine, really. Good-bye.'

The line went dead. Rose slowly replaced the handset

and studied the beautiful little girl sucking her thumb contentedly in her lap.

'When Mummee home, Grannee?' The little face looked up at her with such trust and innocence in her big, blue eyes, that Rose's own filled with tears and she hugged Chloe tightly to her.

'I don't know, sweetheart. I really don't know.'

8

JENNY THREW HERSELF onto the comfortable cream sofa lengthways and smoothed her hair away from her sweating brow.

'Never again,' she shook her head.

'You're absolutely right.' Leah collapsed in an armchair on the other side of the room. 'I am never again helping you move your stuff from one apartment to the other. Really, Jenny, you've only been here for nine months. I can't get over how much junk you've collected.'

Jenny smiled. 'Sorry. But it's going to be worth it, isn't it?' She looked proudly around the new apartment.

The two of them had spent the previous weekend trailing round rental accommodation, until at last they had found their new home. It was not nearly as large as some of the vast lofts they had seen in SoHo, but both girls found too much space intimidating, being used to their smaller, English living spaces.

The apartment was on the twelfth floor of a luxury high-rise building on East 70th Street. Both of them had known the minute that they had walked through the door that this was the one. The apartment had a large sitting room, with doors opening onto a balcony. Along the corridor was a small but serviceable kitchen and dining area, two big bedrooms, both with en suite bathrooms, and a guest room and toilet. It was tastefully decorated in soft beiges and creams, the stripped floors strewn with rugs. The rent was as impressive as the apartment, but Leah's cosmetic company was paying, so that was no problem.

'Yes. I adore it. It has a cosy feel to it. Coffee?'

'Something stronger for me. I think I deserve it. I must have lost pounds lugging all those boxes around today.'

'Okay. You can have a small vodka with lots of ice.' The two girls walked along the corridor to the kitchen. Leah began digging through boxes for a jar of coffee and the bottle of vodka.

'It's a great place for a party. So great that I think we should have a housewarming next weekend. Introduce you to a few people in this town,' said Jenny.

'Fine. We could throw it on Saturday night. That'll give me twenty-four hours to recover from Mexico.'

Leah was flying down to a shoot on Monday morning and would not be back until the following Friday night.

'Leave it to me. I've nothing on at all next week.'

Leah sighed as she fished the coffee out of the bottom of a box. Jenny had had 'nothing on' since Leah had arrived in New York. This, for a top model, was unheard of.

Madelaine had called Leah in the middle of the week and said some worrying things about Jenny.

'I'm glad you're going to be living with her, Leah. She needs somebody to keep her under control. You've noticed the drink problem, I presume?'

'Well, Madelaine. I've noticed Jenny likes a drink but . . .'

'She's turned up on two shoots in the past month stoned out of her mind and pissed. She's put on weight, her skin looks like concrete and the word is getting round. I've told her that the cosmetics company are seriously considering not renewing her contract if she doesn't get her act together. And I'm struggling to find her anything to do while she waits for the new campaign to start. She's got a couple of months to sort herself out. Help her, Leah. I know how close you two are.'

'I'll do my best, Madelaine. I'm sure she'll be fine. She's still one of the best around.'

'Maybe, but there are a thousand beautiful girls out there just ready and waiting to jump into her shoes. This is her last chance. Tell her that from me.'

Leah had had little chance to tell Jenny anything in the past week. She'd been through a gruelling week of shoots, interviews and a big campaign launch for Chaval last night. And she had twenty-four hours before she flew down to Mexico. Hardly the right person to play minder. Tonight, she'd have to have a talk with her.

'There.' Leah put the vodka on the kitchen table and sat down opposite Jenny.

'Cheers. Here's to our new home.'

Leah winced as Jenny downed the entire glassfull in one slug.

'Mmn. That feels better. Do you fancy sending out for some Chinese? I'm starving.'

'Okay.'

'I'll go to the store on the corner and get a couple of

bottles of wine. We'll have a cosy night in. There's a party later on at a model's place, but I think I'm too knackered to move.'

An hour later, they were sitting out on the balcony, eating and watching the sun set over New York. Jenny had ordered a feast of Chinese food and they were washing it down with white wine.

'You realize that is the last Chinese you're going to have for a while, don't you, Jenny?'

Jenny was licking her fingers. 'What do you mean?'

'I spoke to Madelaine last week. She really is worried about you.'

'You mean she's a bossy, interfering old hag who enjoys poking her nose into other people's business.'

'Come on. You know that's not true. You used to adore her. She genuinely cares about us, that's all.'

'Yeah, as far as her bank balance is concerned,' countered Jenny.

'She's a businesswoman and her business is selling us. And when one of her products is not coming up to scratch, she . . .'

'Products!' exploded Jenny. 'You just hit the nail on the head. Well done, Leah. We're not human. We're just walking, talking Barbie dolls with not a grey cell in our heads!'

'I'm sorry, Jenny. I didn't mean it like that.' Leah looked at her friend's angry face, wishing she knew how to approach this more tactfully. 'The thing is, Madelaine thinks you may lose the cosmetics contract.'

'I know. I told you that.'

'Surely you don't want to?'

'Of course I don't want to!'

'Then for the sake of a few drinks, a couple of Chinese meals, no more joints and a few exercise classes, surely it's worth it?'

Jenny stared out into the dusk, then shrugged. 'It's okay for you, Leah. You've handled the pressure magnificently. You don't like alcohol, never touch drugs and could eat chips all day without putting on an ounce. I'm not made like that. I was born to be excessive. Oh, what's the point? It's a vicious circle. I get depressed because I know I'm overweight and drinking too much, so what do I do to drown my sorrows? I eat more and get pissed or stoned. It's all useless!' Jenny burst into tears, stood up from the table and ran into the sitting room, slopping her glass of wine over the patio.

Leah followed her inside and sat beside Jenny on the sofa. She gently put an arm round her shoulders.

'Don't cry, Jenny. I'm sorry I've upset you.'

'Don't be. I know you're only trying to help. And that bastard prince! He's not called me for weeks.' There was a fresh flood of tears. 'Oh, Leah, I just feel so low. Everything was wonderful two years ago. Now I'm in such a mess and I don't know how to start putting it right.'

'Jen, listen to me. You're twenty-three years of age. Most other girls are only beginning their lives and you're talking like yours is over. Don't you realize how lucky you are? You've been blessed with a beautiful face and body, you've made lots of money, been halfway round the world first class and any man would give anything to spend an evening in your company. The pressure's just got to you, that's all. You're strong, Jenny. You can do it, I know you can.'

'I don't know,' sniffed Jenny quietly.

'Well, I do. Remember how you looked after me when I first started? If it hadn't been for you, God knows where I'd have ended up. Now it's my turn. Madelaine's willing to pay for you to go to this health spa in Palm Springs for a week. You at least owe it to yourself to try. If I were you, I'd take up her offer. It certainly can't do any harm.'

Jenny was silent. Then she said, 'You're right. I do owe it to myself. I am going to end up dead if I carry on like this.' She turned and looked at Leah. 'God, you've grown up. However did you get to be so sensible?'

'It must be my Yorkshire blood,' she smiled. 'Now, why don't you ring Madelaine and tell her you'll go?'

'Okay. I'll do it on Monday morning. Jesus, Leah, I'm dreading it. No booze or fags and lettuce leaves for breakfast, lunch and dinner. My idea of hell.'

'Well, I don't think you have a choice. And maybe when you come back feeling wonderful, it might have been worth a little deprivation. And Ranu might think so too.'

'Yes, he hates it when I drink. If I stopped, maybe . . .' Jenny's voice trailed off. She picked up her wine glass and threw the contents into a plant pot beside the sofa.

'To the new me.'

'To the new you,' Leah smiled.

9

EXACTLY A WEEK later, the apartment was vibrating to the throb of music and people were jammed wall to wall.

Jenny was nursing a glass of Coke and smiling through love-filled eyes at her Arab prince. Leah had breathed a sigh of relief when Jenny had called her last Thursday in Mexico to tell her that Ranu was in town, and would be coming to the housewarming on Saturday night. It was just the boost Jenny needed. He had even offered his private jet to fly her to Palm Springs on Monday morning.

Leah was standing in a crowd of people she did not know, mostly models and photographers, artists and designers; the cream of the New York 'in crowd'.

Everyone knew who Leah was and asked her the same set of questions: How was Carlo? Was she really paid half a million for the cosmetic contract with Chaval? How long was she in New York for?

Leah sighed. Maybe it was because she was tired, but she wasn't in the mood for small talk. She wandered out of the sitting room and along the corridor. She went into her bedroom and walked across to her bathroom, wanting some space and a little quiet. She closed the door behind her and stared at her reflection in the mirror.

'The most valuable face in the world.'

That had been one of the headlines last week when the press had got hold of the figure she had been paid for the Chaval contract.

Sometimes she could not reconcile her face with the person she was inside. The first was world famous, the second, well, nobody ever bothered to look. They weren't interested.

Leah propped her face up with her elbows. She thought how lovely it would be to have a day of anonymity, to meet someone who had no idea who she was and treat her accordingly.

The amount of men who asked her out, offered her exotic locations transported by private jets . . . but it wasn't because they liked Leah. It was because they liked 'the face', and the kudos of having her on their arm.

She brushed her hair and wondered if Brett would come. After swinging backwards and forwards all week, she had decided to give Brett the benefit of the doubt. She had left a message with Pat at Cooper Industries, as he had told her to, giving details of the party and address.

Leah realized that she was shirking her duties as hostess, so she reluctantly came out of the bathroom, opened her bedroom door onto the corridor and bumped straight into a tall, dark-haired older man.

'Sorry,' she muttered.

'Don't worry. I was looking for you.'

'Were you?' she answered wearily, not in the mood.

'Yes. My name is Anthony Van Schiele.'

If it was meant to mean something to Leah, it didn't.

'Oh.'

'I believe that you are working for me.'

'Am I?' Leah didn't understand.

'Yes. I own Chaval Cosmetics, among other things.' He was smiling down at her with a twinkle in his eyes.

'Oh dear. I'm so sorry. I had no idea.' Embarrassment was plain on Leah's face.

'Don't worry. Most people who work for me have no idea either. I try and adopt a 'hands off' policy as far as possible. There's nothing worse than a dictatorial new owner, shoving around people who know what they're doing far better than he does. I only acquired the company a few months back.'

Leah was warming to his relaxed attitude, a seemingly rare commodity in New York.

'It's good to meet you, Mr Van Schiele.'

'Likewise. I was wondering, as you are my newest and by far the most expensive acquisition in the past month, if you would allow me to take you to dinner?'

Leah was in no position to refuse. 'Of course.'

'Good. I'll pick you up from here at eight on Wednesday. I have to go now, but I look forward to seeing you then. Good-bye, Miss Thompson.' He bowed formally and walked towards the door. As he pulled it open, Brett stepped in and came towards her.

'Hello, Leah.' He kissed her on both cheeks and offered her the bottle of champagne he was holding. 'Happy housewarming.'

'Thanks, Brett. Come through and I'll get you a drink.'

'Nice place you have here. Almost English,' he smiled as he followed her into the crowded kitchen.

'We like it. Beer?'

'Fine. Some party. Do you know all these people?' Brett whispered in astonishment.

'No,' giggled Leah. 'Unfortunately, they all seem to know me.'

'You do happen to be rather famous. Even my father sounded jealous when I told him I was coming to your party.'

'As you're here and you brought me a bottle of champagne, I shall make an exception and have a glass. We shall toast the British.' Leah yelped as the cork flew off with a loud bang. She suddenly felt as high as a kite and unusually flirtatious.

'To the British,' she toasted.

'To us,' he replied.

They moved through to the sitting room and Brett caught her arm.

'Come and dance. I love this song.'

'Satisfaction' was blaring over the hi-fi and they joined the stamping, shouting mass on the makeshift dance floor in the centre of the room.

'Wow!' As the song ended, Brett picked her up and twirled her round in his arms. 'God, I'm happy,' he said, as he put her down.

'So am I,' Leah smiled.

And she meant it. It was as if she had come alive inside from the moment Brett had walked into the apartment. Her senses were tingling and the world suddenly seemed to be the most extraordinarily lovely place.

A Lionel Richie record came on and slowed down the pace. Brett wrapped his arms around Leah and she nestled into them contentedly.

'Darling, Ranu and I are going to his place. Will you be okay by yourself?'

Leah turned round, irritated at being disturbed. 'Of course. Jenny, this is Brett.'

The two shook hands.

'And this is Ranu, Brett.'

'Hello, Brett, how are you?' Ranu turned to Jenny. 'We know each other already. Brett was six years below me at Eton.'

Brett nodded. 'I fagged for Ranu for a term. He was a hard man to please.'

Although he was joking, Leah could see the obvious dislike in Brett's eyes.

'We must get together and go out to dinner when I'm back from Palm Springs,' said Jenny. ''Bye Brett, 'bye Leah. I'll be back some time tomorrow.' She winked at her friend as Ranu led her out of the sitting room.

'Leah, is Jenny seriously involved with Ranu? He's a first-class pillock with too much money. Everyone disliked him at Eton.'

'I'm afraid so. Don't worry, Jenny can look after herself,' Leah said with a conviction she didn't feel.

For the rest of the evening, Leah played hostess, checking people's drinks and being dragged from group to group to be introduced to the élite of the New York fashion world. Brett tagged along beside her, looking bored. He was feeling incredibly frustrated. It seemed impossible to have two minutes alone with her.

But eventually, the last of the hardened partiers drifted out of the apartment, leaving Leah and Brett standing in the middle of complete devastation.

'Oh God,' groaned Leah, surveying the bottles, glasses and overflowing ashtrays strewn with gay abandon around the sitting room. She collapsed on the sofa. 'I haven't got the energy.'

'Come on. I'll help you. It won't take a minute once we get started.' He pulled her up. 'You'll only have to face it tomorrow morning if you don't do it now.'

For the next hour, the two of them worked hard putting the apartment back together again. The dawn was rising as Leah flopped back down on the sofa.

'Coffee?'

'Mmn. Yes, please.' She closed her eyes.

Brett made two cups of steaming coffee, and sat down on the floor in front of Leah.

'Come on, sleepy. You're far too big for me to carry into the bedroom. Drink this. I'll put the fire on. It's cold in here.'

Leah forced her eyes open and watched Brett lighting the ornamental gas fire. A tremor ran through her as she realized they were alone for the first time.

She sipped the coffee slowly.

'I love the dawn in New York. I've seen it quite a few times in the past week. For some reason, I haven't been able to sleep,' Brett mused as the fire jumped to life. He sat on the big sheepskin rug that Leah had bought that morning and looked out of the balcony windows across the skyline.

They drank their coffee in silence, the sense of anticipation stopping all conversation.

Leah put her empty cup on the floor. As she brought her hand back, Brett caught it and held it tight. He stared hard into her eyes as his face came nearer and he kissed her.

Her mouth opened to him willingly, and his arms locked around her.

As Brett's tongue probed every corner of her mouth, every nerve-ending in her body tingled in ecstasy. She sighed as his mouth travelled down to her neck and he caressed it with his tongue. He pulled her gently down onto the sheepskin rug, and kissed her further, one hand cradling her head, the other exploring the soft curves of her breasts. He propped himself above her as his hand hovered over the buttons of the black camisole top she was wearing.

'May I?' he asked.

Leah nodded shyly, and Brett reverently undid each of the tiny seed-pearl buttons, until the garment fell away to reveal her nakedness.

'Leah, you are so beautiful, too beautiful.' His mouth went to her neck again as his hands covered her breasts. He kissed his way down to her chest, then a warmth suffused Leah as Brett took a nipple in his mouth and sucked it gently. His hands freed, they made their way down to her waist, discovering a concealed zip on the side of her trousers.

Leah lay there, eyes closed, enjoying the new sensations permeating her, but also knowing that she must make a decision. Should she allow this man to take away her innocence? She had guarded it for so long it had become almost sacred.

She suddenly realized why. She had been waiting for him.

Brett must have sensed her thoughts, for he stopped kissing her and looked into her eyes.

'I want, very badly, to make love to you. May I?'

He spoke to her gently, and Leah read the honesty in his eyes.

She nodded, tempted for a second to tell him that he would be the first, but too embarrassed to voice the words.

He kissed her long and hard once more. Leah could feel the new intensity. He knelt upright above her and divested himself of his shirt, trousers and underwear.

Leah watched as a supple, taut body emerged from the garments. Brett unzipped her trousers, and removed them, leaving her naked apart from a pair of silk cami-knickers.

He lay down next to her, and for a second caught a glimpse of fear in her eyes.

'Sweetheart, I won't hurt you, I promise.' He put his arms around her and held her tight. His mouth covered hers and his fingers travelled across her breasts on the journey downwards. He touched her gently through the material, then removed them to reveal a small silken mound.

Leah emitted a gasp as fingers probed inside her, touching her in a place that up to now had elicited no pleasure. It was as if this place was now the core of her, the central pivot which controlled the reactions of the rest of her body. Brett kissed her hard once more, as his fingers probed deeper inside. His thumb flicked over a part of her that responded immediately and sent an involuntary jump through her body.

He released her mouth and knelt above her, his hand travelling down to feel his own hardness. He positioned himself over her and she parted her legs.

As he moved easily inside her, he used his mouth to caress each nipple. Leah's eyes were wide open and she stared into Brett's as he pushed deeper and she gave a small cry.

'I love you, Leah, I've always loved you. I won't hurt you.' Brett's breathing was becoming faster and as the piercing pain inside Leah subsided, she closed her eyes as the pleasure began.

She felt every thrust of him inside her; hard, strong, possessing her completely. That she should be invaded this way, joined together as one with him seemed only natural. A feeling of love filled her. She knew she had always been waiting for him, that no one else could enter her and make her feel complete as this man could.

Physical and emotional feelings locked tightly together into a climax of pure joy, as Brett exploded inside her.

Afterwards, she lay nestled in his arms on the rug in front of the fire, staring up through the windows at the purple glow of dawn.

Leah knew that tonight she had found the key to her future. Brett was the other half of her. He was the missing link to her soul.

Brett felt it too. He had tried to deny it, but as he looked down at her, he knew that loving her was his destiny and would rule his existence from now on.

Perhaps if they had never met . . . deep in their own thoughts, they lay cradled together, knowing with utter certainty that they had just sealed their fate.

10

JENNY FLEW OFF to Palm Springs on Monday and Brett decamped from his fathers' duplex to Leah's apartment.

They spent the evening reminding themselves of the pleasure they had experienced early on Sunday morning and finding it only better than they remembered. Leah was eager to learn how to pleasure him, and found she was able to touch him with her mouth and hands without a shade of embarrassment.

They slept little, and Brett went into the office on Tuesday morning feeling as if he had returned from the moon. His thoughts were distracted, and he was unable to concentrate. As his father talked at him, he found his mind straying to Leah, to her body, her face, the way she had looked as she lay beneath him. He counted the minutes before he was released from the real world to go back to his dream-like existence with Leah.

When he arrived at the door of the apartment, she was there waiting to greet him, hair dripping wet from the bath, beautiful face devoid of make-up.

'I missed you,' he said as he threw his arms around her and drank in her heavenly smell.

Having made love again, Leah padded naked into the kitchen and threw some spaghetti in a pan. Brett showered and then sat at the kitchen table, content to watch her as she expertly prepared a bolognese sauce.

Then they sat down in front of the fire with a bottle of red wine and the pasta.

'Wow, great cook as well. What more can a man ask for?'

Leah giggled. She looked so innocent and vulnerable, sitting there in her robe on the sofa. Brett could hardly believe that this was the same woman whose beauty and sophistication stopped traffic when it was displayed on one of the many bill-boards that were being placed across the length and breadth of America.

'How about I take you out to dinner tomorrow night? I went to the 21 Club with Dad last week and it was excellent.'

Leah's face dropped. 'I can't tomorrow night. I've got to have dinner with Anthony Van Schiele. He owns Chaval.'

A flicker of fear surged through Brett. For the past two days nothing had come between their precious evenings together. The thought of Leah spending an evening with another man made him feel physically sick. But he knew that this was only the beginning of the insecurity he would feel. He would have to learn to deal with it. He was in love with one of the most beautiful women in the world and there was no choice.

'Fine. I understand,' he said with mock indignity.

Leah immediately put down her plate and came to sit on his lap.

302

'I don't want to go, Brett, but I have to.'

'I know you do, darling. I have plenty to catch up on workwise, so I'll spend the evening at home and try and get some sleep.'

Brett felt bereft as he left her at the entrance to the apartment the following morning.

'See you on Thursday. Just remember I love you.'

'And I love you.' She kissed him and climbed into the limousine, waiting to take her to Chaval.

Brett hailed a taxi and rode to work feeling quite ridiculous as tears threatened to fill his eyes at the thought of the next two days.

'Miss Thompson. As always you look quite enchanting.'

Anthony Van Schiele greeted her at the entrance of Delmonico's, and the maitre d' ushered them to the best table in the splendid dining room.

'Can I get you anything to drink?'

'Yes. A bottle of my usual white wine and some mineral water with lots of ice for Miss Thompson.'

Leah was impressed by the fact that Anthony Van Schiele had taken the trouble to discover what she drank.

'Please, call me Leah,' she smiled.

'And you must call me Anthony.'

Leah looked at the man across the table and thought how attractive he was. She would hazard a guess that he was in his early forties, although he looked younger, with his dark brown hair only tinged by grey at the temples. His physique was slim and toned, but his eyes were what gave him his attraction. They were a soft grey, underlined by years of smiling and with a kindness that shone out of them. There was something trustworthy and strong about him.

'So, how is the campaign going? I've seen the posters . . . well, who in New York hasn't?' He twinkled. 'I think they're wonderful and that you are going to earn a great deal of money for our little company.'

Chaval Cosmetics was probably one of the largest and most successful companies of its kind in the world. Leah wanted to laugh at Anthony's choice of description.

'I hope so too. Everything seems to be going well.'

'I trust that marketing vice president of mine is treating you well and not working you too hard?'

'Oh yes. Henry's been most kind.'

'Good. Any complaints, you just give me a call. How are you settling down in New York? Have you been out much?'

'No. To be honest I've been too tired and I was down in Mexico all last week. I have noticed the frenetic pace that this city moves at. It's starting to exhaust me'

'Ah yes. Personally I can't stand it. I find it intimidating and impersonal. I have a house in Southport, Connecticut where the pace is slower and you feel you are breathing real air. Although I must admit that New York seems to be suiting you. You look quite radiant tonight.' Anthony took in Leah's glowing, luminescent skin that would sell so many millions of dollars of Chaval Cosmetics.

In spite of the fact that Leah had been convinced she would have a miserable time, she found that the evening flew by. Anthony treated her with respect and complete decorum, and he also listened with interest to what she had to say. Because of this, she found herself bringing down the usual barrier and telling him things about herself that she usually kept private.

She was amazed when she glanced at her watch in the powder room and noticed that it was getting on for eleven.

'I ordered you a *menthe frappé*. The alcohol content is very small but it refreshes the palate well,' Anthony smiled.

'Thank you.' Leah sat down at the table and took a small sip through her straw. 'So, are you going back to your house in Southport tonight?'

'Yes. I do try to go home every night, unless business keeps me here very late. Then I have an apartment at the top of the Chaval building where I can put my head down for a few hours.'

'I'll bet your wife doesn't see a lot of you,' commented Leah.

'My wife died two years ago, so I'm afraid there is no one at home who misses me,' he answered quietly.

'I'm so sorry, Anthony.'

'Yes. Well, it was a blessed relief. She had been in pain a long time.' He looked off into the distance. 'Sometimes, I still arrive home, expecting her to be there, in her chair by the fire, waiting to greet me. People tell me time heals the pain, and I wait for that to be true.'

A wave of pity for Anthony engulfed Leah as she imagined trying to live life without Brett. Instinctively, she reached across the table and squeezed his hand.

Anthony was touched by her concern. 'I'm sorry, Leah.

I didn't bring you here to depress you. It's interesting, though, isn't it, that others look at rich, successful people like us and only see the outer trappings, which I suppose spell happiness.'

Leah nodded eagerly, finding it refreshing to have found someone who had just voiced the feelings that she herself had.

'I know. Because of my job, no one ever seems to want to take a look at who I am inside. They're only interested in my face, nothing more.'

'I'm interested, Leah,' he said quietly. 'If you ever feel the need to talk, you know where I am. And now it's time to take you home. I can't be responsible for Chaval's most precious commodity arriving for a shoot with bags under her eyes!'

Anthony escorted her from the restaurant. Outside the chauffeur immediately sprang to attention and opened the door of the shiny black limousine. Leah stepped inside and Anthony got in next to her. They drove through the busy streets in companionable silence until they reached her apartment block.

Anthony reached for her hand and kissed it.

'Thank you for a delightful evening. I'd like to do it again sometime.'

To her surprise Leah answered without hesitation. 'Yes, so would I.' She made to get out of the car, but Anthony stopped her.

'You're a real person in a very unreal world. Hold on to that for me, won't you?'

She nodded and stepped out of the car. 'I will. Good-night, Anthony, and thank you.'

As she waited for the lift, Leah thought about the unusual man she had spent the evening with. A peculiar bond had formed between the two of them and Leah knew that she had just made a friend.

11

THE TELEPHONE RANG shrilly through Leah's dream. She forced her eyes open and leaned over to pick up the receiver.

'Hello.'

'*Cara mia.* It is I, Carlo.'

She looked at the luminous dial on the clock.

'Carlo, it's four o'clock in the morning! What are you doing? You know I have to be up at the crack of dawn.'

'*Scusi, cara,* but I could not wait another second to speak to you. I have missed you so much.'

Leah knew that Carlo was waiting to hear that she had missed him too, but the truth was that she'd hardly thought of him since her arrival in New York.

Leah was silent. Carlo continued, 'Are you missing me as I have missed you?'

'Of course, Carlo,' she answered mechanically. An arm was encircling Leah and pulling her back into the warmth of the duvet. When she didn't respond, another arm snaked around her and grabbed hold of a breast.

'Stop it,' she whispered.

'Pardon? Is someone there with you, Leah?'

'No of course not.' Brett subsided next to her.

'Anyway, the show's only three weeks away. We'll see each other then.'

Leah saw Brett open his eyes and frown up at her. 'Look, I've got to go. I want to try and get some more sleep. I've got a big shoot tomorrow.'

'Okay. I understand.' The petulant tone implied that he didn't at all. 'You do miss me, don't you, Leah?'

'Of course, Carlo.'

'I hope that you are behaving and saving yourself all for me. I have spies everywhere that will tell me if you are being a naughty girl.'

'Yes, Carlo. I'll see you in Milan.'

'Yes. I will wait with baited breath until then. *Buona sera, cara.*'

Leah slowly replaced the receiver and lay back against the pillows.

'I presume that was Mr Porselli checking up on his protégée?' said Brett.

'Yes.'

Brett propped himself up on one elbow and stared down at her coldly. 'And what was all that about not being able to wait until you see him in three weeks' time?'

Leah sighed. 'Oh, Brett. Don't be silly. You've got the wrong end of the stick. Carlo was saying that . . .'

'I'm a jealous man, Leah. You and Carlo have been together for a number of years. Is there any truth in the rumours about the two of you?'

'Of course not, Brett.' Leah felt at once irritated and defensive. 'Carlo's been extremely good to me, but there's never been anything physical between us. Never.'

Nor any other man, thought Leah ruefully, wishing she could voice the words. 'I get so angry when the press make up their ridiculous stories. I thought you were above believing all that rubbish they write.'

Brett saw the anger in Leah's eyes. He subsided onto the pillow next to her.

'Okay, okay. I'm sorry. I love you so much, I'm just insecure, that's all.'

'Brett, darling. Please. You have to trust me.' Leah's hand crept under the duvet and found his.

'I love you too. There'll never be anyone else. Ever. Promise.' She squeezed his hand and he snuggled in to her shoulder.

''Night, sweetheart. Sorry.'

Five minutes later, Brett could hear Leah's regular breathing, but sleep would not come so easily for him. The way Leah had talked to Carlo just then . . . he was sure that there had been something between them. He remembered the night of Leah's twenty-first party, when the two of them had danced together. In three weeks' time, Leah would be off to Milan and back into Carlo's clutches. How he'd cope with the thought of them alone together Brett really didn't know.

All thoughts of Carlo were washed away as Brett and Leah spent an idyllic weekend exploring the delights of New York together.

They went skating at Rockefeller Center on Saturday morning, then in the afternoon took a long stroll in Central Park and watched the children play on the carousel. In the evening, Brett took her to Sardi's and they both stared like stage-struck kids as the stars of Broadway sat not inches away from them. Afterwards, they caught a cab back to Brett's father's duplex and sat out on the terrace in the balmy September air sipping coffee.

'This duplex is just beautiful,' said Leah in admiration. 'You must feel like you're slumming it when you come and stay at my place,' she smiled.

'Your apartment has got heart,' shrugged Brett. 'This hasn't.'

Brett persuaded Leah to stay with him at the duplex that night, saying that his father was out of town on business and there would be no embarrassing breakfast meetings for her to endure.

Unfortunately, Brett was wrong, and as the two of them climbed the stairs in their bathrobes to enjoy the superb view over Central Park from the terrace as they ate breakfast, David was already there reading the papers.

Leah stared at Brett's father; David Cooper looked nothing like his son or his sister, Rose. He had blond hair, flecked with grey, a deep tan, and piercing blue eyes that studied Leah with as much interest as she studied him.

'Well, I see we have a guest for breakfast. Leah Thompson, I presume.' He rose to shake her hand and Leah noted that David was slightly smaller than she was, with a firm, stocky body.

Leah held out her hand and David grasped it firmly. 'We've never met, but your face looks awfully familiar,' he joked.

Leah laughed with him, although she had heard that one a thousand times before.

They sat down at the table on the terrace and the maid brought them coffee and croissants. As Brett chatted easily to his father, Leah found herself comparing David Cooper to Anthony Van Schiele. The aura of power he exuded was breathtaking, but just as Anthony Van Schiele was unassuming and rather embarrassed at his vast wealth, David Cooper seemed to wear it like a mantle. Leah felt intimidated by his presence and slightly uncomfortable. She was glad when he stood up from the table, politely said good-bye to Leah and left the two of them alone.

'Sorry about that, Leah. Dad had a change of plans at the last moment,' said Brett, munching a croissant. 'So, what do you think?' Brett glanced casually at a newspaper.

'What do I think of what?'

'Dad, of course.'

'He's not a bit like you,' Leah answered carefully.

'That's what everyone at work says. Most of the staff are petrified of him.'

'I'm not surprised.'

Brett looked at her, his eyes demanding further explanation.

'I mean he just . . . exudes power. He seemed very pleasant, though,' she added.

'He is, once you get to know him. That's one of the reasons I'm glad I've come to work for him. I hardly knew him as a child. He was away so much and my mother always seemed to be frightened of him. I think that fear was passed on to me. But since I've been here in New York, he's seemed different, softer somehow.' Brett shrugged. 'It's probably because I know him a little better now. I really admire what he's done, you know. Built up this huge business from scratch all by himself. So much of the big conglomerates over here are second- or third-hand wealth. What my father's accomplished in thirty-odd years has taken other companies generations. I'm afraid you don't do that by being a sweetie to your employees.'

'Of course not.' Leah was surprised that Brett felt he needed to defend his father.

'Now, what would you like to do today, darling?'

'I don't know. In fact I do. How about taking one of the boats that goes round Manhattan? It looks as if it's going to be a lovely day.'

So they got a cab down to the 42nd Street pier, where they boarded the Circle Line and found themselves a couple of seats at the front of the boat. They enjoyed the cool breeze as the engines rumbled to life and the boat headed out across the river.

They listened to the crackle of the speakers, as the captain gave a running commentary of what they were seeing.

'Wow, look at Ellis Island, and the Statue of Liberty! I've always wanted to come to New York by ship, just to see all this.'

Brett was propped up on his elbows, staring out to sea. 'The immigrant boats used to come in this way, carrying their passengers to a new life in the promised land. I wonder what went through their heads as they saw America for the first time?' he mused. 'I'd love to paint this,' he added quietly.

'Then you must.'

As the boat completed its tour and chugged back towards the jetty, Brett leant over to Leah and took her in his arms.

'Do you ever wish you could hold a moment and the way that you're feeling for ever?'

'Yes.'

'Well, this is one of my moments. I love you, Leah. I've never been happier than the past two weeks. I can't imagine life without you any more.'

Other passengers forgotten, they kissed and held each other until the boat was tied to the jetty and it was time to get off.

'I know where I want to spend the afternoon, if you wouldn't be too bored.' There was a sudden eagerness and a light in Brett's eyes as he thought of it.

'I'm sure I won't. Where?'

'The Museum of Modern Art.'

'Fine. I'd love to go.'

After a light lunch of bagels and cream cheese with smoked salmon, which Leah announced were the most delicious thing she had ever tasted, they left the small delicatessen and decided to brave the subway to take them to the museum.

Leah felt a *frisson* of pleasure as the train rattled through the stations. This was the real New York; the air of tension and danger, the filthy carriage with its smell of sweat, dope and perfume, and its occupants, who lived in the hope of one day joining herself and Brett in their rarefied world of money and comfort.

Leah emerged from the subway feeling as though

314

she'd been on a different planet. As she walked hand in hand with Brett along the street, she was reminded of how much her life had altered in the past few years. And how much she now took for granted. She felt ashamed.

She spent the rest of the afternoon following Brett round the huge collection of priceless paintings in the museum. She listened in awe as he talked knowledgeably about the different styles, periods and movements of the paintings they were witnessing.

On the second floor, Leah studied Van Gogh's *Starry Night*, Picasso's *Les Demoiselles d'Avignon* and Matisse's *Dance*.

Brett seemed to be in a different world, as if something had come alive inside him. Leah knew by the end of the afternoon that Brett had a love and a joy for art that she could only envy and admire, for she herself had no such passion.

'Who is your favourite artist?' asked Leah.

'I can't answer that. I find a painting that I love, that is a pure work of art for its atmosphere, statement and use of colour. Then I'll find another that I can't take my eyes off. I have a soft spot for Manet, Seurat and Degas for the way in which he captured his dancers' vitality and grace so perfectly. I love them all, Leah,' he laughed. 'In some ways I'm glad that I didn't go to art school or choose a fine art course. I don't study paintings from a technical viewpoint because I don't know how. And although all the artists were making visual statements about the world that they lived in, I believe that a painting should be a work of beauty, something that you never cease wanting to look at. If you start to have too much knowledge you can find fault with each one and it takes away the sheer joy of looking at the painting.'

'But you're very knowledgeable. You know so much about all of them.' Leah was holding Brett's hand as they walked out of the museum.

'Oh, I'm no expert,' he sighed.

'You must continue painting, Brett.'

Brett shrugged. 'Maybe. Come on, we'll discuss it over caviar and blinis at the Russian Tea Room. My father said it's a must and we can walk from here.'

Fifteen minutes later they sat on a comfortable red velvet banquette, sipping strong tea. Leah eyed the small pancakes filled with red and black caviar suspiciously.

'Mmn. Wonderful. Try one, Leah.'

'Okay. But I must warn you, I'm a fish and chips merchant myself.'

Brett laughed as Leah bit gingerly into the blini and found she enjoyed the unusual taste.

'Just because you're working for your father doesn't mean you should stop painting. You really do have talent.' Leah was determined not to let the momentum of Brett's enthusiasm at the museum go to waste.

'How do you know I'm talented?'

'Because I watched you when you used to paint up on the moors. It was complete natural ability. If I had a talent like yours . . .' Leah shrugged. 'But I don't. I have no talent at all.'

'What on earth are you talking about, silly? You're one of the most successful models in the world. Surely that takes a little bit of talent,' Brett chastised, mouth full of his fourth blini.

316

Leah sighed. 'No. At least I don't think so. I just happen to have a pretty face and a good body and I wear clothes well. That's not something that comes from inside me, a natural gift for the arts or a superb mathematical brain that can do some good for mankind.'

Brett looked at Leah and mused how she was constantly surprising him. When he had known her that first summer in Yorkshire, he too had fallen in love with her outer packaging and her sweet, gentle nature.

But as he grew closer to her, he was starting to realize that there was so much more to her than her beauty.

'We live in an immediate world, Leah. And the most immediate thing about you is your beauty. You mustn't resent it, because it's part of you and it's brought you success. And, I'd guess, quite a lot of money.'

Leah nodded. 'I know, Brett.' She paused and sighed. 'But sometimes when I'm standing in the same position for an hour or so, I watch the people hurrying around, fiddling with the lights, the camera lens, a stray piece of hair that's out of place. They all care so deeply about it. I mean, one photo. It's hardly going to change the world, is it? It wouldn't really be an earth-shattering disaster if the photo was slightly out of focus. It just seems so false and futile. And there's me, earning all that money for doing nothing, really, when there are people with real talent who are struggling to earn a crust, like the graffiti artist who painted that dragon on the train, or any one of the young actors who work in here as waiters.'

Brett reached for Leah's hand. 'Sweetheart, I understand completely what you're saying. I've lived in a world of luxury and comfort all my life and I've often thought

317

the self-same thing. However, there is an answer to the puzzle, a way that you can reconcile yourself to what you do.'

'And what is that, Brett?'

'Well, you're in a very privileged position. People know you and your face. At present you are an ambassador for a cosmetics company. But in the future, you could use your money and your fame to much better purpose. If you want to do some good for the world, you couldn't be in a better position to do it.'

Leah thought about what Brett was saying. A look of relief crossed her face. 'You're right, Brett. In the future I can do some good. I'd just never thought about it like that. Thank you.'

'For what?'

'For giving me a reason to get up at six in the morning and wear a professional smile on my face for the rest of the day.'

He squeezed her hand. 'Just remember, darling, there are real people around you. And it's wonderful to see that you haven't been sucked in to the hype and false glamour of the world you live in. That's why I love you so much.'

When they arrived back at Leah's apartment, they were greeted at the door by a radiant Jenny, just arrived back from her week in Palm Springs.

'Leah, darling, I've missed you!' Jenny flung her arms round her friend. Then she stepped back. 'How do I look?'

'Absolutely wonderful. Doesn't she, Brett?'

'She sure does,' he smiled.

'Come and sit down and I'll tell you all about it. I've just made some herb tea. Want some?'

Leah sniggered and Jenny gave her a playful punch.

'Okay, okay. I know it sounds weird for your vodka-swigging best mate to be drinking dandelions, but, Leah, I'm converted!' Jenny went to the kitchen, poured some yellow liquid into three mugs and brought them into the sitting room.

'There you go. Try it. It's very good for you.'

Leah raised the cup to her lips and was immediately hit by the familiar, noxious smell. There was a strong memory attached to the smell and, for a moment, Leah felt dizzy and disoriented.

She was back in Megan's kitchen, eleven years of age and terrified.

Leah banged the mug down onto the table beside her, as if to break the spell. The yellow liquid spilled over the edge and formed a puddle around the mug.

'Are you okay, Leah?' Brett was looking at her pale face strangely.

'Yes, I'm fine.'

'It's not that bad Leah, honest,' Jenny giggled. 'Anyway, let me tell you all about the Spa. You have *got* to go. It was absolutely amazing and I feel like a new woman. They've worked out a diet for me and shown me the exercises I have to do to keep the weight down, and I haven't had a drink or a fag since I left New York. I feel fantastic.'

Leah felt a glow of pride for Jenny. She certainly looked one hundred per cent better. Constant exercise had shed the pounds and toned her body back to its old sleekness. Her golden hair was hanging in shiny waves around her shoulders, her skin looked healthy and, most important, her eyes were sparkling with their old zest.

'I'm so pleased, Jenny. Now all you have to do is keep it up.'

'I will, Leah. I have to, don't I?' she said simply.

12

THE TELEPHONE RANG at nine o'clock exactly.

Miranda's heart beat hard against her chest as she picked up the receiver.

'Hello.'

'You are alone?'

He asked that every day.

'Yes.'

'Good. Have you missed me?'

Miranda gritted her teeth.

'Yes.'

'I have also missed you. I am touching myself now while I think about you. Are you doing the same?'

Miranda looked at the hand placed firmly around the neck of her glass of vintage red wine.

'Yes.'

'I do not believe you.'

'I promise I am.' Miranda tried not to let revulsion creep into her voice.

'Ahh, that feels so good. I am stroking it and thinking of being inside you. Put your fingers right inside and imagine it is me. Oh, does that not feel good, Miranda?'

'Yes.' Her voice was little more than a whisper as she concentrated on the silent pictures on the television screen.

'Ahh, I am working myself hard now, I am imagining that I am holding onto your breasts . . . touch your breasts for me, Miranda,' he ordered harshly. 'That feels so good. I am going to come, do it with me . . .' Miranda heard the familiar groan and removed the receiver away from her ear.

'That was so good. Was it good for you too?'

'Yes. Wonderful,' Miranda answered flatly.

'I'm sending my jet to London to collect you on Friday.' Santos' tone had changed completely from a few seconds before. 'Roger will be outside at four o'clock and you will be met at the other end by a limousine.'

'Where am I going?' she asked.

'To the boat. I shall look forward to seeing you for what will be a most enjoyable weekend. Sleep well, Miranda.'

Miranda replaced the receiver slowly. She had come to dread nine o'clock, and as it approached, she would pour herself a large glass of wine and steel herself for Santos' call.

For the first couple of weeks in the flat, he had been sweetness itself. Then the tone of his voice had started to change. He had started urging her to say obscene things to him down the phone. She had tried to protest, but he had shouted at her. Santos frightened Miranda when he was angry, so she'd done as he asked.

Miranda ran a hand through her thick, blonde hair then jumped up from the sofa and went into the bedroom to fetch her case.

She couldn't live like this any more. Things hadn't worked out at all like she had hoped. She'd lived like a princess for the past six weeks, eating sumptuous meals and wearing elegant, expensive clothes. She was chauffeured around in a Rolls and spent afternoons at Harrods increasing her wardrobe or buying gorgeous little dresses that she sent to Chloe in Yorkshire.

But all this she did alone. She saw no one except the hard-faced German housekeeper, Maria, and Roger, the old cockney chauffeur who insisted on following her in and out of every shop she cared to visit. She'd tried to talk to them out of desperation, but Maria could hardly speak any English, and Roger replied to her general chatter in monosyllables.

And she'd started dreaming vividly about Chloe. It was always the same: terrifying; horrifying.

Chloe was running across the moors, a dark figure chasing her, crying and calling, 'Mummee, Mummee! Where are you? Help me!' Miranda would stretch out her arms as the child came nearer, but Chloe would not see her, would run past her. Her screams joined her daughter's as the menacing figure caught up with Chloe, and she stood helplessly watching.

Miranda would be woken by her own sobbing; sweating and shaking uncontrollably.

She'd pace around the flat until the dawn broke, petrified of the darkness, berating herself for the way she had resented Chloe since she'd been born. She'd never shown the child the love and affection she deserved. Chloe had had to find that from others, such as Rose or Mrs Thompson.

323

She wanted to see her child, to make up for the love she had never given. She wanted to wake up in the morning in her own pretty bedroom, in Yorkshire, and hear the curlews crying as they flew across the moors.

Tonight, the homesickness was unbearable. She had to go home. There was no point to all this luxury when she was so terribly lonely and unhappy.

She finished packing her case, called a taxi, and sat tensely on the sofa, waiting for the bell to ring.

The taxi arrived within ten minutes, and she used the stairs so that Maria on the floor below would not hear the lift. With a sigh of relief, she jumped into the back of the car, and thought about how Chloe's face would light up when she arrived home at the farmhouse.

On arrival at King's Cross, she paid the taxi-driver and walked hurriedly to the ticket office. She purchased a first-class seat with one of her credit cards and ran towards the platform from which the train to Leeds was about to depart.

Just as she was handing her ticket to the ticket collector on the gate, a hand was placed on her shoulder.

'Excuse me, miss.'

Miranda turned round to see Roger standing behind her.

The big, burly man was looking at her with menace in his eyes.

'You know I can't let you get on that train, don't you?'

Miranda bit her lip, looking at the guard who was just about to wave his flag and let the train depart. She decided to make a run for it. She wrenched away from Roger's grasp, pushed past the surprised ticket collector and made off down the platform towards the first carriage door. The guard had blown his whistle and the train was starting to move. She caught hold of a handle and swung it open. She put one foot on the step and was just about to swing the other up when big hands forced her back onto the platform and held her as she watched the train snake out of the station. The guard regarded her strangely but assumed it was a lovers' tiff and turned away.

Sobbing pathetically, all fight gone now, Miranda let Roger lead her back to the Rolls. They drove back through the streets in silence until they reached the flat. Roger put on the handbrake and opened the glass panel which he usually kept firmly closed.

'Can I suggest, miss, that you don't try that again? Mr Santos doesn't like that sort of behaviour and I can assure you that you wouldn't get very far.'

'I only wanted to go and see . . .' Miranda stopped herself from saying any more.

'If you want to go anywhere, you know you must ask me to take you. Good-night, miss.'

Roger got out of his seat and held open the door for Miranda. She stepped out wearily, unlocked the front door and went up in the lift to her flat. She dumped her small case in the hall and went to pour herself a large drink from the vast selection in the cabinet. She chose gin and mixed half a glass with some tonic and ice.

Miranda sat on the sofa as she sipped it, large tears dripping down her face.

Tonight she had learned the truth. She had walked in blindly to a situation which was far bigger than she was without even noticing the danger signs. She'd wanted money and luxury so badly that she had never stopped for a moment to think what the price might be.

The price was her freedom. She was a prisoner in a vast amount of wealth, and yet she had nothing. She had even ransomed her own child. And worse, she knew that Santos was not the kind, gentle older man she had assumed him to be. He had an army of spies who worked for him loyally and the kind of power that she could only guess at.

Miranda was scared, very scared. She wanted desperately to run away, but she knew she was trapped.

She sat there for the rest of the evening, swilling the gin down her throat and sinking slowly into oblivion.

When the bell rang next morning, Miranda was still on the sofa. Her head clattering, she staggered to the intercom.

'Hello.'

'It's Ian.'

'Okay.' She pressed the button and a couple of minutes later Ian was standing at the door with a look of concern on his face.

'What happened last night?'

His obvious sympathy made Miranda burst into tears. She sobbed and sobbed and he led her to the sofa, sat her down and waited patiently until she had finished. Then he went to the kitchen and made her a cup of strong black coffee.

'Drink this, and try to calm down.'

'Thanks.'

He sat there silently, watching her. Miranda found his

presence comforting somehow. He was not the kind of man she would have glanced at twice two months ago, with his glasses and his kind, plain face. But now, Ian provided the touch of normality and dependability that was so lacking in her strange life.

'Now, I want you to put your best frock on and I'll take you out to lunch.'

She nodded and retired to the bedroom to shower and change.

'There, you look your pretty self again now,' Ian said kindly. He offered her his arm. 'Come on.'

They went downstairs and Miranda was surprised and pleased to see Ian opening the passenger door of a brand new Rover.

'It's okay. You are allowed. I'm tried and trusted and I thought you'd prefer to go in my car after last night.'

Miranda slipped in, just grateful to be away from that flat and the prying eyes of Roger and Maria.

Ian drove through London in silence, then parked his car down a small cobbled side alley, just off Kensington High Street.

'There's a very good bistro I know along here. I thought we could have a bite to eat and a chat.'

Inside the small restaurant, they sat down at a table in the corner and Ian ordered a bottle of wine.

'Hair of the dog for you, I think. Come on, it'll make you feel better. If you can't beat it, then make it worse. That's what I always say,' he laughed.

Miranda laughed too, which was pleasant.

'Now. I've brought you here because Roger called me to tell me what happened last night and I wanted to talk to you.' Ian's face was serious. 'I don't know how much you know about Mr Santos.'

Miranda shrugged. 'Nothing.'

'Well, that's not surprising. He is certainly not what you would call a high-profile businessman. He could go anywhere in the world and not be recognized. His circle of friends, some of whom you met on board the boat, is small and élite. Most of them have worked for him for a long time and he trusts them. He does not socialize outside this set and it was a rare occurrence that you met him in London at a nightclub. However, his last, er, lady friend had been disposed of and he was on the hunt for a new one. You were it.'

Prey. Hunted, captured, like a helpless fly lured into a spider's web, thought Miranda.

'Does he always treat his . . . lady friends in this way? Like captives?'

Ian looked at her across the table, his eyes soft. He sighed.

'Miranda, I have worked for Santos for over ten years, ever since I came out of school and he gave me a job when I was desperate. He has been a generous employer and I've certainly been a loyal employee. I'm going to break that rule for the next ten minutes because I honestly don't think you realize what you've got yourself into here. Usually, the girls he chooses are professionals; hard, worldly wise and prepared to do anything for a fur coat and a life of luxury. You're not really like that, are you?'

Miranda shook her head. 'I thought I was. I mean, I wanted all those things too. But not like this.'

'Well, I have to tell you that you've got yourself into a hell of a hole. For all Santos' anonymity, he controls one of the most powerful business empires in the world. He has fingers in every pie, although most of the time he'll use a front man to do the negotiating and the other party will not be aware that Santos owns the company. That way, he's managed to collate vast wealth and power across the globe without anybody realizing it.'

'Why does he do that?'

Ian shrugged. 'I've no idea, but it's always been the case. For example, I work for a company in London and only myself and one other director report to Santos. The rest are unaware of the real owner. Strange, I know, but then Santos is a strange man.'

'Ain't that the truth,' breathed Miranda. 'So, am I his only mistress?' she hated using the word, but knew it was the only accurate description.

'Of course I couldn't say for sure, but yes, I believe so. Santos is married and has two grown-up children. His wife is German. I've only met her once. Look, the point is, Miranda, that you mustn't try anything like last night again. You're lucky that Roger told me and I've decided not to tell Santos. Don't do anything to incur his wrath. He's a dangerous man when angry,' Ian said quietly.

A shiver of fear went through Miranda.

'What do you mean?'

'I'm not saying any more, but I don't want to see you get hurt, or your child.' It slipped out before Ian could stop it and he regretted it immediately as he looked at Miranda's horror-stricken face.

'How do you know about Chloe?' Miranda asked, trying to control herself.

'Well, the shopping trips for children's clothes, the phone-calls that Maria has overheard. That's what they're paid such a lot of money by Santos to do and they put two and two together very quickly. Luckily they've told me and not him. I cannot stress to you how important it is that Santos remains unaware of your little girl. It's leverage he'll use if he has to. So, no more phone-calls, letters. You must cut off all contact immediately to protect the both of you.'

Miranda took a few deep breaths to try and calm herself as the fear rose inside her. 'I don't understand why, Ian. Why does he keep me a prisoner? Why does he pay people to spy on me? Why can't I speak to Chloe?' Tears of helplessness sparked in her eyes. This was like some dreadful nightmare.

'Look, I can't say much more. I would be in terrible trouble if Santos found out about what I've told you. He's bought you, and he possesses you. It's the way he is with all his women. If you are good to him and do everything he says, you'll be fine. If not . . .'

The threat hung in the air.

'I'm sorry, Miranda. I don't mean to frighten you. It's terrible that you've become embroiled in all this. But you have and I just had to warn you. I'll do everything I can to help, I promise. Now, shall we order?'

Miranda was shaking her head from side to side in disbelief. 'It's like some dreadful dream. I can't believe this is happening to me.'

The sympathy in Ian's eyes was plain. 'I'm afraid it is. Try not to worry. I'll do my best to look after you.'

Ian tried to lighten the atmosphere for the rest of the lunch, making jokes and telling silly stories. Miranda hardly heard them. She picked at the food on her plate without enthusiasm and was glad when Ian asked for the bill.

She looked out of the window in silence during the journey home.

'I won't come in, as I've work to do. Are you going to be okay?'

'Yes,' she answered in a flat voice.

'I believe you're going off on Friday to join Santos for the weekend.'

'Yes.'

'As I said, just be nice to him. You'll probably have a good time. I'll pop in and see you when you're back. Take care, Miranda.'

'Thanks for lunch.'

Ian watched her as she sadly made her way to the door of her apartment and disappeared inside.

'Poor kid,' he breathed, as he started the engine and drove off down the elegant, tree-lined street.

13

'*BUON GIORNO*, LEAH! You ARE looking radiant, *cara*. It is so good to see you.' Carlo was like an excited little boy as he fussed round Leah, finding her a chair in the crowded salon and ordering one of his assistants to get her a cup of coffee.

Leah looked around the salon and smiled. She couldn't help remembering the morning when Maria Malgasa was the star of the show and Carlo had treated her like a queen. She looked behind and noticed a couple of new, younger faces sitting nervously at the back, as she herself had once done. They were looking at her with awe, and she gave them a friendly smile.

The twice yearly shows were a chance to catch up with the fashion crowd and after her first year, Leah had always enjoyed them immensely. Of course, now she was the star of the September haute couture collection, not just the October ready-to-wear, and photographers were as eager to catch Leah on film as they were Carlo's creations.

But this year, as she listened to Julio go through the running order, she did not feel the same buzz of excitement. Perhaps it was jet lag after the long flight, or more likely that she felt bereft at the thought of being without Brett for the week. And having to face Carlo's smothering attentions after she had become used to life without him.

And this year, Jenny wasn't here. None of the designers had wanted her when Madelaine had suggested her. They wouldn't take her word for it that Jenny was back to her old self. Leah had even gritted her teeth, called Carlo and begged him to give Jenny a chance.

'Even for you, darling, the answer is no. She is *finita*. Washed up, as the Americans say.'

Leah had assured him that Jenny was booze and drug free and looking great, but the fact that her cosmetics contract had been cancelled hadn't helped Jenny's cause. Jenny herself had taken the news relatively coolly when Madelaine had called to tell her.

'It's their loss. There'll be other contracts,' she had shrugged.

Leah had felt awful when Jenny had helped her pack for her trip to Milan, but was grateful that the romance with her prince seemed to be going well. Ranu was taking her on holiday for a few days and Leah was sure that it was the only thing that was keeping her going. She wanted to cry at the amount of work Jenny had put in to her rehabilitation. No one would give her a chance.

'Okay, ladies. Let's set to work,' called Julio.

The spring collection was a huge success, and Carlo had excelled himself this year. Afterwards, the photographers clustered round Leah and Carlo. As always, Carlo insisted on putting his arms tightly around Leah and kissing her. Leah squirmed, but it was too late.

'Is the romance still on between the two of you, Miss Thompson?' one gossip columnist shouted above the throng.

Leah turned away.

'Gentlemen. Enough. Leah, as you know, is shy. We are both tired now,' said Carlo.

'What about the young man you were spotted having dinner with in Sardi's?'

Leah sighed. Someone had caught Leah and Brett leaving Sardi's arm in arm, taken a photo and splashed it across every tabloid in America. 'The model and the millionaire's son,' had run the headlines. Leah had not realized the photo would have reached Italy.

Carlo looked at her oddly, then replied, 'Is it not okay for Miss Thompson to go out with a business associate when she is alone in a new city? Okay, ladies and gentlemen. I think you have enough now. *Scusi.*'

He pulled Leah away from the clutch of photographers. '*Scusa*, I have some people to see, then I wish to take you to dinner.'

Carlo strode away, and Leah knew that she had been issued with an order, not an invitation.

Half an hour later, Carlo came to collect her. They walked outside and Carlo opened the passenger door to his gleaming red Lamborghini.

There was an uncomfortable silence as they drove through the quiet streets of Milan and out into open countryside.

'Where are we going, Carlo?'

'I told you. I'm taking you to dinner.'

Having trusted Carlo completely for years, Leah instinctively knew that something had changed on the night of her twenty-first birthday. The sense of unease inside her grew as they sped further away from Milan.

Carlo turned left through a large pair of wrought-iron gates and up a sweeping drive. He parked the car in front of a large *palazzo*, which was floodlit and looked like a fairytale castle.

'My home,' Carlo said.

Leah could not help but suck in her breath. Carlo was always promising to show her his *palazzo*, but her visits to Milan in the past few years had been busy and she had never managed it.

She got out of the car and followed Carlo up the wide steps to the porticoed front door. As they reached it, the door was opened by a butler.

'Good evening, Luigi.'

'Good evening, sir.'

'Is everything arranged?'

'It is, sir. Follow me.'

Leah followed Carlo and the butler through the exquisite rooms, each one seemingly grander than the last. The high ceilings were delicately painted in pastel shades, depicting religious scenes, and the furniture looked priceless. It reminded Leah more of a museum than a home, and she thought how Brett would appreciate the works of art covering the walls.

At the end of a long marble-floored corridor, lit by countless chandeliers, Luigi opened the double doors and led Carlo and herself into the room.

Leah gasped. She looked up at the ceiling, maybe fifty feet above her. She could barely see the other end of the room, it was so vast.

'The ballroom,' said Carlo. He offered her his arm. 'Come. We will eat.'

The ballroom was completely empty save for one table by the large french windows, which opened onto a large floodlit terrace.

Carlo led her across the great expanse of floor to the table, which was set for dinner.

As they sat down, a waiter appeared from nowhere and opened the champagne resting in an ice bucket. He poured it into two glasses, then went onto the terrace and clicked his fingers. Immediately, the sounds of gentle, classical music floated in from the terrace and Leah saw the string quartet playing outside.

Carlo smiled at Leah's awestruck face. 'See, I told you I was taking you to dinner. It is beautiful here, is it not?'

Leah nodded. 'Yes. It's a fairytale setting.'

Carlo's smile grew larger. 'I am glad you like it. Come. let's have a toast. I know you do not like drinking, but one will not hurt.'

He raised his glass and Leah reluctantly raised hers.

'To us.'

'To us,' she murmured.

The meal that followed was the most sumptuous Leah had ever tasted. Minestrone, Osso Bucco, a shin of veal on a bed of rissotto, delicately spiced with herbs that had been grown on the estate and added in exactly the right amount, and zabaglione for dessert.

Leah threw up her hands in despair when a large selection of cheeses was brought by the waiter and placed on the table.

'Really, Carlo. I can't. I'm going to burst. That was the most delicious meal I have ever tasted. I'm amazed you ever want to eat out when you have a cook like that at home.'

'Yes. Isabella is a wonder. She has been with our family for years. Now, I think it is time we danced.'

The waiter slid back Leah's chair and she stood up. Carlo led her onto the terrace and bowed formally.

'May I have the pleasure?'

Leah nodded and Carlo put his arms around her. They waltzed slowly to the soft music and Leah felt humbled by the beauty of the scene. She only wished that the arms around her were Brett's.

'Oh *cara*, you look more exquisite tonight than I have ever seen you. Your beauty seems to grow with every passing year. Come, I have something to show you.'

Carlo abruptly stopped dancing and escorted her along the terrace and through another set of french windows.

This room was much smaller and almost looked cosy by comparison to the ballroom. Carlo shut the french windows.

'Here. Sit by the fire. The autumn breeze is a little chill.'

Leah sat down in a comfortable red velvet chair and Carlo sat opposite her.

'Would you like a little brandy, *cara*?'

Leah shook her head and watched as Carlo stood up and went to a large, gold inlaid cabinet, on top of which was a selection of heavy, crystal decanters. She noticed that Carlo seemed uncharacteristically nervous. He poured himself a large measure of brandy and threw it back in one. He poured another and brought it back to his chair by the fire.

He stared into the fire, moving his glass round in his hands.

'You are probably wondering why I have asked you here tonight. The past six weeks without you have been unbearable. The separation has confirmed what I have always known. I love you, Leah. I want you to be my wife.'

Carlo took a small black velvet box out of his top pocket, pulled out a shimmering diamond ring and bent down in front of her chair.

'It is only what the fashion world has been expecting. We are meant to be together, you and I. You will live here with me, in the kind of splendour your beauty deserves, and one day you will give me children as beautiful as you.' Carlo took Leah's hand and slipped the ring on her fourth finger.

'Say yes, *cara*, and I will make you the happiest woman alive.'

Leah looked down at the ring on her finger. Suddenly the entire surrealness of the evening hit her and she wanted to laugh.

It was all so perfect. The handsome young prince, proposing to his lady amidst the opulent splendour of his palace. Storybook. The only problem was that she loved another man.

She took a deep breath, and shook her head as she took the exquisite ring off her finger and handed it to him.

'No, Carlo. I can't marry you.'

Carlo looked as though he had been slapped across the face.

'Why not?' His amazement was genuine and Leah realized that not for a second had Carlo contemplated the fact that she might say no.

'Because I'm in love with someone else.'

The amazement turned to horror.

'Who?'

'He's the gentleman you saw me with in the photograph. His name's Brett Cooper and I've known him since I was fifteen.'

'You are telling me that you have been having an affair for all these years, while patient Carlo looked after you, cared for you and never once touched you?' His voice was trembling with anger.

Leah shook her head. 'No, Carlo. I met him again on my twenty-first birthday. He's living in New York and we met up there.'

Carlo stood up and paced around the room.

'*Un momento, per favore!* So this is just a crush. Some little boy who has kept you company while you were lonely in New York. You will get over him, Leah. He cannot offer you what I can, what you deserve. A beautiful home, a title. Do not throw this away. We were made to be together.'

'As a matter of fact, Brett's father is one of the wealthiest men in the world. Not that money matters,' she added. 'Remember, I have my own anyway and I'd love Brett even if he didn't have a penny.'

'After all I've done for you. I made you what you

339

are and now you repay me by fucking some nasty little boy who is still wet behind the ears.' Carlo's voice was rising.

Leah stood up. 'I'm very grateful for everything you've done for me, Carlo. You've been wonderful and I regard you as one of my closest friends. I think I'd better leave now.' She calmly walked towards the door.

'All this time you are acting like the Virgin Mary with me and fucking other men. Well,' Carlo rounded on Leah and she saw the glint of triumph in his eyes, 'it is too late. This afternoon I told the press of our engagement and forthcoming marriage.'

Leah stopped in her tracks. She turned slowly to face Carlo. 'You did what?'

Carlo said nothing, just smiled at her.

'How dare you say that without my permission! Who the hell do you think you are!'

'The man who turned you from a *goffa*, stupid little kid, to the star you are now.'

'Jenny was right. She said you believed that my success is all down to you. But you don't own me, Carlo, no one does. You'd better ring the press tomorrow and tell them there's been a mistake. If you don't, I will.'

'I cannot do that. It will be in all the papers across the world tomorrow morning. *Cara*, please. Let us not argue. I know you love me. You will forget this other boy.' Carlo reached his arms towards Leah but she moved away, trembling with anger.

'Don't touch me, Carlo!'

He followed her and pulled her roughly into his arms. 'I think you owe me a kiss at the very least.' He pressed his lips to hers, trying to prise open her mouth. His hand moved towards her breast.

'Stop it! Stop it!' Leah wriggled free of him, panting. 'As far as I'm concerned, I never want to see you again. Our contract finished at the end of this show and I won't sign another. I want you to call your chauffeur and have him take me back to Milan this instant.'

Carlo's expression changed and his voice softened. '*Cara*, surely you cannot be serious? *Va bene*, maybe I was a little hasty, telling the press before we finalized arrangements ourselves . . .'

'Carlo, for the last time, I do not love you, I do not want to marry you and what you have done is despicable. Call for a car now! Otherwise it will be me who'll be calling the press.'

'Okay, okay.' Carlo rang a bell. 'We will talk tomorrow when you are calmer.'

The butler appeared and Carlo spoke to him in Italian.

'The car is outside.'

'Good-bye, Carlo. I hope for your sake that the damage you have done can be rectified.'

Leah left the room and followed the butler down the long hall, quivering with fury.

On the journey back to Milan she tried to make sense of what Carlo had done. If he was telling the truth, then it was too late to do anything. The story would be in the papers tomorrow morning.

Brett.

Leah bit her lip. She knew how dreadfully insecure he was about her relationship with Carlo already.

The minute she arrived in her room, she put a call

through to Brett's office. Pat said he had just left. She tried the duplex, but only reached the answering machine, so she left a message asking him to call her at the hotel.

She had to try to explain before he saw the papers. Surely he'd understand?

Leah tried to convince herself that he would, but as morning approached, so did the doubt in her heart.

14

'CARLO PORSELLI, THE Italian fashion designer who took the Milan shows by storm this week, yesterday announced his engagement to his muse and top model, Leah Thompson. This is not an unexpected event; the two young lovers have been inseparable for the past four years.

'Miss Thompson spent a romantic evening with Carlo at his *palazzo* on the shores of Lake Como last night to celebrate the forthcoming wedding. She was seen slipping back into her suite at the hotel Principe di Savoia as the dawn was breaking.

'Miss Thompson flies back to New York today to continue her commitments to Chaval Cosmetics, but Carlo assured me that she will return to Milan to live as soon as her contract is up. Congratulations to the both of them!'

Leah studied the photograph of Carlo kissing her outside his salon and sighed. As the taxi taking her to her apartment from Kennedy airport sped through the streets, Leah read the other four articles in further newspapers. They were almost identical, word for word.

'Oh God.' Leah rubbed her forehead in dismay, knowing that there wasn't a hope in hell of Brett not seeing at least one of the papers. She wondered whether she should call her lawyer and sue, but what was the point? The papers had every right to print what Carlo had told them, so she'd have to sue Carlo. By the time she arrived at the entrance to her apartment, Leah's head was spinning.

'Oh no.' Leah let out a sigh of dismay as she saw the paparazzi surging towards her cab.

'Have you set a date yet, Leah?' 'Congratulations, Miss Thompson!' 'What about Brett Cooper, the man who's been escorting you since you arrived in New York?'

'No comment, no comment.' Leah fought through the crowd of journalists and photographers. She needed to gather herself together before she started making a statement. The first thing she wanted to do was to call Brett.

The apartment was silent. Leah flung her suitcase in her bedroom and walked along the hall to Jenny's room.

Her door was shut. Leah tapped on it. 'Jenny, Jenny! I'm back! I need to talk to you.' There was no reply. Leah opened the door and found it in darkness, but could make out the sleeping form in the bed.

'Jenny, wake up. There's a hoard of journalists downstairs and . . .' Leah crept to the bed. Jenny was fast asleep. 'Jen, wake up.' She shook her friend gently. Still no response.

Leah pulled back the curtains and light shone onto the pale, immobile face in the bed.

Then she noticed the vodka bottle lying next to the empty bottle of pills on the duvet.

'Jenny, wake up!' Leah shouted and shook her violently, panic rising in her stomach.

'Oh God.'

Leah picked up the telephone by the bed and dialled emergency.

'Hello. Ambulance, please. Yes.' Leah gave the address. 'I think she may have taken an overdose. Please hurry. I can't wake her . . . what? No, I don't know how long ago. Okay, I'll do that.'

Leah put the receiver down and hurried to get her duvet from her bed. She threw it on top of the inert, lifeless form, then sat holding the cold hand.

'Oh Jenny, please don't be dead. Come on, Leah's here now.' Tears plopped down her face as every second seemed to last forever and all she could do was to sit here uselessly, unable to help. All thoughts of her own problems left her as she prayed that it wasn't too late.

At last she heard the intercom buzz.

She answered and pressed the button and within a minute the paramedics were beside Jenny, testing her vital signs.

'Okay, let's get her to hospital.'

They lifted Jenny onto a stretcher and Leah held the lift as they squeezed in.

'Is she . . .?'

Leah couldn't bring herself to voice the words.

'She's alive, but only just. She's been unconscious for several hours.'

At the doors of the apartment building, the paparazzi closed in as the medics lifted Jenny into the back of the ambulance and immediately attached an oxygen mask.

345

'Who is this, Miss Thompson? Friend of yours?' A journalist pushed her way to the front of the pack.

'You coming with us, miss?' said the medic.

Leah nodded gratefully as she was hauled inside the ambulance and the doors shut.

As soon as they arrived at Lenox Hill, Jenny was taken straight off into emergency, leaving Leah to pace around the deserted waiting room. Tears kept coming to her eyes as she thought of how hard Jenny had tried to pull herself back together again, and how no one had been prepared to give her a chance. Jenny was dying from the pressure of having to be perfect.

Eventually a doctor appeared through the swing doors.

'You are a friend of Jennifer Amory?'

Leah looked up slowly, her face turning ashen. 'Yes,' she whispered.

'Well, Miss Amory is going to be all right. She's in intensive care and will be pretty poorly for the next few days, but she'll pull through.'

'Thank God,' breathed Leah, fresh tears coming to her eyes. 'Was it an overdose?'

The doctor shrugged. 'Yes. Whether it was intended or not we have yet to discover. But whichever doctor prescribed the diet pills we have just pumped out of her stomach should be shot. Mixed with alcohol, they can be lethal. I doubt very much if Miss Amory had eaten anything for the past two days. We found no evidence of that inside her. Was she on a diet, do you know?'

'Yes. But I had no idea the health spa had prescribed her pills.'

'Health spa? Is that what they call them these days?'

346

The doctor raised an eyebrow. 'I'll be telling Miss Amory not to waste her money on such places in the future. The pills these places prescribe are sometimes untested and unsafe. You can't mess around with your metabolism as if it's a second-hand car, you know.'

'Can I see her?'

'Why not? She's sleepy and a little frightened, which is a good sign. Come with me.'

Leah followed the doctor down the corridor and into a small private room.

Jenny was lying in the bed with tubes running from all parts of her body into large monitors. Her eyes were open and they lit up in her pale face when she saw Leah.

'Hello.' Her voice was hoarse and no more than a whisper.

Leah bent over and kissed Jenny's cold cheek, then sat in the chair next to her.

'The doctors say you're going to be just fine,' she smiled.

'I didn't mean to take so many. I . . . I just lost count.'

'Well. No more of those for you in the future. You know what those kind of pills can do to you now,' Leah said gently.

'Yes, but I was so desperate to keep the weight off. I had an important appointment on Monday and I wanted to look my best. Madelaine said it was my last chance and . . .' Tears came to Jenny's eyes and Leah reached for her hand.

'Sshh, I'm going to call Madelaine first thing on Monday morning and we'll get it all sorted out. So don't you worry about that. You just try and get some rest and I'll be back to see you as soon as I can.'

'No!' Jenny grasped her hand. 'I don't want anyone to know. Please, Leah, promise me you won't say a word.'

'Okay, okay. I promise.'

The doctor was beckoning Leah towards the door.

'I have to go now. Try and sleep. Everything's fine. 'Bye, darling.'

Jenny gave a shadow of a smile as Leah kissed her once more, then left the room with the doctor.

'Leave visiting her again until tomorrow. All she needs now is a lot of sleep.'

'She told me that she didn't mean to take so many of those pills just now, so I don't think it was deliberate.'

The doctor shrugged. 'Who knows? Sometimes this kind of thing can be a cry for help. Anyway, we'll make sure our therapist has a good long talk to her before we let her out of here.'

Leah took a cab back to her apartment, feeling cold despite the relative warmth of the late September weather. Her head was reeling from the events of the past twenty-four hours. The journalists had thankfully dispersed. Leah let herself in to the silent apartment. She wearily made her way through to the sitting room where she saw the familiar figure sitting on the sofa.

'Hello, Brett.'

He did not turn to acknowledge her. 'Hope you don't mind. I let myself in with my key. I thought under the circumstances that I'd better return it.'

His voice was flat and cold and his words were slurred. Leah realized he was drunk.

The last thing she felt like was a major confrontation.

She was drained and exhausted.

'Took you some time to get home. Been celebrating the good news, have you?'

'No, Brett. As a matter of fact I've been at the hospital. Jenny, she . . . oh it doesn't matter.' Jenny had sworn her to secrecy. Leah shrugged limply and went to sit in the armchair facing Brett.

'I tried to call you last night and . . .'

'I know. Got your messages. Nice of you to give me prior warning, or was it to ask me to be best man?' Brett spat.

'Look Brett, please. Give me a chance to explain, before you jump to conclusions. I . . .'

'Conclusions! Jesus Christ, Leah! The whole of America knows you were seen slipping back into your hotel room at dawn, having spent a cosy evening alone with Carlo. Are you denying that?'

'No, I . . . but they've got it all wrong. I did go with Carlo to his *palazzo*. He invited me for dinner and I didn't realize what he'd got planned and . . .'

'Ahh, sweet, innocent little Leah, dragged off by big, bad Carlo to his lair. How come it took you until dawn to escape? Was he holding you prisoner or something, or couldn't you be bothered to drag yourself out of his nice warm bed?'

'Enough!' The tone in Leah's voice was that of white-hot anger. 'I am not prepared for you to sit in my apartment and talk to me like this. I'm guilty before I've been tried and you haven't even given me a chance to explain. You're drunk. Brett. I think we'd better discuss this when you've sobered up.'

Brett stood up. 'And wouldn't you be drunk if the girl you loved had lied constantly to you, spent a night with another man, and then announced their engagement to the world? Well, you got what you wanted, Leah. You paid me back well and truly for hurting you when you were younger. I hope it makes you feel good.'

Leah watched Brett lurch towards the door. It was pointless trying to explain further. He was too drunk and irrational to listen. Tears pricked the back of her eyes as she followed him down the hall towards the door.

'Well, good-bye, Leah. It's been nice knowing you. I hope you have many years of happiness with that Italian prick.'

'Brett.' She reached for his arm. 'Go home and when you've calmed down, please call me and give me a chance to explain. And Brett, just remember how I believed you and gave you another chance.'

For a second, Leah saw a flicker of comprehension in Brett's eyes. Then wounded pride and anger returned.

Brett shook his head, turned and wandered unsteadily down the corridor towards the lift.

Leah banged the door shut, fell to her knees and sobbed her heart out. She knew she had lost him again.

Eventually, she dragged herself wearily into her bathroom and took a shower. Feeling a little recovered, she sat on her bed and called the hospital. Jenny was resting comfortably. Leah took the receiver off the hook and crawled inside the cool sheets.

But sleep would not come. Everything was so confused. Carlo, Jenny, Brett . . . Leah gazed at the ceiling and thought how many girls around the world would give anything to be her. Beautiful, successful, rich. But these things came with a very high price. And Leah was unsure whether she was prepared to go on paying it.

15

'WHO WAS THAT?' the pathetic bundle on the sofa asked quietly.

'Anthony Van Schiele. He wants me to go to lunch with him at his house in Southport tomorrow. He's sending a car at twelve. He's probably got cold feet about this Carlo business and thinks I'm about to throw up the contract to become a *principessa*. I'm going to have to go and provide some reassurance. Will you be okay?'

'I'll be fine, Leah, really.'

Leah walked across the room and sat on the edge of the sofa by Jenny's feet. The pale face and skeletal frame hardly resembled the girl she'd once known.

It had been two weeks since Jenny had been let out of hospital. This had coincided with Leah's work for Chaval coming to an end. Leah had cancelled all further assignments and nursed Jenny night and day. But she could not detect any improvement. In fact, if anything, Jenny had deteriorated. She seemed to have lost her fighting spirit and every day seemed to retreat further into herself.

The doctor had warned Leah that depression was one of the symptoms after an overdose, and that the 'cold turkey' of no diet pills nor booze would have a debilitating effect on Jenny's emotional stability.

Having had such a fight to keep her weight down for all these years, Jenny had now gone to the other extreme. Leah was having to force-feed whatever she could get down Jenny's throat. She was nothing more than a bag of bones and Leah thought wryly how pleased Madelaine would be.

'If I make you some of that nice soup I bought yesterday, will you eat a little?'

Jenny shook her head. 'I'm not hungry.'

'But you must eat, darling. You're fading away.'

'Everyone has spent the last few years telling me I need to lose weight and now I'm being nagged to eat.'

'At the moment, you couldn't stand up, let alone show that body of yours to a camera. You have to get your strength back, put on a little weight, and then you'll be in the swing of things again.'

'What's the point, Leah? I know you're trying to be nice, but you know as well as I do that my career's finished. No one will touch me with a barge-pole,' Jenny said sadly.

Leah bit her lip. After her conversation with Madelaine, she knew what Jenny said was true.

'Well, what about Ranu? He'd hate to see you like this.'

'I haven't heard from him since we got back from our holiday. He doesn't know I've been ill and I'd prefer it to stay that way. He doesn't give a damn anyway.'

'Of course he does. I thought you said you had a lovely time in Aspen.'

'We did. But I know he doesn't love me, Leah. Besides,

he wants a renowned, successful sex-symbol to be seen on his arm, not a washed-up old druggie like me.'

'Don't talk like that,' said Leah in despair.

'Why not? It's the truth, isn't it?'

Leah sighed heavily. 'Jenny. You have to pull yourself out of this. You're too young to give up. You have everything to live for. Even if it's not modelling, there are other things in life, things that are much more worthwhile.'

'All I have is my face and my body. I've tried to destroy those and I have nothing left.'

'Jenny, that is the biggest load of crap I have ever heard! That's how photographers and designers make you feel; as though you don't have an inside, and you've fallen for it hook, line and sinker. I'm really disappointed in you.'

'I'm sorry. It's just the way I feel,' shrugged Jenny.

Leah threw up her hands in despair and wandered into the bedroom. It was a glorious autumnal, October Saturday morning and the trees below her window were turning soft shades of yellow and gold.

The beauty of the scene brought tears to Leah's eyes. In some ways, nursing Jenny had at least given her something else to think about. It had given her an excuse to hibernate for the past couple of weeks. She'd needed a break from the camera and the press, to take stock and let some time pass by before she re-emerged into the glare of publicity. She'd discussed the Carlo situation with Madelaine, who had been most anxious when Leah said she might sue.

'No, darling, don't do that. Bad for your image.'

And your agency's, thought Leah wryly.

'Give it some time, let things calm down. The press will be onto another big story next week. In a couple of months, they'll be pairing you off with someone else.'

'But Madelaine, Carlo should not be allowed to get away with this.'

'I know, darling. He's been a very naughty boy, but he did give you your big break.'

Leah sighed. 'Okay. But you can tell him from me that I don't ever want to work for him again and he's not to try to contact me, otherwise I damn well will sue!'

The unfairness of what Carlo had done still ate into Leah day and night. She hated him for destroying her relationship with Brett. Brett had not called, but then, even if he had, it would be impossible to build any trust back into the relationship.

All in all, the past two weeks had been dreadful.

Suddenly, Leah had an urge to get out of the oppressive atmosphere of the apartment. She decided that when she had finished her breakfast, she would shower and then catch a cab to Fifth Avenue. Christmas was just over two months away and she hadn't had a chance to take a leisurely walk round the enticing shops since she arrived.

Having showered, Leah pulled on a pair of Levi's and a sweatshirt and decided that she would treat herself to something new to wear to lunch tomorrow to cheer herself up.

'Hello, Leah. My, you look beautiful. Do come in.'

Leah was overwhelmed by the vast house as she followed Anthony through the simple, but exquisitely furnished rooms. Calling it a 'house' was an understatement.

It was a mansion, set in a large amount of land in Southport, Connecticut.

'What would you like to drink?'

'Mineral water, please.'

Anthony mixed the drinks himself as Leah looked out of the large windows of the elegant sitting room onto the rolling green landscape beyond.

'You have a beautiful home, Anthony,' Leah complimented him.

'Yes, it's a pleasant place to live. We . . . I designed the place myself. Of course, now that my son is only home for the holidays and since my wife . . . well, it's a bit big for just me. I mostly use just the snug and bedroom. I'm thinking of selling it actually.'

'Don't do that. It really is quite beautiful. I can hardly believe I'm only a short distance from New York. The view out here reminds me of where I was brought up.'

'And where was that?'

'Yorkshire.'

'Brontë country. I've read all the great sisters' books.'

'Really? So have I. I'm a huge fan.'

The two of them chatted avidly about their favourite novels, arguing amiably about who was the greatest of the three Brontë sisters.

A maid came through to announce lunch and Leah followed Anthony into the formal dining room, where two places were set at the top of the long table.

'I do feel rather silly having lunch in here, but it's too cold to eat in the conservatory and I thought the kitchen was rather too informal,' Anthony apologized. 'My son and I always use the kitchen.'

'How old is your son?'

'Just turned eighteen. He went off to Yale in September. I have to admit I miss him dreadfully. Anyway, please excuse my indulgence. I have done little else but talk about me and my family since you arrived.'

'Not at all. I'm interested in them,' Leah answered honestly.

After a pleasant lunch, they sat sipping coffee in the sitting room .

'I must ask you, Leah, whether there is any truth to the story in the press that you're going to marry Carlo Porselli and move back to Italy? I know your work for Chaval is finished for now, but obviously we would like to renew your contract for another year.'

Anthony watched as a cloud crossed Leah's eyes.

'No, Anthony. There is not so much as an ounce of truth in it. I was all for sueing, but Madelaine, my agent, advised against it.'

'So the story was total fabrication?'

'No. Carlo told them. I know it sounds bizarre, but Carlo was so sure that I was going to marry him that he didn't bother to consult me first. The irony is that all these years, we've never so much as kissed. Anyway,' Leah shrugged, 'Madelaine tells me it'll blow over. I have to say that I'm still inwardly fuming. As a result of Carlo's actions, a very good relationship with someone that I liked immensely has ended.'

'No chance of a reconciliation?'

'No. But perhaps it's for the best. With my life in the glare of publicity, if it wasn't now, it would be at a later date. I don't think he was mature enough to cope with it.'

'The media can be very dangerous. I have to say that Chaval loves any publicity you get, but not to the detriment of your personal life.'

Leah was on the verge of voicing her disillusionment with her career and life as a whole, when she stopped herself. Anthony might be understanding, but he was paying her a fortune to do a job.

Anthony suggested they went for a walk round the grounds to blow out the cobwebs, and they set off.

Although it was only a quarter to three, the sky was already darkening. They walked through the beautifully kept gardens, Leah admiring the perfection that Anthony's expert gardener had painstakingly created. The space and peace of nature that Leah missed from her childhood in Yorkshire raised her flagging spirits. As she breathed in the clean, fresh air, Leah began to feel some of her natural good spirits return. The city of New York and her problems seemed a very long way away.

'Mmn, I do miss open spaces. I think New York's draining me. It's beautiful here, although to be honest it's a bit too neat for me. I like the ruggedness and wild quality of the moors.'

'I agree, but here there are all sorts of neighbourhood laws about keeping your gardens tidy. The committee would probably have me thrown out if I didn't keep my grass verges under a quarter of an inch,' Anthony smiled. 'You'd like New England. I have a house there. You're welcome to visit any time.'

'Thank you.'

'You were saying that you enjoy the ballet earlier.'

Leah nodded. 'Yes. When I was younger, I wanted to be

a dancer. Mind you, I realized when I reached eleven that I'd have to give up all hope of being a prima ballerina. I wouldn't be able to find a leading man taller then me and they'd have a hernia trying to pick me up,' she giggled.

'You may be tall, but I'll bet you're as light as a feather. Anyway, I'm on the board at the Met and there's a Gala performance in a couple of weeks. Baryshnikov is dancing. Would you like to come?'

Leah's face lit up. 'Oh, I'd love to, Anthony!'

He looked at her seriously. 'Leah, you must only come if you want to. I was thinking this morning that you may have joined me today because technically I'm your employer and you may feel that you can't refuse.' Anthony stopped walking and stared ahead of him. 'I enjoy your company enormously, Leah, but I hope you know that I am not the kind of man to bear a grudge if you don't want to spend your free time with an old fuddy-duddy like me.'

'Anthony, believe me, I made a pact only last week not to do anything that I didn't want to do. Okay, maybe the first time you asked me to dinner I did come because you were my boss, but I enjoy your company too. And there's no way I'm giving up the chance to go to the Met, so I'm afraid you're stuck with me !'

Leah laughed and put her arm companionably through his and they turned and walked back towards the house. Anthony smiled down at her. 'You must have the pick of any man you choose.'

Leah's face clouded. 'No. As a matter of fact, I don't. It's one area of my life that I can't seem to get right, so I decided I'm having nothing more to do with relationships in the future. I'm going to have men as friends, like yourself.'

Anthony couldn't help the small stab of disappointment that sliced through his heart. But he understood the message she was sending him. Maybe in time . . . who knew? Just having her company was better than nothing at all.

Later, as he watched his chauffeur take Leah off back to New York, the feeling of depression that had not left him for nigh on two years since his wife had died lifted.

Anthony went into his snug and poured himself a brandy.

He knew that she wasn't ready at the moment, but he was prepared to wait until she was.

An hour later in New York, Leah felt refreshed and happier than she had for a long time. As the car approached East 70th Street, Leah determined not to let Jenny and her problems get her down.

As Leah stepped out of the lift into the apartment, she could hear the rumble of voices from the sitting room. Her mouth dropped open as she walked in.

Miles Delancey was sitting in the armchair by the fire, and Jenny, far from lying in her usual state of lethargy, was sitting up and talking avidly to him.

'Hi, Leah,' she waved, 'you have a visitor.'

'I can see that. What on earth are you doing here, Miles?'

'Hello, Leah.' He smiled at her and stood up to greet her. 'How are you?'

'Just fine,' she replied. 'Are you on holiday here?'

Miles shook his head. 'No. As a matter of fact I've decided to base myself here permanently from now on.'

'But I saw your spread in *Vogue* last month. You'd just started to make it in England.'

'I know, but the Big Apple is where the fashion scene is really happening these days. I decided that before I became complacent, I should join the migration across the pond and see what happens.'

'Oh.' Miles' reasons didn't ring true, but Leah had no real cause to doubt him.

'Jenny here has made the most entertaining company for the past two hours.' Miles shot her a winning smile and Jenny blushed. Leah had to admit that Miles could be exceptionally charming when he wanted to be.

'Miles has been catching me up on all the British fashion gossip,' said Jenny, looking at him.

Leah could see a light in Jenny's eyes that had been missing for months.

'Yes. Not that there's much to tell. Glass of wine, Leah?'

'No thanks.'

She watched Miles pour himself a glass and felt uncomfortable about the fact that he had made himself so at home in her apartment.

'Miles wants you to introduce him to anyone you might know who could help him get started over here,' said Jenny.

Miles looked into his glass in embarrassment. 'Jenny, really. You shouldn't have put it like that.' He turned to Leah. 'All I said to Jenny was that any help would not be unappreciated. You know what it's like in this business. It's who you know, not what you know.'

Leah felt the same tiny shiver that she had always experienced as Miles looked at her with those penetrating eyes.

'He's also staying in some grotty hotel on the lower east side. I told him that he could come and stay here with us until he sorts himself out, as he's an old friend of yours,' said Jenny.

Leah sighed. Having Miles Delancey stay in her apartment was the last thing she needed. However, he certainly seemed to have provided a tonic for Jenny, and she could hardly say no now.

'Of course. I'm going to take a bath and go to bed. I feel exhausted. Don't keep her up too late, Miles. She's been very sick.'

'I'm fine, Leah. Stop fussing,' said Jenny irritably. 'Sleep tight.' And she turned her attention back to Miles.

Leah went off to her room feeling cross and wondering why she bothered. Her peace of mind had once more been disturbed. Having Miles Delancey at close proximity was something that completely unnerved her.

She climbed into bed and closed her eyes.

She had the dream again . . . a small voice repeating inside her head . . . 'unnatural things, evil things . . . never mess with nature . . . he will find you . . .'.

Leah shot bolt upright, and switched on the light. Her heart was pumping against her chest and her body was drenched in sweat.

Leah knew then, with a terrible certainty, that her childhood nightmare was something to do with Miles.

16

'THANKS FOR LETTING me know, Roddy. Miranda? No, I haven't heard. I'll think about your suggestion and get back to you as soon as I can. Take care, and I'll see you next week. 'Bye.'

Rose put the phone down slowly and gave a long sigh. She felt exhausted and couldn't remember the last time she'd slept properly. She made her way out of her studio and went into the kitchen. She sat at the table and lit up a cigarette, her tenth of the day, and it wasn't even one o'clock.

It was a month since the last telephone call from Miranda. Rose asked herself the same questions over and over as she tried to decide why contact had been so abruptly broken off. The same answers came into her head and Rose shuddered in terror.

She'd been to the police, who had been most unhelpful. Because Miranda was twenty-one, they said that it was within her rights to disappear without telling anyone where she was, that it happened all the time. They'd pointed out that Miranda had contacted Rose from wherever she was at the beginning and there was no reason for

363

the police to assume she was a missing person, or had been the victim of foul play. Rose had left a picture of Miranda with them and asked them to send it down to London just on the off chance that an officer might spot her, but she knew the possibility was one in a million.

Time and again, Rose asked herself if it was her fault that Miranda had gone. She went over and over Miranda's childhood, the numerous arguments and fights coming back to haunt her as clearly as yesterday. Roddy had told her to stop torturing herself, that Rose had taken Miranda in when she was a baby and loved her as if she were her own. That recriminations were pointless. Rose only wished that she had told Miranda how she had fought to adopt her, how she'd moved heaven and earth to become her mother.

And Roddy didn't have to look at the little face that lit up the minute she saw Rose, the pocket version of her missing daughter. Between them, Rose and Mrs Thompson spoilt Chloe rotten, both of them trying to make up for the fact that the child was little better than an orphan, with both parents missing.

Rose ground her cigarette out harshly in the ashtray and decided to listen to the one o'clock news on the radio.

Mrs Thompson came bustling in.

'Put the kettle on, shall I?' Mrs Thompson suggested.

Rose nodded. The two of them listened in silence to the news. It had become routine for Rose to listen to all the news bulletins. The announcer reported that a young woman's body had been found raped and strangled in her bed-sit in King's Cross, north London. Doreen

Thompson watched with sympathy as Rose stiffened and reached again for her cigarettes.

'The woman, yet to be identified, is believed to be in her early twenties. She is a known prostitute who has operated out of King's Cross for the past eighteen months. Other prostitutes in the area have been warned to be on their guard after what police describe as a particularly vicious attack. A full-scale investigation is underway to find the killer.'

Rose breathed a sigh of relief. 'Thank God,' she whispered.

'There you go, Mrs Delancey.' Mrs Thompson placed a steaming mug of coffee in front of her. 'Do you want anything to eat before I pop to the village to collect Chloe from nursery?'

'No thanks, Doreen. I think I'll take this back to my studio.'

'Okay.' Mrs Thompson paused. 'I'm sure she's still alive, Mrs Delancey. She'll come back, I know she will.'

Rose stared out of the kitchen window.

'I hope you're right, Doreen,' she sighed as she stood up. 'Thank you.'

'What for?'

'For all your help with Chloe and for just . . . being here.' Rose shrugged.

'No need for thanks, Mrs Delancey. I worship that little girl. I'll be back in forty-five minutes or so.'

Rose nodded, then wandered back into her studio and gazed at the painting she was working on. She herself could see the fear and frustration that had transmuted from her inner self, through her brush and onto the canvas.

What struck her as so cruel was the fact that her career had taken off since the first exhibition to a point that she had enough commissions to work until she was ninety. Her bank account contained a small fortune and all her money worries were behind her. She was feeling better about herself than she had for a long time. All those years of worrying about Miles, to see him grow into a fine, talented young man, and now it was Miranda who was causing her grey hairs and sleepless nights. Rose stood, picked up a brush and dabbed it into the hookers green and yellow ochre oil paint she had mixed earlier. She made a sweeping stroke on the canvas in front of her and wondered if it was her destiny to live her life without peace.

17

'MIRANDA, WELCOME ABOARD,' Santos smiled and stretched out his hand to help her up the steep steps from the small launch floating alongside the boat.

Miranda grimaced as he kissed her on both cheeks. 'You are looking quite beautiful, as always, my dear. Did you have a pleasant flight?'

'Yes, thank you.'

'Good. Now, I suggest you have a rest in your cabin and join me in the sitting room at eight. We will have drinks, then dinner. Marius will take your luggage down. Follow him.'

Miranda nodded and followed the burly crewman in his smart white uniform down some steps and into the bowels of the vessel. The heavily carpeted corridor had doors on either side and Marius stopped in front of one of them and unlocked it.

Miranda stepped inside, no longer impressed by the splendour and opulence of her cabin. Marius left her alone in the room and Miranda found the drinks cabinet and poured herself a large vodka and tonic. She sat down in one of the comfortable leather armchairs and looked out of the large porthole to the sparkling blue sea beyond.

She took a gulp of her drink. During the flight to Athens, she had decided that the only way she could possibly survive another dreadful weekend with Santos was to get drunk. The thought of him touching her sent a shudder right through her.

He revolted her. That was the only word for it. She had not seen him for over a month and had spent every night before he called terrified in case he would ask her to join him again on his boat. Last time she had spent the weekend with him here, aboard his floating palace with all his lackeys that he called friends, he had behaved outwardly in the same caring manner that he had always shown when she was with him. But later, when they were alone in his cabin together . . . Miranda felt sick at the things he had asked her . . . ordered her to do.

She had returned to London feeling only gratitude to be back safely in her sumptuous prison alone.

She felt as though he had taken her self-worth, that she was no better than some kind of sexual slave without any mind of her own.

During the past four weeks, Miranda had sunk into an abyss of depression. She became obsessed with trying to think of a way to escape from Santos' clutches. She would awake with a new idea, think it through all day with the help of a few double vodkas, then sink back into a terrible black depression as she realized the hopelessness of the situation.

She was trapped. There was no way out. She was doomed to spend the rest of her life like an animal in a cage.

Only Ian's visits had kept her going He had taken to
popping in to see her on a Friday evening, and Miranda
lived for these occasions. It was the only chance she got to
talk to another human being during the whole week. He
bought her books and presents to keep her occupied and
Miranda could see the sympathy for her plight in his eyes.

He'd stay for a drink and tell her about his week. He
would tell her funny anecdotes to try to bring a smile to
her face, but he would have to leave all too soon. He was
usually rushing off home to change for a dinner party, or
to spend the weekend with friends in the country.

'I wish I could come,' she'd sigh sadly.

'So do I,' Ian would answer as he kissed her chastely on
the cheek. 'Take care of yourself, and try not to get too
down. I'm sure things will sort themselves out.'

But Miranda knew that these were empty words of
comfort. Ian knew as well as she that there was little hope
of that.

In the past couple of weeks, she had started to fantasize
about him. She imagined how it would be if things were
different. Ian and she going out to dinner, walking in the
park, going to the theatre. She'd begged him to take her
out again, but Ian had looked wary and said that it might
look suspicious and it was best if he visited her at home.

How could Ian be of any comfort when Miranda knew
that he was just as scared of Santos as she was?

But he was so kind and gentle, unlike any man she had
ever known. Miranda was starting to wonder whether she
had fallen in love with him. She'd never believed in love
in the past, certainly not with someone as outwardly ordi-
nary as Ian. But the feeling she felt when she woke up on

Friday morning, knowing she was going to see him in a few hours' time, was quite magical.

He understood how she felt about Chloe, the guilt she had for resenting the way the baby had forced her to be a mother when she was little more than a child herself. Miranda constantly berated herself for those feelings, wishing that there was some way she could contact Rose and tell her how much she loved her little girl, how sorry she was for ever treating Chloe with anything other than affection and how desperately she missed her.

But she could not. Ian had warned her time and again that Santos would use the child as a weapon. She poured out her pent-up feelings to him and he would sit quietly listening, never judging. And she was finding it harder and harder to watch him leave.

Miranda poured herself another vodka. She listened to the hum of the engines as the boat gently pulled out of Piraeus harbour.

She sat down again and thought how sweet Ian had been last night, popping in on a Thursday evening because he knew she was flying off to the boat for the weekend. When she had heard the key in the lock, she had been sitting on the sofa, tears running down her face, blearing at the television screen.

Ian had fixed her a large vodka and sat down next to her.

'I can't go through with it, Ian. I know what kind of things he'll make me do. Oh God.'

He had taken her gently in his arms and rocked her

while she cried. The feeling of being held by him made the weekend ahead of her even more unbearable.

'I'd rather be dead. Please, don't make me go.'

'Ssh, come on now, Miranda. It won't be that bad. Some women would give anything to be flying off in a private plane to spend a weekend with a billionaire on his boat.'

Miranda looked up at him. 'But I'm not like that. I thought I was. I thought I could handle it. I used to think I'd do anything to live a life of luxury. All I want now is to live in a little house somewhere with my child and have the freedom to take a walk down the street when I want to.'

Miranda also wanted to add, 'and have you with me every day,' but she could not.

'You have to help me, Ian. I can't take much more of this. You know Santos keeps a gun under his pillow?'

'No, but I'm not surprised.'

'I swear, Ian, that if he makes me do anything . . . oh God. I'll kill him.'

Ian looked at the white face and the wild eyes and knew that Miranda was speaking the truth.

'Look. Don't be silly. That wouldn't solve anything. You go through this weekend as best you can, and when you come back next week, we'll have a serious talk. There has to be something we can think of.'

'Do you mean it?' Miranda's face lit up.

Ian nodded. 'Yes. Just promise me you'll be a good girl and do everything Santos tells you.'

Ian had left just before nine, when Santos called, and Miranda had felt able to speak to him normally.

*

And now here she was on the boat, with Ian hundreds of miles away, and at the mercy of Santos.

'Come on, Miranda. Grit your teeth and think of what Ian said. You'll never have to do this again,' she said, and went to take a long, hot bath with another large vodka.

'Good evening, my dear. You are looking beautiful. Here, I have a small gift for you.' Santos handed her a leather-bound box and the ten guests in the salon stopped talking and watched as Miranda opened it.

She drew in her breath as she gazed at the glittering diamond necklace, bracelet and earrings. The set was by far the most impressive that Santos had ever given her. Miranda wondered what it was that Santos would ask for in return later that night.

She stood next to Santos, holding a glass of champagne and listened as he chatted about where they would sail tomorrow. He commanded the complete attention of everyone around him and Miranda suddenly loathed the amount of power that money could bring. The man did not deserve to have his opinions respected just because he was rich. But she had been caught in the trap along with everyone else in the room. And like them, she must pay lip-service.

Miranda's attention was caught by a man who sauntered in through the door and took a glass of champagne from one of the stewards. His face looked familiar and Miranda was struck by how handsome he was. In his late forties, silver creeping in to his blond hair, and a pair of piercing eyes whose glance she knew she'd seen somewhere before.

Santos turned and saw him. 'Ah, David. Welcome. I am so glad you could make it.'

'Yes. I apologize for arriving so late. I was held up in New York on business.' David smiled at Santos. In that moment, Miranda recognized the same revulsion on David's face as she herself experienced every time she looked at Santos.

'Miranda, this is David Cooper. We have become good friends during the time we have been working on a business project in Rio together. I am most honoured that a man as busy as he has graced us this weekend with his company.'

'It's a pleasure to be here,' David smiled.

Miranda held her breath as she stared at David Cooper, waiting for him to recall that he had a niece of the same name whom his son had met during his holidays in Yorkshire years ago.

David did no such thing. He smiled warmly at her and took her hand and kissed it.

'Delighted, Miranda.'

He turned his attention away from her and started chatting to Santos. Miranda let out her breath slowly, trying to still her pumping heart. Thank God Rose and he had had no contact in the past. Miranda realized rationally that there was no reason for David to know who she was. Brett had probably never mentioned her. But it was disturbing standing here under these circumstances knowing that there was a connection between her and this man. If Rose ever discovered that she was a kept mistress who earned her keep through performing lewd sexual acts, why, she may not ever let her see Chloe again.

And yet, there was part of her that wanted to confide in her new-found uncle, to tell him what she was going through and ask for his help. After all, he was by all accounts just as powerful as Santos and the first person she had seen command the same attention from Santos as he commanded from others.

There was a bright flash of light as one of the guests took a photograph of Santos, Miranda and David with his small camera.

'For my photo album,' he smiled insidiously.

'*No!* The voice was a terrifying roar and everyone in the salon jumped. 'Take his camera and dispose of it and the film.' Santos was bright red with anger. One of the crew who had been serving drinks nodded, and removed the camera from the hands of the frightened guest.

'I . . . I'm sorry. Please, I apologize.'

Santos' anger evaporated and he became the charming host once more. 'Do not apologize. It is a rule I adhere to as I am wary of becoming a public figure. I enjoy my anonymity and freedom too much. So. We go into dinner. Miranda, please escort David into the dining room.'

Miranda was studying David Cooper's face. He was staring at Santos with an expression that resembled triumph. He smiled down at her, and offered his arm. They followed Santos through to the dining room. He had taken the arm of a tall, beautiful Eurasian girl.

Miranda was placed between Santos and David at the table, with the Eurasian girl, whose name was Kim, on the other side of Santos. Miranda noted that he seemed to be paying the girl a lot of attention and wondered hopefully if this would let her off the hook tonight.

'Isn't this boat heavenly?' commented David to Miranda with a warm smile. 'I myself have a yacht in the South of France, but it's nothing compared to this and unfortunately I never seem to have time to go cruising. I was thinking of selling it actually, but I think I should wait and see how much I enjoy this weekend.'

'Yes,' said Miranda.

'You're English, aren't you?' David asked, as waiters brought in large tureens of soup.

'Yes.'

'Where do you hail from?'

'Oh, er, London.'

'Really? I'd read your accent as much further up north. But I've spent most of the last twenty-five years in New York, so I've probably lost my ear for the native accents of Britain,' he smiled. 'I love London myself. I spent some of the best years of my life living there. What do you do as a living, Miranda?'

Miranda was nonplussed. Didn't David realize what she was?

'Okay. Let me guess.' David looked at her thoughtfully. 'Well, you're pretty enough to be a model, but something tells me you're not. Do you work for Santos?'

Miranda nodded slowly. She was speaking the truth, after all. She didn't understand why he seemed so interested in her.

'He's a fascinating man, isn't he?'

The words sounded genuine enough and Miranda wondered whether she'd imagined the look of revulsion in his eyes when he'd first arrived in the salon.

'Yes.' Miranda knew that her level of conversation was

not up to the standard of the average ten-year-old, but she couldn't be trapped into making a mistake.

David, however, did not seem to notice. He chatted away to her about his project with Santos and seemed to take it for granted that she knew all about it. Miranda listened and found that she was relaxing a little. He seemed a very nice man, not at all the power-hungry megalomaniac that Brett had hinted he was. He also treated her with an unspoken respect, which restored her self-confidence a little.

After dinner, they went back to the salon and sat drinking liqueurs.

David sat in a chair next to Miranda. He was fascinated by her. She was obviously very young for all her sophisticated outer packaging, and she was also determined to give nothing away about herself. David found this refreshing, as usually once women knew who he was, they would throw themselves at his feet. There was also something vulnerable about her, and he caught a glimpse of fear in her eyes on a couple of occasions when she looked at Santos. She also reminded him distinctly of someone, but he couldn't place who.

He wondered what the set-up was. This girl was surely no whore; she didn't have the world-weariness and jaded quality that marked them out so clearly.

'I think it is time for us all to retire. Tomorrow we will dock at Kos. Breakfast is at eight.' Santos stood up and the evening was immediately at an end for the rest of the occupants of the salon.

'Come, Miranda.' Santos held out his arm. Miranda looked at him, hating him for making it obvious to everyone that she was his possession and would be spending the night with him. She stood up slowly and turned to David.

'Good-night, Mr Cooper.'

David rose, took her hand and kissed it. 'Good-night, Miranda. It's been a pleasure.' He smiled at her somewhat sadly, as she took Santos' outstretched arm and went out of the room.

Santos led her down to his stateroom. 'I think Mr Cooper was quite taken with you, Miranda. Well done. He is an important business colleague and I want him to be kept happy. But now, it is time for us.' He opened the door to the room. The lights were dimmed, but Miranda could see clearly the naked shape of the Eurasian girl lying in the bed.

'I thought you might like some company,' Santos smiled. 'Please, take off your clothes and join Kim in bed while I make us all a night-cap.'

Miranda's heart pounded. Surely Santos wasn't expecting her to . . .

She turned to Santos, desperation on her face. 'Mr Santos, please, I . . .'

Santos gripped her arm in a vice-like hold.

'Miranda. You would not want to upset me by refusing to indulge me in one of my little pleasures, would you?' The words came out of his mouth like melted honey, but the steel in his cold eyes was unmistakable.

'Come here, darling,' purred Kim from the bed.

Santos went over to the drinks cabinet and poured a ready-mixed cocktail into three glasses. Miranda stood, rooted to the spot, fear and disgust coursing through her veins.

'Here, drink this. It'll relax you.' Santos handed her a glass. Miranda took it with a shaking hand and threw the liquid back in one. She had no choice, she knew that. Maybe, if she was drunk, it wouldn't be quite so bad.

'Come, darling, let me help you with your clothes.' Kim had crawled to the bottom of the bed and was tugging at her dress. Miranda let herself be propelled backwards onto the bed and Kim undid the zip of her dress and removed it, revealing the black lace bra and suspenders.

Santos sat in a chair watching intently. Miranda noticed he was massaging his crotch.

'Kiss her,' he ordered Kim.

The darker girl reached for Miranda's lips and pressed her own to them. As her tongue probed Miranda's mouth, a wave of nausea washed over her. She watched as a hand travelled to the swelling half hidden under her bra and covered it completely. Her breast was prised out of the lace cup and Kim's mouth went to her nipple. The room around Miranda started to spin and the whole scene took on a surreal quality, as if it were not really she that was involved, as if her body were someone else's.

'Do the same, Miranda,' ordered Santos. She saw that his trousers were unzipped and he held his erection in his hand.

Like an automaton her head went down to find Kim's nipple. She put it in her mouth and sucked hard. The other girl moaned.

'Wonderful,' said Santos. 'Go down on her, Kim. I want to watch while you lick her.'

Miranda let the other girl push her slowly back onto

the bed, part her legs and climb in between them. Her head felt like lead and her thoughts were woolly. She was just grateful to lie back and close her eyes as the other girl stroked her gently. She felt a tongue probing her and knew that she should be ashamed that the sensation was not unpleasant.

She heard Santos groaning from his chair. 'Climb on top of Miranda so she can please you too,' he ordered.

Miranda found herself looking up into the private orifice of the other girl. It was lowered onto her face. There was a sweet smell emanating from Kim, a feminine, unthreatening smell.

'Lick her, Miranda,' Santos shouted. 'You want to, I know you do.'

Miranda put her tongue inside the other girl and felt a shudder run through her. Her own pleasure was becoming more intense as she felt hands squeeze her breasts and a finger join the tongue working so hard to make her feel good.

The familiar warmth of oncoming orgasm coursed through Miranda. This woman was touching her as only she herself had before, knowing just how to bring her to the peak. She worked hard to do the same for Kim, and could not help but feel more excited as her own tongue produced fragrant juice from the mysterious interior in which her tongue was probing.

Miranda knew she was going to come.

She screamed out in shame and pleasure as wave after wave of the most powerful orgasm she'd ever experienced washed over her.

In the background, she heard Santos bellow in

pleasure. The orifice above her began to contract and she felt Kim go rigid before she too screamed and collapsed onto the bed.

Miranda closed her eyes, swimming in the deep, murky waters of drug-induced drowsiness. Unable to fight them any longer, she let herself sink slowly to the bottom and fell asleep.

18

'ARE YOU OKAY, Leah? You seem awfully quiet lately.' Jenny watched Leah buttering toast in the kitchen as she stood in her dressing-gown holding two mugs of coffee in her hands.

Leah nodded. 'I'm fine, Jenny. I've just been busy, that's all.'

'All work and no play makes Leah a dull girl,' she commented. 'Have you seen Brett recently?' Jenny put the two coffee cups down on the work-top.

Leah had known that Jenny would ask at some point. Although it had been over a month since their relationship had been so abruptly and unpleasantly terminated, Leah had not mentioned Brett's demise to Jenny. In the past couple of weeks she had been up to her eyes with work and Jenny had been out most evenings in the company of Miles. Anyway, it was not something she wished to hold a post-mortem on.

'No. Brett and I are finished, and to be honest, I'd prefer not to talk about it, if you don't mind.'

Jenny looked genuinely upset. 'Oh, Leah. I really thought that you two . . .' Jenny stopped as she saw Leah's face harden. 'Okay, I'm sorry. I won't mention another word.'

'You and Miles seem to be getting on well.' Leah looked at her friend and could hardly believe it was the same girl. She knew that Miles had achieved in two weeks what she had not been able to achieve in months. Jenny's eyes were sparkling, she had put on weight and the colour had returned to her cheeks. Whatever Leah felt about Miles, she was happy that he seemed to have provided the tonic Jenny needed to set her on the road to physical and mental recovery.

Jenny's face lit up and she smiled coyly. 'We are. He's the best thing that's happened to me in ages. I feel a new woman. Isn't he gorgeous, Leah?'

Leah nodded uncertainly. Although Miles had shown nothing but kindness towards Jenny since he'd been at the apartment, her instincts about him would not disappear. She remembered how Miles had seduced her own mother and Rose into believing he was the perfect gentleman.

'I think I'm in love,' Jenny whispered. 'We just get on so well. We've spent more or less every second together, and he keeps telling me how beautiful I am and I'm actually starting to believe him,' she giggled. 'Anyway, I'd better take his coffee to him before it's stone cold. See you later.'

As Jenny lifted the two mugs from the work-top, the sleeve of her satin dressing-gown fell back to her elbow and Leah saw a large purple bruise running round the circumference of Jenny's arm.

'Jenny, how on earth did you bruise your arm so badly?'

Jenny blushed and shook her arm so that the bruise was once more covered by her dressing-gown, slopping coffee over the floor at the same time.

'Oh, I fell yesterday. You know how clumsy I am. I don't think I've got my sea-legs back from being sick. I'm fine, really.'

Leah watched Jenny go out of the room. Something about the shape of the bruise and the way Jenny had blushed when questioned told Leah that her friend was lying.

The following evening, Leah let herself wearily into the flat. It had been another long, hard day, but she was looking forward immensely to the prospect of going to the ballet with Anthony tonight. The flat was quiet and she presumed Miles and Jenny were out. She made herself coffee and took it through to her bedroom. She showered, then dried her hair and tried to decide which gown she would wear tonight. She chose a favourite Lanvin dress, put on a little make-up and slipped into the gown. She tried on a variety of different necklaces, and finding nothing to suit, remembered that Jenny had a tear-drop diamanté necklace that would look perfect. She went out of her bedroom and down the corridor and knocked on Jenny's door, not expecting a reply.

'Leah, I'm busy,' Jenny's voice, unusually harsh, replied from the other side.

'Sorry, but I was wondering if I could borrow your diamanté necklace to wear to the ballet tonight.'

'I've lost it, sorry.'

'But I saw it yesterday on your dressing-table. Can you have a look for me?'

'Please, Leah. Go away. I'm busy.'

Thoughts of vodka bottles and tablets filled Leah's mind. This time she wasn't taking any chances. She tried the door. It was locked.

'Jenny, let me in now, otherwise I'm calling that doctor at the hospital.'

'I'm fine, just leave me alone.'

Leah acknowledged that Jenny did not sound drunk, but God knows what was going on behind that door.

'I mean it. If you don't let me in, I'm calling Lenox Hill now. They told me to if you started acting strangely. Come on, Jenny, open this door.'

'Okay, okay.'

The door opened and Jenny's face appeared, half hidden by the doorframe.

'See? I'm fine.' Jenny held out the diamanté necklace. 'There you are. Enjoy yourself tonight. I'll see you later.' Jenny moved to close the door, but Leah was too quick for her. She pushed the door wider and marched in, looking for evidence. There was none to be seen. Feeling rotten that she'd obviously been mistaken, she turned round to Jenny to apologize.

'Jenny, I'm sorry, I just thought . . . Jesus!'

Jenny was staring at the floor. The right side of her face was bright purple and her eye was half-closed.

'Jenny? What happened? How on earth did you do that?'

Jenny shrugged. 'I did it last night when I went to get a glass of water from the kitchen. I didn't bother to turn the lights on and I tripped over the hall table and fell.'

Leah immediately remembered the screams she had heard, and the bad purple bruise she had seen on Jenny's arm yesterday.

'I don't believe you. Start telling the truth or I'm calling the hospital.'

'Look, Leah. It's none of your damn business and if you don't believe me, I don't care. I am telling the truth. Just stop interfering in my life, will you? It's like having an over-protective mother watching my every move! I can look after myself, thank you.'

Anger rose inside Leah. 'Oh really. And what would have happened if I hadn't come back from Milan and found you? I don't expect to get thanks for looking after you like I have done, but Christ, Jenny! Don't treat me like an idiot! I'm not the enemy, I'm your best friend who loves you and I know that Miles did that to you, didn't he? Didn't he?'

Suddenly Jenny crumpled. Tears came to her eyes and she sank down onto the bed. 'Don't shout at me, Leah, please. I'm sorry I've been ungrateful, but I knew you wouldn't understand. Okay, Miles did get a bit rough last night, but he was so apologetic. He's promised never to do it again.'

'Really? And what about that bruise I saw on your arm yesterday? This is ridiculous, Jenny. Apart from anything else, how can you expect to start working as a model again when you're covered from head to toe with bruises? Miles is leaving here tonight,' Leah said firmly.

'Oh no, please. Don't make him go. He's helped me so much. I just wanted to die before he arrived and he's been so good and kind. I love him, Leah. I need him. And I believe him when he says he won't hurt me again. He just gets a little too passionate, that's all.'

Leah gave a long sigh. She was in a no-win situation. If she told Miles to leave tonight, Jenny would blame her for it and sink back into the black depression of before. If she let him stay, well, she was surely putting Jenny in danger of another kind?

'Please, Leah,' Jenny pleaded, 'I promise it'll never happen again. Give him one more chance. I don't know what I'd do without him.'

Leah went to sit on the bed beside Jenny. 'You say you love him, Jenny. What about Ranu? You were madly in love with him for years and you've only known Miles a couple of weeks. How can you love anybody who tried to hurt you like Miles has done?'

Jenny shrugged. 'He didn't mean it, honestly. He's told me how much he loves me. And he was worried about going for his interview today, that's all. I'm sure that when he gets a job and his green card sorted out, he'll calm down. As for Ranu . . . well, I never felt like this about him.'

Leah could hardly believe the way Jenny was protecting Miles. In her book, for a man to even think about using his physical strength against a woman was heinous crime enough, but to actually do it . . . Leah looked at Jenny, pity in her heart, fear in her mind.

'Okay, Jenny. I'll let him stay. Personally, I think you're crazy to even contemplate having him near you again, but as you said, I'm not your keeper. However, this apartment is in my name, and as your landlady, if that man so much as touches you in anything other than a gentle way again, he's out. No more chances, no more excuses. I'm not happy about it at all, but . . .'

Leah was cut off in mid-sentence as Jenny's arms were flung around her. 'Thank you, Leah. I swear it'll never happen again. I know it looks dreadful, but Miles isn't like that, really.'

'Who's he been to see today?'

'*Vanity Fair*. I gave him the contact and he called and mentioned your name. I hope you don't mind, but I know once he gets started, he'll feel much better.'

The last thing Leah wanted was some brutal maniac who beat up women getting a job on her recommendation, but what could she do? She stood up.

'I've got to go. I'm meeting Anthony at seven and I'm going to be late. For God's sake, look after yourself and inform Miles that from now on, I don't want him to use my name to get him through any more doors, okay?'

Leah left the room, quickly donned the necklace, threw a wrap over her shoulders and went to hail a taxi. She sat in the back feeling frustrated and depressed. First Carlo, then Brett, and now Miles. Why did men seem to use women the way they did? Couldn't Jenny see that Miles couldn't love her if all he wanted to do was to hurt her? That he was using both of them for their contacts and a place to stay in New York. And he was preying on someone who was weak and defenceless.

Leah's current resistance to men went up another few notches as the cab approached the Metropolitan Opera House in Lincoln Center. The cab pulled up, she paid the driver and got out.

Anthony was waiting for her, as arranged, in the bar. He kissed her on both cheeks and sensed that she was uptight.

'Are you okay, Leah? You look disturbed about something. Anything I can help you with?'

Leah shook her head as she took a glass of bucks fizz from him. 'No, I'm fine, really Anthony. And I can't wait to see the ballet. Thank you so much for inviting me.'

As the overture of *Swan Lake* swam softly around the packed auditorium and then Baryshnikov appeared on the huge stage in front of her, Leah relaxed.

Her eyes filled with tears at the end, and she could hardly speak as they left the theatre after ten standing ovations for the brilliance of the famous male dancer.

'That was absolutely wonderful,' Leah sighed. She felt on a high as they walked out of the theatre.

'Hungry, Leah?'

She smiled. 'I can always be persuaded to eat.'

'Then we shall go and find some supper.'

The limousine drove them to the GE Building in Rockefeller Center. Leah followed Anthony inside and up in the lift to the sixty-fifth floor. They entered a spectacular dining room. The aubergine silk walls, green leather chairs and waiters dressed in pastel tails created a thirties' timewarp. A dance band played and the customers sitting round the edge of the dance floor were impeccably dressed.

The maitre d' greeted Anthony warmly and led them to a table by the window. Leah looked down sixty-five giddy floors to the street way below.

'Where is this?'

'The Rainbow Room. One of my favourite haunts. Slightly old-fashioned, like me,' Anthony quipped.

'I love it,' Leah enthused.

Anthony ordered two steak tartare and a bottle of dry white wine. 'Are you sure there's nothing wrong? You've been very quiet tonight,' he asked.

'No, really, there's nothing.'

'You're sure?'

Leah nodded, feeling guilty that Anthony had noticed.

'Okay, Leah, but I hope you've realized by now that I'm your *friend* as well as your boss. Any time you want to talk, feel free. I'll always be there to listen. Actually, I hope you won't think me forward, but I was wondering what you're doing over Christmas?'

'I promised to spend it with Jenny, my flatmate.'

'Oh. Well, you know I told you that I have a house in Vermont?'

'Yes.'

'I'm going up there and my son, Ben, is going to join me. I wondered if you'd like to come along. Jenny would be welcome too. It's a big house and if it snows, it's quite beautiful.'

'Thanks for the offer. I'll speak to Jenny and ask her.'

'Fine.'

An hour and a half later, Anthony dropped Leah at the door of her apartment building. Leah frowned as she got into the lift. Her lovely evening with Anthony had cheered her up, but she wondered what she would find in the flat.

Jenny was in the sitting room, calmly sipping coffee alone.

'Hi, Leah, did you have a good evening?'

'Yes, it was lovely. Where's Miles?'

'In the spare room. Honestly, Leah, he was so repentant. He bought me a huge bunch of flowers and I read him the riot act and told him he wasn't coming back into my bed until I said he could. But the good news is, he got a three-page spread from *Vanity Fair* this afternoon. Isn't that great?'

'Yes,' said Leah insincerely. 'Now, I have a suggestion to put to you. Anthony has invited me to spend Christmas with him and his son in Vermont. I want you to come with me.'

Jenny's face dropped. 'Oh. But what about Miles?'

'Jenny, I wouldn't get a moment's sleep if I thought you were here by yourself with Miles. I'm sure he'll be able to fend for himself for a few days and I really do think a break would do you the world of good. Besides, I think it might be fun. Anthony's a really nice chap.'

'I don't know, Leah. I'll have to ask Miles and . . .'

'I'll make a bargain with you. I'll promise to turn a blind eye to what he's done if you agree to come to Vermont with me. You owe me one, Jenny.'

'Okay, okay,' Jenny sighed. 'Miles won't be happy, though.'

'Tough shit. It's time he realized that you do have a mind of your own. Now, you just watch it. I'm going to bed. See you tomorrow. Good-night.'

'Good-night. Leah?'

'Yes?'

'Thanks. And really, Miles will never hurt me again.'

'As long as you're sure.'

'I am.'

Leah nodded and went to her room, still unconvinced about Miles.

But as she lay in bed, she began to look forward to Christmas. And she had to admit she liked Anthony. In a world full of arrogant, selfish, aggressive males, his gentleness and sensitivity shone out like a beacon.

He gave her hope for the future.

19

MIRANDA HEARD THE key in the lock. She sat deadly still on the sofa, twisting a hanky round her fingers. She listened to the footsteps in the hall, her heart a slow thud against her chest. Every time the key turned, she froze with fear, thinking that it might be him, that he might have decided to fly to London and check up on her.

'Hello, Miranda. I thought I'd pop in and see how your weekend with Santos was and . . .'

She was in his arms before he could finish, sobbing pitifully. He placed his hands on her heaving shoulders, desperate to comfort her, but nervous that she was so close.

'Oh God, Ian, I can't face it any more. The things he made me do, I . . . I can't tell you. I'm so ashamed.'

'Come on now, Miranda. It can't have been as bad as all that. I'll get you a drink.'

But she clung on to him. 'It was, it was. Oh God, I want to die.'

Miranda was becoming hysterical. Ian led her back to the sofa and sat her down. He tried to move away but she would not let him. She looked at him, her eyes pleading with him.

'You have to help me. I can't stand it any longer. I'll kill myself before I'll see him again. Please, Ian. Help me.'

'Okay, okay,' he soothed. 'Let me get us both a drink and we'll talk this through.'

Miranda let go of his arm and he went over to the drinks cabinet and poured them both a stiff Scotch.

'Here. This'll calm you down.'

Miranda took the glass from him and sipped the whisky.

'There now. Nothing's worth getting in this state about, is it?' he smiled gently. 'Tell me exactly what happened.'

After a lot of coaxing and two more whiskys, Ian managed to get the story out of her. The tale of what Santos had made her do filled him with loathing and disgust.

'The worst part was that he drugged me with something, but I can remember everything that happened. I can't go through it again, Ian, really.'

As he put his arms around her, a sudden instinctive feeling that he must protect this girl from the monster that he called his boss surged through him. He'd tried to pretend for the past few months that he was only carrying out his duty by visiting Miranda regularly, but the truth was that he could hardly wait to see her.

Ian could deny it no longer. He had fallen in love with her.

What this meant to his nice, well-paid job and career prospects he was not prepared to think about, but he could not stand by and watch the woman he loved endure that kind of treatment from Santos again. Miranda had no self-respect left and her shame was pitiful to witness.

'Miranda, darling Miranda. Believe me, I'll do all I can to help you.'

'You will?' The look of gratefulness in Miranda's eyes as she stared up at him washed away any doubts he may have had before.

'Yes.'

'Thank you, Ian.' She threw her arms around him and held him tight. She muttered something incoherent over his shoulder.

'Pardon?'

Miranda pulled away from him and looked down at her hands.

'I said, I love you, Ian.' She sighed deeply. 'I don't expect you to feel the same way about me. After all, I am a paid whore and . . .'

This time it was Ian who took Miranda in his arms.

'Oh darling, that doesn't matter. You don't realize what I went through at the weekend, thinking of you with *him*, imagining what he was making you do. I've tried to stop myself feeling like this, but I can't help myself. I love you too.'

He took her face gently in his hands and kissed her lips timidly, knowing that she may back away in fear. But she did not.

He took her there, on the sofa, neither of them able to break away from each other, unleashing all the pent-up emotion and need for physical relief for their feelings.

For the first time in her life, Miranda understood how

sex could be the ultimate manifestation of love, pure and beautiful, and she knew that never again could she let another man use her body as a vessel for his own pleasure.

At last, sated and exhausted, they lay wrapped naked in each other's arms.

Ian stroked her hair gently. 'I promise you, Miranda, whatever happens, I will never allow that man to touch you again.'

The dreadful fear of the past few months had left Miranda for the first time. She lay in his arms, realizing how wrong she had been to think that the world was about power and money. She would give anything at this moment to be in a little house with Ian and Chloe: if they had nothing, they would have love and freedom. And that was all that really mattered.

'I'm going to think of something, darling. I'm going to get you out of here. We'll start again somewhere else, where Santos can't find us and –'

The harsh jangling of the telephone broke into their new-found peace. Both of them jumped and the look of fear appeared on Miranda's face once more.

'Answer it, sweetheart.'

'I can't.' Miranda bit her lip and clung onto him tight. 'Make it stop, Ian, please.'

'Come on, darling. We mustn't let him think anything is wrong. He'll become suspicious and that'll make it even harder for us. You must answer it. I promise you won't have to speak to him for much longer. Go on.' He reached over to the table, picked up the receiver and handed it to her.

'Hello.' The agonized look on Miranda's face was too much for him to bear. Ian stood up, walked out of the room and went along the hallway to the bathroom.

He leant against the door and wondered if Miranda knew what the consequences of their actions tonight could be.

20

LA GUARDIA AIRPORT had a holiday atmosphere, the sense of expectation and smiling faces making a change from the usual harassed businessmen anxious to get to their next meeting.

Leah and Jenny made their way through to their departure gate and settled themselves on the plane.

'Tell me a little about our host. Are you involved?' asked Jenny.

'Absolutely not. Anthony's a very good friend of mine. He really is an awfully nice man. I'm sure you'll like him. His son'll be there too. Anthony lost his wife two years ago and he still misses her dreadfully.'

'So you don't think he's got you down for Christmas under false pretences?'

Leah shook her head. 'No, I'm sure of it,' she smiled.

As the aircraft took off, Leah hardly noticed. She remembered how frightened she'd been when she'd first flown to Milan. Now it had become second nature to her.

After a short stop-over in Boston, the plane touched down at Lebanon Airport. Anthony was waiting there to

397

collect them. His face lit up as he saw them and came to help with their luggage.

'Goodness. You're only staying for a week. It looks like you've come for ever, Leah.'

'That's what comes of being Santa Claus. I haven't brought anything to wear, just lots of presents,' Leah giggled. 'This is my friend Jenny, by the way.'

'Hello, Jenny. Welcome. It's good to meet you.'

'Thanks. It's very nice to be here.'

Jenny and Leah followed Anthony out to his Jeep. The air was bracing but crisp. As they set off, Leah gasped as she looked out of the window.

'It's so pretty here, Anthony. It reminds me of England.'

'Yes. That's why they named it after your little country. I thought you'd like it.'

There was a festive atmosphere as they drove along the country roads to the quaint village of Woodstock, nestling at the foot the mountains. Anthony chatted away about his plans for the week.

'It's anything goes, really. Do what you want, when you want. There is snow up on Suicide Six and plenty more expected, so we can ski if you'd like.'

Leah shook her head. 'I don't ski.'

'Oh, I do!' enthused Jenny. 'I adore it.'

'Great. So does my son, Ben. I don't ski much myself, so it'll be fun for Ben to have company on the slopes. And I thought it might be pleasant to take a walk down to the church in the village tonight to celebrate midnight mass. Here we are, girls. Home sweet home.'

Anthony's house was on the outskirts of Woodstock, set

in rolling countryside with a view of the mountains beyond. It was painted a bright white, with green shutters framing the leaded windows. A porticoed terrace encircled the entire structure, around which Anthony had erected fairy lights.

'Oh, Anthony. It's so . . . picturesque.'

'Yes, it does look rather nice. It was my grandparents' house originally. They lived here for fifty years and when my parents died, it was passed to me.' Anthony dragged the suitcases out of the boot and Leah and Jenny followed him up the steps to the front door. As they entered the large hallway and followed Anthony into the sitting room, Leah felt like a little girl again. A real ten-foot Christmas tree was standing in the corner, lights twinkling and presents piled high underneath. The big fireplace was a blaze of orange warmth and the mantelpiece was covered with holly. The New England Sheraton mahogany sofa was strewn with patchwork cushions and the stripped wood floor was covered in a priceless Sarouk rug.

'Oh, it's like something out of a fairytale,' breathed Jenny.

'It reminds me of a ballet I once saw, *The Nutcracker*. It's beautiful,' Leah smiled.

A young man came bounding down the wide stairs two at a time. He entered the sitting room and smiled warmly at the two girls.

'Now, let me guess. You couldn't possibly be Anthony's son by any vague chance, could you?' smiled Jenny.

'You noticed the resemblance, then? I'd like to say that Dad got his boyish good looks from me, but . . .' the young man shrugged. 'Now who is who? I know both of you are superstars and I shall dine out for the next six months at college on the fact that two of the most beautiful girls in the world came to my house just to spend Christmas with me, but . . .' Ben studied Jenny. 'Are you Leah?'

Jenny shook her head, secretly delighted that Ben thought that she may be the famous model his father employed.

'Shows how well our massive advertising campaign penetrates into the great American public's psyche, doesn't it, girls?' said Anthony, his eyes twinkling. 'Let me introduce you all. This is my son, Ben. Ben, this is Leah, and this is Jenny.'

Ben shook hands with them. 'It's good to meet the both of you.'

'Is either of you hungry? I've made some soup for lunch,' said Anthony.

Jenny nodded. 'I have to admit that I'm starving.'

'Good, good. Ben, why don't you take Jenny and Leah upstairs and show them to their rooms while I organize lunch. Half the fun of coming here is that we do everything ourselves.'

Leah followed Jenny and Ben up the stairs.

'Okay, Leah, you're in here.' Ben led her into a large bedroom.

'If you want to wash up and unpack, we'll see you downstairs for lunch in twenty minutes or so. Come on, Jenny, follow me to your quarters.'

They left the room and Leah immediately went to the window. She wondered whether Anthony had purposely arranged for her to have this room, for the view over the rolling green countryside was quite breathtaking and suddenly made her feel very homesick. She wondered what Mum and Dad were doing. That life seemed like a million years ago.

There was a big window seat and she perched on it, half enjoying the sweet pain of reminiscence. But then Brett leapt into her thoughts, as he always did when she was caught for the smallest moment off guard. She allowed herself to wonder where he was spending Christmas Eve, how he was feeling, whether he was missing her like she was missing him.

But remembering was a pointless exercise. Brett had gone, for ever, and she had to put back on her mantle of protection that allowed her to live life without the constant pain, but yet made everything else that she experienced a little less than it might have been.

She opened her suitcase and started hanging her clothes in the sturdy oak wardrobe. Her bedroom was furnished simply, but she knew that the blue and white check curtains and the big oak bed covered in a matching blue and white patchwork quilt were the best money could buy.

She freshened up in the en suite bathroom, then set off downstairs with her mountain of presents.

'Here, let me help you with those, Mother Christmas,' Anthony laughed as she staggered into the sitting room.

Together, they placed the presents under the tree.

'Fancy helping me in the kitchen?' Anthony was wearing a flowered apron over his jeans.

'Of course. I think you could start a new trend in men's

fashion in that,' Leah said as she followed him into the big comfortable kitchen that reminded her immediately of the one in Rose's farmhouse in Yorkshire. The familiar smells of good home cooking were emanating from the stove and carols were playing softly on the radio. A sense of well-being filled Leah and she started to feel very glad she had come.

'Yes, I do look rather good in this, don't I? I was wondering whether I should wear it to the next shareholders' meeting. Some mulled wine for you, Leah? It's not very alcoholic.'

Leah went to peer inside the big pan simmering on the stove. The smell was delicious.

'Okay, I'll try it.'

'Good. It's my own special recipe. And I have to warn you that Christmas luncheon tomorrow will be prepared, cooked and served by yours truly.' Anthony ladled some mulled wine into two glasses and handed one to Leah. She took a sip and loved the warm, spicy taste.

'This really is very good. And I'm impressed by your proficiency in the kitchen. I'm hopeless.'

'I'm sure you're not. All cooking takes is time, patience and a little imagination. I find it a wonderful way of relaxing. Where are Ben and Jenny? Luncheon is about to be served.'

'I'll call them.'

While Anthony started serving the soup into four bowls and placing them along with freshly baked bread onto the scrubbed pine table, Leah called Jenny and Ben.

They bounced into the kitchen, laughing about something, and Leah was thrilled to see Jenny's eyes sparkling.

'Before we tuck in to what I know is going to be a spectacular repast, I'd just like to say, on behalf of my son and I, how glad we are that the two of you are here. Now, please begin, before the soup gets cold.'

Lunch was a jolly affair, with mulled wine flowing, and the food tasting almost as good as Mrs Thompson's cooking. Jenny and Ben had struck up an immediate rapport and the quick wit that Jenny had been renowned for in the modelling world seemed to have returned to her.

By the time they had finished lunch, it had gone three o'clock and the sky outside was darkening.

'I don't know how anyone else feels, but I could do with a nap before the evening's festivities. It's a tradition that we invite a few long-standing friends in for a drink on Christmas Eve. Then we all walk to the church for midnight mass.'

Everyone agreed that they could use a rest and once the dishwasher had been stacked and turned on, the four of them retired to their rooms.

Leah lay on the comfortable bed, a sense of peace inside her. She could feel herself starting to relax, the cares of the past few months slipping away in this tranquil atmosphere . . .

She awoke to a knock on her door.

'Leah, it's seven. Our guests arrive at eight.'

'Goodness me! I've been asleep for ages. I'll be down in a jiffy. Thanks Anthony.'

'No rush, Leah.'

After a hot bath in the big deep tub, she donned a simple Saint Laurent cocktail dress. All the clothes that Carlo had made her had been confined to boxes in the bottom of her vast wardrobe in her apartment.

She brushed her hair and put on a light make-up.

'Hello, sleeping beauty,' Ben smiled as she came down the stairs into the sitting room. 'We wondered if you'd ever wake up again.'

'I'm sorry, I . . .'

'He's only teasing, Leah. That's what this place does to you. Can I just say how lovely you're looking tonight,' said Anthony.

'Yes, you clean up quite well, don't you Leah?' Jenny teased.

'Ignore her. Sit down and have a drink.' Ben patted the sofa beside him and handed Leah a glass of champagne. 'Dad says you don't drink very much, but it is Christmas.'

'You make me sound so boring, Anthony,' Leah smiled at him across the room. 'I notice you're not wearing your pinny to greet your guests.'

'Er, no. A guy's got to ring the changes and I will be in it all day tomorrow.' Anthony was dressed impeccably in a pair of grey flannels and a beautifully cut blazer.

'This all looks so perfect,' Leah mused. The fire had been stacked high with logs, the wall-lights were on their dimmest setting and the Christmas tree sparkled in the half-light.

There was a knock on the door and Ben jumped up to answer it.

An older couple bearing gifts came down the steps into the sitting room. Anthony kissed them, provided them with a glass of champagne and introduced them to Jenny and Leah.

The doorbell rang again and again. Soon the sitting room was full of people.

Leah chatted to them, enjoying the fact that they all seemed as relaxed and as pleasant as Anthony himself. There was not a business-like New Yorker amongst them and not once did any of them mention her modelling contract, although it was obvious they all knew who she was.

Leah went to the kitchen for a glass of orange juice and Anthony followed her.

'Are you enjoying yourself, Leah? I hope you don't mind my friends coming round. I know how often you have to stand and make small talk at drinks parties.'

'Not at all. I think your friends are lovely. They seem so much more relaxed than other Americans I've met. More real,' she shrugged.

'Yes. Although it might surprise you to know that most of them have large businesses based in New York. But they all come here for Christmas and it's an unspoken rule that no one talks "shop" when we're here. Bill, who we were speaking to before, he's the head of a big electronics company, and Andy runs a PR firm in Manhattan.'

'I'm amazed,' said Leah genuinely.

'Well, I'm glad you're enjoying it. We'll all set off for church in a few minutes, although you don't have to come if you don't want to.'

'I'd love to come. I haven't been to midnight mass for years.'

'Great. I'm so happy you and Jenny are here. It's made it feel . . . well, almost like a family again.'

'Thank you for having us.'

'Come on, you'd better find your coat. It's freezing out there and the forecast said to expect snow.'

Leah felt as though she was in a time-warp as she entered the small village church, lit by candles and with the choir in their traditional robes. She had done this every year with her family in Oxenhope.

Everyone sang their heart out on the familiar carols, and Leah went forward with Anthony to receive communion. She looked at his head bowed next to her at the altar and felt a wave of affection run through her.

When they came out of the church, tiny flakelets of snow were starting to fall.

Everyone drew in their breath at the perfection of the scene. They kissed each other and went on their separate ways with cries of 'Merry Christmas'.

Anthony offered Leah his arm.

'It may look lovely, but snow on ice can be lethal.'

Leah took his arm and they set off with Jenny and Ben following behind.

'I have to say that this is my favourite night. And this place never fails to provide the perfect setting.'

'I haven't felt as Christmassy as this for years,' agreed Leah.

'You poor old world-weary thing, you. How old did you say you were? Fifty?' Anthony smiled down at her.

Leah looked terribly serious.

'I was only joking, Leah, really,' said Anthony, studying her face with concern.

'I know. But you're right. I'm twenty-one and sometimes I do think like I'm fifty. Do you realize that I'm only three years older than Ben?'

'It has crossed my mind, although it's hard to believe. You've just led such different types of lives. I don't think you're any the worse for it as long as you acknowledge your maturity the way you just have.'

They had reached the front of the house and Anthony took her hand and pulled her up the rapidly whitening path. 'Come on, let's get inside by the fire and thaw out.'

The four of them sat near the warmth of the fire, drinking cocoa.

'You realize that when you wake up tomorrow, the outside world will be completely white. We could be cut off for days. It has been known,' remarked Ben.

'Well, I for one wouldn't mind,' Jenny replied. 'It's heaven here. I'm off to bed, if no one minds, otherwise Santa will see we're still awake and won't come and deliver any presents.'

'If he does drop down the chimney, he ain't half gonna have a hot ass!' smirked Ben.

'Thank you, son, for that festive comment. We all like to believe in fantasy, however old we are.'

'Anytime, Dad. I'm going to take a leaf out of Jenny's book and hit the sack, just in case Santa does come a-calling. 'Night, you guys, and Merry Christmas,' Ben smiled and followed Jenny up the stairs.

Anthony checked his watch. 'A quarter to two. Enough hours into Christmas day to open my special bottle of port.'

He stood up and went to the drinks cabinet. He came back and filled two glasses.

'Not for me, Anthony.'

407

'As a matter of fact, it's not for you anyway.' He placed the glass on the hearth of the fire. 'It's for our merry friend, just in case he should pop down the chimney to visit us. We have a glass of port together every year. Cheers.' Anthony raised his glass to the chimney and sipped the ruby liquid. 'I have to be up at the crack of dawn to check the turkey. I put it on low the minute we arrived back from church. It's an absolute monster and it should just be cooked by lunchtime. The rest of you can sleep in until eleven if you want, when breakfast will be served. Please, if you're tired, feel free to go to bed. I always stay up into the small hours on this special night.'

Leah did not feel in the least bit tired. She just felt wonderfully relaxed and peaceful. She stared into the fire and thought how good it was to be with a man whom she did not find in the least bit threatening, and with whom she could be herself.

'It's sad, isn't it, how we all grow up and stop believing in magic,' she remarked.

'Yes,' said Anthony slowly. 'But there is magic all around us. As we grow up, our minds just become too cluttered with practical thoughts and we lose touch with it. That's why nights like tonight are special. It's time out from the real world. Time to dream and recapture our lost innocence. When I'm here, I remember that the world is a wonderful place, full of beauty. But as you grow up, you have to search harder for that beauty. It's there, but it's hidden.'

Leah nodded in agreement and once more felt a glow of genuine affection for this deep, sensitive man.

They sat by the fire together in companionable silence.

'Right, as I'm only going to get a couple of hours' sleep before I come on duty, I think I ought to go to bed.'

'Mmn.' Leah stretched. 'I feel so relaxed. Couldn't I just curl up by the fire like a cat and go to sleep here?'

'Anything you want, Leah, but you may be a little more comfortable in a bed.'

'You're right.' Leah moved reluctantly and stood up. Anthony did the same.

'Good-night, Anthony, and thank you for such a lovely day.' She reached up and kissed him on the cheek.

'Don't thank me, Leah. I can't tell you what it means to me that you're here.' He took her hand in his and kissed it.

She smiled, then walked slowly towards the stairs. She paused on the first step. 'Merry Christmas. Anthony.'

'Merry Christmas, Leah.' He watched her lithe, perfect body move gracefully up the stairs, than bent down to grasp the extra glass of port. He drank it slowly, savouring the taste and thinking about Leah.

She was an unusual woman. Under that perfect exterior, she had such maturity and depth. He wondered whether she knew that their previous conversation held such relevance for his feelings towards her. He had searched and had indeed found hidden beauty.

21

LEAH WOKE UP six days later with a feeling of foreboding. The thought of going back to New York later today was anathema to her relaxed system.

She could hardly believe how wonderful the past few days had been. No stress, no problems, just good company, a lot of great food and, most important of all, no timetable. She had been able to get up when she liked, eat when she was hungry and sleep when she was tired.

Anthony had made the most cordial host, always full of ideas for things to do, but assuring Leah that if she wanted to lie by the fire all day eating mince pies and reading a novel,then that was fine too. And in fact, while the weather had been so bad, that was how the two of them had wiled away the hours. Jenny and Ben had struck up a great friendship and were usually out before Leah was up, heading for the ski slopes. They would return around four, ready to take on Leah and Anthony in a massive snowball fight.

It warmed Leah's heart to see the way Jenny had blossomed and thought how much good the break seemed to have done her too. She wondered if Jenny and Ben were having an affair, and hoped that this meant Miles was out of the picture, but Jenny and Ben's relationship seemed to be that of great buddies rather than anything physical.

The four of them had uproarious dinners in the evening, drinking too much wine and laughing. Then they would spend the rest of the evening playing one of the many board games that Anthony had at the house for long, snowy evenings. Jenny and Ben would usually disappear off to bed early in preparation for another day on the slopes. Anthony and Leah would settle down in front of the fire for a nightcap and a chat, which had become routine since Christmas Eve.

As she took her clothes from the wardrobe and started packing them into her suitcase, she knew she would miss his constant company when she got back to New York. She had spent some time mulling over whether she was attracted to him and decided that yes, she was. Not in the all-consuming passionate way that she had been for Brett, but in a calmer, perhaps more mature way.

She had little idea how Anthony felt for her. He had certainly never given the slightest indication that he regarded her as anything other than a very good friend, which, under her present circumstances, was all she wanted.

But as she walked down to breakfast, she felt sad that their holiday together was over.

'Good morning. It's pancakes and maple syrup to set you up for the journey back to the city.' Anthony placed a plate piled high with calories in front of her. For a change, Leah did not feel hungry.

'Don't remind me,' she moaned. 'I have this big ball

tomorrow for New Year's Eve that Chaval want me to attend.'

Anthony sat down and began to make inroads into his plate of pancakes.

'I know. I'm going too. We could both play hookey and stay here instead.'

'Don't tempt me. I love it here. The thought of New York fills me with horror.'

'What did I tell you? I gave you three months to become sick of the place and you have.'

'Well, Anthony, you shouldn't have brought me here. I could quite happily stay here for ever reading books and eating chocolate beside the fire. You're so lucky to have this place.'

'I know. I haven't used it half as much as it deserves, but this year, as one of my resolutions, I'm going to make an effort to come here regularly. After all, it's no distance from New York. You're welcome to come with me any time you want.'

'Thanks. That makes me feel a little better. Where are Jenny and Ben?'

'Out having a sledging race. They've been like kids ever since we got here.'

'I think it's great. Jenny has had such a rough time recently and it's been good to see her smiling again. When are you going back to New York?'

'Tomorrow. I'll spend this evening clearing the place up and catch a flight mid-morning. Do you want me to pick you up before the ball tomorrow night?'

'That would be lovely. I hate going to these things by myself, and at least I'll be arriving with the president of the company,' she quipped. The employer-employee situation had generated a series of running jokes all over the holiday period.

'I must say that it has been a pleasure having you here, Leah. As I said, any time.'

'Thanks, Anthony. Now I suppose I'd better go and get on with my packing.'

Three hours later there were sad good-byes at the airport. Jenny and Ben seemed heartbroken to be leaving each other.

'God,' sighed Anthony. 'It's like when you were a kid and had to say good-bye to your best buddy because you were going off to school.'

Ben smiled and turned to kiss Leah good-bye. 'It's great to meet you. Thank you for coming here. You're so good for Dad. Take care of yourself.'

The last call for their flight came over the Tannoy and Leah and Jenny waved good-bye as they hurried to their departure gate.

The flight took off on time and Leah looked sadly out of the window as they left the snow-covered countryside far below and headed for New York.

'Well, I have to say that that was the best Christmas I have ever had,' said Jenny.

'Me too,' said Leah. 'Come on then, spill the beans. When's the wedding?'

'I think I should be the one asking you that, Leah,' Jenny said slyly. 'Honestly, it wasn't like that at all. Ben's the brother I've never had. We just got on so well. It was wonderful to be with a man I really liked without the complications of sex. Ben has a serious girlfriend at college and I have Miles.'

Leah's heart sank. 'Oh.'

'I can't wait to see him. And anyway, what about you? Anthony is charming. I can't believe he's the boss of such a big company. He's so modest. And boy, is he in love with you.'

Leah swung to face Jenny. 'I don't think he is, you know. It's the same as you and Ben. We just enjoy each other's company. It's odd really, because there's a twenty-year age-gap, but we just click.'

'How do you feel about him?'

'I like him enormously.'

'But you don't fancy him?'

Leah paused. She didn't want to analyse what she felt for Anthony for fear she might spoil it. 'I don't know.'

Jenny shrugged. 'Leah, if I had a lovely man like that who so obviously adored me, I'd never let him go. You two are good together. Very good. Don't be too hasty, will you?'

Leah looked at Jenny. She shook her head slowly.

'I won't.'

22

MIRANDA HEARD THE knock on the door and rushed to greet Ian. He picked her up in his arms.

'Happy New Year, my love,' he whispered.

'And to you.' Miranda nestled in his arms, so happy that the interminable hours of the past week were over and Ian was here, holding her.

Ian put her down. 'Come on, let's go through to the sitting room. I have some presents for you.' He put an arm round her.

Ian was immediately hit with guilt and sorrow as he saw the small Christmas tree that Miranda had erected. She rushed to collect the three presents that were underneath it.

'For you,' she said excitedly.

'Oh darling, I feel so dreadful that I had to leave you alone over Christmas. We just couldn't afford Santos smelling a rat, that's all. You know I missed you dreadfully? I spent every day counting the hours until it was over.'

'So did I,' Miranda breathed. 'Thank God for television. I've watched everything from *Sesame Street* to *The Guns of Navarone.*'

Miranda did not tell him how she had spent Christmas Day in a haze of tears and alcohol, thinking of what Rose and Chloe were doing in Yorkshire. Only the fact that Ian would be back from his family on New Year's Day had pulled her through.

'But the best Christmas present of all is, guess what?' Her eyes sparkled.

'What?'

'Well, Maria came to see me yesterday to tell me that she was going back to Germany for a week to see her family. She went off yesterday evening and won't be back until next Tuesday. So, you could stay here tonight if you want. There are no spies.'

Ian already knew, for Maria herself had telephoned him three weeks ago. This had given him time and the perfect opportunity to put his plans into action. He pulled Miranda close and hugged her. 'Of course I want to.'

'There's champagne on ice. I thought we'd have our own Christmas and New Year together.'

'Well, let's have a glass of champagne and we can open the presents.'

'Yes,' said Miranda excitedly. She held him close again, as if unable to lose touch with him for a minute in case he disappeared.

'Go on, silly, get the champagne. I've got a surprise for you.'

Miranda jumped up and went into the kitchen. She removed the champagne, the best and most expensive she could find, and found two glasses. She went back into the sitting room and Ian popped the cork and poured it into the flutes.

'Here's to us,' said Miranda.

'Yes. I promise you, Miranda, that I will do anything I can to make this New Year better than last.'

Then they got down to the serious business of opening presents. Miranda had gone wild on one of her credit cards, finding it a huge pleasure to spend Santos' money on Ian. It was the only way she could think of defying him.

'My goodness, Miranda, these are all fantastic.' Ian was overwhelmed by the Cartier watch, the Dunhill cufflinks and expensive aftershave.

'Well, you know it's Santos' money, but I did spend hours choosing everything. I wanted to get the watch engraved but, as usual, Roger was lurking in a dark corner watching my every move.'

Ian leaned over and kissed her. 'Thank you, darling. They're all wonderful. Now, it's time to open yours.'

Ian handed her a slim envelope, wrapped in pretty paper and tied in a bow.

Miranda opened it like an excited child. When she saw the contents, tears filled her eyes and she could hardly speak.

'Oh Ian, I . . .' She studied the tickets carefully. Two flights to Hong Kong booked in the names of 'Mr and Mrs Devonshire'. There was also a marriage licence in the same names.

'Oh Ian . . . are you asking me to . . .?'

'Yes, my love. To marry me, to run away and start afresh together where Santos can't find us. I've got everything lined up. We get married in a registry office, then catch a taxi straight to Heathrow. We board a plane that afternoon which will take us to Hong Kong. I've a friend in business over there who's offered me a job. I'm afraid I won't be keeping you in the lap of luxury, like you're used to, but we'll be free and far away from Santos. We have to do it this week because Maria's absence will make it that much easier for us. And I also know that Santos is on his annual Christmas break with his wife and children. He's on his boat until January the tenth, so by the time he gets back, we'll be long gone.'

'But Ian, I'll need a passport and . . .'

'Hush, Miranda. Tomorrow morning, Roger will be busy helping me at the office. What I want you to do first thing is to go out and have your hair dyed a darker colour. Then I want you to have some passport photos taken. I'll call round for them tomorrow night. If you go out in the car with Roger, wear a scarf. I'll have new passports for both of us by Friday. All my contacts during my years working for Santos came in very useful. Of course, I didn't mention that they were for us.'

'Do I really need to have my hair dyed, Ian?'

'It's an added precaution. I don't want to leave anything to chance. If this goes wrong, well . . .' Ian shrugged.

Miranda burst into tears. 'Oh God, thank you Ian. I'm so happy.'

Ian wiped the tears away from her cheeks. 'You look it,' he smiled wryly.

'I'm sorry. They're tears of happiness, I promise. I can't believe that this whole nightmare is going to be over. I love you.' Miranda kissed him with such passion, Ian was almost overwhelmed. He was filled with huge desire.

'Come on, let's go to the bedroom. Make this night last.'

A thought crossed Miranda's mind and her face darkened. 'Ian, what about Chloe?'

'I've thought long and hard about it. There is no way we can kidnap Chloe and get her out of the country with us. So I decided that number one was to get you and me out. Once we're thousands of miles away, you can contact your mother, let her know you're okay and take it from there. I'm sorry, Miranda, but while you're a virtual prisoner here, you're never going to see Chloe again. At least there's a chance if you're free.'

'You're right,' said Miranda quietly. 'Do you think I'll ever see her again, Ian?'

Ian squeezed her hand. 'Of course you will, my darling,' he pulled her to her feet. 'Come on now, I want my future wife to show her prospective husband how much she loves him.'

They walked slowly to the bedroom, arms tightly clasped around each other.

The vehemence and passion of their love-making that night was beyond anything either of them had experienced before. They could not get enough of each other. They interspersed their love with arrangements and contingency plans for the following Friday. They were still awake when the dawn broke and Ian rose to leave.

'We won't have time to discuss things tomorrow when I call round for the photos so, remember, only one small bag. We want it to look as if I'm just taking you out for lunch. I'll organize some clothes for you, but wear something pretty. After all, it will be your wedding dress.'

'Won't Santos assume that we've both gone together, once Roger tells him I was last seen with you?'

'Yes. But there's no simple way round it. I'm the only other person trusted to take you out, so it has to be me.'

Ian walked back towards the bed. He kissed her gently on the lips and turned to leave.

Suddenly, fear coursed through Miranda's veins as she saw Ian go.

'Ian!' she almost shouted.

'What is it?'

'I'm scared. What if something goes wrong?'

'Nothing will. I promise. Everything's arranged. Just remember, this time next week we'll be man and wife and all this will seem like a bad dream. I love you, Miranda.'

'I love you too.'

He blew her a kiss as he walked out of the bedroom.

Miranda settled back on her pillows but knew that sleep would not come. She crept to the window and drew back the curtain.

She could see him in the half-light, walking at a brisk pace away from her and the flat, to his car which he had secreted a few streets away.

'Good-bye, my love,' she whispered quietly as she dropped the curtain back into place.

23

'HELLO, LEAH. HOW was the flight over?' Anthony kissed her on both cheeks as she got into the back of the limousine and they drove off towards the Museum of Modern Art.

'Absolutely fine. It's hard to believe I left Woodstock only twenty-four hours ago.'

Anthony studied Leah as she lapsed into silence, looking out of the window.

'Is everything okay? You seem a bit quiet.'

'I'm sorry, Anthony. No. Everything's fine.' Leah smiled at him.

In truth, she did not feel fine at all. But she could not put her finger on it. Miles had greeted them both pleasantly when they had returned yesterday. He'd kept the apartment spotlessly and Jenny and he were off to some party in the East Village tonight.

A sense of impending doom was with her and she could not shake it off. But it was unfair to Anthony to be down when it was New Year's Eve and she had no particular reason to be anything less than happy.

Their limousine drew to a standstill along Fifth Avenue

421

as a group of shouting and cheering New Year revellers, dressed up in outrageous costumes, crossed the road. They were all young, probably the same age as Leah, and suddenly Leah realized how she had missed out on the freedom of being neither a grown-up nor a child. She had gone from one to another without so much as stopping to pause for breath.

For a second, as she watched the smiling young faces, she desperately wanted to throw off her elegant evening gown, escape from the restrictive confines of the rarefied, privileged world in which she lived and run to join them.

Anthony saw this. He knew exactly what she was thinking. It made him feel old, sad and guilty for wanting to take Leah away from this for ever. But in some ways, if he asked her tonight, wouldn't he be giving her back her freedom? The freedom never to have to stand in front of a camera again, to do with her days as she wished, to help them both become young again, as she had done for the past week in New England.

As the car drove slowly along Fifth Avenue and proceeded across West 53rd Street, he gently touched her arm.

'Don't look so sad, sweetheart. The power is yours to change your destiny, if you so wish.'

Leah looked at him carefully. She was amazed that Anthony had understood how she felt.

'I'm being spoilt. After all, who back there would not swap their lives to be me? With my money, fame and youth, I'm the American dream.'

The limousine pulled up in front of the Museum of

Modern Art and Anthony helped Leah out. They joined the be-jewelled throng entering the museum, and Leah could not help but remember who she had been with the last time she had been inside this building.

Leah left Anthony to remove her long velvet evening cloak and then freshened up in the ladies.

When she returned to the vast downstairs room where the ball was taking place, Anthony was surrounded by people, some of whom she knew from Chaval. All eyes in the group turned as Leah walked towards them and a hush descended.

Even a professional model who graced catwalks and billboards all over the world had nights when her radiance was staggering. And tonight was one of Leah's.

She was dressed in a Jean Muir ball-gown, its black satin bodice covered in threaded silver. The skirt, made of layer upon layer of black tulle, moved as softly as a ballerina's around her ankles. Her hair was coiled in curls upon her head, and threaded with silver to match her dress.

Anthony held out his hands to her.

'Leah. What can I say? You look, I have to say it, a picture! I think you know most of the people here?'

Anthony introduced the guests she did not know, and they went to take their places at one of the tables, laden with crystal and antique china plates.

The dinner was lovely, and Leah soon brightened up. Anthony watched in admiration as Leah held the table spellbound with anecdotes from her travels around the world. He watched the other men entranced by her beauty and charm and thought once more what a fascinating woman she was.

Once the meal was finished, the band began to play and people started to dance.

'May I have the pleasure?' Anthony asked.

'Of course.' She took his outstretched hand and they went onto the dance floor.

As they began to move to the steady rhythm, Leah saw David Cooper dancing not inches away from her. He saw her, waved and smiled. Anthony saw this too and also smiled and acknowledged David Cooper.

'I didn't know you knew David,' he said.

'I don't, well, not very well. I've only met him once.'

'He's a strange one. A bit of an enigma in the business community of New York. Everyone knows his vastly successful companies, but no one seems to know him. In fact it's unusual to see him at a public function such as this. He keeps himself very much to himself, especially since his wife died a few years ago. Mind you, I know how he feels. You become very anti-social.'

The band stopped playing and Leah and Anthony returned to their table. The director of the museum stood up and made a speech about how much good tonight's ball would do for the museum and asked everyone to raise their glasses to the oncoming New Year, which was fast approaching.

Everyone joined in the countdown and twelve o'clock struck. Anthony hugged Leah tight and kissed her chastely on both cheeks.

'Happy New Year, Leah. I hope it brings you happiness and peace.'

'And to you, Anthony.'

They went onto the floor to join hands with the rest of

the guests and sang the traditional Auld Lang Syne.

The dance band turned the tempo up and sedate ladies picked up the hems of their ball-gowns and jived.

'Not really my scene, Leah. But you carry on,' said Anthony.

'May I?' It was David Cooper.

'Hello, David. Yes, with pleasure.' Anthony released Leah into David's arms.

Leah, faced with the choice of being blatantly rude, or dancing with David, nodded and began to move to the beat.

'How are you?' he asked.

'Fine.'

'You look stunning tonight.'

'Thanks.'

'A great pity about Brett and you. I had a feeling it was serious.'

This was all she needed tonight! A post-mortem with Brett's father.

'I was very surprised when Brett asked for his trip abroad to be moved forward.'

So Brett had gone away.

'Yes,' she replied ambiguously.

'So, you're seeing Anthony Van Schiele?'

'No. He's my boss and we've become good friends.'

'Leah, no need to be coy with me. I understand the way the world works. Just because you had a fling with my son doesn't mean you have to enter a convent now it's over,' David smiled.

Leah wanted to scream. This man had no idea of her feelings for Brett and the way he was dismissing their affair as a 'fling' made her feel sick. David Cooper was so cold. She could never imagine him loving anyone.

'I don't intend to enter a convent, I can assure you! Now, if you'll excuse me . . .' Leah extricated herself from his arms and walked towards the powder room.

She washed her hands, which felt clammy, then lingered on, reluctant to go back to the party. She wanted to go home.

Eventually she went out into the lobby and saw Anthony holding her cape.

'Time to go?' he asked.

Leah nodded gratefully. 'How did you know?'

Anthony led her out of the building to the waiting limousine.

'I watched you with David Cooper. I have to admit I'm intrigued to know your relationship. By the way, do you want to come back to my apartment for a nightcap?'

'Okay.' Leah realized that it was silly to be coy when they'd spent the past week under the same roof.

'It's not far from here.'

They rode the rest of the way in silence, until they reached the front of the skyscraper inhabited by Chaval.

They walked past the security guard, who wished them a Happy New Year.

'And to you,' Anthony smiled as they made their way to the lift.

The journey that Leah had made so many times before took them up to the sixty-seventh floor.

The apartment turned out to be a comfortable, spacious set of rooms with a lovely view over New York. Like Anthony's house in Southport, it was sparsely but elegantly furnished.

'Will you join me? I get embarrassed drinking by myself,' said Anthony.

'Okay. I'm not anti-alcohol for moral reasons, I just don't particularly like the taste.'

'I'll make you a *crême de menthe frappé.*'

Anthony mixed the drinks and sat down opposite her. 'So, how do you know David Cooper?'

'It's a long story.'

'We have all night.'

'Okay. You remember I told you that first time I came to your house that I'd just ended a relationship?'

'Yes.'

'David Cooper is his father.' Leah recounted meeting Brett when she was younger and then the fact that they'd met up again just before she'd left for New York. She told him that they'd had a bad argument, and that Brett had left the country without a good-bye.

Anthony sat quietly listening, nodding occasionally.

'The whole affair has put my trust in human nature down to zero. I promised myself that I'd never get involved with a man again.'

'I can understand you feeling like that, Leah. When you feel deeply for someone, as you obviously did for Brett, and they let you down, it does funny things to you. I hate to sound patronizing, but you will eventually get over it.'

'I know. But meeting David Cooper tonight brought the whole thing back.'

'Look, Leah, it may be the wrong moment after what you've just told me, but we've always been honest with each other, haven't we?'

Leah nodded.

'Well, the thing is . . .' Anthony, usually so eloquent, struggled to find the right words. 'When I first met you, I thought that you were an exceptionally beautiful woman and, like all men, I desired you. Then, as I started to get to know you better, I realized how much more there was to you. Your beauty masks your other qualities very successfully and it has been a constant pleasure to discover your depth of character, and your genuinely good soul. This may sound like a typically American tribute, but what I'm trying to say is that the past week confirmed what I thought. I've done something I never believed I'd do again after Florence, my wife, died. I've fallen in love with you.'

Anthony studied his brandy glass as Leah watched him. She knew he had more to say.

'The thing is, I'm not the type of man who runs around in the fast lane with lots of different women, and when I first realized I loved you, I felt guilty because of Florence, and also because of the age-gap between us. I tried to convince myself that it could never work, that you needed someone young, like Brett. But then, after spending time with you, I started to think of what I could give you and that perhaps, having grown up so fast, you needed someone older. In short, I have to tell you that I want you to marry me, Leah.'

Silence reigned heavy in the apartment as Leah sat, stunned by what Anthony had just said.

'Having just heard about Brett, I understand that it will take time for you to get over him. I know what it feels like. Losing someone close is the most painful experience in

the world, but you have as much time as you wish. I just
thought that, before we proceeded any further with our
relationship, you should know my ulterior motive.
There's no pressure, and I promise that if you don't feel
the same as I do, we can carry on our friendship as
before.'

'Anthony, I . . .'

'Hush, you don't have to say anything. I'm not looking
for answers tonight. I'm sure what I've said has come as a
shock and I want everything to go on as before. When
you feel ready, you give me your answer.'

'Thank you for telling me. I know it must have taken a
lot of courage and I feel honoured that you have asked
me to marry you. I don't know how I feel, because I've
never thought about our relationship in those terms
before, but I promise you I will think about it.'

'Good. That's all I ask. Now, I have to fly to France
tomorrow for a meeting and I shall be away for a couple
of days. May I ring you when I get back?'

'Of course.'

'Right. I'll call Malcolm and have him bring the car
round to take you home.'

Anthony escorted her to the door of the lift, and kissed
her once more on both cheeks.

'Take care, Leah. I'll see you soon. And I mean it,
there's no pressure, so don't worry about what I've said to
you tonight.'

'I won't. Thank you, Anthony, for a lovely evening.'

The lift door closed and Leah went down to the lobby
where Malcolm was waiting. She followed him out to the
car, and stepped inside. She was driven across town,

hardly seeing the remnants of the New Year revellers still drunkenly celebrating in the streets.

'Thank you, Malcolm,' she said before she went through the lobby of her apartment building and took the lift to her floor.

She turned the key in the lock and stepped into the darkened apartment. She switched the lights on and walked towards her bedroom. A noise stopped her. It was very faint, and sounded almost like a wounded animal. The sound was coming from the sitting room. She crept silently down the hall and into the pitch-black room. She fumbled for the light-switch and turned it on to its dimmest setting.

There, sitting huddled in the middle of the floor, was Jenny. She was naked, shivering and rocking herself to and fro, emitting small, keening cries. As Leah stepped closer and stood just five yards away, she drew in her breath in horror.

Jenny's body was covered in violent purple bruises.

24

LEAH STOOD FOR a second trying to calm herself. Jenny was still unaware that she was in the room. She knelt down next to Jenny, frightened she may startle her.

'Jenny, it's Leah,' she said softly. Jenny jumped as she put a hand on her shoulder.

'Oh God,' Jenny moaned.

Leah took off her velvet cape and wrapped it around the shivering girl's shoulders. She stood up and deftly lit the gas fire.

'Come on now, let's sit you by the fire. You'll catch your death.'

Slowly, Leah manoeuvred Jenny across to the warmth of the flames. She was weeping softly to herself and all Leah could do was to hold her tightly in her arms.

'Oh, Jenny, Jenny,' she whispered. 'Why did he do this?'

'I . . . I mentioned what a lovely time we had in Woodstock and how well Ben and I hit it off. He accused me of sleeping with Ben. He . . . he called me a . . . whore . . . he tried to strangle me and . . .' Jenny could go no further. She looked up at Leah, who could see the harsh red marks around the delicate skin of Jenny's neck already turning grey and blue.

'Where is Miles?'

'In my bed, fast asleep. He was very drunk. He probably won't remember anything about it in the morning.'

The thought of the perpetrator of this dreadful crime being less than a few yards from where they were sitting sent shivers down Leah's spine. Her mind whirled as she thought of what was best to do.

'I'm going to call the police.'

'No! Don't do that!' A look of dreadful anguish came onto Jenny's face. 'Please, Leah,' she begged, 'don't don't *don't*!'

Jenny's voice was rising and she was becoming hysterical. The last thing Leah wanted to do was to wake Miles.

'Okay, okay, shush. I won't call the police. But I think we ought to take you to the hospital to get you checked over.'

'No!' This time there was fear on Jenny's face. 'He didn't hurt me really badly. It's just the shock. I'm fine, honestly.'

'Are you sure nothing hurts?'

'Positive. My neck feel sore, but that's all. Please don't make me go to the hospital, Leah. They'll ask who did it and I can't face answering all their questions tonight. If I'm not feeling right tomorrow, I promise I'll go.'

'You know that this can't carry on? That Miles has to leave?'

Jenny nodded slowly. 'I didn't realize before tonight, but he could have killed me.'

Once more, guilt for not following her own instincts

432

came back to haunt Leah. She should have got rid of Miles the last time.

'Come on, let's get you into bed. You can sleep with me tonight, then tomorrow morning first thing I want you down at the doctor's to get yourself looked at. You're not to come back until after lunch. I have a few things to say to Miles.'

'Oh Leah, why is my life such a mess?' Jenny said sadly. 'In Woodstock I really felt that I was beginning to win. I felt . . . happy. I was really looking forward to seeing Miles and getting my career on the go again. And now? It's useless. Why, Leah, why?'

Leah shook her head slowly, as she helped Jenny from the floor.

'I don't know, Jenny, I really don't.'

25

THE FOLLOWING MORNING, Leah dispatched a forlorn Jenny off to the doctor's, with instructions not to return to the apartment until after lunch.

Leah made herself a cup of hot, strong coffee and sat in the sitting room to wait for Miles.

At eleven o'clock, she heard Jenny's door open. Her heart beat steadily against her chest as Miles, dressed in Jenny's bathrobe, came into the sitting room.

'Morning. Want some coffee?'

'No thanks. I've got some.'

She followed Miles into the kitchen and watched as he calmly filled the kettle and switched it on.

'Happy New Year, by the way,' he smiled. 'Boy, last night was quite a night.'

'Yes. You could say that. Sit down, Miles. I want to talk to you.'

Miles looked vaguely surprised at the stern way Leah spoke to him.

'Okay. Where's Jenny, by the way?'

'Out.'

'Oh. I wouldn't have thought that she'd have been up

so early. We both had a little too much to drink last night at the party we went to.' The kettle boiled, Miles filled his cup, added milk, then came to sit down opposite Leah.

The fact that Miles had returned to his normal, charming self after his brutal actions of the night before unnerved Leah.

'Miles, I found Jenny crying when I got home at three in the morning. She was very distressed. She said that you'd tried to strangle her.'

A look of genuine amazement crossed Miles' face. 'What!' He laughed loudly. 'She obviously had too much juice last night.'

'I don't think so. She was covered in bruises, and it's not the first time it's happened. A month ago, she had a badly swollen face and a black eye.'

Miles' face darkened. His black eyes glittered. 'Are you saying it's me who's been inflicting these injuries?'

'Yes. Not only has Jenny herself told me it was you, but it's hardly likely to be anyone else, is it? You were with her all of last night.' Leah thought how ridiculous the conversation was. 'I was all for asking you to leave a month ago, but Jenny wouldn't have it. She said that you always apologize afterwards, and that you'd promised not to do it again. So I let you stay because of Jenny. But, Miles, this can't go on. I want you out of this apartment today.'

Miles sat silently, staring at Leah. The look on his face was the same one he had used when she was a child. It made her feel almost unclean.

'You believe Jenny, then?' he said slowly, still staring at her.

'Yes. Of course I do. I saw the bruises for myself. I have

435

no reason to doubt her. Now, I'd like it if you'd pack your bags this morning and leave by lunchtime. You're lucky Jenny has refused to call the police. If you go away and promise never to try and contact her, I won't either, for the sake of your family.'

'My family? What family?'

'Rose, Miranda and Chloe, of course. They'd be devastated if you ended up in court accused of beating up a woman.'

Miles stood up and walked over to Leah. He towered over her and, for the first time, Leah felt fear course through her veins.

'And what do you know of my family? Eh? You were always trying to get in on the act when we were kids, sucking up to Rose and seducing that wet cousin of mine. Telling other people how to run their lives! Miss Pure, Miss Perfect.'

Miles brought a hand towards her face and, for an instant, Leah thought he was going to hit her. Instead, he gently traced the contours of her face, his fingers moving down her neck towards her breast. This galvanized Leah into action. She jumped up .

'Stop it, Miles! Don't you dare touch me! Get out of here, now! Otherwise I'm calling the police!'

'Okay, I'm going.' Miles sauntered towards the door, then stopped and turned round. His black eyes glinted as he stared at her.

'You'll regret this, my dearest Leah.'

Miles left the room and ten minutes later appeared at the door of the sitting room. He threw the front door key onto the floor. 'I'll let myself out. *Ciao.*'

436

Leah heard the door slam and listened to the lift taking Miles down and out of her life. A terrible cold fear was lodged inside her, rendering her incapable of moving.

Come on, Leah. He's gone now. He won't come back. He knows what would happen if he did.

Eventually, she stood up and wandered into the kitchen to make some more coffee.

She went back into the sitting room and slumped onto the sofa.

A deep weariness gripped her as she heard the key in the lock and thought of the struggle she would have to convince her dearest friend once more that life really was worth living.

Jenny came into the sitting room. She looked pale and dreadfully miserable.

'Has he gone?'

'Yes.'

'Oh.' Jenny promptly burst into tears. Leah went and put her arms round her friend.

'I really loved him. What will I do without him?' Jenny wept.

'Carry on and look to the future. I'm sorry, Jenny, but really, you must see that you're better off without him? I've known Miles a long time and there's always been something about him that makes me uneasy. Any man who could do what he's done to you has to be evil.'

'I know. But he gave me a reason to live. Before he came, I was so depressed. Now he's gone.'

'Oh Jenny. Look how happy you were in Woodstock. Why not give Ben a ring? He'll cheer you up.'

'No. He's gone away for New Year with his girlfriend. I'm not number one in anyone's book.'

'You're number one in mine. We've got each other. Oh, Jenny, please, you have got to fight on. There'll be other men who'll love you and take care of you, not hurt you like Miles did.'

'Is it worth it, Leah?'

Leah wiped the tears from Jenny's face. She wanted to answer that she didn't know, but Jenny needed her.

'Of course it is, silly. You've just had a really rough time, that's all. Things will get better, trust me.'

Jenny grasped Leah's hand. 'Oh Leah. You're so strong. I wish I was like you. You've been so good to me. I just seem to cause you nothing but problems.'

'That's what friends are for. And all I want in return is to see you get over this as quickly as you can. You must try. Promise?'

Jenny shook her head forlornly. 'I can't. Miles was all I had. Everything else has gone.'

'Come on, Jenny, you mustn't think like that.' Leah was desperately trying to think of something she could say to cheer Jenny up. 'What did the doctor say?'

'Not a lot. You know what they're like. He didn't believe that I'd fallen down the stairs, but said there was nothing he could do unless I'd tell him the truth. He checked me out and I'm fine. He gave me a prescription for some sleeping tablets and some Valium.'

'Well, give them to me. We don't want to start all that again.'

'I didn't even get them,' said Jenny quickly.

'Okay. Well, promise me you won't. Pumping yourself

full of drugs won't help, you know that, don't you?'

Jenny nodded.

'Why don't you go and have a lie down? You must be exhausted. I'll make you a cup of tea and bring it in.'

Jenny nodded. 'Yes, I am a bit tired.' She squeezed Leah's hand. 'Thanks, for everything.'

'Any time. Go on. I'll be in in a minute.'

Jenny stood up and wandered slowly out of the kitchen. Leah filled the kettle, wondering what she should do. She was not qualified to deal with someone as badly depressed as her friend and after last time, well, the responsibility weighed heavily on her shoulders. She decided to ring Jenny's consultant at Lenox Hill.

The receptionist told her that the consultant was on holiday until tomorrow and she should call then. Leah put down the phone. There was nothing more she could do now, but she would ring first thing tomorrow if Jenny was as unstable as she seemed at present.

'There you go.' Leah handed the hot steaming tea to the pathetic figure in the bed.

'Thanks.'

'Would you like me to stay with you?'

Jenny shook her head. 'I'll be fine. I feel very sleepy. I'm sure I'll nod off.'

'Okay. But call if you need anything. I'll be in my room.'

Leah closed the door behind her, and went into her bedroom to try to catch up on a little sleep herself.

The wonderful week in New England floated into Leah's thoughts. The feeling of being protected and secure in a safe haven made her feel vulnerable now she was alone.

The thought of Anthony's proposal last night came into her thoughts for the first time. With Jenny and Miles, she hadn't had a chance to think about it.

Did she love Anthony? If feeling enormously comfortable with someone, knowing that he understood who she was and being able to relax completely in his company was love, then yes, she loved him.

And yes, she found him attractive.

But marriage? She didn't know.

At half past ten that evening, Leah went into Jenny's bedroom. Jenny was sitting upright, eating an apple and watching her portable television. Her hair was brushed and shining and Leah thought she looked remarkably well under the circumstances.

'Hi, Leah.'

'How are you? You look much better.' Leah sat on the bed and took Jenny's hand.

'I am.'

'Do you want to come and sleep in my room tonight?'

'No. I'll be fine in here.'

'Sure?'

'Absolutely.'

'I'm proud of you, Jenny,' Leah said warmly. 'You know where I am. Good-night, sleep tight.' Leah stood up.

'Leah?' Jenny reached out her hand and pulled Leah towards her. 'You've been fantastic over the last few months. The best friend I could have hoped for. Thank you so much. I love you.' Jenny flung her arms round Leah and held her tight.

'I love you too. Happy New Year, darling.'

'Yes, Happy New Year. You deserve the best of everything. Just hold on to who you are and you'll always be fine.'

As Leah walked out of the room, Jenny waved.

'Good-bye,' she whispered through her tears as the door closed.

At nine o'clock the following morning, Leah took a steaming mug of coffee into Jenny's room.

Before she saw anything, the familiar alcoholic smell told her the worst had happened.

Leah switched on the light and moved towards the still, pale body of her friend. She removed the empty bourbon bottles and Valium packets from the duvet. She checked Jenny's pulse.

Leah gathered the girl into her arms and held her tightly.

'Oh, Jenny, my darling Jenny.'

Leah wept.

26

MIRANDA STOOD IN front of the mirror, checking her appearance for the last time. After much deliberation, she had decided on a simple Zandra Rhodes suit of cream silk, trimmed with ermine.

She had spent the last night sleepless, and had eventually risen at five and spent hours fixing her new dark hair.

Miranda looked at her watch. Five to ten. Ian should be here at any minute to take her and her small overnight bag out of this nightmare and on to a new life together.

Yesterday, she had called Roger and had him drive her to her bank. There, she had drawn out every penny that was in the account Santos had opened for her. She had hardly touched the account since, as she had found it more convenient to use the credit cards Santos had given her. So there was twenty-five thousand pounds still in the account. She had taken five thousand in cash and the rest on a cheque made out to the new name on her passport. Ian would worry if he knew what she had done, but by the time Santos found out, they would be hundreds of miles away, and the money would give them a start.

Miranda went through to the sitting room and sat

down. Her hands were clasped nervously together and she could not help but watch the small clock on the mantelpiece, the seconds ticking away.

'Please, don't be late, Ian,' she murmured. The nightmare scenario of last time she had tried to walk out of Santos' clutches had haunted her for the past week. She had woken in cold sweats from vivid dreams of Santos turning up at the airport, trying to stop them getting on the plane.

The clock ticked past ten o'clock as Miranda sat, in an agony of waiting. She remembered Ian's words.

'If I don't arrive by half past ten, pick up your bag, get out of the flat, and run like hell until you can find a taxi. We'll meet at the registry office. Failing that, get a taxi to Heathrow and I'll see you in the departure lounge.'

Miranda knew Ian had arranged for Roger to go off on some kind of job this morning, and Roger had told her yesterday that he wouldn't be available until lunchtime. The coast was as clear as it would ever be.

For the hundredth time, Miranda checked in her small clutch-bag for the address of the registry office. She knew it off by heart now anyway.

The clock ticked on to quarter past and Miranda could stand it no longer. She got up and poured herself a good measure of vodka. The tasteless liquid flowed down her throat.

At twenty-five past ten, Miranda was in such a dreadful state of trepidation that she had taken to pacing the floor.

'Oh God, please, come, please come,' she repeated silently again and again.

The silence in the room was deafening, and she

switched on the television, hoping that it would give her something else to concentrate on. She would wait until twenty to eleven and then do as Ian had asked and take a taxi to the registry office.

She stared blankly at the ten thirty news bulletin.

Then she saw Ian's face appear on the screen.

Miranda wondered whether she was hallucinating. She moved forward and listened intently to what the newscaster was saying.

'. . . killed in a hit and run accident at eight o'clock yesterday evening. Police are appealing for any witnesses who might have seen the driver of the car. And now, onto the weather. The cold snap is set to . . .'

Ian's face disappeared from the screen. Miranda sank to the floor, believing she was going to faint.

'No, no, oh God, no . . .'

She rocked to and fro, her mind unable to take the news in.

Her fingers and toes were tingling as her heart raced dangerously inside her chest. She took deep breaths, trying to control herself.

The faintness passed. Miranda stood up unsteadily and reached for the vodka bottle. She took a huge swig straight from it and sat down on the sofa.

Something told her that it was vital that she took hold of herself. She forced herself to think about what she should do.

Ian was dead. Had it been an accident? Miranda knew that she could not tell herself that it was.

If it hadn't been an accident, then Santos must have found out about them.

All that Ian had told her about Santos came rushing back into her mind. He had warned her that the man was evil enough to kill.

Miranda knew she was in mortal danger and there wasn't a second to lose. In a giant effort, she put her grief and anger to the back of her mind. This was survival. If she didn't move quickly, there was every chance that she could end up dead like Ian.

Instinct took over. Miranda grabbed her overnight bag and headed for the front door. She opened it.

'Nooh!!' She tried to push past him, beating her knuckles into his chest, but he picked her up and carried her kicking and screaming back inside the flat.

'Shut up! Shut up!' Roger slapped her repeatedly across her face as Miranda screamed hysterically.

'Murderer! Murderer!'

'Do you think we're all blind and stupid? I'm warning you, madam. If we have any more trouble, that little brat of yours in Yorkshire is dead! Do you understand me?'

Roger threw an envelope into Miranda's lap.

'I'm leaving you here to calm down. Look inside the envelope and don't forget what I've told you. Mr Santos isn't happy, not happy at all. And we all know what happens then.'

Miranda heard the front door slam.

She opened the brown envelope.

Inside were pictures of her daughter, Chloe. Chloe was standing outside her nursery school in Oxenhope village, holding tightly to Mrs Thompson's hand. She was wearing a dress that Miranda had bought her just before she left.

The sight of her beautiful daughter and the happy family scene made the tears fall once more.

They could hurt her at any time. Chloe was in danger because of her selfishness.

She ran to the telephone and picked up the receiver. The line was dead.

She ran to the front door. It was locked from the outside.

She was a prisoner.

Miranda finished off the rest of the vodka, then started on the whisky. Three hours later her mind was numbed.

The answer was simple. Miranda went into the kitchen and drew out the big bread knife. If she was dead, Chloe would be safe, Santos would move onto another whore.

Miranda positioned the knife at her wrists. She touched the skin and drew blood.

She stopped, then threw the bread knife to the floor. No, that was a coward's way out. She was the only person alive that could make Santos pay for destroying her and killing Ian.

Strength surged into Miranda's body. She picked up a priceless antique figurine that rested on a mahogany table in the corner of the sitting room.

She hurled it towards the sitting-room door. It shattered into hundreds of small pieces.

'Bastard! I'll never forgive you for this. I'll find a way to make you pay, Santos. For both of us,' she added quietly.

27

'ASHES TO ASHES, dust to dust. . . .' The vicar intoned quietly.

Leah watched the older couple, holding onto each other for support, move towards the open grave. The woman threw a pink rose on the top of the coffin, then turned into the comfort of her husband's arms and began to weep softly.

The grey January morning seemed to reflect the couple's grief. As the woman passed Leah, she grasped her hand and Leah saw the same beautiful blue eyes that Jenny had had.

'Thank you, Leah. I know you did everything you could. Jenny loved you like a sister. She was always telling her dad and me about how good you were to her.' The woman stared into space, squeezed Leah's hand, then moved away. The rest of the crowd gathered round the grave moved respectfully to let the couple pass through them. The vicar followed them.

The crowd began to disperse. Leah moved forward, steeling herself to look down into the hole in the cold, hard ground.

'Good-bye, Jenny. Love you,' she whispered.

Tears stung the back of her eyes, but she was unable to let them fall. The whole thing was too surreal. She could not imagine that the oak casket strewn with flowers had anything to do with her young, beautiful friend.

Others at the funeral had wept copiously, Madelaine in particular.

Leah moved away from the grave and felt an arm on her shoulder.

'You okay?'

The voice was strong and comforting and she turned her eyes up to Anthony. Ben was standing next to him, eyes full of sadness.

'Yes. We'd better get back to the apartment. I think I've spoken to most people to give them directions.'

Anthony nodded, put his arm around her and they followed the last few mourners out of the graveyard.

Leah was silent on the short journey back to the apartment in Anthony's limousine. All conversation seemed banal in the light of what had just taken place.

When she opened the door of the apartment, the sitting room was already filled with guests. The caterers were handing round glasses of sherry and soft drinks.

As Leah moved through the crowd, she felt faintly sick as she heard snatches of conversation. They were talking about the latest young British modelling sensation and last month's issue of *Vogue*.

It was as if Jenny had never existed.

'Darling, what can I say? It was so, so, tragic. Jenny was one of the best I've ever had.' Madelaine, the picture of elegant grief in her black Lanvin suit with veiled pillbox hat to match, stood in front of her.

Leah wanted to scream at her. Madelaine hadn't given a damn about Jenny when she was in trouble. All she'd cared about was making sure that her 'product' didn't screw up her commission by going off the rails.

Leah felt real loathing. This woman, along with all the other hypocrites in the room, was just as responsible for Jenny's death as Jenny was herself. They had all been happy to make as much money as they could out of her when things were going well, but had dropped her like a hot potato as soon as she ran into problems.

Leah fought to control her anger. 'Anthony, this is Madelaine. She runs Femmes.'

Anthony held out his hand and Madelaine took it. 'It's good to meet you, Mr Van Schiele. Leah has told me so much about you. Her campaign for Chaval seems to be going very well. I hear that sales have increased by a quarter since Leah began. Well worth the little fee I negotiated, don't you think?'

Madelaine batted her eyelashes flirtatiously. Leah wanted to claw her eyes out.

In the past week, numb from grief, shock, and guilt at being unable to prevent her friend's death, Leah had paced around the eerily quiet apartment, trying to make sense of it all. She had come up with no answers, but she had made a decision. The false world in which she lived had destroyed a young, beautiful girl who should have only been starting out on life, not lying in a box five feet under. It was a corrupt world and although Leah guessed that it was probably no worse than any other type of business, she needed breathing space to try to recapture the joy of just being alive and young. She had all the money she could ever want, a beautiful apartment and a successful career. These meant nothing to her. At twenty-one she felt like an embittered old woman. She wanted out.

As Leah stared at Madelaine, she realized that she had at her fingertips the only weapon that could genuinely hurt this hard, cold woman who had treated Jenny so cruelly.

'You two are good together, very good.' Jenny's words came back to her.

A great rush of satisfaction rose inside her and she reached for Anthony's hand.

'I have something to tell you, Madelaine. When I've finished the assignments I'm booked for, I'm giving up modelling for good.'

A look of horror replaced the smile on Madelaine's face. The money she had earned from Leah had bought her a very nice house in Cap d'Antibes and a Porsche 924.

'I . . . but . . . why, Leah?'

Leah had never heard Madelaine lost for words and she relished the pain on the woman's face. She just hoped that Jenny was here somewhere, watching and enjoying. She looked up at Anthony. A flicker of surprise was in his eyes, but it disappeared quickly.

Madelaine repeated the question. 'Why?'

Leah was still staring up at Anthony. She grasped his hand tighter and smiled at him.

'Because Anthony and I are to be married as soon as possible.'

Part Three

New York, March 1984

1

LEAH WOKE TO the soft chirping of the birds hailing the coming spring. She kept her eyes closed, enjoying the few peaceful moments between sleep and wakefulness, when every muscle in her body felt relaxed and refreshed.

Reluctantly, she opened her eyes and glanced at the clock positioned on the bedside cabinet. Half past eight. She hadn't even heard Anthony leave this morning.

Exhaustion had hit her during the first three months of her two previous unsuccessful pregnancies, and again, at ten weeks, she was feeling weary and washed out.

Leah rose slowly out of the big comfortable bed and walked towards the en suite bathroom. She filled the large round tub with water and bath essence and climbed in. She put her flannel over her face and breathed deeply, thinking of what she would do with the day that stretched before her.

Anthony and Dr Adams, her gynaecologist, were insistent that she did as little as possible. No riding, no swimming in the beautiful indoor pool, in fact nothing that would tax her above turning the page of a book.

Leah stepped out of the bath, wrapped herself in a big

towel, and padded into her dressing room to find something to wear.

She stood naked in front of the full-length mirror. Her body was still as firm and toned as it had been when she'd graced the cover of magazines across the globe.

Leah sighed deeply as she put on a soft all-in-one cashmere jumpsuit. Although she could never admit it to Anthony, sometimes she missed those days. The feeling of being needed, the fact that if she didn't turn up for a booking, it would cause countless problems for the assembled crew hired on the shoot.

For the past two years she could have spent every day in bed and no one in the world except Anthony would have noticed.

'Come on, Leah, stop it, you sound so spoilt,' she said to her reflection. She left her dressing room, walked along the heavily carpeted corridor, down the sweeping staircase and crossed the large hall.

A light breakfast of croissants, fruit and decaffeinated coffee was waiting for her in the conservatory where she liked to sit in the morning and look at the beautiful gardens. This morning, the view was more exquisite than usual. The last of the snow had been washed away by a light March rainfall, and the first proper sunshine of the year was in evidence, heralding the re-birth of nature. Leah sat down at the table, poured her coffee and hoped this was a good omen for her own baby's birth.

There were only four weeks left until she passed danger point. The previous two babies had both miscarried at twelve and fourteen weeks respectively. Dr Adams was sure that if she could get past that, she would carry the baby full-term.

Leah hated the unfairness of it. She, who had never smoked and hardly drunk alcohol in her life, who had kept incredibly fit and seldom suffered a day's illness, didn't seem to be able to produce what millions of other women accomplished with ease. Although she'd had stringent tests after both miscarriages, the specialists seemed unable to quantify the reason. They told her that she was in good health and there were no problems at all with her insides. Rather than making her feel better, this news made her feel worse, for she had no excuse for her problem.

They both wanted a baby so badly. Anthony, in his midforties, was aware that the years were passing all too quickly. And yet, he was producing his side of things with no problems at all, whereas, at twenty-three, Leah was struggling to do the same.

If she lost this baby she knew that she could not go through it again. The mental agony of every twinge, any sudden slight pain, which under normal circumstances she wouldn't have noticed, now threw her into a panic.

Leah knew objectively that she'd become unhealthily obsessive about her problem. It had completely taken over the past year and put a strain on her otherwise happy marriage. Anthony had shown nothing but kindness, love and understanding, whereas she had become irrational, short-tempered.

If only she could produce this one baby . . . Leah was sure it would stop her feeling so terribly depressed. After all, she had everything a woman could want. Her marriage was successful, she had a beautiful home and enough money to do whatever she wanted.

Anthony had insisted that her earnings from her days as a model were not to be touched, as he had enough for both of them, so her invested earnings were making a small fortune.

Sometimes Leah sat and berated herself for her selfishness. She had become so caught up in her problem that her dreams of doing some good in the world with her money had been lost. She would sit alone, blushing guiltily as she watched the news telling of another disaster in some far-flung corner of the world; of starvation and blood-shed which left thousands homeless and dying; and tell herself how lucky she was and that she must do something to help. Then she would feel a pain and become caught up once more with her troubles, and do nothing.

Once this baby's born, she told herself, as she cut a kiwi fruit into neat little pieces, once it was born, then she'd set about doing something worthwhile with her life.

The post was sitting neatly on a silver tray. Leah leafed through it, taking out the letters addressed to both of them and leaving Anthony's to one side. All of them were invitations to charity functions, gallery openings and official dinners. They depressed her as she knew that until the baby was born, she wouldn't be going anywhere.

Her heart lifted as she saw her mother's familiar writing. She opened the envelope eagerly. They spoke every week, but it was over two years since she had last been to England. With the miscarriages, the depression that followed, then the new pregnancy, there never seemed to be the opportunity. And now it would be at least eight or nine months before she could go. That was, if she kept the baby.

Mum kept her up to date on the gossip in Oxenhope. She still worked part-time for Rose – although she didn't need to anymore since Leah had provided her parents with a comfortable yearly income – but Mum said it got her out of the bungalow and she enjoyed it. Leah was fascinated by the mysterious disappearance of Miranda. Apparently, she'd not been seen since Leah's twenty-first birthday party in London. She'd gone off, leaving little Chloe all alone, and hadn't been heard of since. The things that Mum called her were not kind, but Leah knew that Miranda had never done much to endear herself to anyone. Still, leaving her child was about as low as you could sink, Mum said. Leah could hear in her voice how she worshipped Chloe. It sounded as though Mrs Thompson had stepped in as surrogate mother to the seven-year-old child, while Rose locked herself in her studio to paint.

As for Miles, her mother was always asking Leah if she had seen him lately in New York, as she was sure that they would be mixing in the same circles now that Miles was such a successful photographer. Leah would say no, she hadn't seen him, then quickly change the subject. She had told nobody about the way he had treated Jenny, just watched with horror as his name began to appear in the credits of large spreads in American *Vogue, Vanity Fair* and *Harpers & Queen*. She prayed that Jenny had been a one-off, that by her keeping quiet she had not endangered the lives of other women that crossed his path.

And Carlo? Well, she'd heard nothing from him since the night he'd asked her to marry him. Leah supposed that Carlo had heeded Madelaine's warnings to leave her alone. She'd read in the papers that Maria Malgasa was once again his love and his top model. The whole incident had left a horrid taste in her mouth, souring what should have been pleasant memories.

Leah read her mother's letter slowly, biting her lip when she read that her dad was due to go into hospital some time in the next three months for a replacement hip operation. His own had crumbled because of his arthritis, and although Mum was cheerful about it, saying that the doctors had assured her that her father would be fine, Leah could sense the underlying current of anxiety.

If only she could go over and be with her parents for the operation.

Leah decided she needed a walk. She let herself out of the conservatory and stepped into the biting air, trying to put all unpleasant thoughts out of her head. Stress was bad for the baby, and the tiny creature inside her was the most important thing in her life.

2

ALTHOUGH IT WAS four o'clock in the morning, David was wide awake. Olympic Airways flight OA412 had left Kennedy airport five hours ago for the long journey east towards Greece.

David rose and went upstairs to the deserted bubble to have a drink. He sat in one of the comfortable chairs nursing a brandy.

Tension surrounded him, making every nerve-ending quiver with a gut-wrenching anticipation. He wouldn't call it fear. No, fear was what he had experienced in Treblinka. It was more that he felt as if he were heading towards his destiny, as if his whole life had been guiding him towards this journey across the world to take revenge on the man who had murdered his mother and father and violated his beloved sister.

Everything was in place. There had been a flurry of calls between himself and the organization in the past week. There was a boat that would surreptitiously shadow Frankl's boat in case of trouble. There was also a member of the organization on board, posing as one of Frankl's crew. David had been issued with a gun which he had been taught to fire with accuracy. It was to be used only in an emergency, to protect his own life. The organization wanted Frankl alive. They had devised this plan so that Frankl would be extradited by his government and forced to stand trial in Europe for his crimes against humanity.

David had to get through an evening of perfectly normal behaviour, then once Frankl had put pen to paper to sign the warrant for his own arrest, David would be removed from the boat and it would be over.

David comforted himself that in forty-eight hours' time, he would be back on a plane on his way to St Tropez. He wanted two weeks of peace and quiet before he flew back to New York to begin his life free of the nightmare of Frankl. Of course, if all went well, then he would have to appear at his trial.

David checked the time. He needed to sleep, to relax.

He went back downstairs to his seat. He closed his eyes and sent up a prayer.

Frankl was waiting to greet David in the magnificent salon.

'David, it's a pleasure to see you again.' He shook his hand warmly. 'You know Miranda, of course.'

David stared at the pathetically thin girl standing just behind Frankl. He remembered her from three years ago as being exceptionally pretty and blonde. The girl he looked at now had lank brunette hair and had aged maybe ten years since he had last seen her.

'Of course, although I think you've changed your hair colour.'

'She has. A female whim, but I think it rather suits her, don't you? I asked her to leave it that colour, didn't I, dear?' He smiled at Miranda, who nodded sullenly.

David smiled at Miranda. 'Well, it's good to see you again, Miranda.' He looked for a reaction behind the dull, expressionless blue eyes and wondered what on earth had happened to the girl to effect such a change in her.

'We will be setting sail in twenty minutes. I thought we could go onto the deck with a bottle of champagne,' said Frankl.

The engines were humming as the boat moved gently out of its mooring.

'We are alone this weekend?' David enquired. 'Usually there are so many people aboard.'

'Yes, well, sometimes a man needs a little solitude and as we have business to attend to, I felt it was better to keep the party small. Others may join us tomorrow when the business has been completed, but for the present, it is just the three of us and my captain. Let us toast to an enjoyable and fruitful weekend, shall we?' Frankl raised his glass.

A warning bell rang in David's head, but he put it down to his own neuroses.

Half an hour later, it was becoming breezy and there was a chill in the air.

'It is time to go in. Dinner will be at eight, after which we shall get to work. Relax and enjoy.'

Frankl waved as he walked inside and disappeared down the stairs.

*

'So, my dear, would you mind if you left us men to work out a little business? I am sorry, but once it is done we can spend the rest of the weekend enjoying ourselves.'

Miranda shook her head. David did not miss the look of relief on her face.

'Good-night, David.' She rose from the table and walked towards the door.

'Now. I suggest we go into the salon and I shall pour some liqueurs while you prepare the papers for signature. Yes?'

David nodded in acquiescence. He stood up and followed Frankl through the large glass doors and into the salon.

He tried to steady his hands as he unlocked his briefcase and drew out the papers. As he did this, he pressed a knob to start the tape recorder, hidden in the bottom of the case. He had practised this move many times and performed it fluently now. He put the case on the floor. The feel of steel pressing into his right-hand side underneath his jacket comforted him.

Not long now, David. Just keep calm. Everything is going according to plan.

He handed the papers to Frankl who put them on the marble table and raised his brandy glass.

'We must have a toast before we proceed. To our continued co-operation and fruitful partnership.' Frankl knocked back the brandy in one.

'Yes.' David sipped his brandy slowly. He needed a clear head.

'I have to tell you, David, that I was a little surprised when you put this proposal to me. You were the last person I would have expected to be involved with, how can I put it, a rather shady group of militants in South America. By approaching me and asking me to supply arms to this group, sworn enemies of my own country, it would mean immediate arrest and then expulsion if the Bolivian government discovered my involvement. So obviously I went to a great deal of trouble to make sure that you were all you seemed.' Frankl eyed him.

David's body turned to ice. 'And what did you discover?' he said slowly.

Frankl paused for a long time. Then he smiled. 'That you were indeed all you seemed. A clean-cut rich businessman. My men could find nothing to mar your record.'

David relaxed and he chuckled with Frankl.

Frankl leant forward towards David, the expression in his eyes changing instantly. 'But this made me even more suspicious. Why should a man such as yourself suddenly decide to enter a deal such as this?' Frankl shook his head. 'I'm afraid I wasn't convinced, David.'

David sat there watching Frankl, his mind travelling back to the last time he'd seen that expression in his eyes. They glinted evil.

'So I did some more investigation. After all, when we sign this agreement, I will be putting the safety of my home government at risk, not to mention myself. I then discovered that you were half Jewish. That was not a problem. I have done many deals with Jews in the past. No, it was you that gave yourself away.' Frankl leant back in his chair, crossed his arms and laughed.

'Oh dear, perhaps I should not make fun of you. After all, your experience in Nazi hunting is limited, is it not, David?'

David's body was rigid as he listened to Frankl's slow, hypnotic words.

Frankl knew who he was. There was nothing left. Years of work had been ruined. So he had to ask.

'How?'

'Your more experienced friends should have told you that you would be watched by me and your apartment searched. Under the circumstances, was it not a little stupid to have a Rose Delancey painting entitled *Treblinka* hanging in your study? At last the pieces fell into place. David Delanski. Brother of the delightful Rosa. After that, it was easy. Your merry band of intrepid hunters have been known to me for years. But I have to say that it was a clever plan. It nearly worked.'

'You bastard,' David breathed.

Frankl chuckled. 'Come now, David. You Jews, you think you are so clever, you think you will rule the world. But you are all so stupid, scum who will never achieve the power you long for.'

David stood. 'There are others on the boat, you know. At any minute they will . . .'

Frankl lifted his hand. 'Of course. My faithful Captain. He has worked for me for two years. And then I discovered his links to your little organization. He is, er, tied up on the bridge and shall not be coming to your aid. I shall dispose of him later.' Frankl brushed a piece of fluff from his jacket and shrugged. 'I decided that it was best to get rid of you at the same time. Neat and tidy, like the old days. You may have escaped from Treblinka, but there is no escape this time.'

David realized that Frankl was still living in the days

where he could murder someone on a whim.

'So, how are you going to dispose of me? For I presume that is why I am here?' he asked as calmly as he could.

Frankl nodded. 'Yes, you are right. One of my men could have picked you off long before now, but I felt that it was only right that I completed the job I began forty years ago. And I didn't want to ruin your little plan,' Frankl shrugged. 'A nice, simple drowning is what is needed. The poor major tycoon that fell overboard while enjoying a pleasant break on his friend Santos' yacht.'

Something inside David burst. A well of hatred and anger opened itself and poured into his brain. He reached inside his jacket and pulled the gun on Frankl.

'Enough! It has to finish, Frankl! I was sent here to make sure that you paid for what you did in Treblinka in front of the world, but now I see that it is my own destiny to kill you. I swore vengeance when I left Treblinka. Stand up! Now!'

David trained the gun on Frankl, who smiled, shrugged, then did as David had asked. He stood up slowly.

'As you wish, David Delanski. You're in charge.'

'Turn around! Move!' David roared. With one hand pressing the gun into the small of Frankl's back, he steered Frankl towards the sliding doors of the salon and led him onto the deck. He knew he should lock Frankl in a cabin downstairs and radio for help, but pictures of the night Frankl had murdered his father and Rosa's terrified face after he'd raped her were scudding through his mind.

They reached the edge of the deck and David bent

Frankl over the low rail, gun to his temple. Adrenaline pumped through his veins making him light-headed and nauseous. His breathing was coming in short, sharp bursts.

'I've waited a long time for this moment.' David was trembling with emotion. 'I swore that I would take revenge for what you did. This is for Mama, Papa, Rosa and all the others. May God show mercy on your soul!'

David fired. And fired again. Two hollow clicks cut through the breeze and echoed around the deck. David pulled the trigger again and again, but there was no explosion. Then he heard something more frightening. The sound of laughter. Hysterical, victorious laughter.

The big hand was round his throat and a gun pointed to his head before David had time to move. His own, empty gun dropped out of his hand and skidded along the deck as he was forced into the position that Frankl had occupied only seconds before. The weight of Frankl's body was pressing against his own. David grasped the rail to stop himself from toppling overboard.

'You foolish, pitiful little man. While you showered, I emptied your gun. It does not have any bullets. But this one, my friend, does. It is not I who am destined to die tonight, but you, David Delanski.'

'One question before you dispose of me. Did you ever feel any remorse for murdering thousands of innocent people?'

'Never. You may say a prayer if you wish. You Jews usually like to pray before you die.'

The gun was pressing harder into his neck. David looked down and saw total blackness beneath him.

'Good-bye, David. It has been interesting reacquaint-ing myself with you.'

Forgive me, Rosa, I tried. I've lost, like all the others before me.

There was the sound of a sickening crack behind David. Frankl let out a scream and the gun fell from his grip. Then another crack, the sound of bone splintering. Frankl groaned, fell forward on top of David, lost his balance and toppled lifelessly over David's head and into the ocean.

David so very nearly joined him, only his knees locking round the rail as he used what little energy he had left to heave himself back onto the deck.

He crumpled to the ground and sat gasping for air.

Eventually David looked up and saw the figure silhou-etted in the moonlight. She was holding his empty gun and staring straight ahead of her.

'Thank you, thank you,' panted David. 'Are you all right?'

The figure nodded. 'Do you think I killed him? I hit him very hard on the back of his head.'

'I don't know, but I doubt anyone could survive a blow of that kind for long in the water.'

'I wanted to kill him, David. I didn't do it to save you, you know. I did it for myself, and for Ian.'

The calmness with which she spoke frightened David. The girl was obviously in shock.

David stood up. 'Miranda, why don't you go to your cabin and have a lie down? I think we ought to leave here as soon as possible. I'm going onto the bridge to see the Captain.'

'Yes. I do feel tired. And cold.' Miranda held out her arms. 'Come and hold me.'

David walked towards her as Miranda began shivering violently. He folded the girl into his arms.

'It's okay, it's all over now.'

She looked up at him. 'Yes. Take me home to Rose, David.'

In the depths of the water, Frankl was regaining conciousness. As water filled his lungs, he coughed and struggled to move his limbs. With all the strength panic could muster, Frankl kicked for the surface.

David made his way to the bridge, and found the Captain gagged and tied to a chair. He released him quickly.

'The plan has gone wrong. He was on to us months ago. I'm afraid Frankl will never be brought to trial. He is either dead or dying in the water.'

'David, you did all you could. I will radio the other boat to arrange a rendezvous. We will leave immediately.'

David nodded and slumped into a chair, not even able to begin thinking about what Miranda had just said.

Something slapped hard against Frankl's face, preventing him from swimming further upwards. He reached out. A blade cut through his finger and he screamed.

A deep rumbling came from close at hand as the boat's engines stirred into life. Before Frankl had time to move, the propellers started to turn.

Frankl's body was sliced into a hundred pieces of unrecognizable flesh.

3

ROSE PUT DOWN the telephone and sank into a chair. The shock of hearing his voice again as much of a revelation as knowing Miranda was safe.

Rose closed her eyes and took five long, deep breaths. She was going to see David again after all these years. He'd been brief on the telephone, promising to explain all when Rose arrived in France. David was sending his private plane to Leeds Bradford airport to pick her up and fly her across the Channel. He had told her that Miranda was alive and well, but he thought it best if they met in St Tropez without Chloe so that they could all talk.

Rose knew she could not begin to work out how David had found Miranda on a boat in the Greek islands. Surmising was pointless and in less than twenty-four hours she would know the truth.

As the Lear jet landed at Nice airport, Rose applied a new coat of lipstick and brushed her thick titian hair. She studied herself and felt glad that the worry over Miranda and a strict diet had shed pounds off her figure. She was amazed to find that it still mattered that he thought she was beautiful.

As she emerged from customs, she saw him. He looked older, of course, the grey streaking his blond hair.

Her feet were carrying her towards him, nearer and nearer.

He saw her and his eyes lit up.

'Hello, David.'

'Hello, Rose.'

'Good flight?'

'Not bad.'

'You must be tired.'

'I'm okay.'

The banal conversation continued as Rose followed him through the airport and out to the car park. David unlocked the passenger door of a Mercedes and helped her in.

'You look beautiful. You've hardly altered at all.' David was staring at her.

'You look well too.'

'Thank you.'

David got into the car and started the engine. They drove in silence, neither of them knowing how to bridge the gap between where they were now and where they had left off twenty-eight years ago. Anything they could think of to say was either too lightweight or far too heavy for them to handle. Rose looked out of the car window at the breathtaking view of the Mediterranean.

Fifteen minutes later, David pulled the car over into a small parking area. There was a deserted bay below.

'Let's go for a walk. I have things to tell you that you need to know before you see Miranda.'

Rose nodded and stepped out of the car.

*

The windswept figures spent two hours on the beach. As the grey March day sent the waves skidding into the shore, they walked along side by side, keeping their distance. Then the woman stopped, sank to her knees and put her head in her hands. The man reached down to comfort her, cradling her in his arms.

Eventually, they stood, and continued walking, his arm around her shoulder.

The light was growing dim as Rose and David returned to the car.

Rose was shivering, not only from cold, but from shock and emotion. David helped her in and she sat staring in front of her. He walked round to the other door and climbed in behind the wheel.

'You are sure that he had no idea she was my adopted daughter? Was that the reason he's treated her the way he has?'

David shook his head. 'No, Rose. Miranda used her real mother's surname mainly because she didn't want you finding out where she was.'

Rose turned to David, her face ashen.

'And did she tell you what her real mother's surname was?'

David shook his head. 'No. Does it matter? At least Miranda is not tied to any of this by blood.'

Rose's eyes filled with tears. 'Oh, David, that is where you are so wrong.'

*

'Rose, oh Rose!' Miranda flung herself into her mother's arms, crying piteously. Rose stroked her daughter's brunette hair, her heart breaking. She knew that it wasn't over for her daughter yet.

The three of them went down the narrow stairs of David's yacht and into the salon. David poured them all a stiff drink and sat down on one of the comfortable sofas.

'We have a lot to tell you, Miranda, about your past, and about ours. I wanted Rose to be here before I began.'

'You start, David.' Rose sat down next to Miranda and held the shivering girl tightly in her arms.

'Do you have any idea why I was on Santos' boat this weekend?'

'Business?'

'You could call it that. Frank Santos' real name was Kurt Frankl. He was deputy commandant at Treblinka, a death camp for the Jews in Poland during the war. He murdered my mother, father and countless others. He did unspeakable things to Rose.' David paused before he began to tell the full story. The pain of doing so, of speaking it aloud, was almost more than he could bear.

Miranda grabbed Rose's hand as David recounted the atrocities of the man she had just killed. He told her of Anya, who'd helped them escape, and how she'd been raped by Frankl and other SS officers.

'But once Anya, Rose and I escaped from Treblinka, we realized the battle for survival was not yet over,' sighed David. 'We lived on our wits, hiding in forests, using the money I had stolen from Treblinka to buy what food we could find. Anya gave birth to her baby in a barn near the Polish border. She was very sick afterwards, but eventu-

ally she recovered.' David looked at Rose and knew that
she too was reliving the terror. 'The war came to an end
and we managed to make our way to Austria. Do you
remember Peggetz, Rose?'

Rose nodded. 'Yes. A terrible place, a terrible time . . .'

PEGGETZ CAMP, AUSTRIA, 1945

There seemed to be hundreds of men, women and children heading for the displaced persons camp run by the
British army, all of them nursing the hope that this would
be their way home.

Convoys of army trucks filled with soldiers advanced
across the mountainous countryside around Lienz.

Rosa and Anya were dropping with exhaustion and
Anya's baby, Tonia, grizzled ceaselessly as she was
bumped up and down in the makeshift baby carrier slung
round Anya's back.

Peggetz camp stretched endlessly along the Drau valley. It was a German barracks, now filled to the brim with
refugees of all nationalities.

There were thousands of Cossack soldiers, their horses
grazing for miles in the green countryside surrounding
the camp.

'David, it looks like Treblinka,' Rosa said uncertainly as
David followed the others through the wooden gates.

'Hush now, Rosa. We won't be here for long. All we
have to do is to speak to a British officer and tell him we
are half English. They will help us.'

The four of them spent their first night in Peggetz

under the stars, as there was no room for them inside the dormitories.

The next morning, David left Anya and Rosa chatting with a young Cossack soldier and went to find someone who could help them.

He saw a British officer in uniform and went up to him.

'Excuse me, sir.' David had not spoken English for many months and struggled to remember his former fluency. 'My sister and I have family in Britain. We want to go there as soon as possible. See.' David showed the officer his mother's British passport.

The officer, surprised at the dishevelled boy's good English, studied the passport.

'You say this is your mother?'

'Yes, sir. And I have the address of my grandparents. Is there a train we can catch to England from here?'

'I'm afraid it doesn't work quite like that, my boy. There are hundreds in this camp who wish to leave, and many who would like to go to England. However, the Red Cross is in that hut over there. If you go and see the officer in charge, they might be able to help you.'

The officer turned away and David's heart sank. He knew that his mama had run away with his papa and hadn't spoken to his grandparents since. They didn't know that Rosa and he existed. He wandered miserably over to the hut that the officer had pointed to, and went inside. There was a line of people waiting to see the Red Cross official, who sat at a desk. Eventually, it was his turn.

'Name.'

'David Delanski. And Rosa Delanski, my sister. We want to go to Britain to our grandparents.'

'Do you indeed?' The official looked sceptical.

David explained as best he could about their situation. The official's expression, hardened by hundreds of similar stories, didn't change.

'Right, well, all I can do is to write to this couple and see if they corroborate your story. Do you have any identity documents?'

'Yes. My mother's passport.'

'Anything else?

David remembered the locket, now back round his neck. He unclasped it carefully.

'Here. Send that. My grandmother gave it to my mother.'

'Good. It may be some time before we hear. Post is still struggling to get through and we have a lot of cases to deal with.'

'What about our friend, Anya? She has no home and she wants to come to England too.'

'What nationality is your friend?'

'Ukrainian.'

'Ahh. What is her name?'

'Anya, er, I don't know her second name.'

'I'll see what I can do. In the meantime, remain in the camp.' The officer watched as the boy left the room. For him and his sister, there was a slim chance, but for the Ukrainian girl, none. They had just received orders that all Soviet citizens were to be repatriated, by force if necessary. The thousands of Cossacks and other Russian refugees would be moved out in a few weeks' time, back to Russia to face an unknown fate.

*

David discovered, while he was waiting in the queue to see the Red Cross official, that in the village of Lienz it was possible to buy bread and fresh milk, albeit at extortionate prices. He went back to Rosa and Anya who were still sitting where he'd left them with the Cossack.

'When are we going to England?' Rosa asked him.

'Not yet, Rosa, but soon, I promise.' David did not want Rosa to see the fearful doubts that were in his mind.

Rosa stood up and hugged him. 'Good. I don't like it here.'

'No, but we just have to wait until they contact our grandparents. Then we'll be off.'

Anya stood up. 'David, this is Sergei. He says there is a tent near his that has just been vacated, but we must go now before someone else finds it.'

'Thank you, Sergei. If you would take the girls with you to the tent, I will go into Lienz and find some supper.'

Anya translated into Russian and Sergei nodded.

That night, David and Sergei built a fire over which they cooked the sausage that David had purchased earlier. It was a beautiful hot night, and some of the Cossacks began singing and dancing with the women. David was urged to accompany them on his violin. Anya stood up and danced with Sergei, while Rosa held little Tonia. Anya didn't come back to the tent until dawn was breaking and Tonia was grizzling with hunger.

'David, there is a rumour among the Cossacks that there is to be forcible repatriation for Russians and Ukrainians.' Anya came and sat next to David after breakfast. 'Can it be true?'

David shrugged. 'I don't know, Anya.'

Her eyes were filled with fear. 'My family fled the Ukraine ten years ago to escape the Communist regime. I couldn't bear to go back there. Sergei says we would all be punished.

'But why, Anya? You have done nothing.'

'I know, David, but Stalin; he is a . . .' Anya pulled at a blade of grass. 'Anyway, the Cossacks are going tomorrow for a meeting with Field Marshal Alexander. I think they will explain everything then.' Anya turned and looked into David's eyes. 'I cannot go back to Russia. I would rather die.'

David nodded. 'If there is a problem, we will leave here immediately,' he said simply.

'Thank you, David. But if anything did happen . . . I . . . would you take care of Tonia for me?'

'Of course, Anya, but I think you're worrying for nothing.'

'Maybe,' Anya looked over the beautiful Austrian countryside, a rock of fear in place of her heart.

The following day, David watched with Anya as the Cossack officers were loaded into trucks.

That evening, the trucks came back empty.

The following day, Major Davies, the officer in charge of the camp, announced that the rumours were true. Forcible repatriation had been agreed between Stalin, Churchill and Roosevelt. People were to be moved back to Russia as from tomorrow.

All hell let loose in the camp. Thousands of Russian refugees, men, women and children, were living there.

Some started to pick up their meagre possessions and walk, like automatons, away from the camp.

Later, a makeshift platform was erected in the main square of the camp. The priest was going to hold a service of prayer before the loading began tomorrow morning.

David searched through the milling, wailing crowds for Anya. She was nowhere to be seen.

He didn't understand. He knew that the Cossacks should be considered enemies of the Soviet Union for fighting with the Germans, but surely, innocent women and children wouldn't be punished?

David returned to the tent. Tonia was fast asleep, wrapped up in a blanket. David saw there was a piece of paper pinned to her.

He removed it and read it.

'Dear David,

Sergei and I have left the camp. We face certain death if we stay. You may not understand, but believe me, it's true. We are heading for Switzerland, where we hope we can find asylum. We may not get there alive and that is why I ask you, *please*, David, to take care of Tonia until I send for her.

I will find you in England.

Thank you, my dearest friend.

Good luck and good-bye.

Anya.'

The following day, David watched through a window of one of the now empty dormitories as people were loaded, screaming and kicking, into trucks. Shots rang out time and again. It was like revisiting his worst memories of Treblinka. He had foolishly believed the war was at an end. But he understood now, and thanked God that Anya had left.

'May God go with you.' he whispered, as he hugged Rosa and Tonia to his breast.

David shook himself to bring him back to the present. Miranda was staring at him in shocked silence. She turned to Rose. 'Why did you never tell Miles and me about your past? I know that it has little to do with me, because I'm adopted, but surely . . .?'

'Darling,' Rose gripped Miranda's hand. 'Forgive me, for that is where you are so wrong. David, please continue.'

David nodded. 'After Anya left and the rest of the Russians were repatriated, news came from England to tell Rose and me that our grandparents were willing to take us in. But Tonia, Anya's child, was unable to come with us. The authorities at the camp told us not to worry, that the baby would be adopted. Before we left the camp, we wrote a letter to baby Tonia explaining how her mother had escaped being repatriated to Russia by running away. We told her that Anya had sworn to come and find her once she was settled and how we both loved her and wished she could come with us to England. We wrote down our full names and our grandparents' address in London. We asked the Red Cross to put the letter in Tonia's file for safe-keeping until she was old enough to understand. We left for London and a new life.'

'And what happened to Anya?' asked Miranda.

David studied Rose's guilty face.

'We don't know, Miranda. We think that she and Sergei were probably caught and shipped back to a labour camp in Siberia. Not many escaped.'

'And Tonia? The baby?' She looked up at Rose, who was deathly white. Rose looked at David, remembering his reaction to what she had told him earlier. David nodded imperceptibly.

'Rose has something else to tell you, Miranda. Then you might understand why this has so much to do with you. I'll be in my cabin. Call me if you need me.'

Rose nodded as David left the room. Rose looked at her daughter. The time had come.

'Darling, I want you to be very brave, like you have been so far. I'm going to tell you about your real mother.'

4

OXENHOPE, YORKSHIRE, 1960

THE WRITING ON the envelope was strange, written in
an unfamiliar hand. Rose picked it up from the mat and
saw that it had been readdressed from her grandmother's house in London, then sent on to her old
London address. It had then been redirected, along with
the rest of her post, to her new home in Yorkshire.

She heard Miles crying in the kitchen, so she took the
letter with her and opened it with one hand, while she
spoon-fed her three-year-old son with the other.

The English was appalling, broken and badly spelt, and
it took her a long time to work out the first sentence.

'Deer Miss Delanski . . .'

Just the use of the name that seemed part of a long ago
distant person, removed from herself, made her shudder.

'My name is Tonia Rosstoff. I am locking for you or
David Delanski. My Mother was Anya Rosstoff. You

481

knew her at Peggetz. Please, very urgent' – this was underlined – 'I meet with you. Please to come to address at top of page. Quickly pleese.
Tonia Rosstoff.'

Rose realized that Miles was screaming as the hand holding his apple sauce had stopped inches away from his mouth as she read the letter.

She glanced at the top of the letter. The address was in east London somewhere.

First things first. She concentrated on feeding her hungry son, then cleaned him up and put him in the makeshift playpen she had erected in the corner of the kitchen. Miles sat happily playing with a toy truck and Rose sat down to read the letter again.

It sent shivers up her spine. Her first instinct was to call David . . . no! That was impossible. She would have to deal with this by herself.

The thought of even having to travel back to London was bad enough; but to see the little baby whom they had abandoned to her own fate made her heart palpitate. It brought back a whole wave of memories that she just couldn't deal with.

On the other hand, the girl was obviously desperate to see her. She checked the original postmark and saw that the letter had taken over three weeks to reach her up here.

There was nothing for it. She would have to go. Her conscience would not let her ignore it.

She couldn't take Miles and yet, having lived here in Oxenhope for over three years, she still knew no one.

The community was very tight-knit, and because she was a single woman with a baby, who had bought the big farmhouse on top of the hill, the locals eyed her with obvious suspicion.

She decided to take a walk down to the village and enquire in the post office whether there was anyone who would like to earn a bit of extra cash childminding.

As she expected, Mrs Heaton, who ran not only the tiny post office in the centre of the village, but the local gossip grapevine too, was unforthcoming.

'Childminding, you say . . . mmn.'

Rose stood there trying not to become irritated by the fact that the woman was obviously dying to enquire where the boy's father was. But Rose wanted to live here for the rest of her life, so she smiled at Mrs Heaton.

'Yes. I have to go to London tomorrow and I don't want to take Miles with me. I'll be back in the evening. It really is quite urgent.'

'Poor mite. No one to look after you, eh?' clucked Mrs Heaton disapprovingly. 'Well, I might know someone,' she said slowly.

Rose's face lit up. 'Wonderful, who?'

'Doreen Thompson. She's got a two-month-old baby. She might do it. She's a good lass, is Doreen. She stays at home *all* the time, to look after Leah,' hinted Mrs Heaton.

'Where does she live?'

''Cross t'road, off t'square. She'll be in. Say I sent you. Number eight.'

'Thank you, Mrs Heaton.'

Rose manoeuvred Miles' pushchair round in the cramped space and walked towards the door.

'Good-bye,' she called as she went out onto the narrow path and crossed the road into the square.

Number eight was a small terraced back to back at the end of the row, with a line of white nappies hanging on the line in the tiny yard at the side of the house. Chickens complained and scattered as Rose unlocked the gate and pushed Miles through the narrow opening.

She knocked on the door and a woman holding a baby peered at her through the kitchen window.

'Mrs Heaton from the post office sent me,' she called through the glass pane.

The frown lines on the face of the woman disappeared and she opened the door.

'Mrs Thompson?'

'Yes.'

'Er, Mrs Heaton told me that you might be interested in a spot of childminding, seeing as you have one of your own. Hello, sweetheart.' Rose extended a finger to the baby, who happily curled her small fat hand round it and locked it in a vice-like grip.

'Well, I . . . I don't know. I . . .'

'The thing is, Mrs Thompson, that I have to go urgently to London tomorrow and it's too long a journey for Miles. It would only be a day. I hope to be back from London by seven, but I will have to catch the first train tomorrow morning. I really am desperate, Mrs Thompson. And Miles is a good baby. He won't cause you any problems, will you, darling?'

Miles was fascinated by a chicken that was hovering near his pushchair. He reached out his arms to grab it, but it ran smartly away.

'Well, I ought to ask my husband, but . . .' Mrs Thompson's face softened as she looked down at the beautiful little boy in the pushchair, ' . . . I'm sure it won't harm just this once.'

'I'll pay you, of course. Would two pounds be enough?'

Mrs Thompson looked as if she might faint. Then she shook her head. 'No, I couldn't take that. After all, he'll cause me no extra work, seeing as I'm here with Leah any road. Ten bob'll do fine.'

'No . . .' Rose was delving into her handbag to find her purse. 'I want to pay two pounds because I'll have to bring Miles here early tomorrow morning and you've been so good to help out at such short notice. Here.' Rose handed the amazed woman two crumpled notes. 'Thank you. I'll be round tomorrow at six, equipped with everything he'll need. 'Bye.'

Rose smiled to herself as she wheeled Miles through the gate and started on the long walk up the hill. She instinctively knew that Miles would be fine in the capable, motherly hands of Mrs Thompson.

As the train pulled into King's Cross at a quarter past eleven the following day, Rose felt almost physically sick. The way she had closeted herself off in her isolated home with only Miles for company suddenly seemed like the perfect way to lead her life. Walking down the crowded platform towards the taxi rank, she forgot the many times when she had literally wept out of sheer loneliness and frustration at her inability to put a brush near a canvas.

She climbed into the taxi and gave the driver the

address on the top of Tonia's letter. She just wanted to get this over and done with and be back on the train to Leeds, headed for the safety and security of her peaceful life.

The taxi drew up in front of a run-down block in Tower Hamlets.

'The flat you want is in that building over there, but I'm not taking you any further. It's not a nice area, this, miss.'

Rose could see that perfectly well for herself.

She walked across the courtyard and looked up at the small, crumbling balconies draped with grey washing. There was an echo of children's voices, but they were unseen.

She opened the door to the block she wanted and started up the cold stone steps. Cold filled Rose's bones. The acrid smell of rotting rubbish was distinctive and one she remembered well.

The peeling door to the flat was scuffed with black boot marks and part of the pane was missing.

Rose took a deep breath and rang the bell, which didn't work, so she knocked on the letterbox.

There was no reply. She knocked again, louder, this time.

Still nothing.

The door on the other side of the landing opened and a pair of black eyes peeped out.

'Gone away.'

'Sorry?'

The Asian woman studied Rose, and opened the door further.

486

'Gone. In ambulance. Two weeks. Very sick. Maybe dead now,' the woman shrugged.

'Do you know which hospital?'

'Perhaps Whitechapel. Very near.'

'Thank you very much. I'll try it.'

Rose started down the steps. She knew where Whitechapel hospital was and decided it was faster to take a brisk ten-minute walk rather than get a cab. She prayed that she wasn't going to be too late.

She asked at information, hardly daring to breath as the woman looked down her lists.

'Yes, here we are. Tonia Rosstoff. Ward Eight.'

The woman gave Rose instructions and she walked along the pale green corridors, hating the smell of sickness and disinfectant that a blind man could identify as a hospital.

Rose asked the sister behind the desk which bed Tonia was in.

The sister looked grim. 'Are you a relative?'

'No.'

'Oh.' The sister thought for a moment. 'I was hoping you might be as Tonia doesn't seem to have any family. She is a very sick girl. Unfortunately, she came in too late. If we'd have caught her earlier, then maybe . . .' the sister shrugged.

'Is she going to be all right?'

The sister shook her head. 'I'm afraid not. She has tuberculosis, but at a very advanced stage. There is little we can do now. Poor thing. We nurses aren't meant to get attached to our patients, but Tonia, well, you'll see what I mean in a minute. So much sadness in those young eyes,' the nurse sighed. 'And her poor child. She was brought into the hospital with Tonia, suffering from malnutrition. She's fine now, and ready to leave the ward, but God knows what will happen to her when her mother dies. Taken into care, I suppose, as there's no family. Anyway, follow me. I'm afraid her English is not good and she's very weak,' the sister whispered as they walked into a small side ward.

The pathetic sight that lay in the bed brought tears to Rose's eyes. Tonia seemed dwarfed by the hospital bed, with the life-preserving paraphernalia surrounding her.

Rose walked nearer and saw that Tonia was asleep. She was tiny and dreadfully thin. Her cheekbones stuck out of her hollow, white face and there were huge black marks around her eyes.

Lying there, with her blonde hair spread across the pillow, she looked no older than a twelve-year-old child, although Rose knew the girl must be eighteen.

'I'll leave you,' whispered the sister and quietly closed the door.

Rose sat down in the uncomfortable wooden chair by the bed.

'Tonia,' she whispered. 'It's Rosa. Rosa Delanski.'

No response. Rose took the girl's hand and squeezed it. She tried some Polish.

'Tonia, *kochana*, Tonia darling.'

The eyelids fluttered, then parted. Tonia looked up to the ceiling, as though she supposed she was having a dream.

Rose squeezed her hand gently.

Tonia, *kochana*, do you understand Polish?'

Tonia turned very slightly, as though the movement might bring about great pain. She looked at Rose, then nodded.

It was a long time since Rose had used her native tongue and she began carefully.

'I am Rosa Delanski. You wrote me a letter asking me to come and see you.'

'Yes.' The voice was no more than a whisper. 'I never believed you would come. Thank you.'

'What was it that you needed to see me about?'

The pressure on Rose's hand tightened and Tonia heaved herself upright.

'I have a baby. Three months old. In ward in hospital. Please, look after her when I . . .' this effort seemed to have exhausted Tonia and she fell back onto the pillows. '. . . die.'

'Oh Tonia, what has happened to you? There are so many things I want to ask. When we left Peggetz, the Red Cross assured us you would be adopted and . . .'

Tonia shook her head violently. 'No. Orphanage. Terrible. Please, not my child. Please. I have written letter . . . in cabinet . . .' Tonia inclined her head slightly, '. . . look inside.'

Rose did so. There was an envelope and nothing else.

'In case you came. It asks for you to look after Miranda. Request from mother, see?'

Tonia's difficulty with speech did not help Rosa's confusion.

'Can I open it?'

Tonia nodded.

The letter was again in bad English, but it told the

reader that Tonia requested that either David or Rosa Delanski should have custody of Miranda Rosstoff if Tonia died.

'Understand that I would kill my baby rather than leave her, as I was left, to grow up alone in a terrible place. No love, only hunger, tears, unhappiness.' Tears were spitting out of Tonia's eyes as passion gave her strength to speak.

Rose's heart was breaking. Tears fell down her cheeks too.

'Oh Tonia, why oh why did you not contact us sooner? If only we'd have known, I . . .'

'I did not know about you before. Only twelve months ago. In prison – had to steal and take men to earn money to eat – and social worker asked me about family. Said none. She got my file from authorities and in it was your letter. I wrote, but no reply. I came to England to find you. Then pregnant. Then get sick. Have baby, then this.'

Tonia was panting hard.

'Sshh. Take it easy, Tonia. You have time to rest.'

Tonia's wide eyes gazed at Rose, full of fear.

'No. I think I die soon. I'm frightened . . . oh dear Lord, I'm frightened.'

Rose leaned over and gathered the girl up in her arms. She hugged her to her, feeling the fragility and the life ebbing away. She stroked her hair, her tears dampening Tonia's head. Never had she felt so utterly helpless. The effects of the past and the futility of life were never more apparent to her than now.

'I'm here now, *kochana*, Rosa is here and she'll look after your baby for you, I promise. Oh, my darling.'

Tonia pulled away and stared at Rose, her eyes full of

relief. 'Thank God you came before it was too late. You knew my mother, Miranda will have family. Now please call the sister.'

Rose gently lay Tonia back on the pillow. 'Do you need something?'

'Yes.'

Rose went to the door and called the sister, who came running down the corridor.

'Is she all right?' her face was a picture of concern.

'I don't know. She said she wants to see you.'

The sister moved to Tonia's bedside and leant near her patient. Tonia whispered to her for a long time, struggling with the words. Eventually, the sister nodded and raised her head.

'I think she said I'm to promise that I'll let you take her baby home. That you are the only family she has; that you loved her mother and she wants you to be Miranda's mother. Can you ask her in Polish if I'm right?'

Rose did so and Tonia nodded. 'Yes. Not orphanage, pleeze, promise.'

The sister's eyes too were full of tears.

'I promise. Why don't I go and get Miranda now?'

A smile broke on Tonia's face and the sister hurried out of the room.

Rose sat down once more and took Tonia's hand. 'There, now, *kochana*. You see? You're not to worry. Miranda is coming here now and I swear she will leave with me. I'll love her and look after her as if she is my own. You just concentrate on trying to get better.'

The sister brought in a white woollen bundle. Tonia signalled that Rose was to hold her.

Rose could not help letting out a small cry as the baby was placed gently in her arms.

'Isn't she beautiful?' whispered Tonia, studying the two of them.

'Yes. Just like her mother and grandmother.'

'Rosa, let her grow up believing she is yours. She does not need to know.'

The sister watched the three of them; dying mother holding the fingers of the tiny baby she had so bravely handed onto her new mother. She did not think she had ever seen a more heartrending scene.

Tonia's eyes were closing.

'It's time to leave now. Tonia must be exhausted.'

Rose nodded.

'Good-bye, Tonia. I'm going to come back in a couple of hours' time and we can talk again.'

Tonia opened her arms for the baby. Rose placed Miranda in them and Tonia held her tight.

'*Do widzenia, kochana*, good-bye, my darling.' Tonia gently kissed the top of Miranda's head, then handed the baby to Rose.

'She is yours now, Rosa. I thank you from the bottom of my heart.'

'You can see her again later, my love,' said the sister.

Rose kissed Tonia.

'Good-bye, Tonia. I'll keep my promise, I swear. You rest now.'

Tonia nodded. Her eyes followed Rose and her baby out of the door. She blew a small kiss, then lay back and closed her eyes.

*

When Rose came back to the hospital two hours later, the tear-stained sister shook her head sadly.

5

ROSE OPENED HER eyes. She had closed them to shut out the present and take herself back to that bleak hospital room. The entire event was etched so clearly on her memory and she wanted, at the very least, to be able to tell Miranda everything her mother had said before she died.

Miranda was sitting very still. Rose wanted to continue to the end.

'I have to say that I was not able to take you straight home to Yorkshire as I promised Tonia. Both that dear sister and I knew when we promised Tonia that day that the world didn't work like that. But at least your mother died happy, believing that you wouldn't have to suffer what she herself had suffered. After Tonia died, you were placed in the care of foster parents. I applied immediately to adopt you, but because of the fact that I was unmarried, I was thought unsuitable. It took me three years and numerous court hearings before I finally brought you home with me. That sister kept her vow. It was her statement and Tonia's letter that finally convinced the court to let me adopt you. I'll never forget the day I finally held you in my arms and knew you were mine. Of course, there was one vow I couldn't keep to Tonia. By the time you finally came home to Yorkshire, you were almost four years old. You could talk and you were very confused as to who your mummy was. Tonia hadn't wanted you to know that you were adopted, but I had to tell you that I was your new mother, because you never stopped asking. You seemed worried that I might disappear, as you had been shunted from one foster family to another in the years I had been trying to adopt you. Oh Miranda, I swear that I loved you as my own, and yet you always felt second best to Miles. Sometimes I wanted to tell you how I'd fought for the right to adopt you tooth and nail, just to prove to you how much I cared.'

'So I took revenge for my real mother and my grand-mother, and from what you say there is every possibility that Santos – I mean Frankl – was my grandfather?'

Rose nodded slowly. 'Yes, although Anya, your grand-mother, was forced to have relations with other SS offi-cers, so it is something we will never know for certain.'

Miranda looked up at Rose. 'He deserved to die, didn't he?'

'Oh, my darling, yes, yes. Not just for us, but for what he has done to you.'

'He threatened Chloe. He took pictures of her and said he'd hurt her if I tried to contact her. I . . . love her . . . so much. And he killed the man I loved. For the past two years he's kept me locked up, like . . . an animal in a cage, because I'd tried to run away. I –' Miranda's voice broke and she could not continue.

'When David first told me about the way that Frankl had treated you, I presumed that it was because he knew you were my daughter. But he didn't know, Miranda. He had no reason to treat you in that way, other than the fact that he was a twisted, diabolical, evil man. His cruelty did not end at Treblinka, it would never have ended.'

Miranda was silent. Then she said, 'I'm scared, Rose. Will they send me to prison?'

'No, darling. David and his organization are making sure that will never happen. As far as the authorities are concerned, you were not on that boat. David has told the Greek police that Frankl was missing from the boat when he and the Captain awoke in the morning. They still haven't recovered Frankl's body. And even if they do, the organization that David has been working with is very powerful, reaching to the very highest level in America. The case will be taken no further. There are hundreds that wanted Frankl dead, believe me.'

'But they wanted him alive so he could be extradited and stand trial. I ruined all those years of planning.'

'I believe it's for the best. I, for one, would not have been able to go to court to give evidence against him. The thought of seeing that man ever again . . .' Rose shuddered.

'He made me do some terrible things, Rose. I . . . can't tell you.' Miranda gripped Rose's arm.

'Oh, my darling. I, too, suffered in the same way. I was no more than eleven. I'd blocked it out in order to survive, but the pain is still there. Miranda, we have to help each other through now. We both have to try and start again, for Chloe's sake, if not ours.'

496

'How is she?'

Tears came to Rose's eyes. 'Beautiful.'

'I'm desperate to see her, but I'm so scared she may have forgotten me.'

'Darling, not a day went past when we didn't talk of you. Miranda, you've no idea how terrified I've been. I haven't slept properly since you disappeared. The things I imagined . . .'

As Miranda saw the agonized look on Rose's face, a ray of sunshine streamed into her mind, clearing out the deep cobwebs of insecurity, hate and anger. She saw with clarity that all through her childhood, Rose had shown her nothing but patience and love, but her own vulnerability had made her unable to recognize this.

Miranda felt an enormous sense of guilt for the pain she had caused not just Chloe, but Rose. Her mother, who so obviously loved her.

'I can't deny the fact that I put you and Chloe through such a terrible time because of my own selfishness, but I believe that I have been punished. I fell in love with someone who was neither rich nor handsome. And through him, I began to understand the true values in life. I've lost him, and I don't think that I will ever love again. But I know now that I can be a good mother to Chloe. And I hope that we can become friends.' Miranda paused. 'I'm going to need your help in the next few months.'

Rose stretched out her arms.

'And I yours, darling. And I yours.'

Mother and daughter talked through the night, and only as dawn was breaking, did Miranda rise.

497

'Yesterday, I felt my life was over, and you've helped me to see things about myself and my past that I needed to understand before I could go forward.' Miranda sighed. 'I'm so dreadfully tired now.'

'Go and sleep and don't worry. Rose is here now. The nightmare is over.'

'Yes. Good-night, Mother. I love you.'

Miranda left the salon.

Rose sat still for a long time, then she went up on deck to watch the dawn heralding another day.

There were so many things that, like Miranda, she had to work out. Feelings that had been revitalized, rekindled with the kind of overpowering strength that had always been there, but buried.

'How did she take the news that Frankl may be her grandfather?' A hand was placed on her shoulder. A tremor ran through Rose. She did not turn round.

'As well as could be expected. There is so much for her to take in, to understand. The things she has been through . . . it seems so cruel, history repeating itself. Why Miranda? Why Tonia's daughter?'

'Why you? Why me?' The hand massaged Rose's shoulder. 'We are not here to question why. The older I get, the more I believe that our destiny is mapped out for us before we give our first scream of existence.' David paused. 'I've missed you, Rose.'

The sudden intensity in his voice brought back overpowering memories. This was dangerous. The spell had to be broken. Rose moved away.

'Miranda and I will return home to Yorkshire as soon as possible.'

498

'Please, Rose. Stay a little longer. Surely Miranda needs a little more time to adjust? And there is something I wish to talk to you about.'

'What is that?'

'Brett. As you tried to protect your children, so I did the same. He knows nothing of the past. Oh Rose, I have been a dreadful father. Selfishly dissuading him from his obvious artistic talent because I couldn't handle it. But now I have to sort it out, try and put things right to make sure my past does not damage my son any further. And I need your help.'

'How can I help?'

'Well, this is what I plan to do . . .'

6

'INDUSTRIALIST FRANK SANTOS, who was reported missing from his boat during a short holiday in the Greek islands, is believed to have fallen overboard. Shreds of his clothing have been discovered and it is thought he may have become entangled with the propellers of the boat. The alarm was raised by Mr David Cooper, a close friend and business associate of Santos, who was the only other person aboard apart from the Captain. Greek police do not suspect foul play. Although Mr Santos owned companies across the world, he shunned the limelight, preferring to live a quiet life in . . .'

Brett caught the bulletin just as he was leaving his apartment for Kennedy airport, the news making him more confused. He'd received a call from his father last night, asking him to catch the next flight to Nice, where David would meet him.

Eleven hours later, when Brett emerged from Arrivals at Nice, there was his father, looking dapper in a pair of casual trousers and designer sunglasses.

'Hello, Brett.' His father slapped him on the back

warmly. 'Thanks for coming at such short notice. Let's get off, shall we? We're meeting Rose and Miranda in St Tropez for dinner.'

'Rose and Miranda? Why?'

David walked swiftly to his hired Mercedes, threw Brett's holdall in the back and opened the passenger door. He started the engine and they set off out of the airport.

'Brett, I have about two hours to put you in the picture. I feel dreadful for never telling you any of this, guilty for being such a bad father and a complete shit for never listening to anything you tried to say to me.'

David concentrated on a bad right turn as Brett's mouth dropped open.

His father continued speaking completely calmly.

'An enormous number of things have just happened which you have a right to know about. I'm going to start from the beginning and I suggest you hear me out. Save any questions for when I've finished. You'll be shocked, amazed and sickened, but I have to tell you everything.'

So, as they drove through the magnificent scenery along the coast of the South of France, David told him his story, beginning in Poland and finishing with the events a few days ago on the boat.

'I know it's an outrageous amount to ask anyone to take in at one go, but I think it was best to get it all out. I'm sure you have a list of questions and I shall do my best to answer them.'

'Oh, Dad,' Brett's voice broke with emotion. 'Why didn't you tell me? If only I'd known. I would have helped, you know. You shouldn't have shouldered all this alone. I'm sorry if I'm not responding to it very well. But it is a revelation. And part of me too. You shouldn't have protected me. I had a right to know my heritage.'

'I know that now. But if I had told you, then I could never have escaped. It would have been part of my future, and yours.'

'But the whole point is, Dad, that it has been. It's had a huge effect on you, and therefore on me and Mum,' Brett said sadly.

'I did what I thought was right, for all of us. I'm sorry if I was wrong. I'm so sorry, Brett, for being so blind. It's so difficult to explain how I've felt, I . . .'

'Try, Dad. I might understand better than you think.'

'Okay.' David thought for a minute. 'Well, would you understand it if I told you that making money was almost an obsession for me; that because it was an unemotional currency, and yet so powerful, I was able to block off all the confusion and hate that was the legacy of my past, and concentrate on that. It couldn't hurt me; I was in control of it and it made me feel safe. I was also very good at it. I was unable to touch my emotions, and money filled the void.'

'Poor mother,' whispered Brett, almost to himself.

'Yes.' David knew there were other reasons he had been unable to show his wife love, but they were secrets he would take to the grave with him, that his son would never understand.

'Did you love her?'

'Sorry?' David was deep in his own thoughts.

'Did you love her?'

'Yes, Brett. And like you, she tried very hard to reach

502

me. It was entirely my fault that she wasn't able to.' David wished to go no further. He changed the subject. 'Look, obviously I brought you over here to tell you all this, but there's another reason. How happy are you working for Cooper Industries?'

Brett shrugged. 'I enjoy it.'

'I've been honest with you, Brett, so please be honest with me.'

'Okay, Dad,' Brett said slowly. 'Five years ago when I first came into the company, I hated it. I felt resentful that you'd never asked me what I wanted to do with my future, that you'd always assumed I would follow in your footsteps. My business acumen has never and will never match yours. I don't thrive on making mega-deals. But over the years, I suppose I've learned to accept it better. I've settled down and tried to forget all those dreams I had of being an artist. If you ask me if I'm happy I'd have to say, no, not really. But I feel ashamed then, because of all the millions of people who would swap their poverty-stricken lives to be me.'

'Mmn,' pondered David. 'The thing is, Brett, that a lot of this is my fault. After all, if you had been poverty-stricken, then nobody would have cared if you'd gone off to France and spent the rest of your life painting. So, in fact, having a wealthy family has hemmed you in, when it should have helped you.'

'There's one last thing. Was it because of your need to break from the past that you didn't see Rose for all those years?'

This was a question David had been dreading, but his answer was prepared.

'Partly. We also had a very bad argument. It was blown up out of all proportion and both of us were too proud to say sorry. So stupid, really. We wasted twenty-eight years. Anyway, it's all mended now. And your Aunt Rose and I have cooked up a plan for you. It was her idea and I want you to know it has my full blessing.' David pulled the car to a halt. He reached over and squeezed Brett's hand. 'Forgive me, Brett. I hope I'm going to be able to make amends.'

Brett saw the tears in his father's eyes. He nodded.

The moment was gone quickly as David jumped out of the car, but it was the first time in his life that Brett had seen his father show any true emotion towards him.

'So that's the plan. What do you think?' Rose's eyes were shining in anticipation.

The sea-front restaurant was empty, the first of the tourists not expected until April when the weather began to improve. Rose had been waiting for them when they arrived, a bottle of white wine on the table.

Brett was stunned at the proposal Rose had just put to him. He eyed his father nervously.

David smiled at him. 'Brett, I told you that I gave this plan my full blessing. If it doesn't work out, there will always be a place for you at Cooper Industries.'

'We thought that it was the perfect way for you to find out if it's what you want,' Rose continued. 'There'll be no pressure, and rather than sailing straight into art school, you'll be able to work at your own pace.'

'You'll also have one of the best teachers there is to guide and help you,' smiled David. 'Well? What do you say?'

Brett looked from one to the other of them. He was overwhelmed. Rose had suggested that he come to England with her and work alongside her in her studio for a few months. After that, he'd be free to either continue painting and go to art school, or slip back into Cooper Industries in his present situation.

'I . . . Dad, I . . . but what about my work at Cooper Industries? I can't just walk out and leave you in the lurch?'

'We'll cope, just,' smiled David. 'It is what you want, isn't it, Brett?'

'Well . . . yes, oh God, yes!' Brett laughed.

'Miranda and I are flying back to England in a week. We want to spend some time together before we go back to Yorkshire and see Chloe, her little girl. You're welcome any time after that.'

'Well, I have some things to tidy up at work, but . . .'

David brushed Brett's remonstrations away with a flick of his wrist. 'Nothing that can't be sorted out.'

Brett banged the table with his hands. 'Okay then. You've got yourself a deal!' Brett's eyes were shining and he looked as if an enormous weight had been lifted from his shoulders.

'I'm just sorry it's taken this long. How I could have ignored my own son's talent, coming from the background he does, I'll never know,' said David sadly.

'Hold on a minute, Dad. I haven't put brush to canvas in years. I may not be able to do it any more.'

'Believe me, Brett, you will. I didn't paint for almost twenty years. It never leaves you,' Rose said.

Brett was interested to see his aunt and his father

together for the first time in his life. There was an intimacy, a warmth between them, that belied any rift that had separated them for so long. Brett felt overjoyed. For the first time in his life, he felt as though he was part of a family.

A figure was standing just outside the restaurant, searching the tables with her eyes.

'Miranda! Over here!' David waved.

She smiled at him shyly and walked over. David stood up and pulled out the spare chair.

Brett studied the thin, dark-haired girl with astonishment. He could hardly believe it was Miranda. David had told him that Miranda had been through a tough time, but the shy, almost pathetic shadow of the girl he had once hated produced a wave of sympathy. 'Hello, Miranda. How are you feeling?' he asked gently.

She raised her eyes and looked at him nervously. 'I . . . better, thank you.'

'Good. It must have all been a terrible shock. Never mind, it's over now. And it looks as if I'll be joining you in England in a couple of weeks. You must be looking forward to seeing your daughter,' he said kindly.

Miranda's face lit up and her eyes cleared. As she looked at Brett, her eyes were filled with an unspoken gratefulness.

'Yes,' she said simply.

7

LEAH WOKE UP and saw that the sun was shining
through the cracks in the curtains. She lifted herself from
the bed and opened them. It was a beautiful April morning and her spirits rose.

After all, she had every reason to be happy. She was
past the danger point by three weeks and was feeling
good. Her gynaecologist had confirmed that the baby was
fine and that there was absolutely no reason why she
shouldn't be optimistic about carrying this one to term.

As she climbed out of bed, a slight pain in her side
made her wince. Leah ignored it, knowing that it was perfectly natural to get the occasional pain. It soon passed
and Leah decided to go next door and look at the
nursery. She hadn't done this for the past four months,
scared stiff that it might be a bad omen, but today she felt
relaxed and positive about her pregnancy.

The nursery had been fitted out two years ago when
Leah was pregnant for the first time. The cradle was
swathed in dust sheets which she quickly removed, and
the cupboard was filled to the brim with all manner of
expensive baby clothing.

'What a lucky little baby you're going to be,' she said to the lump in her stomach.

She left the nursery and went to take a shower.

By the time she arrived in the conservatory for breakfast, she was starving.

She made short shrift of the orange juice and croissants, then tucked into a bowl of fruit as she leafed through the mail. There were three letters for her this morning. Two she recognized as charity circulars and the third was in an unfamiliar hand.

She opened it. And gasped in horror when she saw what was inside.

It was a photo of her from four years ago, in one of Carlo's dresses, taken at the spring collections in Milan. The photo had been torn out of a four-year-old April edition of *Vogue*.

Her face had been slashed lengthways and across with a knife.

She held the photo with shaking hands, unable to tear her eyes away.

She checked inside the envelope. There was nothing else.

'Oh my God,' she breathed.

Carlo.

Things had been too quiet on that front. She had not heard a word from him in the past two years, although there had been rumours that his business had taken a nose dive since Leah had left.

A pain in her side made Leah wince. Tension. She mustn't worry or get uptight. She needed to call Anthony and tell him. He would know what to do.

Leah stood up and walked through the sitting room towards the telephone.

Another pain made her cry out as she doubled over.

'No! Oh, no!'

Betty, the housekeeper, came rushing in, having heard Leah's cries. She found her mistress crouched on the floor, her face a picture of agony.

'Call an ambulance, Betty. And Anthony. I'm losing the baby. No!' she groaned, then passed out.

8

LEAH LAY BACK on her pillows, having hardly touched the breakfast tray that Betty had brought her. She hadn't been hungry since she'd arrived home a week ago.

Anthony had suggested they fly to the house in Woodstock where they'd spent so many idyllic Christmases. Leah had shrugged and said that if that was what Anthony wanted, it was fine by her.

Anthony was urging her to see Doctor Simons, a psychiatrist, but Leah did not want to be told that she was depressed. She knew she was depressed.

A small tear caught in the corner of her eye when she thought of the little white bundle that in five months' time she would have been holding. Was she a murderess? That was what she felt like sometimes, especially with the last one. At four months, the fetus was developing into a tiny, perfect human being and she, as its mother, had failed to give it life.

She didn't want to talk to anyone about these thoughts. Anthony would tell her she was being silly and Doctor Simons that it was part of her post-miscarriage 'guilt trip'. Fine. Put a name to these feelings, but that

510

didn't halt them or make them easier to deal with.

Leah opened her post without enthusiasm.

There was another one, her face and body slashed to ribbons, this time taken from Carlo's autumn collections a year later.

Her eyes filling with tears, Leah rolled the photo into a tight ball and threw it into the wastepaper basket. She knew she ought to tell Anthony, but she wasn't up to interviews with the police, or dealing with threats.

At present, she didn't really give a damn if she died.

Betty brought the slashed magazine page to Anthony after she had cleaned their bedroom.

'I think you ought to see this, sir.' Betty was very fond of the sweet young girl who treated her and the other staff so gently. She was as worried about her present state of mind as Anthony was.

Anthony took the tatty piece of paper, looked at it and sighed.

'Oh dear.'

'I found it in the wastepaper basket after breakfast. She could have done it with her fruit knife, sir.'

'Thank you, Betty, for bringing this to me.'

'That's all right. I'm concerned for her, sir. That lovely picture of Madam, it looks as though she was thinking of . . .'

'Yes, Betty. Thank you.'

'Very good, sir. Madam will be down in a few minutes. Her luggage is just being brought downstairs.'

Betty left the room.

Anthony folded up the piece of paper and stuffed it in

his pocket. This was the wrong moment to deal with it. Maybe when they had relaxed for a couple of days at the house in Woodstock, he would ask her.

Leah came into the sitting room. She was looking thin and pale, but quite beautiful in a Donna Karan soft woollen trouser suit.

'Ahh.' He went to her and kissed her on the cheek. 'Stunning as always. Ready to go, darling?'

Leah nodded silently.

'Come on then. We don't want to miss that plane, do we?'

Leah shook her head.

'Sweetheart, I promise you that these few days will do you the world of good. You love the house and we don't have to move beyond the front door if you don't want to. Could you manage a small smile for me, darling?'

Leah tried, but it was a pretty rotten attempt.

'Pathetic,' Anthony chuckled. 'Well, let's go.'

He steered her out of the room and five minutes later they were in the car heading for the airport.

'How are you feeling this morning, darling?'

Anthony set down the tray of orange juice, coffee and croissants at the bottom of the bed.

'Okay,' came a muffled voice.

'Shall I open the curtains? It's a beautiful day.'

'If you want.'

Anthony sighed in frustration. He was bitterly hurt that Leah had insisted on separate bedrooms when they'd arrived at the house. He had acquiesced, praying that after a couple of days of complete rest and relaxation,

512

Leah would realize she was being silly and move back into their bedroom.

So far, that was not the case. Day after day he'd suggested nice things to do; places to visit, restaurants he knew she loved, but there had been little response and no enthusiasm.

If he was honest, Anthony was getting to the point where he wanted to physically shake his wife, to tell her that she was becoming her own worst enemy and that she had to snap out of it. But she seemed a million miles away from him, and now that she refused to share his bed, well, he knew that was the beginning of the end.

He kept telling himself that it was just depression, that the change that had been wrought in Leah would pass; that it was not because her feelings towards him had changed. Every day, however, as she cold-shouldered him, it was getting harder to hang on to that belief.

Anthony knew he mustn't give in. If he did, he knew he would lose her completely.

He took a deep breath to steel himself against her frostiness and opened the curtains.

'There. Look at that.'

Anthony came and sat down on the bed as the sun streamed in through the windows. 'Anything you'd like to do today, sweetheart?'

Leah sat up slowly, pushing her magnificent hair away from her face and shielding her eyes against the bright sunlight.

Anthony had rarely seen her look more beautiful. He restrained his desperate urge to take her in his arms and make love to her. It had been over five months since the last time, for Leah would not let him touch her while she was pregnant in case it hurt the baby. His efforts to seduce her since she had returned home had been greeted with a grimace, as if his touch revolted her. Now, he was almost mad with desire.

'Not particularly,' she shrugged.

Anthony made a huge effort to drag his eyes away from her breasts, tantalizingly covered with a layer of white lace. He felt like a dirty old man; unloved and unattractive.

'I was thinking we might take a drive into Woodstock, do some shopping at that little boutique you love, then have some lunch at the Woodstock Inn. What do you think?'

'I'd prefer to stay here, to be honest. But if you want to go, then . . .'

Something inside Anthony snapped.

'No! It's okay, Leah. You just stay here and feel sorry for yourself! Jesus Christ! You're twenty-four! You have everything most women dream of and . . .' Anthony stopped himself as he looked into her eyes. The expression there had not changed. He ran a hand through his hair distractedly and stood up.

'Look, I'm sorry. I'm doing my best to understand how you're feeling, but . . . I'm going out for a walk. I won't be long.'

Leah watched as Anthony left the bedroom. She knew she should feel something about what he had just said, but she couldn't. There was only the same, aching numbness that prevented her from reacting, as though everything was not quite reality.

She heard the door slam and supposed she should worry.

Anthony marched out of the house and down the long driveway, berating himself for ever mentioning that he would like another child. So far as he was concerned, he loved Leah to distraction and although having a baby would cement their love, Anthony was only concerned that Leah should not lose out for marrying an older man. As it turned out, he had proved himself quite capable of being a parent, and the sadness was that Leah was unable to prove herself in the same way.

He had prayed for Leah's sake that this pregnancy would be successful and he'd been equally devastated for the same reason when it was not.

Leah's doctor had explained time and again the clinical reasons for Leah's change of personality, that it was a state of mind she could not help. He had begged Anthony to show patience and understanding, but he was only human. The deterioration since her first miscarriage had been a gradual, but noticeable process and Anthony longed for the bright, happy girl that he'd married.

Anthony sometimes pondered the theory that Leah was bored and that was why she had focused her energies on having a baby. Her quick, enquiring mind needed more than the daily routine of being a businessman's wife, especially after the hectic life she had led before she married. He had asked her time and time again if she'd like to go back to modelling, or indeed chose some other career that enabled her to put her brain to good use. Leah had always refused.

As he strolled down the wooded avenue, listening to the calling of the cuckoos in the evergreens high above him, Anthony found himself wondering once again why Leah had so suddenly decided to marry him. At the time, he had been so overjoyed that she had agreed, he had not stopped to think too deeply. But now, as he witnessed their relationship deteriorating before his eyes, he had to ask whether Leah had ever really loved him to begin with.

Anthony was scared. Losing Leah was a nightmare he couldn't handle. A wedge was forcing them apart and Anthony didn't know how to bring them back together.

Later, they sat together on the terrace. Anthony had returned full of apologies and Leah had made an effort to be pleasant.

Anthony stood up and went to her. 'Why don't we go out for a nice romantic dinner? You could put on the new Christian Dior dress I bought you last week. Mmn, darling?' He put his arms round her neck and kissed her lightly on the cheek.

Leah struggled out of his arms and shook her head. 'I'm too tired to go out. You go if you want. I'm going to have a lie-down.'

She disappeared inside.

Anthony shivered, even though the May night was warm. He sighed and picked up a copy of the *New York Times* to try to take his mind off his problems.

His attention was caught by a photograph on page fourteen. It was of the model Maria Malgasa in her heyday, looking stunning in one of Carlo Porselli's designer gowns.

Anthony read the paragraph below.

'Maria Malgasa, known to millions in the mid seventies as the world's highest paid model, has been found strangled in her hotel room in Milan, where she was on a shoot for *Vanity Fair*. The crew discovered her body when she did not appear at the airport for the flight back to New York. Her long-term lover, Carlo Porselli, is helping police with their enquiries. Details are still vague, but it is believed that there was evidence of sexual intercourse and strangulation. Ms Malgasa's body is being flown back to New York today, where pathologists will identify the exact cause of death.'

Later, Anthony showed Leah the article.

'You knew her, didn't you?'

Leah nodded as she looked at the photograph. Anthony watched as her face turned deathly pale.

'Oh . . . God. Anthony, I've been receiving pictures of myself through the post, slashed.'

'I know, darling. Betty showed me one she fished out of the bin. We thought that it was your doing.'

Leah shook her head. 'In the photographs, I'm always wearing Carlo's clothes at Carlo's shows. The postmark on the envelope was Milan. If he's doing this to me, don't you think it's possible that he . . . Maria?' Leah could not voice the words.

'I don't know. But what I do know is that we're calling the police now.'

9

'*PER FAVORE*, PLEASE believe me. I left Maria straight after dinner. She said she was tired and wanted an early night.' Carlo swept a hand through his dishevelled hair as he gazed across the desk at the police officer.

'But, Signor Porselli, traces of your semen have been found on the sheets on Miss Malgasa's bed. Your fingerprints are on her body and all over the room. The hotel chambermaid assures us that clean bed linen was put on the bed on the afternoon of Miss Malgasa's murder.'

'But I've told you!' Carlo banged his fist down on the desk in frustration. 'Maria and I made love before we went out to dinner that evening, not afterwards. I said good-night to her by the hotel lift and returned to my apartment alone.'

'It is a pity that nobody in the hotel lobby can verify that. The porter swears he saw a dark-haired man who fits your description accompanying Miss Malgasa up to her room, fifteen minutes after you say you left. And that he saw the same man leave at half past four in the morning.'

Carlo sighed deeply. '*Non lo so*, I don't know who that man was. It was not me. I loved Maria! She was my top model! Why would I wish to murder her? I have no track record of violence, do I? Ask any of the models I have worked with over the years.'

'We have, Signor Porselli.' The officer threw a clear plastic wallet across the desk. 'Take a look at those.'

Carlo drew out the shredded photos of Leah.

'Attch! These are *nauseante*! Depraved!'

'We think so too, and so does Mrs Van Schiele, who has been receiving them through the post. The last one carried a Milan postmark.'

Carlo opened his mouth to speak, but stopped himself. He knew by the way the officer was looking at him that he believed he was guilty of both crimes.

'Was she to be your next victim, *Signor* Porselli?'

Carlo felt tears of self-pity and indignation pricking at his eyelids. To think that he, Carlo Porselli, the great designer, was being held in this pigsty of a Milanese police cell, wrongly suspected of murder.

'I shall leave you now to think about what I have just said, *signore*. We have enough evidence to charge you as it is.'

'When my friends hear of this, you will suffer!' Carlo shouted as the officer moved towards the door of the cell.

The officer smiled. 'I think, *signore*, that you don't have as many friends as you thought. *Buona notte.*'

The cell door banged shut.

Carlo put his head in his hands and wept.

The two-hour flight from Linate airport arrived on time at Heathrow. The passengers made their way through passport control, customs and out into the fresh May air.

He bought a newspaper as he waited in the queue for a taxi. As the cab sped away from the airport, he smiled as he read the headlines. Carlo Porselli had been charged with Maria Malgasa's murder.

He'd planned it that way, to pay Carlo back for the way he'd stolen Leah from him and turned her into an arrogant, self-serving whore who'd treated him like scum.

Maria and the others had satisfied his need for a short while, but now it was time to claim the woman that had always been his. He'd sent her warnings and now all he had to do was wait. He knew she'd come to him.

The cab took an hour to reach King's Cross station. He boarded the train and settled down for the long journey north.

10

ROSE WANTED TO weep as she watched Miranda nervously fiddling with the buttons on her coat as the taxi drove up the hill towards the farmhouse. She grasped Rose's hand.

'What if she doesn't remember me? I look so different.'

'She will,' Rose replied, exuding a confidence she didn't feel.

Brett waved the two women away and said he'd help the driver with the luggage and pay him.

Miranda, still holding tightly onto Rose's hand, walked towards the front door.

It opened before Rose had time to insert the key.

Mrs Thompson's face appeared from behind it.

'Is everything all right, Doreen? Chloe?' she asked as calmly as she could.

'Chloe's fine,' said Mrs Thompson. 'Here you go, love. I told you your mum was coming home today, didn't I?'

A beautiful seven-year-old child appeared shyly from behind Mrs Thompson. She looked nervously at the two women standing on the doorstep. For one dreadful moment, Rose thought Chloe was going to run into her arms.

'Hello, Granny,' she smiled sedately.

Then she turned her eyes to Miranda, who was standing stock-still, staring at her.

'Hello, Mummy,' she said and reached out her arms towards Miranda.

With a cry, Miranda swept Chloe up in her arms and hugged her as though she would never let her go.

The two older women's eyes were cloudy as they watched. Rose felt a hand on her shoulder. She turned and saw that Brett's eyes were misty too. They watched as Miranda carried her child inside and into the sitting room.

'Oh my darling, my baby.' she wept. 'Mummy's home now, Mummy's home.'

11

BRETT AWOKE TO the sound of the family of thrushes that were nesting under the eaves of the farmhouse outside his bedroom. He squinted in the half-light at the clock and saw that it was six in the morning. He bounded out of bed, donned an old sweatshirt and jeans, and slipped downstairs to his studio. He smiled as he entered the room. It had been Rose's before she had converted one of the barns and she had passed it on to him. He stood for a second, glorifying in the smell of paints and general clutter that had been of his own making.

Brett studied the painting on his easel carefully.

He knew that this was by far the best of anything he had painted up to now. The colours were so subtle, blending into each other in a perfect, natural harmony.

This painting had identity. It was not just Brett Cooper apeing another artist. It had an individuality and uniqueness of its own.

It had taken nine paintings and three months of solid work to get him to this point. The rest, scattered around the studio, were good, but lacked singularity. Rose had been very encouraging, telling him that he must continue and that, eventually, his own personal style would start to blossom. She told him that he had a natural talent that needed to be cultivated, worked on and given freedom to express itself.

Brett knew that, at last, he had done just that.

In his formative years, he had taken an object or landscape and emphasized it at its full beauty. But since he had started painting again, he felt he wanted to say something on the canvas, give the painting a meaning. The one he had just completed was of a beautiful young girl, reaching for the heavens. The top half of the painting was full of glorious colour; the sky was blue, the sun was shining, the apple blossom trees around the girl's head were in full bloom, and Brett had used romantic expressionism to the full. But for the bottom half of the painting, he had used much darker colours. There were male hands grasping at the girl's ankles, and the ground below her was cold and black. One of the male arms was stretching up towards her barely covered midriff.

Brett stared at it for a moment. 'Woman in Chains,' he murmured.

He would bring Rose in to see it today. Half the joy of living here was the long conversations over a bottle of wine that went on deep into the night. Rose would tell him of her days at the Royal College and they would discuss the works of Freud, Bacon and Sutherland, and her contemporaries in the fifties, taking hours over each painting from Rose's huge collection of catalogues.

But as Brett looked at his new painting, he knew the time had come to move on. There was no question of his returning to work for his father in New York. He needed to be in an institution full of young artists, to grow with them. His Aunt Rose was keen on his following her into the Royal College, but Brett knew where he wanted to go. To Paris, where his grandfather Jacob had lived and learnt his craft. It was beckoning to him; he dreamt of it at night so vividly that he awoke in the morning questioning the reality of the new day.

He decided that the time had come to discuss his future with Rose, tell her that he wanted to go to study at the Sorbonne. Brett took his palette and a brush and began to work, putting the finishing touches to the new painting. As always when he worked, his mind turned to Leah.

He had read of Carlo's arrest for the murder of Maria Malgasa with a large degree of horror and a small degree of satisfaction. Brett had often wondered why Leah had never married Carlo, after the announcement in the papers. He had presumed that they had fallen out in some way, but now this had happened, doubt was beginning to creep into his mind. He'd been so drunk and angry when he'd confronted Leah, not really giving her an opportunity to explain. What if she had been telling the truth? After all, the man had just been charged with the brutal murder of another model.

Brett sighed. It was pointless torturing himself. Leah was happily married to another man. The relationship was not meant to be. He was destined to spend the rest of his life dreaming of a woman that could never be his.

Brett knew his father thought it odd that his interest in women had been non-existent for the past five years. But Rose understood how he felt. She would often tell him how she had loved one man when she was younger, and how circumstances had made it impossible for them to be together.

Brett put his paintbrush down and realized that he was hungry. He opened the door to his studio, walked down the hall and paused to pick up the post.

Miranda and Chloe were already in the kitchen eating breakfast. Chloe's face lit up when she saw Brett.

'Hello, Uncle Brett. Have you been painting more pictures?'

Brett nodded and handed Miranda a typewritten envelope.

'Yes, Chloe. Two for you, Miranda,' he smiled.

'Thanks, Brett.'

Brett often experienced a feeling of *déja vu* when they were sitting round the table at breakfast. Mrs Thompson bustled round the kitchen and Brett would let his mind wander back to that first holiday he had spent here. So much time had passed, so much water under the bridge.

Rose arrived in the kitchen.

'Morning, everyone.' She looked exhausted.

'Sleep well?' enquired Brett politely.

'No. I suddenly had a major panic about the New York exhibition at three o'clock in the morning. I've been in my studio ever since.'

'Honestly, Rose. I know you've never shown over there before, but your work is superb, really,' comforted Brett.

'Thanks, dear, but it's less than two months away and I've still got another four paintings to complete.'

'We'll be there to support you, Mother,' said Miranda gently.

'I know you will, darling. I'm sorry if I'm being neurotic, but it matters so much that I'm a success over there.'

'You will be, promise. Now, would it be all right if I took your car into Leeds this morning? I want to buy a couple of outfits for Chloe for our trip.'

'Of course, darling.' Rose looked at Miranda. 'Are you feeling okay? You look awfully pale.'

'Oh, yes. I'm fine. Come on, Chloe. Let's go and get you dressed, sweetheart.'

'Okay, Mummy.'

The two of them left the room.

Rose sighed. 'Miranda worries me, Brett. She's so up and down. I'm hoping the trip to New York will do her good, although I'm not going to have much time to spend with her. It's a shame she and Chloe can't stay over with me for the whole month, but Chloe has to be back to start school.'

'I'm sure they'll have a wonderful time. Dad's duplex is stunning and right in the centre of everything. Dad told me he's going to take some time off work while you're staying with him to show Miranda and Chloe around.'

'That'll be nice.'

Brett rose. 'I'd better get back to work. Could you come to my studio later, Rose? I have something to show you, and I want to have a chat.'

'Of course.'

Rose sat at the table and yawned.

If she went to New York, she wondered if she would ever return home.

*

Miranda stood in the queue at the bank in Bradford with Chloe waiting impatiently at her side. Her heart was thumping steadily as she stared at the envelope she had addressed earlier. When it was her turn, she handed in the cheque made out for five hundred pounds cash. She asked for it in fifties, then took the money and sat down at one of the small tables placed around the room.

'What are you doing, Mummy?' asked Chloe, watching Miranda carefully wrapping the money inside a sheet of foolscap paper.

'Posting a letter, darling. But it's a secret. We mustn't tell anyone.'

'Who are you posting it to?'

'That's a secret as well. Come on, let's go and have an ice cream.' Miranda took Chloe's small hand in hers. Outside the bank, she popped the envelope in the post-box and walked down the street towards the ice-cream van.

12

LEAH MOOCHED AROUND the beautiful sunny garden, viciously cutting dead heads off roses.

She checked her watch. Ten past ten. An entire day stretching before her. Then an interminable evening of strained conversation over supper when Anthony arrived home.

She could not believe the way she was feeling inside. Dead, numb, with not the slightest flicker of interest in anything.

Even when the police had interviewed her and she had shown them the slashed pages sent to her through the post, she had not really felt anything. It was as if she were a bystander, watching her life take place from a distance. She had felt nothing when Carlo had been charged, her evidence only compounding the fingerprints found in Maria's hotel room. The police said they may ask her to go to court as witness for the prosecution, but Leah didn't want to think about that.

She was sure that she didn't love Anthony any more. Though it still pained her to watch how she could so easily wound him with a word.

529

They had not slept in the same bed for over three months, ever since they had arrived back from the house in Woodstock.

The thought of sex with him repulsed her; only reminding her of her inadequacies and the deaths of her three babies. She had known it was pointless to keep trying. So she had decided to stop.

She pondered often whether Anthony was having an affair. It was only natural that he should take comfort with another woman. But he was never late in and he called her constantly when he went away on a business trip.

In some ways, she thought it would be better if he had got someone else. It would halt the guilt. She wished that he would show some anger, like that time in Woodstock, but he accepted the way she was towards him with resignation.

She had refused therapy time and time again. After all, she was not ill. Just unhappy.

Anthony had suggested that they tried again for a child, and when Leah had refused point-blank, had suggested adoption. She had still refused. To adopt a child would be a public confirmation of her inadequacies.

So, she went from day to day, just waiting until it was time for bed and she could slide into sleep and have her wonderful dream. It was recurring: a baby in her arms; small and soft and dependent, and Brett standing proudly by, looking with love in his eyes at both of them.

She wouldn't think of him for weeks at a time, then she'd have the dream and would spend the following day remembering how she had felt about him, how perfect their love had been. It stirred in her sexual feelings that she thought long since dead and she guiltily thought of Anthony and how he would feel if he knew.

But then there was the other dream; the one she'd had since she was a child. The dark figure, chasing her across the moors until she could run no further . . . and hearing Megan's voice over and over warning her . . .

Leah shook herself and tried to bring herself back to the present. Instinctively, she knew that she was wasting precious time; that her life had fallen badly off course and she wasn't doing a thing to help put it back on track.

It was as if she was in limbo, waiting for an event that she *knew* would come to save her from herself.

Until then, life must go on.

Leah picked up the fallen dead roses from the ground and made her way back towards the house.

The telephone was ringing. She picked it up.

'Hello.'

'Oh, Leah. It's Mum. I . . .'

There was a choking sound from the other end of the line.

'Mum? Are you all right? What's wrong?'

'I . . . I'm sorry. Leah, it's your dad. As you know, he's been recovering fine from his hip operation, but last night, the hospital called me. He's had a heart attack, Leah, a bad one. They don't know whether he'll pull through. Oh, Leah, I'm so frightened. I don't know what to do.'

'Mum, listen to me. I'm going to catch the next Concorde to England. I'll fly to Leeds from Heathrow. Is Dad in Airedale hospital?'

'Yes.'

'I'll meet you there as soon as I can. Mum, hang on, and tell Dad to do the same. I'm on my way.'

'Thank you, Leah. I . . . we need you.'

'Keep calm, Mum. I'll call you from the airport when I know what time I'll be arriving at Leeds.'

Leah put down the phone and immediately dialled British Airways reservations. She got the last seat on the lunchtime Concorde to London. It arrived at half past ten in the evening, missing the connecting flight to Leeds. She'd have to hire a car and drive through the night up to Yorkshire.

She ran upstairs to throw some things into a suitcase, came downstairs and wrote a note to Anthony:

'Family crisis in England. Dad has had heart attack.

Call you when I get there. L.'

Malcolm drove her to the airport and she rushed through passport control as she heard the last call for her flight.

As the plane took off, Leah experienced a rush of emotion. It almost took her breath away with its power. There was deep pain, yes, but something else too.

For the first time in months, she felt needed.

Leah arrived at Airedale hospital at four in the morning. The nurse directed her to the intensive care ward. Doreen Thompson was sitting in the waiting room, staring into space. Leah bit her lip as she saw how her mother had aged since she'd last seen her. Small patches of grey had spread through her hair and her face was tired and haggard.

Leah threw her arms around her. They held each other for a long time as Mrs Thompson wept quietly.

'Thank you for coming, Leah. I was going mad with no one to talk to.'

'How is he?'

Mrs Thompson shrugged. 'They say he's the same. No better, no worse. He looks dreadful. So pale . . . he's wired up to all these machines. He opens his eyes sometimes, but he can't talk.'

'I'll go and see him.'

'Do you want me to come with you?'

Leah shook her head. 'You stay here and try and get some rest. You look all in.'

Leah walked slowly up the quiet corridor. She saw other relatives sitting by their loved ones, even though it was the middle of the night. There were no set visiting hours in intensive care.

The nurse pointed to the room in which her father was lying. Leah took a deep breath and walked in.

She choked back a sob, nothing preparing her for the sight of the father she worshipped looking so frail and still. He was lying flat on his back, with monitors and drips attached to him.

'Dad. Dad,' she whispered softly. 'It's Leah.' She leant right over so that if he opened his eyes, he'd see her. But he didn't.

Leah sat down heavily in the chair placed by his bed. She reached for his claw-like hand, misshapen after so many years of steroids and other drugs. His poor body had taken so much suffering and Leah had never heard so much as a word of complaint from him. He was forty-eight and looked sixty-five.

'Dad, Leah's here now. I want you to concentrate on getting better very soon, so Mum and I can take you home and we can be a family like we used to be.' Tears rolled down Leah's face as she thought of all the times she could have flown back home to see them. But she'd been so wrapped up in her own selfish problems. And now it might be too late.

'Dad, do you remember when I was a little girl, and you used to take me for walks on the moors and tell me the names of all the different birds as they flew above us? And my first day at school when I cried and wouldn't go in? You told me that you'd stay the whole day outside and if I didn't like it, I could come out and you'd be waiting to take me home. Of course, once I got in there, I was okay, but you were waiting for me at hometime. I've often wondered whether you did really stay outside for the whole day.' Leah smiled through her tears, as she watched her father's eyes flicker open and a slight smile appear on his face.

Leah sat there for two hours. She went down the corridor to the Ladies, then found her mother looking a little brighter in the waiting area.

'The doctor makes his rounds shortly. Why don't we pop along to the canteen and have some breakfast? You must be starving after your journey.'

The last thing Leah was thinking about was her stomach, but she probably did need to eat.

The canteen was bustling with the change over from night to day staff. Leah and her mother managed to force a cooked breakfast down them.

'How long before the doctors know whether . . . well, the danger is passed?'

Mrs Thompson shrugged. 'They don't, really. On top of everything else, Dad's running a high temperature and is weak anyway from the hip operation. That's what did it, Leah. It was too much for his poor heart to cope with. They don't know at the moment how badly the heart attack has affected him. I've never been one for prayer, Leah, but I've sent a few up in the past couple of days. Me and your dad, well, he's the only man I've ever known. We married at seventeen. Twenty-five years. I know I sometimes get irritable with him, but he's my two eyes, Leah. I couldn't live without him.'

Leah held her hand as her mother sobbed, then quickly dried her tears with her sodden hanky. 'Anyway, no time for tears,' she said briskly. 'We've got to be strong for Dad now, Leah. Keep believing he's going to pull through. He's got to,' she said simply.

For the following two days, Leah and her mother kept a constant vigil by his bed. They talked to him, read to him, held his hand and stroked his forehead. The nurses suggested they went home and got some sleep but neither mother nor daughter would hear of it. 'We want him to know we're always there,' said Mrs Thompson firmly.

On the third morning since Leah had flown in from the States, the doctor called them both into his office.

'Good news. We're taking Mr Thompson out of intensive care this morning. We think he's going to pull through.'

'Oh, thank God, thank God,' Mrs Thompson wept.

'But he's going to be in hospital for another three

weeks or so, and after that he'll need careful nursing. Now, as we know he's out of danger, I suggest you two go home and get some rest. We don't want another couple of patients, do we?'

'Thank you, doctor, thank you.' Leah led Mrs Thompson down the corridor, and they popped their heads round the door of her father's room. A nurse was removing the monitor from his chest.

They walked to the bed. Her father's eyes were open and alert. He mouthed hello.

'We're just popping home to get some shut-eye for a few hours, love. Prepare ourselves for your return.' Mrs Thompson raised her eyebrows and Leah was thrilled to see her mother's normal banter returning.

Mrs Thompson leant over her husband and kissed him on the forehead. 'If you ever do that to me again, Yorkshire puddings are off the menu for good.'

Mr Thompson smiled and nodded. He mouthed, 'See you later.'

Mother and daughter left the hospital with a spring in their step, drove back to Oxenhope in Leah's rented Escort, and slept like babies for the rest of the day.

13

A WEEK BEFORE Mr Thompson was due to come out of hospital, Leah made an appointment to see his doctor.

He ushered her inside and she sat in a chair in front of his desk.

'How is my father, doctor?'

'Making very good progress, Leah. As I said, he will need very careful nursing for some time to come. We can provide back-up, for example the district nurse will check on him every other day, but I'm afraid the majority of work will fall into your mother's hands.'

'This is what worries me, doctor. My mother is completely exhausted. She's looked after Dad for twenty years now. I can stay for a few more days, but eventually I will have to return home to the States. I thought of hiring a nurse, but the bungalow is small and Mum's useless at delegating. So I've come up with an idea. What if I sent them both away to a convalescent home for a few weeks? It would mean Mum would be with Dad, but she'd be able to have twenty-four-hour nursing back-up to do all the things that have to be done, and at the same time have a break herself. She needs the rest as much as Dad

537

does. I've rung a few private homes and I've found one near Skipton that looks lovely in the brochure and takes husbands and wives. It sounds more like a hotel than a convalescent home and it would get Mum off to a flying start and stop me worrying quite so much.'

'I think it would be splendid. But they're very pricey.'

'That doesn't matter. I just wanted to know whether you thought it was a good idea.'

'Definitely. For both of them.'

'Good. That's settled then. I wonder if you'd tell Mum, doctor? If I tell her she'll go on about the money and tell me that she doesn't want a fuss made.'

'Of course.' The doctor smiled understandingly.

'Now, you two. Go away and don't worry about anything. Dad, try and make Mum relax, will you?'

'I'll do my best, lass.' Mr Thompson was lifted into the back of the ambulance taking them to the convalescent home twenty miles from the hospital.

'Good. 'Bye, Mum. Have a rest. That's the whole point of your going.'

'Yes, Leah, but really, me and your dad would have been fine at home.'

'Shut up, Mum!' Leah hugged her tight. 'I'll be flying over to see you when you get home.'

'If you get a chance, tell Chloe I'll miss her and I'll be back soon.'

'Yes, Mum.' Leah blew them both a kiss as the ambulance doors were closed. She watched it drive out of the hospital grounds and sauntered to her car.

As she let herself into the bungalow, depression hit her.

The past two weeks had been completely taken up with worrying about her father and supporting her mother. She had not had time to think about her own problems. But now, with the bungalow so empty and quiet, her mind moved to Anthony and her troubled marriage. She'd rung him a couple of times to let him know how things were going. He'd been as sweet as always, saying that of course she must stay for as long as she wanted, that she only had to ask and he'd be over to England and by her side in an instant. Leah had said she wanted to spend a week or so tidying up loose ends before she flew back and Anthony had accepted this without question. She'd reckoned some time alone was exactly what she needed to sort herself out.

Leah mooched around the bungalow, putting the cups on the drainer away and straightening the already perfectly placed sofa cushions. Eventually, she sat down and gave a long sigh. Maybe it was reaction from the past two weeks, but today was not the day to start down a path of soul searching.

She grabbed the keys to her car and left the bungalow. She knew where she wanted to go.

The Parsonage had had a new coat of paint since she was last here. An extension had been added, containing a souvenir shop and extra space for exhibits.

The queue to get in was enormous, but Leah stood happily in the sunshine, listening to the American coach party, bedecked with video cameras, chattering loudly in front of her. She found it odd to think that she had spent the past three years among them; they seemed so foreign out of their own country.

Inside, the Parsonage was exactly how she remembered it. She wandered round slowly, soaking in the atmosphere she'd loved as a young girl. The last time she had been here . . . was that why she had come? To evoke memories that were so pleasant, yet so painful still?

She pondered this as she walked down the cobbled main street, stopping at the Old Apothecary to buy herself some mustard seed bath powder.

She paused in front of the Stirrup Café. What the hell! If she was going to wallow in past memories, she could at least do it properly.

Leah sat down at a table by the window so she could watch the world go by, and ordered a shepherd's pie.

Just as she was about to take a sip of coffee, she glanced out of the window and saw a tall figure with a familiar head of titian hair walking up the street. No, surely she was seeing things? Her mother hadn't mentioned that he was in Yorkshire visiting Rose. It must have been someone who looked like him. He seemed to glance in her direction, but then continued walking until he was out of view.

The most dreadful disappointment swamped Leah. She slurped her coffee, deep in thought.

The little bell by the door tinkled, but Leah didn't look up .

'It *was* you. I wasn't sure at first, but . . .'

He was standing in front of her, smiling nervously.

'Hello, Brett.'

'I . . . hello.'

'What are you doing here?'

Brett looked surprised. 'I live with Rose up at the farm-

LUCINDA EDMONDS

house. Didn't your mother mention it?'

'No. But she has had other things on her mind recently.'

'Yes. I was dreadfully sorry to hear about your father. Rose told me. But he's recovering well, isn't he?'

Leah smiled. 'Yes. It was pretty touch and go for a while though.'

Brett hesitated. Then he said, 'Would you mind if I sat down?'

Leah shrugged nonchalantly. 'Sure.'

Brett put two loaves of bread on the floor by his chair. 'Rose loves the bread from the baker up the street. I come in to Haworth to get it for her.' Brett wondered why he was apologizing for being here when this part of the world was now his home.

'I'm starving. Are you eating?'

'Yes.'

'I'll have whatever you're having.' Brett caught the eye of the waitress.

'Yes?' said the waitress, pad at the ready.

Leah blushed. 'Another shepherd's pie, please.'

'Right you are.'

Leah looked at Brett and knew immediately that he remembered too.

'How long are you in England for?' he asked.

'Another week. I'm staying at the bungalow. So you don't work for your father any more?'

'No. It was his suggestion that I come over here for a few months to paint. Then if I was sure it was still what I wanted, I could apply to art schools. As a matter of fact I had some good news this morning.' Brett fiddled in the

541

pocket of his jeans and drew out a creased letter. 'The paintings I submitted to the Sorbonne School in Paris have been accepted. They want to see me for interview in ten days' time. Oh God, Leah, I want to go and study there so badly. It was where my grandfather studied, you know.'

The waitress arrived with the food.

'No, I didn't. But I'm thrilled for you. I can't believe that last time I saw you, you were so sure that your father would never let you leave his business.'

'I've done this with his full blessing, Leah.' Brett sighed as he lifted his fork and began to eat. 'So much has happened to our family in the past year. It's too complicated to explain, but Dad was hiding all sorts of wounds which made him the way he was. He's been through a pretty gruelling time and the experience has changed him completely. He's a different man. And so am I.

'Leah, you must come up to the farmhouse for a drink. I know Rose would love to see you. She's off with Miranda and Chloe to New York for her first American exhibition in three weeks' time.'

'Really? And how is Miranda? Back from her mysterious absence, then?'

'Yes. And like my father, a changed person. As a matter of fact, Miranda and I get on like a house on fire these days. She's a regular sweetheart and that little girl of hers is adorable.'

Leah did not reply. She didn't know how to. Brett ranting on about how wonderful Miranda was, hurt, really hurt.

'I 've got to make tracks, Brett.'

'Sure. Look, Leah. I really do think we should talk. I behaved like a first-class idiot last time you saw me. Could I ask you to join me for dinner tonight?'

'Not tonight.'

'Oh.' Brett looked disappointed. 'Tomorrow, then?'

'Okay.' It was out before she could stop it.

'We'll go to Steeton Hall. Rose says the food is terrific. I'll pick you up at eight from the bungalow.'

'Fine. See you then, Brett.' She took some money out of her purse and placed it on the table. ''Bye.'

Brett watched her as she left the restaurant. Ten minutes later, he strolled up the High Street, hands shoved deep in his pockets.

Leah, Leah. She was here. He had just spoken to her, not fifteen minutes ago.

Brett made for the moors at the back of the Parsonage where he had first kissed her. He sank down into the sweet-smelling grass. The sun was still high in the sky and he closed his eyes.

Was it over? Instinct told him not.

But to start it up all over again . . . Brett felt scared. Scared of the pain of throwing himself open to his emotions after locking them up for so many years.

His father had locked up his heart and thrown away the key. It was safer that way, it brought no surprises, no suffering. On the other hand, thought Brett, it made life flat, colourless, like one of his charcoal sketches that hadn't been filled with the living, breathing beauty of colour.

He still loved her.

The past was the past. And he wanted a future.

*

543

The following evening, Leah was reminded of the first time she had been due to meet Brett in New York. She tried on every outfit that she had brought with her, and for the life of her could not decide what to wear. Usually, she was able to go straight to her wardrobe and pull something out, knowing instinctively that it was right.

She felt like a teenager again and mused how she never had these problems when she was going out for dinner with Anthony.

But then, Brett had always made her feel like this: self-conscious and as nervous as a kitten.

She had spent a sleepless night at the bungalow. She thought it was a mixture of being alone for the first time, and struggling with her conscience over seeing Brett tomorrow.

A couple of times, as the dawn broke over the moors, she thought of calling Anthony, but she didn't. He might hear the guilt in her voice.

For goodness' sake, Leah, you're only going out to dinner with an old friend, that's all.

But her heart wouldn't agree.

Brett drove down into Oxenhope village. He turned onto the new estate and the bungalow appeared before him, the sight of it bringing a wave of apprehension.

Leah had seemed so calm yesterday, as if their meeting had not affected her at all. He'd been a bag of nerves and had talked far too much, he thought. He'd been in such a state that Rose had nearly murdered him when he admitted he'd left her bread somewhere in Haworth.

Every nerve ending in his body tingled with anticipation as he drove up to the front door. He switched off the engine.

Come on, Brett. She's a married woman. This is a pleasant dinner for two to apologize for past misdemeanours.

They were both sensible, mature adults now.

His heart told him otherwise.

'Hello. You look very nice.'

'Thank you, Brett.'

He stood on the doorstep, unsure whether he should go in, or whether Leah had plans to go straight to the restaurant. Then he realized that it was probably his job to decide.

'Shall we make our way straight there? It's a very pleasant drive and we can have a drink before we eat.'

'That's fine. Come in while I try and find my keys.'

Brett stepped into the hall as Leah disappeared into the sitting room, then re-emerged, triumphant.

'I put the keys in the plant pot so I wouldn't lose them, then couldn't remember for the life of me what I'd done with them,' she laughed. 'I've been hunting everywhere for the past half-hour.'

She shut the door behind her and they walked towards the car.

The journey to Steeton took under twenty minutes. Rose had donated her battered Range Rover to Brett for the duration of his stay and Leah enjoyed the distinctive smell of old car; a mixture of leather and petrol.

They managed small talk successfully for most of the

journey, arrived at Steeton Hall and made themselves comfortable in the bar. Brett ordered a pint for himself and a white wine for Leah.

'You drink these days, then?'

'Only on special occasions.'

'I am truly honoured, ma'am,' replied Brett, wondering whether he should launch into his explanation immediately, or wait until dinner. He decided the latter.

'So, why did you give up modelling?' he asked.

'I'd had enough. And when my friend Jenny died, it was the last straw.'

'I'm sorry, Leah. I had no idea.' Brett looked genuinely upset. 'What was it? Booze, drugs?'

'She attempted suicide twice, the second time successfully,' replied Leah.

'That's tragic. So how long have you been married?'

'Almost four years.'

'Happily?'

'We've had our problems, but, mostly, yes. Anthony is a very good and kind man.'

'He's a lot older than you, then?'

'Twenty-two years. He's only forty-six, no age at all these days.'

'Shall we go through?' Brett saw the maitre d' beckoning them.

Leah followed Brett into a candlelit conservatory. A table for two was laid by the window.

'This is charming,' said Leah, as she picked up her fork to make headway into her advocado and prawns.

'Yes.'

All through dinner, Brett kept finding the right moment to begin his speech, then losing courage and talking of something else.

In the end, he ordered two coffees and a cognac, and steeled himself.

'Look, Leah. I want to apologize for the way I behaved that night in New York. I was dreadfully drunk, angry and upset. I didn't give you a chance to explain.'

Leah shook her head. 'No. You didn't, did you?'

'I was so devastated when I read all the newspapers telling me the girl I loved was about to marry someone else. I flipped.'

Leah surveyed Brett calmly. 'Just for the record, Brett, I was telling you the truth. I had never had an affair with Carlo, and I was livid when he told me he'd informed the media that we were getting married. I wanted to sue, but Madelaine, my agent, stopped me.' Leah shrugged. 'Anyway, it's all water under the bridge now, and I can understand why you were so upset.'

Brett sighed. 'When Carlo was arrested for Maria Malgasa's murder, I began to realize that I never gave you a chance to explain. I suddenly thought that Carlo may have taken you to his *palazzo* that night under false pretences.'

'Yes, he did as a matter of fact, as I tried to tell you.' Leah shrugged. 'I don't know, Brett. Carlo was a lot of things: spoilt, selfish, arrogant, but I can hardly believe he is a murderer. But on the other hand, he was sending me photos of myself through the post slashed with a knife. I went to the police and I think that helped corroborate the evidence against Carlo. His trial's in six weeks' time.

Anyway,' Leah shuddered. 'Let's talk of happier things. Where did you go when you disappeared into the blue yonder?'

Brett told Leah of his travels around the world, visiting his father's properties, until he noticed that they were the only couple left in the restaurant.

'I think we'd better let the poor staff go home to bed.' He paid the bill and they wandered out to the car.

Brett pulled the Range Rover out of the car park and drove down the long path. Using the darkness to hide his embarrassment, he said, 'Look, I have to ask you. Can you forgive me and could we start again?'

'Yes, Brett. I'm sure we can become friends again. It was all a long time ago.'

It was not the reply he'd wanted.

They lapsed into silence as Brett drew up to the front of the bungalow.

'Thanks for dinner,' Leah said, as Brett turned off the engine.

'Anytime. I can't tell you what a load it is off my mind to be able to explain everything to you after all this time.'

'I'm glad you did.'

Leah opened the door.

'Good-night, Brett.'

'Good-night, Leah.'

She closed the car door and walked towards the bungalow. She fiddled in her bag for the key. She heard the engine turn over.

She unlocked the door and walked inside, shutting it behind her.

Leah sank onto the floor, a mixture of relief and

thwarted anticipation making her feel quite faint. Oh God, she had wanted to invite him in so badly, but . . . no, the relationship had ended in New York, and whatever the reasons, he was her past, not her future.

She picked herself up, threw off her shoes and walked down the passage to the kitchen.

She filled the kettle and turned on the radio to fill the quiet. She sat down at the table, feeling enormously proud of her self-restraint.

She made herself a cup of coffee and padded down to the sitting room.

The coffee cup smashed with a crash to the floor, spilling its boiling contents everywhere as she saw the face silhouetted at the window.

It took all of her self-control to prevent a scream leaving her lips as her hand went to her mouth.

'It's me, Leah! Brett! Let me in! My car won't start!'

14

AS LEAH LAY in Brett's arms the next morning, she knew that it had been inevitable the minute she had opened the door to let him in.

Neither of them had been strong enough to fight it.

They had tried, Brett insisting that he would walk home, then drinking gallons of coffee to put off the moment when the decision had to be taken.

Dropping from weariness, yet every part of her alive with suppressed desire, Leah had at last stood up and suggested Brett could sleep on the sofa, as she was in the bungalow's spare room, rather than make the long walk home.

He'd apologized profusely for the inconvenience, and accepted the duvet that Leah handed him with thanks and a promise to call the nearest garage first thing in the morning.

'Good-night, then,' she had said, as she turned to leave the room.

He'd caught her hand. 'I love you, Leah. I've never stopped loving you.'

Then he'd pulled her close and kissed her as she had

dreamed of him doing so many times over the past years.

They had made love there on the floor, unable to draw apart for even a short time and find the bedroom.

She had gazed with longing at his firm, muscular body, feeling her innermost part cry out for attention.

He had been everything she'd known he'd be: tender, loving, passionate; words she'd almost forgotten the meaning of. And she had responded in a way that amazed and frightened her. She wanted to explore, touch and caress every single part of his body.

Months of repressed feelings rushed to the surface as he entered her and she climaxed almost immediately, he not long after.

'Oh God, Leah. Oh God.' He looked down at her with tears in his eyes. 'It's you, it's always been you right from that first summer. And there'll never be anyone else. I know it. I feel it so deeply. Oh my love.'

And she had lain there, unable to feel guilt or sadness, only suffused by the pure joy of being loved by him once more.

Later, when they had climbed into bed and made love again, Leah reached for Brett's hand in the darkness.

'I have to go back, you know.'

He couldn't expect any more than she had given him. 'I know.' He squeezed her hand. 'Then let's make the most of the time we have.'

Never had Leah known it possible for the days to fly by so fast.

Because they both realized that each second they spent

together was precious, they made every moment special and filled to the brim with love. Leah had put away thoughts of the future and had decided she must pay the price of the time she spent with Brett at a later date.

Rose knew immediately, of course, when Brett arrived home the following afternoon, explaining embarrassedly that the Range Rover was still broken down in front of the bungalow. The happiness in Brett's eyes was unmistakable and she could not help but be glad for him. She did not preach to her nephew about the consequences of what he was doing; she knew that he was fully aware and had decided to accept them.

Leah, only fleetingly feeling a pang of guilt, revelled with Brett as they took an unashamedly romantic trip back into the past. Hand in hand they went back to the Parsonage, they strolled up onto Haworth Moor and kissed where they had first kissed; they lay in the grass by the farmhouse and made love under the burning blue sky. At night, they drove to Haworth and joined the tourists eating at any one of the cosy pubs or good restaurants, before making their way back to the bungalow for a night of love.

All was as it had been. And the figure watched them now, as he had watched them then.

Four days, three days, two days . . . Leah woke next to Brett on the morning before her flight back to New York and was sick in the bathroom.

Brett found her, pale and miserable, staring into space at the kitchen table.

'What is it, Leah?' He hoped he knew.

'Nothing,' she replied.

'You look ill.'

'I'm not feeling too clever. It must have been that chilli we ate last night.'

Brett was desperate to persuade her to admit the truth. He sat down next to her.

'Is it because you have to go back to America tomorrow?'

He had said it, voiced what they had both tried not to think about for the past, six heavenly days.

The spell was broken and Leah burst into tears. Brett let her alone, unsure of what to do or say.

'I'm sorry.' Leah fumbled in her dressing-gown pocket for a tissue and blew her nose. She stood up, a surge of pride replacing sorrow, and walked out of the kitchen and back into the bathroom.

As she showered, the full consequences of what she had done hit her. Tomorrow, she had to fly back to her husband and try to pretend that nothing unusual had happened, when she was sure her feelings for Brett were written all over her. Anthony wasn't a stupid man. Surely he'd guess? Waves of shame filled Leah as she thought how Anthony had only ever shown her love and affection, and she had repaid him by having an affair the minute she was out of his sight.

Leah sat naked on the bathroom floor, head in her hands. If Brett asked her – which so far he hadn't – to stay, would she?

Oh God, she didn't know. Having thought that the time alone in Yorkshire would give her space and time to think about the state of her marriage, all it had done was to complicate things beyond logical thinking.

There was no doubt in her mind that she loved Brett, but then she saw Anthony's dear face, looking down at her. A knocking broke into her thoughts.

'Are you okay, Leah?'

'Yes. I'm just coming out.'

Leah unlocked the door. She walked straight into Brett's arms and five minutes later, into bed.

Their last evening together had been planned down to the finest detail. Champagne at the bungalow, then to Old Haworth Hall for dinner.

It was a disaster. The sight of Leah's half-packed suitcase in the bedroom was enough to ruin the evening before it had begun. Brett had booked a flight to Paris for his interview at the Sorbonne so that the two of them could travel to Heathrow together. They were leaving in Leah's rented car at five tomorrow morning, which meant that good-byes, and last-minute advice for Brett from Rose had taken place earlier that afternoon. He returned to the bungalow as miserable as sin.

Neither of them touched their food at the restaurant and they made a last, silent journey back to the bungalow in the newly repaired Range Rover.

Leah made coffee and they sat in the sitting room, deep in their own thoughts.

This is the last night I'll ever spend with her.

How can I bear the thought of leaving him?

'We ought to go to bed. We have an early start tomorrow,' she murmured.

'Leah, I . . .'

'Sshh,' Leah put a finger to his lips. 'Don't say anything.' She led him into the bedroom and they made love for the last time. There was a desperation and a tenderness in the physical act that mirrored feelings neither could voice. But they both knew they would never forget it for as long as they lived.

They did not sleep, but arose at four and made a final check of the bungalow. Leah closed the front door and posted the keys through the letterbox, then they set off in her rented car.

Leeds Bradford airport at seven in the morning was a depressing a place. Thankfully for them both, the shuttle to Heathrow was on time.

An hour later, they made their way through to the check-in desks for Leah's ten thirty Concorde flight to New York. Leah watched her luggage disappear on the moving belt. The next time she saw her suitcases, she would be minutes away from seeing Anthony too.

Brett was chalk white and his eyes were bloodshot.

'Coffee?'

She shook her head, knowing she was causing herself more pain by prolonging the inevitable.

'I think I'd better go. My flight will be called soon.'

'Okay.' Brett checked himself. The lump in his throat was threatening to spill over into his eyes.

He walked alongside her, the distance to passport control agonizingly short.

She stopped, only feet away from the divide that would swallow her up and make her disappear for ever.

'Good-bye, Brett.' Her eyes were lowered.

He could hold out no longer. The tears ran down his face and he didn't care who saw.

'I love you,' he whispered.

She turned and walked towards the desk.

He stood watching her. As if life had suddenly wound to slow motion, he saw her give her ticket to the security girl.

'*No!*' Brett hardly knew it was his voice. She had passed the desk and was about to disappear behind the screen.

He was galvanized into action. '*Leah! No!*' He ran towards her, bypassing the astonished security girl, and grabbed hold of her.

Shaking, he stood and turned her to face him.

'You can't go, you can't do this to me. I know you love me. Please, please, Leah. We were always destined to be together. Admit it!' he almost shook her. 'You love me, Leah, you love me.'

She looked at him, at the tears pouring from his eyes.

At that moment she chose her future, for better for worse.

'Yes, I love you.'

Two hours later, as Air France flight A300 left the ground heading for Paris, Brett smiled at the beautiful woman sitting next to him.

'You won't regret this, my darling. I promise.'

Leah smiled at him. Then she turned and looked out of the window and shook her head slowly.

15

ANTHONY PUT DOWN the telephone slowly. He stood in the magnificent hall, the chandelier above him glittering even more brightly as he looked at it through the tears in his eyes.

He willed his body to move, to take him into the sitting room where he could pour himself a large brandy.

She wasn't coming back.

The thought repeated itself over and over in his head, and still his brain would not register it as a plausible event that was going to happen. Surely, in a few hours' time, he would drive down to the airport and greet his wife on her return from England? He would bring her back to their home, and life would continue as normal.

No. Leah was never going to be inside these four walls again. She had fallen in love with another man and had left him.

It happened all the time; to his friends, neighbours, to people all over the world, every single day. And now it had happened to him.

Anthony felt as if he'd had a severe physical blow. His legs were no more than two sticks of quivering muscle and he grabbed a brandy glass and poured a large measure before they deserted him altogether.

He sat down heavily, spilling a little of the brandy on the cream sofa.

The Fabergé clock ticked as usual on the marble mantelpiece.

Silence. The silence that would be Leah's legacy to him; his only companion.

The sense of devastation that filled him was total. Even when his first wife had been so ill, he had not felt like this. But then he'd had time to come to terms with losing her, as he'd watched the life seep slowly out of her.

It was the shock. Never once during Leah's extended time away from him had he considered she wouldn't return. Thinking back, Anthony knew that it shouldn't come as a surprise. She'd been so desperately unhappy for so long. It was obvious now that this had been because she no longer loved him.

While she'd been away, he'd thought constantly of how he could bring her to see what she was doing to herself. On the telephone she'd sounded much brighter and Anthony had been happy to let her have as much time as she needed if it would return to him the old Leah.

But he now realised the reason she'd sounded so happy was because she had fallen in love with someone else.

The pain was terrible. Anthony felt physically sick when he glimpsed in his mind's eye Leah making love to another man, the pleasure that he had been denied for over a year.

He should have known when he first married her that

she was too young to be tied down to an older man such as himself. Brett was the same age as she. Strong and fit; he was sure Leah would have no problems bearing a child with him.

He refused to believe, however, that any man could love a woman more than he loved Leah.

He loved her totally, unselfishly and to the exclusion of all others. Anthony wept.

16

'ARE YOU HAPPY, my darling?'

Leah lay in Brett's arms, wishing she could answer him yes, with no reservations or doubts.

She nodded slowly, hating the fact that she was in the most romantic city in the world, planning her future with the man that she had loved for all these years, and yet she couldn't rid herself of a terrible sadness.

The freedom and joy that she had found with Brett in Yorkshire had vanished the second she'd made the collect call to Anthony from Heathrow Airport.

He had sounded heartbroken, devastated. But he had not begged her to return. He had said that he loved her, that he would always love her, that he wouldn't stand in the way of her happiness.

Leah wished he'd ranted and raved and then she wouldn't be feeling quite so guilty. Now, every time she and Brett made love, she pictured Anthony's face, looking down at her with tears in his eyes.

Leah had kissed Brett good-bye outside the Sorbonne yesterday. His interview had taken most of the morning, so she had spent the time visiting old friends in their designer salons along the Avenue Montaigne. Her luggage was presumably still at JFK Airport and she had only the dress she stood up in. The designers had welcomed her into their sanctums with open arms, and when she had told them that she may be moving to Paris permanently, they had begged her to return to her old profession and work for them. She had protested that surely she was too old now, and they had laughed and said that twenty-five was nothing these days; look at Jerry and Christie and Marie!

She'd left feeling gratified, but confused. The realization of what she had done hit her. She went to sit in a café and had a *citron pressé* and a *brie baguette.*

Leah had celebrated with Brett on the evening of his interview. He had been told he had been accepted at the Sorbonne. They had dined at Maxim's and Brett had asked her how she felt about living in Paris for the next few years. She had said that tonight was not the moment to start planning the finite details, but that she was sure she wouldn't mind at all. Brett was so dreadfully happy and she didn't want to spoil it for him with her own doubts.

The offer of modelling work was tempting in one sense; after all, she would have to have something to do while Brett was studying, but Leah was convinced that there were other things she could do that she would prefer.

Brett's face had lit up when she had told him.

'That's fantastic, Leah. Me at the Sorbonne, you working again. After all, you've told me that you've been bored with nothing to do save weed the garden for the past few years. Are you going to think about it?'

Leah nodded. 'Oh yes.'

Brett couldn't understand how she felt about modelling, how deep Jenny's death had cut . . . Leah knew she couldn't expect him to.

Leah kissed Brett and arose from the big comfortable hotel bed. She went to the bathroom and turned on the shower.

One day left in Paris before they returned to Yorkshire and the start of her new life.

Maybe when they arrived back at the place that held all their memories, she would feel more secure and positive about the future.

The hot water ran over her body.

The decision was the right one. It had to be. Once the pain and guilt of leaving Anthony had lessened with the passage of time, she would be able to appreciate once more what she had with Brett.

Think, Leah, think how unhappy you were for the past year.

Then she saw Anthony's strong features and heard his gentle voice, and she couldn't remember.

17

'THE THING IS, Rose, that I was wondering whether you'd be able to put up an extra person for the next few weeks, just until we fly off to Paris.'

Brett was standing in the kitchen at the farmhouse, looking at the floor. He felt terribly embarrassed.

Rose sighed. 'Where is she now?'

'At her parents, breaking the news. They arrived back from the convalescent home yesterday and she thought it was better to get it over and done with immediately. We would rent something just for the next three weeks or so, but everything is chock-a-block. It's right in the middle of the tourist season.'

Rose nodded slowly. 'Of course Leah can stay here. Presumably, I won't have to make up an extra bed?' Her eyes twinkled.

Brett blushed. 'No.'

Well, you and Leah will be here by yourselves then, because Miranda, Chloe and I fly to America in a week's time. The farmhouse will be empty. Goodness knows what Doreen Thompson's going to make of all this. Leah has told her husband, hasn't she? I'm not going to have him turning up here with a couple of heavies and destroying the place, am I?'

'No. Apparently, he took it reasonably well. I don't think they've been happy for quite some time.'

Rose looked at Brett's sparkling eyes and felt glad for him. 'Leah's okay about moving to Paris with you?'

'Well, we haven't discussed it seriously, but I think so. I'll probably leave for Paris in a couple of weeks to give me time to find an apartment before term starts. Leah will join me as soon as I've found one.'

Rose's face became serious. 'Leah must love you a hell of a lot to do what she's done. Even if the relationship with her husband wasn't the happiest, she's given up everything for you. Don't let her down again, Brett.'

'I won't, Rose. You know how I feel about her. I'm so lucky to have been given another chance. I want to marry her the minute she's free.'

'Good.' Rose smiled. 'I have to pop into Leeds this afternoon to buy some clothes for America. Anything you want?'

'No, thanks. I think I'll go into my studio until Leah arrives. My fingers are itching after five days of rest.'

Brett walked over to Rose and put his arms round her. 'Thank you, Rose. I knew you'd understand.' He kissed her and went out of the room.

Rose watched him go. She hoped that nothing would happen to stop her still idealistic nephew finding happiness with the woman he loved.

The way that she had been stopped.

'Leah! I thought you were safely back in America with Anthony! What are you doing here?' Mrs Thompson's face was filled with happiness as she ushered Leah inside the bungalow.

'I'll tell you in a minute. First of all, I want to hear about you two.' Leah followed her mother into the sitting room and hugged her father. 'I must say, you both look like new people.' Leah squeezed her father's hand, feeling dreadful at having to impart such upsetting news when they were both looking so well. Leah drank a cup of tea slowly and listened to her mother expound the wonders of the convalescent home.

'So. Now we've told you our news, tell your dad and me why you're still here.'

Leah took a deep breath and did so. She wanted to weep at the shock on both of their faces.

'I'm sorry.' It was all she could think of to say.

After a long silence, Mrs Thompson spoke. 'Are you absolutely sure you're not making a terrible mistake? Anthony's such a nice, kind man. He's been so good to you.'

Leah wanted to cover her ears. Her mother was right, but it was more than she could bear to hear.

'I've been unhappy for the last year, Mum. And Brett, well . . .' Leah wrung her hands. 'I love him.'

'He let you down before, Leah. He can do it again. No sense of responsibility, that young man. His head's up in the clouds, like his aunt.'

'He won't let me down, Mum. He's changed, grown up. He's not a boy any more. He's a man.'

'I knew that young man was going to be nothing but trouble the first minute I set eyes on him nine years ago,' ruminated Mrs Thompson. 'So where are the two of you going to live?'

'Brett's asking Rose if she wouldn't mind putting me up at the farmhouse until Brett and I go to Paris in September.'

'Paris, is it? And what will you do with yourself there while Brett's involved with his paintings?'

'I've been offered jobs with two of the fashion houses.'

Mrs Thompson's eyes glinted. 'Now who was it that told me not so many years ago that she would never step on another catwalk for as long as she lived?'

'I know, Mum, but things have changed,' Leah answered, irritated that her mother had picked up on this. 'I've been bored silly doing nothing for all these years. Anyway, I haven't decided yet.'

'Don't you think you're going to find it a bit difficult living with a student after Anthony? After all, that's what Brett will be. He's going over there to work, night and day. How much time will he have left for you?'

Her mother was voicing every single fear that Leah had kept to herself over the past few days.

'Enough. Anyway, I need my own life, free from depending totally on a man. That's what went wrong with me and Anthony.'

'If you know that, surely you should go back and try and work it out with your husband and not go waltzing off with another man?'

Leah's head was splitting. She had known this would be difficult, but with her own rock-solid conviction missing, she could stand no more of this.

'Look, I have to go. I'll come and see you tomorrow. I really am sorry that I've upset you.'

She turned to her father, who sat silently in his chair.

'What do you think, Dad?' Leah looked desperately at him. He stared at her for a moment, then he shrugged.

'The main thing is that our Leah's happy. Are you happy, love?'

'Oh yes,' answered Leah, looking him straight in the eye. 'Very.'

18

THE NIGHT BEFORE Rose, Miranda and Chloe were due to leave for America, Leah and Brett joined them for an uproarious supper at the kitchen table.

'May I propose a toast to Rose Delancey, who I know will take America by storm. To Rose.' Brett lifted his glass.

'To Rose,' chorused Miranda, Chloe and Leah.

'Thank you for that tribute, Brett dear. And here's to you and Leah and your new life together in Paris. I hope one day to be wheeled round the Tate in my bath chair to study your paintings. You better not become more famous than me, mind you! Cheers!' giggled Rose.

Leah stood up. 'And I'd like to say thank you, all of you, for making me feel so welcome here. I'm very grateful.' Leah glanced down at Miranda, who smiled shyly back at her.

'Right. Well, what do you say that we all lend a hand with the washing up?'

Miranda shook her head. 'No, Mother, you go into the sitting room. I know you want to have a chat with Brett. Leah and I will do the washing up, won't we?'

Leah nodded. 'You wash, I'll dry.'

'I'll help you, Auntie Leah.'

'Okay, Chloe.'

Leah studied the dark head bent over the sink and decided that being a brunette personified Miranda's new personality. Subtler, deeper and much more interesting. Leah could sense a sadness in Miranda, and understood why Brett had found her so much easier to get on with. Miranda had shown Leah nothing but kindness since she had moved into the farmhouse two weeks ago, although they had had little chance to talk.

'Are you looking forward to America, Chloe?' Leah asked, as the little girl conscientiously wiped a plate.

'Oh yes. We can see Mickey Mouse,' she nodded.

'Well, Chloe, Uncle David's said we might be able to if you're a good girl,' Miranda answered, winking at Leah over Chloe's head.

'Do you like my dungarees, Auntie Leah? Auntie Doreen bought them for me today as a present.'

'They're very smart, Chloe,' smiled Leah. There had been a tearful farewell between Doreen and Chloe earlier. The little girl seemed more attached to Mrs Thompson than she was to her own mother or Rose, which was not surprising.

The washing up done, Miranda hung the tea-towel over the radiator. 'Chloe, why don't you go upstairs and get into your pyjamas? Mummy will be up in a minute.'

'Okay. Will you come and tell me my bedtime story, Auntie Leah?'

'Of course.'

Chloe's eyes lit up and she skipped happily out of the kitchen.

'Chloe seems to have taken a real shine to you, Leah. And your mum's been so good. Chloe thinks the world of her.'

'She's a lovely little girl, Miranda. You must be very proud of her.'

Miranda smiled. 'I am. Leah, I . . .' She fiddled embarrassedly with a clean coffee cup. 'In case I don't get a chance before you and Brett go off to Paris, I just wanted to apologize for what I said on the night of my sixteenth birthday. I was so jealous of you and Brett and . . . the things I said were a pack of lies. Brett and I did little more than kiss and that was under duress on Brett's part. I knew he loved you then, and I hated him for it. I'm so sorry. You two would have been together ages ago if it hadn't been for me.'

Leah sat down at the kitchen table. 'Miranda, please, forget it. I have. Okay, so I was devastated at the time, especially when I thought that Brett might be Chloe's father . . .'

Miranda's face darkened. 'He wasn't. I mean, he isn't. I swear, Leah.'

'Well, I just presumed he was when you kept so quiet about her father.'

Miranda nodded slowly and looked up at Leah. For a second, Leah recognized in Miranda's eyes a desperate need to unburden herself, but the look passed in an instant.

'I'm so glad that you and Brett are together. I'm not the person I was when I was younger and I loathe the way I behaved. I was hoping that maybe in the future we could be friends.'

'I'd like that very much, Miranda.' Leah smiled. 'You have a wonderful time in New York. It's a marvellous place and I'm sure you'll love it. When you come home, maybe we could go for lunch in Haworth before I go to Paris. Now, I'd better go up and see Chloe.'

'Yes. Thank you, Leah.'

Miranda sat in the kitchen staring into space. There were tears in her eyes as she struggled to bury the memories that had haunted her since she was no more than a child.

'Are you okay, darling?' Brett nuzzled the side of Leah's face. 'You seemed a bit quiet tonight.'

Leah stared up at the blackness. They had just made love, and once more, the passion and excitement had been missing for her. She'd done her best in the past few weeks not to let Brett see.

'Yes, fine. Just a bit tired, that's all. I've not been sleeping too well recently.'

'It's been a long day. We were up at five driving Rose, Miranda and Chloe to the airport. They'll be in New York by now. I can't believe that this time last year, I was living there too. Isn't it strange the way life has turned out?'

'What do you mean?'

Brett sighed in the darkness. 'Well, last night I sat at the kitchen table thinking how we're all so different, each one of us, and yet, we're back here, together again. It's as if that first summer affected us all; our lives and our futures. There was a sense of destiny in the air.'

'There was,' said Leah quietly.

'Good-night, darling.' Brett kissed her and wrapped his arms around her.

Leah closed her eyes.

And it came again. Every night now, she had the dream; every night it was the same. Only tonight, for the first time, she saw his face.

'*Noooh!!*'

She sat bolt upright and reached for the lamp switch.

'Darling, what is it?' Brett sat up next to her, alarmed.

She could sense him, so near that she could still hear his breathing.

'I'm sorry. I had . . . a nightmare.'

'Oh, sweetheart. You've been having a lot recently. Come here. I'll look after you, Brett's here.'

He rocked her in his arms gently, his hand caressing her hair.

Even surrounded by his love, she knew with a certainty what prevented her sleeping for the rest of the night, that no one could protect her from the man who had haunted her dreams since she was eleven years old.

Fate . . . Megan . . . evil . . . fear ground in her stomach until the dawn broke.

She was back here of her own free will. She had fulfilled her side of destiny and she knew that it would not be long before he fulfilled his.

19

'ARE YOU SURE you'll be okay by yourself, darling? I hate to leave you all alone in this big house.'

Brett's suitcases were packed and standing ready in the hallway. The two of them were in the sitting room, watching for the taxi.

Leah smiled reassuringly. 'Of course I'll be okay. Mum and Dad are only down the road if I get lonely. And Miranda and Chloe will be back soon.'

Brett pulled her closer to him. 'I'll start apartment hunting tomorrow. I reckon I should be able to find something in the next couple of days. You'll probably be on a flight to Paris by the end of the week.'

'Yes.'

'Will you promise to speak to Rose's solicitor about getting a separation from Anthony? The longer you leave it, the longer it will be before you're free.'

'Yes, I promise.'

Brett tipped her chin up towards him and kissed her gently on the lips. 'You don't know how much I'm going to miss you.'

'Me too,' replied Leah.

They saw a car climbing slowly up the hill.

Brett stood up. 'Well, darling, this is it.'

Leah followed him into the hallway and picked up a suitcase.

Brett opened the front door and the taxi driver took the suitcases from them and went to place them in the boot.

'I love you, darling. Take care and I'll call you when I reach the hotel.'

Brett hugged her.

'Good-bye, Brett.'

'Good-bye, Leah.'

She watched the taxi make its way down the hill, and waved until it was out of sight.

She turned, and went back into the house.

It was strangely eerie being all alone. Leah pondered whether she should go to her parents', then decided against it.

She went into the kitchen to fix herself something for supper. Soup and bread sufficed.

She checked the clock. Half past six. A whole evening alone.

Leah made her way into the sitting room, admiring once more how Rose had managed to turn the run-down house into a cosy, comfortable haven.

She sank down onto one of the deep sofas, picked up the remote control and switched on the television. She flicked from channel to channel, and seeing there was nothing that took her fancy, turned it back off again.

There was a pile of magazines on a coffee table. She

heaped them onto her lap and turned over the pages without registering anything in them.

Ten to seven. Leah was appalled at how bad she was at being alone. She used to be able to keep herself amused for hours when she was younger and the days spent by herself at Anthony's house had been regimented, following a strict routine. Most of the time she'd been so pre-occupied with thinking about the babies, or the loss of them, that she hadn't noticed much else.

It suddenly struck Leah that she had no idea who she was any more.

Her life was in a dreadful mess and that sensible, cen-tred girl she'd been when she was younger had slipped out of her grasp without her realizing it.

What about that dream of doing some good with her money, making the world a better place? She'd let that disappear the minute she encountered problems of her own.

Leah moved from the sofa and walked tentatively towards the well-stocked drinks cabinet. She took out a bottle of gin and stared at it thoughtfully.

It was her decision to take and she wanted a drink.

She poured herself an inexperienced measure of gin and added some tonic.

The bitter taste caught in her throat and she spluttered helplessly. She added a little more tonic and went and sat back down again.

Men. They had ruled her life since she was fifteen. First Brett, Carlo, then Anthony. Even though she'd had such a successful career, her entire life had centred around what was happening in her personal life.

But that was the way of the world, she mused. All the successful, dedicated career girls she'd ever met seemed only to be happy if their love-life-cum-domestic situation was going according to plan.

Why couldn't women have both? After all, men did.

And yet, if women did have both, there was the constant feeling of not coming up to scratch in either department. At the end of the day, one would suffer. Striking the balance seemed impossible and those who tried it looked permanently exhausted.

Leah realized that she'd settled for one and it hadn't been enough. Too much time to brood had made her problems with having a child grow out of all proportion.

Leah got up and poured herself another gin.

She suddenly resented being female enormously. Mischievous hormones and women's lib did not weld comfortably together. Her body and emotions wanted a man and a baby; her mind wanted a career, something that was hers and hers alone.

First things first, Leah. Which man do you want?

Leah shivered as she voiced this thought for the first time, and immediately blamed it on the gin.

She didn't know. Brett was kind, generous, he loved her to a fault, but he was so . . . Leah searched for the right expression . . . immature and idealistic. This had been fine for dreams, but not reality. She was used to the down-to-earth maturity of Anthony.

Leah burst into tears. She cried as she had not cried since the night that Jenny died.

She thought she'd been so in charge of her own destiny, when in fact she'd been as much manipulated by others and her own feminine weaknesses as her dead friend had been. She cried for Anthony, who had always received so much less than he deserved from her. In the past two years she'd become a miserable, selfish female, completely wrapped up in her own problems, and Anthony must have been through hell. She cried because the world was so difficult and beautiful and cruel and wonderful and because for the first time tonight she could see herself so clearly.

Leah got through half the bottle of gin, but she didn't feel drunk. The startling clarity with which her life came into focus made any hangover worthwhile.

And the dreams? The dreams were manifestations of her unhappiness, a way of telling her that things weren't right. Relief flooded through her. Yes, that was it.

Five days at most. Five days alone to sort herself out. An oasis that she was sure she'd been granted for a reason.

Leah went upstairs later knowing that physically she would suffer tomorrow, but mentally she had a sense of freedom that she relished.

She knew she would find the answers now.

Peaceful, for the first time in months, Leah crept into one of the spare bedrooms, crawled under the duvet, and fell into a dreamless sleep.

He saw the lights go out.

An owl hooted from somewhere in the barn.

No, not tonight. It was too risky. The others had been gone for about ten days now, but Brett might come back.

He knew the moment wasn't right.

He would wait.

20

ANTHONY WAS WOKEN from a restless sleep when he heard his doorbell ringing incessantly. He checked the time on his alarm. Half past six. Who the hell wanted him at this time on a Sunday morning?'

'All right, all right, I'm on my way,' he mumbled, as he met Betty, repleat with bright pink satin robe and matching mules, approaching the door from her quarters.

'It's okay, Betty. I'll deal with this.'

Betty shrugged and disappeared down the corridor.

Anthony looked through the eyehole and saw the familiar uniform of a policeman. A plain-clothes man was standing next to him. The man flashed an ID card through the eyehole. Anthony nodded, switched the alarm system off and unlocked the door.

'Can I help you?'

'Detective Cunningham, FBI. Sorry to bother you this time of the morning, sir, but is Mrs Van Schiele at home?'

'No, I'm afraid she's er . . .' Anthony could not bring himself to say it. 'She's on holiday.'

'I'm sorry, sir, but could I ask you where exactly she's gone?'

'England. Yorkshire, actually. To visit her parents.'

Cunningham gave a frown of concern. 'In that case, sir, I think we'd better come in.'

'She's all right, isn't she?'

'As far as we're aware at present.'

Anthony guided them to the sitting room.

'What exactly do you want to speak to my wife about?'

'These, sir.'

The detective took a thick polythene envelope from his briefcase. He handed it to Anthony.

Anthony took the envelope and studied the contents. There were back copies of American *Vogue*, *Vanity Fair* and a couple of English editions of *Harpers & Queen*.

He looked nonplussed at the detective. 'I don't understand.'

'Shall we sit down, Mr Van Schiele?'

Cunningham patted the seat next to him on the sofa and the officer positioned himself in a chair opposite.

'Has your wife received any more odd mail recently?'

Anthony shook his head, thinking through the pile of post still waiting for Leah in the hall unopened.

'No, I don't think so. I haven't opened it since she's been away though. But anyway, Carlo Porselli is locked away in an Italian jail awaiting trial.'

Cunningham nodded. 'Unfortunately, this is our fundamental problem. We don't believe that it was Mr Porselli who sent your wife those slashed magazine pages.' Cunningham waved the magazines at Anthony. 'We found these during the course of another investigation, and other things besides.'

'I . . . I'm sorry. I'm terribly confused. Could you explain?' said Anthony.

'Sure. A couple of days ago, the police were called to an apartment in New York. The downstairs neighbours were complaining of a noxious smell coming from the apartment above them. The police broke in and discovered the rotting corpse of a prostitute under the floorboards. We reckon she'd been there for about three months. She had been raped and strangled. I was called to the scene. In a room in the apartment, we discovered hundreds of photos of your wife pinned to the walls. They had been slashed violently with a knife and defaced. There was also a charcoal sketch of your wife when she was much younger that had been ripped to shreds. We also found these.' Cunningham picked up one of the magazines and opened it at a previously marked page. 'In all four of them, there is a page torn out. We thought nothing of it at first, but having asked the magazines in question to send us identical copies, we saw there was a link. In each magazine, the page that had been torn out was a photo of your wife, Mr Van Schiele. And when we checked with those slashed photos you handed in to us five months ago, we discovered they were the missing pages.'

Cunningham surveyed Anthony's pale face silently. 'There is no doubt that it was this man who sent the pages to your wife. We are also pretty sure now that the wrong man has been locked up for the murder of Maria Malgasa. The prostitute found under the floorboards was murdered in an identical way to Malgasa. We've got on to forensic and confirmed that there were other unidenti-

580

fied fingerprints found in the Milan hotel room in which she was murdered. They match not only with those on the New York prostitute, but also with another unsolved, identical murder of a prostitute in Britain, committed three years ago. There is another connection. The man who rents the New York apartment in which we found the body is also known to have been in Milan at the time of Malgasa's death. In fact he was the photographer on the shoot.

'He also left Britain for New York three years ago, the day before the body of the prostitute was found.'

Anthony could stand it no longer. 'Who is this man?'

'Miles Delancey. The fashion photographer. Unfortunately he's gone missing. He has not returned to his New York apartment since he was in Milan on the photo shoot with Maria Malgasa. We believe he flew straight to Britain. And we're almost sure his next intended victim is your wife.'

21

'THE TELEPHONE RANG this afternoon, love. I was asleep when I first heard it and it stopped before I could get it. When it rang again, I picked it up with my claw, but I'm afraid I dropped it.' Mr Thompson pointed to the receiver, lying on the floor by his chair and giving out a monotonous bleep.

Mrs Thompson picked up the instrument and re-placed it on the set. She raised her eyebrows. 'I wonder who it could have been? I've just left Leah up at the farm-house, so it couldn't have been her. Never mind, I'm sure they'll try again if it's urgent.'

Mr Thompson nodded, once again feeling the inade-quacy of his frail body.

'I'm going to go and make your dinner, love. It's your favourite; Yorkshire puddings and beef stew.' Mrs Thompson smiled at her husband and went into the kitchen.

He was awoken by the sound of a car in the distance.

He listened intently, as the noise receded. He had no idea how long he'd been asleep, but the barn was in blackness. He found his torch and shone it on his watch. Ten to ten.

He'd been having a dream, about her. He felt himself through his trousers. He was rock hard.

He couldn't hold out any longer.

It had to be tonight. He'd watched the house for four days and no one except her mother had visited. She was alone now and he must make his move before anyone came back.

Another hour, and he would go to her.

He relished the thought of what he would do to her, slowly caressing himself.

Once he'd loved her, worshipped her. She was so perfect, too perfect to be touched physically by a man.

But then she had thrown him out of her apartment, onto the streets. She'd threatened him and treated him like scum.

And three weeks ago he'd watched her screwing that cunt, Brett, on the moors.

Then he'd known for sure that she was no better than the rest.

She was his. She always had been.

And now it was time.

He went to the edge of the barn and peered round. The upstairs lights had gone out.

There was no need to break in. After all, this was his home and he had the key.

There were no outside lights and he crept stealthily along the outside of the barn, the half-moon making him a noticeable silhouette against the sky.

He ran swiftly to the front door, put the key in the lock and opened it slowly.

The hall was in complete blackness. He closed the door and stood behind it, trying to make out the stairs.

As his eyes adjusted he saw a figure in a long robe coming down the stairs. He slunk back into the shadows and allowed himself a smile.

She was coming to him.

His penis pulsated as he watched her descend the stairs, long dark hair falling over her shoulders.

She reached the bottom and crossed the hall.

Miles made his move. His hand went over her mouth as he grabbed her and dragged her along the corridor and into the sitting room.

She struggled, but was helpless against his inhuman strength.

He threw her on the floor, face down.

'You know who I am. And you knew I'd come for you, didn't you?'

'Miles, I . . .'

'Shut up! If you make another sound, or move, I'll kill you.'

It was so important that she didn't talk, didn't ruin the moment he'd been waiting for.

He tore his trousers from his body and massaged himself.

He bent down and ripped the robe from her. Her round buttocks shone white under the cold light of the moon.

Yes, he would take her as she lay.

He plunged into her, hands going round and under

her and squeezing her breasts violently. They were fuller than he'd imagined.

She was emitting small kittenish noises as he savagely tore into her, but he couldn't hear them any longer. His hands moved to her slender neck and closed round it. He squeezed, laying the full weight of his body on top of her.

'You bitch! You've wanted this since you were a little girl. You've always been mine, always. And I thought you were so perfect, so pure, and all along you were screwing that bastard . . .!'

He could feel his semen roaring up towards the tip of his cock. His hands tightened round her neck with an unlockable grip.

'Aargh! Jesus!'

He shot into her, and sank onto her, feeling her legs twitching beneath him. Then they stopped.

He knew that moment all too well.

He released his hands from around her neck, and lay there, panting, atop the immobile body.

All feeling left him, as it always did. Next would come the guilt. He had to get out of here as quickly as possible. He could take Rose's Range Rover.

She kept the keys in the bureau by the sitting-room door.

Miles staggered upright, and fumbled for his trousers. He put them on, made his way to the bureau and found the keys to the car in their usual place. He put them in his pocket and turned back to the door.

A small figure was standing there. A hand reached for the light by the door on the wall.

Miles blinked.
The figure looked past him to the body on the floor.
She emitted a small cry.
'Mummy!'
The blue eyes looked up at him.
'What have you done to Mummy?'

22

THE LITTLE GIRL ran past Miles and knelt by the body on the floor. She shook her and began screaming at a piercing level when she could emit no response from it.

Miles stood there, paralysed. He didn't understand, he . . .

'Chloe, what on earth?'

Miles swung round to see Leah standing behind him in the doorway. She clapped her hand over her mouth as she stared into his eyes. Then she looked beyond him to the scene on the floor.

Miles shook his head, trying to make sense of the situation. He had just taken the girl standing in the doorway. She was lying dead on the floor.

'Chloe, come to Leah. Come on. Mummy will be okay. Come to Leah.'

She saw his black eyes boring into her. His hair had grown long and was unkempt and greasy. His face was dirty and he smelt odorous.

But it was his eyes. She saw they were full of madness.

He seemed confused. He had come for her, as she'd dreamt he would. But Chloe was here and that had not

587

been in the dream. Her only thought was to get Chloe and then get out of this house, away from him. There was nothing she could do now to help Miranda.

And she had to do it while Miles was caught off balance.

'Chloe, come on darling.' She beckoned to the child, unable to focus on the naked body on the floor, dark hair covering the face.

'Let's go to the kitchen and get a drink, sweetheart.' Her eyes never left Miles'.

She steered Chloe out of the room, very slowly, then turned and walked towards the kitchen. She closed the door behind her with a slam and locked it. She bent down to talk to the hysterical little girl.

'Now, Chloe. I want you to do everything Aunt Leah says and be a very grown-up girl. We have to run as fast as we can to get help from the village for Mummy. Okay?'

Chloe nodded.

Galvanized into action, Leah stood up and pulled Chloe across the kitchen to the back door. With trembling fingers, she unlocked it, grabbed Chloe's hand and fled out into the night.

Miles stood immobile, staring at the body on the floor. He walked across to her and knelt down. Heart pumping against his chest, he smoothed the thick hair back from her face and rolled her over.

The piercing blue eyes stared up at him, lifeless.

An animal howl left him as he pulled her close to him and held her to his chest.

'Nooo! Please, No!'

Not Miranda, not the only person who had helped him when he needed help, the only woman he'd ever trusted.

She had understood him, had taken him into her bed since they were small children and comforted him when he was having one of his terrible dreams. He rocked the motionless body in his arms, caressing the dark hair that had led him to murder her. Tears streamed down his face. He kissed her, willing life back into her.

A fleeting movement outside caught his attention. He sat up, dropping Miranda's body onto the floor. He saw the two figures fleeing down the hill.

Immediately, he was filled with hatred. This was her fault. She had caused Miranda's death and she had to be punished for it.

He stood up and ran to the front door.

'Come on, darling. You can do it. Keep going.'

Leah was panting and dragging Chloe behind her.

'Please, can we stop, Auntie Leah? I can't run no more.'

'You have to, Chloe, you have to for Mummy.'

Leah was trying to formulate in her mind what she should do. Run down to the village, to her mum and dad's and get help from there. The most important thing was to get away from him. He was insane, he would kill them both.

'Ow!' Chloe screamed as one of her slippers flew off her foot and the harsh gravel cut into her tender skin. She stopped and ran back for the slipper, and as she did so, two headlights came over the hill and began bearing down on her at a frighteningly fast pace.

'Quick! Onto the moors!' Leah turned left onto the grassland. She would have to go across country to the village, down past the reservoir. He couldn't follow them that way.

She heard the noise of the car slowing down, then the rumble as it turned and started across the moors.

'Oh God, oh no!'

Chloe was screaming now at the top of her voice. All Leah could think of was getting to her parents, to safety, to help.

'Please, don't let him catch us, please God, help us!'

She pulled Chloe down and across towards the reservoir. The car was getting nearer and she could almost feel the white light of the headlamps boring into her back.

There was nowhere to hide, no cover to protect them and Chloe's little legs were unable to keep up with her own.

Then an idea flashed through Leah's brain. It was not Chloe he was after, but herself.

She looked behind her. The car was no more then five hundred yards away. There was no escape. He would catch them and kill them both.

At least she could give Chloe a chance.

With a surge of strength that Leah did not know her exhausted body could give her, she hurled Chloe away from her and down the hill to the side of her, praying that the child would make a safe landing. She checked behind her and saw that the car had not stopped, but was continuing after its prey.

Then she kept on running. Running across the moors,

running for her life, as she had in the dream time and again.

She saw a low wall two hundred yards away from her and for the first time, a ray of hope entered her head. He could not follow her in the car, he'd have to get out.

Her chest heaving painfully now, she begged her legs to go faster as she ran towards the wall.

He was so close now. She could not look behind.

She reached the wall and heaved herself up onto it. The reservoir shimmered below the steep incline of the moors, and on the other side, the lights of Oxenhope twinkled.

She jumped off the wall and landed, screaming in pain as her weight fell on her ankle and there was a sickening crack.

'No please, don't let me pass out, I'll die, I'll die.'

She hauled herself onto her haunches and stood up, the pain from her ankle so dreadful that she felt dizzy and sick.

'Must keep going, must keep going.' Tears were falling freely down her face as she heard the car screech to a halt behind her. Then the sound of a door opening.

Hobbling as fast as she could, she saw blue flashing lights against the sky, and willed herself once more not to pass out from the pain.

'It's no good, Leah. I'm coming for you. I'm so close behind you, inches away. Give up now.'

'No! No!'

A tufted hillock sent her flying headlong to the ground.

It winded her. She tried desperately to move, but she could not.

She lay there, waiting.

Now there was no escape.

She heard his breathing behind her. She closed her eyes and said a prayer as she heard the scrub crackle and he knelt behind her.

Hands went round her neck and squeezed. She could not struggle any longer.

This was her destiny.

She felt her breath draining from her.

Then a shot rang out.

The pressure round her neck stopped instantly. Leah knew she should try and move, but she could not.

'Stand up, arms in the air, and you will not be harmed.'

Woozy from lack of oxygen, Leah thought she was dreaming as the male voice rang out across the moors.

He knelt upright, looking above him.

'Give yourself up and we will not harm you,' the voice repeated. 'Move away from the girl.'

Miles blinked as a spotlight was switched on, bathing the moors in light.

'Never, never. She's mine.'

The hands went back round her neck.

'Oh God no, please no!'

Then another shot rang out. Miles jumped and screamed in pain. He rolled off Leah and lay, clutching his leg.

'Come on! Come on! Get up!' Miles stood, blood darkening the material of the trouser covering his shin. He pulled Leah to her feet. He put his arms around her chest and dragged her towards the wall.

'Let the girl go now, Miles.'

The foul stench of his breath washed across Leah's face.

'They won't shoot while I've got you to protect me, see?'

They reached the wall and he heaved them up onto the top of it and they rolled down together onto the other side.

'We're going to get in the car and you're going to drive.'

'I . . . I can't. My ankle.'

He was dragging her towards the car. He opened the driver's side and lifted her into it. Then he crawled across her and landed in a heap in the passenger seat.

'Drive! Drive!'

Leah fumbled with the keys in the ignition. The car started and she gingerly put her foot down on the clutch, and yelled in pain as her ankle took the strain.

'Shut up, you stupid bitch! Drive! Downwards. Away from those bastards!'

Leah put her foot on the accelerator. The car jolted forward. Miles was struggling to remove his trousers to see if he could stem the blood from his leg.

'We're heading towards the reservoir, Miles. We have to go back up to reach the road.' The steep incline below Leah with the shimmering pool of water at the bottom filled her with terror.

'No! Drive downwards and we'll cut across country when we reach the reservoir.'

'But Miles, it's too steep, we'll . . .'

'Just do it!' he roared.

'Okay, okay.'

She could see in the mirror that there were headlights following her down the hill.

'Faster! Faster! They're catching up!'

'I can't! We'll crash.'

'For Christ's sake!'

Miles pushed her foot off the accelerator and placed his own on it. His hands went round the steering wheel.

'Stop! Please stop! We're going to go into the reservoir!'

But Miles wouldn't listen. The car went careering at great speed down the hill, the water coming closer and closer.

Leah knew they faced certain death at the bottom.

'Oh God, oh God!' she wept. She moved her foot away from the pedals, her entire weight pressing against the door.

There was only one thing she could do. She fumbled behind her and found the handle.

Using all of her strength, she tugged at it and it opened.

She tumbled out of the car and was thrown to the ground.

There was an explosion not yards from her as a bullet from a marksman hit one of the tyres.

She managed to lift her head and watch as the car toppled over and over, burst into a ball of orange flames and plunged into the water below.

Then she passed out.

ROSE'S FACE WAS ashen as she watched the coffin being lowered into the ground. Her eyes were red from crying.

There was nothing left to bury of Miles; the police had found pieces of his clothing floating in the reservoir, and particles of his blood that had been analysed from a sample of the water.

Anyway, what clergy would give a service for a man who had murdered his sister, even by default, and others?

Rose felt faint as she listened to the vicar intone the blessing on Miranda's soul.

Others around her placed wreaths beside the grave, and began to walk away.

'Come, Rose. It's time to leave.' Brett put an arm round her shoulder.

She shook her head. 'No, Brett. I want to stay a while longer. Would you mind seeing to the guests at the farmhouse until I get back?'

'Of course not.' Brett shrugged uneasily. 'Don't stay too long.'

'I won't.'

Rose watched the others walking off into the distance.

The drone of the cars died away and all she could hear on the balmy September afternoon was the twittering of the birds in the trees.

She walked towards the grave and knelt down.

'Miranda, sweetheart. I don't know whether you can hear me. If you can, I ask you to listen to what I have to tell you. I must tell someone, explain why it is my fault that you are lying down there. I pray you'll understand and forgive me.'

Rose wiped the tears from her face and took a deep breath.

24

OCTOBER, LONDON 1946

AT TILBURY DOCKS on a cold and grey November morning, a large white ship sailed slowly up the foggy estuary and pulled alongside the quay.

An hour later, the passengers began to disembark. Among them was a thin young man, one hand clutching a battered violin case, the other holding tightly to the hand of a skinny, ashen-faced girl. She stumbled as she walked down the gangplank, and the young man picked her up in his arms and carried her the rest of the way.

Ladies dressed in green uniforms were waiting to receive the motley group of passengers. One of the ladies tried to take the girl from the boy's arms, but he held on fiercely to her and his eyes filled with fear.

'Do you speak English?' she said.

'Yes. Not for many years. Excuse.'

The lady looked irritated. 'What are your names?'

'David and Rosa Delanski. Our grandparents are meeting us from the ship.'

The lady checked down a long typewritten list.

Her face changed to surprise as she read. 'Yes, here you are. Lady Brown is meeting you at King's Cross. Board that bus over there.' She pointed behind her. 'I say, is the girl all right?'

'Yes. She has the sickness sea. Bad, from Bremerhaven.'

'Sea-sickness. Ah well, some rest and hot drinks should sort her out,' the lady said briskly as she passed onto the next in the queue.

David carried Rosa to the bus and sat down thankfully. Another lady in a green uniform was handing out tea and biscuits.

David took them with a nod and gulped them down. He tried to persuade Rosa to try a little of the biscuit, but she turned green and would only sip at the tea.

The same lady came round again ten minutes later with a box of woollen jumpers and cardigans.

'Take one for each of you. We don't want you to catch cold now, do we?'

David shook his head, remembering when he couldn't feel his feet for days on end in Treblinka. The cold here was nothing compared to that.

However, he dressed Rosa in a grey jumper that was far too large for her and she snuggled into his shoulder and promptly fell asleep.

David stared out of the window as the bus moved off. Although he was nervous at stepping into an unknown country to meet unknown relatives, he once more felt grateful for the chance to begin a new life. In the camp at Peggetz, he had watched as others were left to fend for themselves as best they could, with no family or means of escape from the poverty. He had seen people commit suicide, children separated from their brothers and sisters and taken off to orphanages.

Nothing could be worse than that dreadful place.

David's one regret was having to leave baby Tonia at the camp. She was not family and he could hardly ask his grandparents to take her in too. But the Red Cross official had assured him that Tonia would be well cared for and adopted as soon as a home could be found for her.

No one had been more surprised than he when the Red Cross official had informed him of the letter from his grandmother. He had started to think that a reply would never come, as the days turned into weeks, and those into months. But at last, the Red Cross official had called David into his hut and informed him that his grandmother had written saying that she was happy to give them a home once they arrived in London. She had enclosed some money to arrange a berth on a ship as soon as possible.

David watched the deserted road become more and more built up as they approached London by way of the A12. The East End was still showing the signs of the severe bombing it had received during the war. Buildings with their insides hanging out for the world to see; huge patches of land laid to waste in the middle of neat rows of houses, surrounded with makeshift fences.

As they drove further into the city, David witnessed the massive construction job under way to rebuild London, a task that would take years to complete.

The bus pulled to a stop outside a large, imposing building.

'King's Cross, ladies and gentleman. Will all those who are going on to the camp at Wigesly stay on the bus for the time being. David and Rosa Delanski, please come forward. Your grandmother is waiting.'

David woke Rosa up and pushed her along the aisle to the front of the bus.

He climbed down the steep steps, then turned to help Rosa down.

'David? Rosa?'

A small, beautifully attired woman was standing behind him.

David burst into tears and fell into his grandmother's arms.

25

EVEN ROSA SEEMED wide awake as the magnificent Bentley drove them through the streets of London.

Lady Victoria Brown sat between them, an arm around each of them. She seemed nervous, watchful.

'Is that your violin, David?'

He nodded proudly. 'It's a Stradivarius. I'll show you.' David opened the case and touched the instrument reverently. 'It is the Ludwig.'

'My, that is beautiful,' said Lady Brown admiringly. 'And worth quite a large sum of money, I'll bet. We'll have to take it to Sotheby's in New Bond Street to get it valued for insurance.'

Their grandmother looked anxiously out of the window as the car drew to a halt in front of a beautiful white house on the edge of a park. It was exactly how David had imagined it when his mama had described it to him all those years ago.

'We're home,' their grandmother said.

She took their hands as they walked together up the flight of steps that led to the door of the house.

A maid in a crisp white uniform opened the door.

'Good afternoon, madam.' The look of surprise on her face was obvious as she stared at the two ragamuffins on either side of her mistress.

'Helen, what these two need is a good bath. There are clothes laid out for them in the pink and blue rooms respectively. Once they've bathed, dressed and eaten, would you bring them to me in the drawing room?'

'Certainly, madam. Come on, children.'

Rosa was loathe to leave this lovely, kind lady that looked like her mother.

'Go with Helen, Rosa. She won't hurt you.'

Lady Victoria watched her grandchildren go up the stairs. Her heart bled for them. She had no idea exactly what they'd been through, but the fear in their eyes bore testament to the torment they'd suffered.

When she had received the letter from the Red Cross, a mixture of elation and sadness had swept through her.

The locket, the one she had given her daughter Adele on her eighteenth birthday, brought tears to her eyes when she had withdrawn it from the envelope.

Then she'd read that Adele had been murdered in the gas chambers at Treblinka, along with her husband, Jacob, but that their two children had survived. Victoria and her husband were apparently the only known relatives of the two Jewish orphans.

Victoria had cried for a long time, mourning the beautiful daughter who had loved a man enough to leave her family and then walk into death with him.

She'd only admiration for Adele, and merely wished she'd had the courage to follow her own heart when she was younger. But she had not. And now, she was almost sixty years old, living with a biased, bigoted man whom she had loathed for the past forty years.

As Victoria and the rest of the British nation had listened in horror to the reports of the atrocities that the Germans had committed against the Jews, her husband, Robert, Lord Brown, had sat unmoved.

He was anti-Semitic, anti-German, anti-everything but the British. His years in India had made him the worst sort of British ex-patriot and his views were narrow-minded and arrogant in their certainty.

When Beatrice had called from Paris to say that Adele was missing, and it had then become obvious that she was never going to return, Robert had completely cut her from his mind and his life. He had told all his friends that she had died in a tragic car accident near the Arc de Triomphe. He had even insisted on going away to their house in Somerset the week that the funeral was meant to be taking place.

Victoria had begged him to help her search for their daughter, but he had, with some aggression, ordered that Adele's name was never to be mentioned in his house again. That she was dead.

Victoria knew that this was because he had worshipped his daughter – she honestly thought that Adele was the only person Robert had ever loved – and Adele had betrayed him.

So, it was on that slim premise that two months ago, she had begged him to take in Adele's two children. He had read the letter with a face like thunder, almost exploding when he saw that his daughter had married a Jew. He had thrown the letter on the fire and told his wife never to mention the subject again. The answer was absolutely and utterly no.

'Let them rot in hell, like their Yiddish mother,' he had growled as he left the room.

After Victoria had recovered from her husband's unbelievable inhumanity, she had sat down and composed a letter to the Red Cross official at the camp in Austria.

She told him the children were to come to her as soon as possible. Of course they would find a home with their grandparents. She had enclosed money for their passage to England.

So now Victoria sat in her drawing room, contemplating how she would break it to her husband that she had gone against his wishes.

She had been denied their daughter. What she had left of Adele, not even her husband could take away.

Victoria sighed. To have loved as Adele obviously had, even for a short time, was better than never having loved at all.

'Come in, children, and sit down.'

Victoria looked on in pleasure as the two children gazed with awe at the beautiful corniced ceiling, high above them, crowned by a sparkling chandelier throwing out crystal-reflected light. They looked like different people after their bath. Rosa was wearing one of Adele's old dresses, and for an instant, Victoria felt breathless. Rosa could be Adele. The dress was too young for her and looked terribly old-fashioned, but the sweeter she looked, the better.

Her heart filled with love.

'Now. I want to tell you something very important. Later, you will meet your grandfather. His name is Robert. I . . . I haven't told him you were coming because . . . I wanted it to be a surprise. You must be on your best behaviour.

'Of course,' answered David politely.

He was such a handsome boy.

'How old are you, David?'

David had to think about this one.

'Seventeen.'

'Why, you're almost a man!' Victoria imagined her husband taking David to his heart, enrolling him for Sandhurst, watching him follow in his footsteps.

'And you, Rosa?'

Rosa looked at David for guidance.

'She's fourteen, I think.'

And terribly undernourished, thought Victoria. She looked at the way Rosa smiled up at her brother and slipped her hand into his. They were obviously very close. 'Now, what I'd like you to do is to tell me, right from the beginning, what happened to your family.'

So David began the story from the moment Adele had met Jacob in Paris. He tried to repeat it exactly as his mama had told him. With prompting from Rosa, he told Victoria in halting English, that improved with each sentence, of the ghetto in Warsaw, then Treblinka. He did not tell her of the atrocities that had been committed against them by Frankl. That was something he doubted he could tell anyone, ever.

Nevertheless, tears appeared in his grandmother's eyes.

'We've heard of these kind of things, in England, of course. But knowing now for definite that it was all true, and worse, is very hard.'

Victoria thought that her husband must soften his heart if he heard their story. Only a monster would feel no compassion for these tragic victims.

After years of going half mad with frustration at her empty, pointless life, Victoria was suddenly filled with a mission; to halt the pain David and Rosa had suffered and give them as much love and care as she possibly could.

'I know I can never make up for what you've suffered, or bring back your mother and father, but I promise I will try and help you forget what you've been through. I want you to go up to your rooms in a minute. When Robert returns I want to talk to him alone. We have plans to make. David, you must decide what you would like to do with your future.

'David. He play the violin good,' said Rosa timidly.

'And Rosa has a great talent for painting. She shall draw for you, won't you, Rosa?

Rosa nodded eagerly.

'I'd like that very much, Rosa dear,' Victoria said quietly. 'Ask Helen for some paper and pencils. I'm sure we have some somewhere.'

The two children went up the grand staircase and along the deeply carpeted corridor to their sumptuous adjoining rooms.

Rosa followed David into his room, looking nervous.

'What is it, sweetheart?'

She ran to him.

'David, will you let me sleep with you tonight? I do not want to sleep by myself.'

He nodded. 'After everyone is in bed, you can creep in. But there is no reason to be frightened.' He stroked her soft titian hair. 'We're safe now.'

'I cannot believe what you're saying to me, Robert! For pity's sake! These are your grandchildren, your own flesh and blood!' Victoria wrung her hands in despair. 'At least allow me to bring them down to meet you.'

The heavy-set, balding man put his hands on the mantelpiece and shook his head.

'No, Victoria. I said four months ago that I would not have them in my house and you disobeyed my wishes. I should have you put out along with them.'

'Please, Robert! If you saw them, heard what they've been through . . . Rosa is the image of Ade –'

'Don't mention that name in my house!' Robert roared.

Victoria sat down heavily in a chair. It was hopeless.

'So, what do you want me to do? If we refuse to take them in, they will be deported as illegal aliens and sent back to a displaced persons' camp in Poland. They have suffered so much already. I cannot believe that even you would wish that on any two children, least of all your own flesh and blood.'

'They are not my own flesh and blood! My daughter is dead. She died twenty years ago. These Yids are obviously imposters. I want them out of my house by tomorrow morning.'

Victoria felt the bile rise in her throat as she listened to him. He was sick, cruel, but worst of all, he was a hypocrite. He could stand at the Cenotaph, publically paying tribute to all those English war dead, and yet he would turn his grandchildren out of the house, onto the street, because they were half Jewish.

Something snapped inside her. She'd put up with his arrogance, ruthlessness and petty prejudices for long enough. A tidal wave of anger and hatred swept over her. She could stand no more. She would leave with her grandchildren as soon as possible.

Rosa crept down the dimly lit staircase, holding her picture in her hand. She had spent the past two hours painstakingly drawing it and she wanted to give it to the lady whom she hoped would become her new mama.

She stopped outside the drawing-room door, which was slightly ajar. She could hear her grandmother's voice, then a man's.

'Well, Robert. I only hope you can live with yourself after what you're about to do. If those two children are sent back to a camp in Poland, they stand no chance of any kind of life. There is every possibility that they will perish there. The poverty and starvation in these places is well documented. I ask you one more time to please, reconsider.'

There was silence from the room. Outside, Rosa's face turned pale and her heart began thumping against her chest.

'No, Victoria, never. I want them out by tomorrow morning, otherwise I will call the police and have them deported.'

Rosa turned and fled up the stairs.

Victoria studied her husband calmly, quietly.

'All right, but if that is how you feel, I shall leave this house with them. We will go as soon as possible.' She rose, with as much dignity as she could muster, walked to the door, then stopped.

'I have always disliked you, Robert. But now I despise you. You are contemptible and inhuman. You will be hearing from my solicitor. Good-bye.'

She closed the door and walked up the stairs to her dressing room.

An hour later, belongings hurriedly thrown into a valise, and having decided that the three of them would stay in a hotel tonight, for she could not bear to be under the same roof as her husband a moment longer, she went and knocked gently on David's door.

There was no reply. She tried again, then opened it. The room was empty.

She tried Rosa's door and received no reply. She looked inside and saw that it, too, was deserted. The window onto the balcony was wide open, sending blasts of freezing cold air into the room.

On the bed was a sketch.

Victoria picked it up and saw that it was the most exquisite drawing of her daughter, Adele.

It read, 'To Grandmoter, with lov, Rosa.'

Victoria slumped on the bed and cried.

26

DAVID AND ROSA spent their first night in London huddled close together under a hedge in Hyde Park.

David had never felt such sheer hopelessness. He knew that it was because he'd been fooled into believing that they had at last found sanctuary.

When Rosa had told him what she had heard at the drawing room door, he knew that there was no time to waste. Being deported back to the living hell of further incarceration in Poland was not an option David could risk. Rosa might not even survive the return journey. He watched her sleeping, nestled into him against the bitter cold.

She'd had such a terrible life so far, more than anyone should have to endure. She had seen such pain and suffering and she did not know what comfort, love and security was.

As David looked down at her, a little strength seeped into his bones. He had promised Mama he would take care of Rosa and he would.

He had to find a way of making a life for both of them. He now knew for certain that the only person he could rely on was himself.

He gingerly opened his violin case, his hands almost completely numb from the cold. He felt under the lining and drew out the remaining coins.

Four left. And they were a mixture of German and Polish currency. He knew he could not use these here; it would arouse too much suspicion.

Then he would have to sell his violin. There was no choice. The Stradivarius was hugely valuable and if he could get a good price, it would provide food and shelter and give the two of them a chance.

Having held on to it for this long, David felt guilty that all else had failed.

Once the dawn broke, David woke Rosa and they crossed a big roundabout into a road called Oxford Street.

'I'm so hungry, David. Do we have any money for something to eat?'

David shook his head. 'No, Rosa, but we will have by lunchtime.'

'How?'

'Never you mind. Come on, let's go down there. It's a subway of some kind. It'll be warmer.'

They walked down the steps at Oxford Circus tube station. There was a bench in the corner of the station and David led Rosa to it and sat down.

'What are we going to do, David? What if the police come after us?'

'We'll make sure they don't find us, sweetheart.'

He checked the clock on the other side of the station. Ten to eight.

He stood up and went across to the ticket office.

'Excuse me,' he enquired to the sleepy clerk. 'Could you tell me how I get to Suddeby's? I believe it is an antique shop in Bomb Street.'

The clerk chuckled. 'I think you mean Sotheby's in New Bond Street. Yes. It's not far from here at all. It's just up the road.'

David listened to the clerk's directions. 'Thank you, sir.' David went back to Rosa and held out his hand. 'Come on, Rosa. We're going to find some breakfast.'

'Come in, come in.' The man ushered David and Rosa into a small room, crammed with valuable and beautiful objects.

'My name is Mr Slamon. My assistant tells me that you have a rare object you would like to sell. Can I see it?'

David nodded and placed his case on the man's desk. He removed the instrument and handed it to him.

Slamon's eyes lit up as he fingered the delicate pine wood of the front of the instrument. He turned it over and surveyed the unmarked maple back. The workmanship on the violin was exquisite. He checked the facsimile label as his excitement mounted. He reached for the pernambuco and horsehair bow, and noticed three of the strings were broken.

'Beautiful, quite beautiful. Where did you get it?'

'My mama and papa bought it for me for my tenth birthday. We lived in Warsaw.'

'You are a very lucky young man to have parents who would buy you such a treasure. Did your parents ever tell you if the violin has a name?'

'Yes. The Ludwig.'

612

Slamon studied the young man opposite him carefully. It was highly unlikely that if he had stolen the violin, he would know its name.

'Of course, we will have to check that it is authentic, which will take a couple of days . . .'

'No!' said David. 'I want to sell it now.'

Slamon coughed. 'I see. Umm, have you any proof that the instrument is yours? I mean, Sotheby's could never be seen to handle stolen goods.'

David's eyes lit up with anger and he grabbed the violin from Slamon.

'If that is how you feel, then I shall take my violin elsewhere.'

'Now, now, calm down. I do apologize, but since the war, we've had all manner of individuals offering us possessions that couldn't possibly be theirs.'

'Play, David,' Rosa said quietly. 'That will convince him.'

David felt deeply hurt at having to prove that he was no thief, but then he saw the hunger in his sister's eyes and nodded.

'All right. I will play for you.'

He nestled the violin lovingly under his chin and placed the bow across the strings. He closed his eyes and played.

Slamon was finally convinced. The familiarity between instrument and player was an infinitesimal something that could only be built up over a number of years. The boy played the instrument exquisitely. And the sound was that of a rare and beautiful violin, fashioned by the great master himself.

'Thank you. That was very beautiful. And I do apologize for doubting you. Obviously, I will still have to have a second opinion from my colleague, but having heard you play, I am convinced that it is indeed authentic. May I take the instrument, please?'

David handed it to him, his eyes wary.

'You may accompany me if you wish, or I could ask my assistant to bring some tea and biscuits in here while you wait.'

Rosa's eyes lit up.

'We'll wait here,' he said grudgingly.

Half an hour later, Slamon was back, smiling.

'My colleague agrees with me. It is indeed the Ludwig, made by Stradivarius in 1730.' Slamon sat behind his desk. 'Now, we conduct auctions every Wednesday and Sotheby's would take a ten per cent handling fee of course. I reckon something like this could fetch . . .'

'Please, sir. I told you, I'd like the money today.'

'I see. Well, what we could do is give you an advance of some kind, until we have a purchaser. As a matter of fact, there is one particular gentleman who I know will be very interested. How say you I give you a two-hundred-pound advance, with a receipt stating that the remainder will follow as soon as we have sold the violin?'

'And how much will you sell it for?'

Slamon tapped his fingers on top of his desk. 'Mmn. Now let me see. I reckon we'd put a reserve price of twelve hundred pounds, so that would be the minimum you would receive. But with a piece as rare as this, it could go for up to two or three times the amount.'

'I'm sorry, sir, but how much is that in zlotys, Polish money?'

'I couldn't tell you off hand. What about French francs? Could you calculate, er, zlotys from them?'

David nodded.

Slamon did some figures and related them to David.

David quickly did some sums in his mind. His eyes lit up. The amount was a fortune, enough for Rosa and he to live on for years.

'All right. I shall take the two hundred pounds, but I wish you to sell the instrument as soon as possible.'

'Fine. I'll just make the cheque made out to . . .?'

David shook his head. 'Cash, please.'

Slamon shrugged. 'All right. It will take a little longer though. More tea?'

An hour later Rosa and David emerged into the watery November sunlight.

He swung Rosa round and hugged her tight.

'See? I told you David would sort it out. Right, let's go and find a café and have the most enormous breakfast you've ever seen!'

They spent the next two nights at a small hotel just off the Bayswater Road. David bought himself a suit and went to see letting agencies to find a place they could rent.

The first office he visited asked him to fill in a form.

At the top, he had to put his name.

David thought quickly. He did not want to write his real name down there, just in case the police were after him. What was it that the man in the café had called policemen? Co . . . Coo . . . Coopers! That was it

He wrote his new name in the box and smiled. David

Cooper. It sounded good and very English. David and Rosa Delanski were dead from this moment on.

He told the secretary at the letting agency that he was looking for a small flat for himself and his wife, thinking that a young brother and sister looking for somewhere to live might arouse suspicion.

She gave him the address of two places to visit and he bought a map of London and hopped onto a red bus. The first flat, in a place called Notting Hill, was small and poky and the landlady was nosy.

The second, a stone's throw away from the hotel in the Bayswater Road where they were staying, was much more pleasant.

The only problem was that there was only one bedroom, with a big double bed in it.

Never mind, thought David, thinking how Rosa hated sleeping by herself. He could always sleep on the couch in the sitting room if Rosa preferred.

The flat was on the top floor, with a landlord who lived off the premises. It was small, but spotlessly clean and would do them well to begin with.

David said he'd take it and move in immediately. He got round the problem of providing references by giving the landlord six months' payment in advance. In the grim days of post-war recession, that sort of hard cash softened anyone's rules.

Rosa loved it. She danced around the flat, as pleased as punch. She laughed when David told her that she would have to pretend she was his wife.

Later, they went off in search of food for supper. With rationing still in force in London, David and Rosa had to

616

part with a fistful of money as the shopkeepers surreptitiously produced hidden wares from under the counter.

But it was worth it as they tasted Rosa's wonderful meal of chicken rissoles and 'little hoofs', a tasty potato dish that their mama used to make. They washed it down with a bottle of wine that went straight to their heads.

'A toast, to Mr and Mrs David Cooper!'

Rosa giggled helplessly at this.

'And I think you should become Rose from now on. It's much more English.' David wanted to say less Jewish, but he didn't.

They climbed into the comfortable double bed at midnight. Rosa fell asleep immediately, but David was wide awake.

The stirring in his loins as he felt the soft skin of Rosa's back pressed against him was unmistakable.

He turned over, feeling guilty and ashamed that he should feel this way about his sister.

But he couldn't help it. Rosa was so unaware of her beautiful, blossoming body. She would parade naked in front of him, as she had always done at home, innocently unaware of the effect it had on her brother. She was such a child in some ways, but so adult in others, and David would find himself fantasizing about her all hours of the day and night.

It was no good. He couldn't share the same bed with her any more. He was getting to the stage where he couldn't trust himself.

He pulled back the covers, heading for the bathroom, where he would relieve himself of his problem and then retire to the couch, but a small hand pulled him back into the warmth.

'Where are you going, David?'

'Just to the bathroom, sweetheart. And then I will sleep on the couch, as I am restless and will disturb you.'

'No, David. Don't go,' she said quietly.

'I must.'

Her fingers were trailing a soft line down his back.

'Come and hold me, David.' The voice was husky, that of a much maturer woman.

He lay back and she folded herself into his arms. David bit his lip. Her naked body so close to his was an ecstatic torture.

She rose and propped her head on her elbow, looking down at him.

'I love you, David. I love you.'

She bent down and kissed him on the lips, her tongue probing inside his mouth.

He wanted to stop, wanted to tell her that this was so wrong, but the sheer joy of having her kiss him made it impossible to think sensibly.

David groaned as her hands slipped downwards and touched him where he was so hard and ready to burst. He reached for her developing breasts, with their nipples out of proportion to the soft burgeoning flesh around them.

'I understand, David. Let me help you, then you'll sleep. I love you.'

Her hands closed around his shaft and began massaging him until he shot his milky seed all over her fingers.

David turned over and cried in shame. The way that Rosa had learnt about what she had just done was too terrible to contemplate. Rosa's arms went around him.

'Don't cry, David. It's natural if two people love each other. And we do, don't we?'

David thought for one dreadful moment that his sister had no idea what natural was, but as her lips closed over his once more, he could only follow his body and love her as she wanted to love him.

27

DAVID AND ROSA lived as man and wife for almost two years. The Ludwig had sold for two and a half thousand pounds and financially they were secure. David had never known such sheer happiness. They were everything to each other; it seemed to him impossible that two people could experience greater joy. They had no friends, no one they knew in London, but David did not miss that. He had Rosa. His love, his sister, his genius. They spent twenty-four hours a day together, revelling in exploring London, exulting in the security of their tiny flat. After so much terror, pain and uncertainty, the sanctity of their small home and each other became their rock.

They neither of them discussed the rights or wrongs of their relationship. It was too painful and David had pushed it to the back of his mind. He sometimes dreamt that Rosa wasn't his sister, but his wife, and that they didn't have to pretend any more. For he would marry her tomorrow.

He had been insistent on one thing. He had booked Rose into a clinic under the name of Mrs Cooper. There

620

she had got herself fixed up so that she wouldn't have babies. David knew that would be terribly wrong.

David would lie on the couch, content to watch Rosa as she stood at the easel he'd bought her and sketched him and anything else she could find.

Slowly, her paintings began to change from the purely representational work she had always done.

Sometimes, she would throw the brush down in a sulk and hurl herself on the bed in frustration.

'Oh, David, I've a thought that wants to come out, but I can't transfer it.'

David took Rosa to as many galleries and exhibitions as he could find. They went to the National Gallery, the Tate and wandered down Cork Street to study the *Miserere* series by Georges Rouault at the Redfern Gallery. But the exhibition that fascinated Rosa most was that of Graham Sutherland's work at the Hanover Gallery. She stared at *The Thorn Cross* for hours.

'It's so . . . brutal.' Rosa turned to David. 'I want to go home and paint.'

Later that week, David studied a painting that Rosa had just finished. He shuddered as he looked at it. There was something dark and bleak about it; distorted faces and eyes staring at him from behind bars at strange angles.

'Rosa, what have you called this?'

'Treblinka,' she answered lightly.

David knew it was time for Rosa to move on. She needed to have her talent fostered.

It scared him; the thought of Rosa knowing other people, going off and leaving him for hours while she was at art school. But very soon he would have to find work anyway, especially if he was to pay for Rosa's tuition.

They discussed it that night over dinner.

'Oh, David, do you really think they'd accept me at the Royal College?'

'I'm sure they will, once they've seen your work.'

The following day, David hailed a taxi and stacked four of Rose's canvases on the back seat.

'Exhibition Row, please, driver.'

The taxi pulled up in front of the grand entrance to the Royal College of Art, and David heaved the paintings inside.

'Well, Mr Cooper, this isn't really the way we do things around here,' said the flustered receptionist. 'You need an application form and . . .'

'Could you ask someone to look at these, please, and contact us if he thinks my sister might have talent?' David wrote down his name and address on a piece of paper.

'Good day to you.' David nodded at the startled woman and walked out of the building, supremely confident that someone would spot the genius he knew Rose possessed.

He was right. Ten days later, Rose received a letter asking her to come to the college the following Monday. She would have to spend two days at the college doing life drawings and pass through numerous interviews.

Rosa was in a frenzy of nerves the night before.

'You'll pass with flying colours, I promise you.' David kissed her gently on the cheek.

*

Three months later, in the September of 1948, Rose began her diploma course at the Royal College of Art. Although only seventeen, and growing more beautiful by the day, thought David, the school had recognized her talent and accepted her.

The first day without her was unbearable. David mooched round the empty, silent flat, not knowing what to do with himself. He felt desolate without her.

But he had things to do, plans to make. He had to start thinking about his own future. They still had money to live on for the next couple of years, but Rosa's college course was going to take a big slice out of it.

David found a pencil and a pad and sat down at the kitchen table. He made a list of various jobs that he thought he may be suitable for, then crossed each one off.

None of the things on the list appealed to him in the least. He wanted to be his own man, start his own business where the sky could be the limit. He was so different to others of his age that he knew he could never fit in to an everyday office environment.

He wandered round the flat, hands in his pockets, thinking.

At half past three, he gave up. He had just made a cup of tea when the doorbell rang.

David opened the door and saw that it was his landlord.

'Come in, Mr Chesney. I have the rent for you.'

'Thank you, Mr Cooper. I like my tenants to be on time with their payments,' he nodded.

'Do you have many?' asked David, handing him an envelope.

'Oh yes. About twenty-five. I own seven houses. Bought them for a song after the war and converted them. Best thing I ever did. Good-bye, Mr Cooper.' Mr Chesney tipped his cap and disappeared down the stairs.

David closed the door and went back to the table to drink his tea. He mulled over what Chesney had said. The man had given him an idea.

The following day, David went to visit a number of local estate agents. He was astonished to see how cheap the price of an average terraced house was. He took details on a cross section of the properties back home and sat down and worked out some figures.

David checked and rechecked them, to make sure he had not made a mistake.

He hadn't. The money to be made was excellent, if he was prepared to risk the initial capital. He suspected it was a growth market, with more and more young people preferring to move and have a place of their own. Many could not afford to buy or rent houses, but they could afford flats.

David made detailed notes and drew up cash flow projections. Then he went into the City of London to try to find a bank to help finance his project. Each one said no. David came home disheartened but not prepared to give up.

He knew he had to make a decision. The only way he could do it was to take the rest of the money from the sale of the Stradivarius, leaving enough for Rosa and him to live on for the next six months. With that, he could afford to buy either two small houses or one large one and turn them into self-contained units.

He went home with a bottle of champagne and celebrated with an ecstatic Rosa, still overwhelmed by her first week at college. He did not tell her about the gamble he was taking.

'Here's to us.' David raised his glass. 'To the property tycoon and the greatest painter of the next half of the century.'

28

IN THE FOLLOWING three years, David's business went from strength to strength. With the onset of the fifties, David found that demand was outstripping supply. He acquired a reputation for providing quality conversions at a very reasonable rent. His tenants were happy and word spread.

By 1951, David owned fifteen houses around London. He started looking at land that had been bombed which he could buy cheaply to build office blocks in the City. The banks were now falling over themselves to lend him money.

Everything was perfect. Except for one thing.

Rosa. During her first year at the college, nothing much had changed. David had worked hard at his business during the day and they had spent the evenings together as usual. Then during the second year, Rose had started staying out late. She'd come in after midnight, talking avidly of the Colony Room in Dean Street, where she and other students from the college had drunk with Muriel, the proprietor, and artists such as Bacon and Freud.

LUCINDA EDMONDS

She started going to part-time evening classes at Borough Polytechnic, along with others from the Royal College.

'Oh, David, Bomberg's techniques are so exciting. He rejects anything that's artificial or concocted. He's teaching me so much.'

David listened patiently and nodded and smiled in the right places. He was happy that Rosa was developing her talent, and tried not to mind that she had little time or energy left for him.

But during the third year, David hardly saw her. Rose blamed it on her work load at college, that she had to stay late to get paintings finished, but often there was alcohol on her breath and sometimes she wouldn't appear until the early hours of the following morning.

What could he do? He could hardly accompany her; he was sure their intimacy would be noticed.

And during her last term, Rose often did not come home at all.

David often pondered if she had another man. How would he understand if she had? What right did he have to stop her? He was her brother, for God's sake.

His love for her had not diminished and the pain with which he witnessed Rose become more and more removed from him did not ease. But she was a young girl; she deserved a normal life and he must not prevent it.

She still slept with him and they made love occasionally, but not with the abandon and tenderness she had once shown him.

On the night after Rose's graduation from the Royal College, David took her out to dinner. She had just been granted her first showing at the Redfern Gallery. She was tingling with excitement.

'Can you believe it, David? Me, having an exhibition! And it's all thanks to you.'

'No, Rose. It's your great gift. And to celebrate, here.' He handed her an envelope.

'Can I open it?' she said excitedly. David nodded, knowing how she loved surprises.

She read the enclosed document and her face dropped.

'What's wrong?'

'Oh, David, I'm so sorry.'

David was filled with trepidation.

'Why? What do you mean? I thought you'd be thrilled to move to a new apartment in Chelsea. I own it, Rose. We own our own home.'

Rose looked at him across the table. Then she dropped her eyes.

'I . . . I wanted to speak to you about this before, David.'

'What? For God's sake, tell me, Rose.'

'I think it's best if we don't live together any more. Roddy, my friend from college, has got a spare room in his flat.'

David was aghast. 'Why, Rose. For God's sake, why?'

She looked him straight in the eye. 'You know why, David. It's wrong. What we've being doing is wrong.' Her eyes filled with tears.

'But, Rose, nothing matters if we love each other. You said on that first night that –'

'I know what I said. But I was a child then. I didn't know any better.'

'But I know you still love me, Rose and . . .'

Rose stood up from the table, tears tumbling down her face.

'No, please, David. I can't listen. I'm sorry, David. I'm truly sorry.'

She ran from the restaurant and out into the night.

She did not come home that evening, or the night after. Two weeks later, David realized that she was never coming back when Roddy arrived at the flat for her things.

David felt unable to escape Rose. As her fame grew in the following four years, every paper and gossip column he opened was full of the beautiful young Rose Delancey . . . David noted the subtle change of surname.

The art critics embraced her strong, individual work, John Russell of the *Sunday Times* noting the similarity to Bacon. The undertones of her life during the war were present in all her paintings.

By 1955, twenty-four-year-old Rose Delancey was the toast of London. Her paintings had been shown at the Beaux Arts Gallery to rave reviews. She had everything; beauty, talent, intelligence and a mysterious past.

Eligible bachelors flocked around her and she was seen with a different man every week.

One morning, David read in a newspaper that Jean de Plessey, a particularly handsome French count, had been seen with Miss Delancey constantly for the past few weeks. There were rumours of a proposal and a summer wedding.

David could not bear to read any more. As usual, he

spent the rest of the day concentrating his emotions on his business empire, which was fast moving him towards paper millionaire status.

Then, two months later, the telephone rang late one night.

'David Cooper.'

'Hello, David. It's Rose.'

He gulped. Just the sound of her voice was enough to turn him to jelly.

'Hello, Rose.'

'I . . . I was wondering whether I could come and see you tonight? Are you busy?'

David looked at the mountains of paperwork in front of him and said, 'No, not at all. Come round.'

'I'll be there in half an hour.'

She looked better than he remembered her; slimmer, slightly taller and incredibly beautiful. The radiance she emitted when she walked into the room was staggering. David understood why every man in London fell at her feet.

She pulled a cigarette and a holder out of her clutch bag and lit up. She paused by the window to see the view from his apartment and David thought how sophisticated she had become.

'Would you like a drink?'

'Yes. Do you have Campari?'

'No. Only wine and beer, I'm afraid.'

'Wine will do fine.'

David took a large gulp from the bottle as he poured the wine into two glasses in the kitchen and went back into the sitting room. She was sitting on the sofa, legs tantalizingly crossed under the expensive Chanel black dress.

'Thanks.' She took the glass.

'Why did you want to see me?'

'I . . . I wanted to apologize for not contacting you during the last few years. I . . . couldn't.'

She looked up at him and David saw that the love was still in her eyes.

'Do you understand, David?'

'Yes, Rose.'

'It wasn't because I had forgotten you, I just felt that a clean break was the right thing to do.'

'Yes.' Monosyllabic answers were all he could manage as he gulped back the tears.

Rose sighed. 'It was wrong, David, what we had. I began to realize it as I grew up. It was because there was no one else. We were so dependent on each other for so many years before, shared so much tragedy together. I can see the reasons why, but that doesn't make what we did right.'

'No.'

'Anyway, I also came to ask you if you'd come to my wedding.'

David felt as though someone had just thrown acid in his face. As though he were drowning, and couldn't get his breath. Rose, his Rose, was marrying someone else.

He couldn't let her see.

'I may be in America. I'm sailing over there in a week's time and won't be back for six months. I'm thinking of expanding my business there. But thanks for the invitation.' David was proud of his control. Now he wanted her to leave, so that he could let his grief out alone.

'You might be back. We haven't set a definite date yet.'

'We'll see. I presume you're marrying the French chap?'

Rose nodded, not a flicker of emotion showing on her beautiful face. 'Yes. Jean de Plessey.'

'You'll still continue painting, though?'

'I think so, but to be honest I feel a bit wrung out at the moment. The last couple of years have been wonderful, of course, but I feel as if I'm on a production line. I could use a break.'

David sensed his sister's exhaustion.

'Well, you have been a very busy young lady in the past few years. I must congratulate you on your success.'

'Thank you. It's all down to you paying for me to go to the Royal College,' she smiled. 'And a bit of Papa, too, giving him his gift. I also wanted to tell you that Lady Brown, our grandmother, came to my exhibition three months ago. She saw a photograph of me and put two and two together. Apparently, she decided to leave her husband the night he refused to take us in. When she came to tell us, we had already left. She's divorced Grandfather now, but managed to hold on to the house. She'd love to hear from you, David. She's very lonely. Would you go and visit her?'

David shrugged. 'Maybe, but I'd prefer not to go back into the past.'

'I understand.' Rose looked up at the wall. 'You have *Treblinka* up there. I hate that painting. Why have you hung it?'

David could have said that it was because it reminded him of the glorious days that the two of them had lived in their cocoon, the happiest time of his life.

Instead, he shrugged. 'I like it, that's all.'

Rose checked her watch nervously. 'I must go, David. I'm meeting Jean at half past eight.' She stood. 'It's nice to see you again.'

Rose walked towards the door and he followed her.

She turned with her hand on the handle.

'Good-bye, David.' She pecked him lightly on the cheek.

The love and passion welled up inside him and he pulled her to him and held her there.

She struggled. 'No, David! Stop it! Don't! Please.'

He shook her. 'You still love me, Rose, I know you do. I can see it in your eyes. Say it, Goddamn you!'

She beat him on the shoulders and shook her head violently. '*No! No!* I don't, I don't, let me go, David, please! It's wrong!'

He held her chin with one hand and pressed his mouth against hers. She continued to struggle. He probed every corner of her lips until his tongue found entrance.

Her warm mouth tasted of cigarettes and wine and he chased her tongue to make contact with it.

He found it at last and she stopped struggling. She went limp in his arms as her body responded.

He took his mouth away from hers and looked at her. Tears were streaming down her face, mirroring his own.

'You do still love me, don't you, Rose?'

'Oh God, David. Yes, I still love you.' She shook her head from side to side as the tears flowed down her cheeks. 'I still love you,' she shouted again, '*I still love you, I still love you . . .*'

29

ROSE REALIZED THAT the sky was getting dark. She
checked her watch. She'd been sitting by Miranda's grave
for over two hours. She wiped away the tears with the
back of her hand.

'So you see, Miranda, I went back to David of my own
free will, knowing that I couldn't resist him. We made
love that night, and David went off to America a week
later. He made me promise I'd wait for him until he
returned. Oh God, I was so confused, so exhausted from
the past few years.

'I continued to see Jean, but I knew it wasn't right. The
only man I could ever love was David.

'Five months later, it was confirmed that I was pregnant. Why, you ask, could I not marry Jean and pretend
the baby was his?'

Rose paused. 'Well, I had never slept with Jean. I'd
never made love with anyone other than David. I
couldn't, you see.

'Obviously, I cancelled the wedding. And that was
when I decided to come up here to Yorkshire. The press
would have had a field day if I had stayed in London and

produced a child. I couldn't have handled that.

'I needed to be alone. At twenty-four, I was washed out, emotionally and mentally. I knew that I could never love another man, but that the man I loved could never be mine.

'It was too late for an abortion by the time I found out, just like you.

'I knew I could never see David again, that he must never know that I had his child.

'Miles, David's baby.'

Rose voiced the words for the first time.

'That is why you are lying down there, Miranda. Because I was too weak to stop myself from loving my own brother. I produced a child who was doomed from the start. I prayed he'd be all right, watched him for any tell-tale signs and found none. Miles was so clever. He was always so charming towards me.

'But I was blinded by love. I should have seen long ago what I'd created. A monster.

'So you mustn't blame Miles,' Rose whispered. 'What he became was no one's fault but mine. Oh Miranda. I'm so, so sorry for what I've done. Please, if you can hear me, forgive me, please forgive me.'

Rose sobbed again. Then she looked up as she saw a line of birds settle in the tree above Miranda's grave. The wind rustled and then the birds started twittering, until there was a rousing chorus of life.

It was almost dark.

Rose smiled.

'Thank you, Miranda,' she whispered. 'It's over now, isn't it?'

'No, Rose. It has only just begun.'

A male voice made her jump.

She turned and saw David standing behind her. He took her gently by the shoulders and pulled her upright.

'Come with me, Rose.'

She looked up at him. It was where she belonged and she could fight it no longer.

'Yes.'

He kissed her gently on the lips.

The two of them walked slowly off down the path, arms wrapped around each other, until they were but specks in the distance.

Epilogue

_____

Paris 1992

'MY LORDS, LADIES and gentlemen. I welcome you all here tonight. Thank you from the bottom of my heart for coming to this evening's fashion show, here in the Grand Ballroom of the Ritz. I would like to thank the manager for loaning us this magnificent room free of charge.

'As I'm sure most of you are aware, the Van Schiele foundation was set up four years ago. It is a charity with a difference, because it does not discriminate against any form of human suffering.

'Suffering can come in many disguises; whether it is a young man dying from AIDS, or a war veteran whose pension is not enough to support him with even the simple comforts that every person deserves.

'In the past three years, we have helped over one thousand needy causes, some of them disasters on a national scale, some a single human being.

'Tonight, however, we are helping the Holocaust Foundation to continue their good works. They are a group of men and women who have elected to make sure the killing of six million people is not forgotten and will never be repeated in history again. They also counsel and help victims, and relatives who have lost loved ones, to come to terms with what has happened to them.

'This is not a madness that is only in the past. At this moment in time, with the Berlin wall falling and the rise of Nazism once again sweeping through the streets of Germany, I believe that we should all welcome and support this organization.'

There was heartfelt applause from the audience.

'In a moment, I should like to introduce you to David Cooper, a man I'm sure you all have heard of, who is the President of the Holocaust Foundation. But first, a few words from the Vice President of our organization, my husband, Mr Anthony Van Schiele.'

Anthony came up onto the dais beside Leah. He kissed her and squeezed her hand and she sat down to listen to what he had to say.

'Good evening, ladies and gentleman. Thank you for being with us tonight. My wife has steered brilliantly at the helm of an organization which when it was launched took up one room in our home. Now, it commands an entire floor of my block in New York and she has a larger office than I do.'

There was muffled laughter and more applause at this.

He waited until the audience was quiet.

'There is little more to say, except, thank you, once more, and let me welcome David Cooper.'

As David began his speech, Leah slipped off the platform with her husband.

'Is she here?' she asked him anxiously.

Anthony nodded. 'She's here. Her flight from Moscow was delayed, that's all.'

'I must find Brett and tell him.'
Anthony nodded again.

The star-studded audience bid almost fifty thousand pounds for the sumptuous range of clothes in the new Carlo collection. Carlo himself, a humbled, much more likeable man since his spell in jail awaiting trial for murder, embraced Leah warmly. He had apologized long ago for his misdemeanours, and Leah, knowing what he had suffered, and feeling partly responsible for putting the wrong man behind bars, had been glad to accept.

Rose, David, Brett, his wife Cecile, Chloe, Anthony and Leah sat round the table chatting and enjoying the excellent dinner.

Leah looked round the table with happiness, musing how strange it was to see all the people who had had such an effect on her life reunited once more.

After the tragedy eight years ago, Rose had left Yorkshire to go to New York, fleeing the terrible memories that the farmhouse held for her. She had never returned, staying with David at his duplex ever since. Tonight Leah thought how content brother and sister looked.

Chloe had elected to stay with Mrs Thompson in Yorkshire, flying to stay with Rose in America for the school holidays. Leah couldn't help but be glad that her parents had Chloe to keep them company. With her hectic schedule, her visits to Yorkshire were less regular than they should be.

She'd regained consciousness that terrible night on the moors and found herself in Anthony's arms. She had looked up at him and known then that she loved him with a depth that she could never feel for Brett. Anthony had taken her straight back to New York the following day and they had taken refuge in the house in Woodstock. There had been no recriminations, no arguments. The ghost of Brett had at last been exorcised. Anthony recognized that. Leah felt only grateful that he'd given her another chance. It had taken her many months to recover from the shock of that night in Yorkshire. With Anthony's love and understanding, she had done so. During the past eight years, their relationship had grown stronger as the months had passed. There was still no baby, but they were looking into adoption. And who knew what tomorrow may bring? For the present, Anthony and the foundation gave Leah all the joy she needed.

Leah glanced at Brett across the table. It was good to see that he too had finally found happiness. His new wife obviously adored him, and Brett's career as an artist was beginning to take off. It had been eighteen months before she'd found the courage to write to him, to try to explain why she had left him to return to Anthony. He had not responded. So she'd been surprised when she had received a call from Brett, out of the blue, at her office just over eighteen months ago.

'Leah, I need your organisation's help,' he'd said. Then he had told her the story.

It had taken an enormous amount of effort; leads that led frustratingly to brick walls, bureaucracy and red tape thwarting them time and again.

Then they had found her.

And, finally, she was here.

Brett was tingling with excitement.

'Have you met her?' he asked.

'No, but Anthony has.'

He put his hand on hers. 'Thank you, Leah. For everything. You don't know what this means to me. And I understand now. We were past, not future, weren't we?'

'Yes.' Leah smiled at him and realized that, at last, they could be friends.

Leah rose from her seat. 'David, Rose, Chloe. I wonder if you can come with me. I have someone whom you might like to meet waiting for you.'

Leah left the table, and the others, bewilderment on their faces, followed her through a side door and out of the ballroom.

Leah led them along the corridor and knocked on a door.

A faint voice answered.

Leah opened the door and went in. David followed.

He stared at the frail lady sitting in an armchair. The face, it was so familiar, and yet he couldn't place it.

She spoke. 'Hello, David.'

Tears filled his eyes as he ran to her, held her, covered her with kisses. As Rose joined her brother, Chloe stood watching in fascination.

'Anya, Anya . . . I thought you were dead. Oh God . . .'

Leah quietly closed the door and left them alone.

Outside, Anthony was waiting. He saw Leah's eyes were filled with tears.

'Darling, I have something for you.' He handed Leah a heavy square parcel, wrapped in brown paper. Leah tore off the paper and gasped as she saw the painting.

'I commissioned Brett to paint it. It's based on the original charcoal sketch that he did of you when you were fifteen. But Brett wouldn't accept payment. He said it was a thank you present for all you've done to help find Anya. It's called *Hidden Beauty*. Brett and I decided the name was perfect.'

'I don't deserve this.'

'Yes you do, darling. And a lot of people here tonight agree with me. Brett was so anxious to trace Anya for his father's sake. He thought that bringing the past into the present would help David finally come to terms with what has happened to himself and Rose. They suffered so much together and now life has come full circle for all three of them. You've done something wonderful by getting Anya out of Russia and bringing her here. I love you, Leah.'

He lifted her face to his and kissed her gently on the lips.

Inside the hotel suite, a camera flashed.

'Not now, Chloe. You can take photos of your great-grandmother later.'

The pretty sixteen-year-old glanced up at Rose and smiled.

'Sorry, Granny.'

Rose shuddered.

She'd seen that look before.